SNOWFLAKES OVER THE STARFISH CAFÉ

JESSICA REDLAND

Boldwood

First published in Great Britain in 2021 by Boldwood Books Ltd.

Copyright © Jessica Redland, 2021

Cover Design by Debbie Clement Design

Cover Photography: Shutterstock

A CIP catalogue record for this book is available from the British Library.

Paperback ISBN 978-1-80162-406-0

Large Print ISBN 978-1-80162-402-2

Hardback ISBN 978-1-80162-401-5

Ebook ISBN 978-1-80162-399-5

Kindle ISBN 978-1-80162-400-8

Audio CD ISBN 978-1-80162-407-7

MP3 CD ISBN 978-1-80162-404-6

Digital audio download ISBN 978-1-80162-398-8

Boldwood Books Ltd
23 Bowerdean Street
London SW6 3TN
www.boldwoodbooks.com

To my older brother Mike and my younger brother Chris, with love always xx

'With courage, nothing is impossible.'

— Sir William Hillary, 1823

Founder of the Royal National Lifeboat Institution (RNLI), Est. 1824.
(Originally known as the National Institution for the Preservation
of Life from Shipwreck)

1

Bonfire Night, eight years ago

'These are the last two crates,' I said, reaching the bottom of the stairs at The Starfish Café. I weaved between the pine tables and placed them down at the far end of the room beside several other crates of Christmas decorations.

Angie looked up from unpacking the seven-foot artificial Christmas tree. 'How is it Bonfire Night already? I swear the summer tourists only went home yesterday.'

'I hear you! Am I best not to mention that tomorrow is exactly seven weeks till Christmas Day?'

'Argh, don't! I haven't even *thought* about presents yet.' She ran her hands through her greying bob and shuddered, but I knew she was only joking. Angie loved the countdown to Christmas as much as Mum and I did.

'Hot chocolate time!' Mum announced, coming towards us with a tray of three mugs. I smiled at the squirty cream topping, peppered with mini-marshmallows and chocolate buttons. Extremely indulgent but absolutely delicious.

'Cheers!' she said, handing us each a mug. 'Let the full-on festive fabulousness commence!'

We clinked our drinks together, laughing, and I experienced the same warm and fuzzy sensation I had at this moment every year as the countdown to Christmas commenced. Fifty days to go!

Christmas had always been a huge thing in our family and it was double celebration time for me as I was born on Christmas Eve, resulting in the uber-Christmassy name Hollie Gabrielle and the pet name 'Angel'.

Mum loved her traditions and putting the tree up at The Starfish Café on Bonfire Night was one of them, started twenty-one years ago when the café opened.

Mum's parents had owned the land at Starfish Point – a five-acre site a couple of miles south of the North Yorkshire seaside town of Whitsborough Bay – since the 1950s, bought when my granddad saw the potential for catching crabs and lobsters along the coastline. The sand and shingle beach was home to a small colony of seals, making it a popular destination for visitors, so, throughout the summer season, my Granny ran a café called Norma's Nook from a prefabricated unit.

Mum worked in Norma's Nook straight after catering college and took over as the new owner a few years later when Granny retired. For the next decade, she ran it just as Granny had but it was time for major changes: new name, larger premises, and a plan to open all year round.

An eternal optimist, Mum was never afraid to take risks and refused to listen to the critics who said there was no way she'd have enough business to survive through the winter. She adored Kevin Costner and put her own spin on a quote from his film, *Field of Dreams*. 'If I build it, they will come,' became her mantra. So she built it and they *did* come. Although I think her amazing skills in the kitchen and her bubbly personality had a lot to do with that.

The first ever Christmas that the new and improved café was open, Mum went for 'full-on festive fabulousness', putting the tree up on Bonfire Night and decking out the café with shiny garlands and lights everywhere, convinced it would help build the winter trade. Those who visited occasionally when going for a walk started coming more regularly, drawn by the Christmassy ambience and Mum's amazing comfort food.

After a successful first winter opening, a tradition was born with Bonfire Night set in stone as the night each year to put up the decorations. At first it was only Mum and Angie but, after I started a summer job when I was twelve, the decorating team became a trio and, now aged twenty-six, this was my fifteenth year.

'Tree first?' Mum asked, a little pointlessly. It was *always* the tree first.

I opened out the base unit and began teasing out the branches on the bottom section while Mum and Angie each took another level.

'Lovely clear night,' I said, glancing towards the terrace. 'Perfect for the fireworks.'

The annual display started at 7 p.m. over South Bay and the view from the café was fantastic, so every year friends and family would join us for drinks and a buffet while enjoying the fireworks.

'It's quite mild tonight,' Mum said. 'Should be able to go out onto the terrace.'

Angie shook her head. 'I'll stay in here, hiding in the storeroom with a napkin stuffed in each ear.' Poor Angie hated the loud bangs.

'We'll send out a search party when they're finished,' Mum said with a giggle.

'Thanks, Heather.'

They smiled at each other affectionately and it gave me a

warm glow. I loved their friendship. They'd met at primary school aged four and had remained the best of friends ever since. They studied catering together at college and, as soon as Mum took over running Norma's Nook, she offered Angie a job. Three decades of working together could have damaged some friendships but I'd never seen even the slightest of niggles between them. They were so aligned that they often finished each other's sentences. 'Like the same person inhabiting two bodies,' Dad would say.

I considered myself lucky that I had the same sort of friendship with Katie, although we didn't meet until we were fourteen. Her parents were going through a nasty divorce at the time and she didn't have a great relationship with her older sister so I became her shoulder to cry on. Keen to avoid the tense atmosphere at home, she spent more time at our house – Sandy Croft – than hers.

'What time does Craig think he'll make it tonight?' Angie asked, holding the stepladder for me as I added the angel to the top of the tree.

I smiled at the thought of seeing him. 'Hopefully by half seven. He's gutted about missing the fireworks, but it was the only time the husband and wife were both free so he didn't have much choice.'

My boyfriend Craig was an independent financial adviser who often worked evenings to catch working clients. It meant we only got to see each other two or three times a week but that worked well for me. He was my first serious boyfriend and much as I loved our time together, I also valued the space after so many years being single and doing my own thing.

For the next ninety minutes or so, the three of us sang along to Christmas songs while we transformed the café ready for the guests. They'd start arriving from half six, giving them time for a drink and a chat before the fireworks display.

While Mum and Angie brought out the buffet food, I took the

empty crates and spare decorations back up to the first-floor storeroom.

Before returning downstairs, I looked out the window at the front of the café, overlooking the woods and car park, and smiled to myself. Such a stunning setting.

The Starfish Café is a beautiful two-storey building clad in rich, warm European Redwood timber. Surrounded by pine trees, it feels very alpine. If it wasn't for the North Sea below, visitors could be fooled into believing they were in a mountainous ski resort instead of North Yorkshire.

Mum had carried the alpine feel inside the café with pine tables, wooden cladding and even a Swiss cuckoo clock on the wall. The décor was perhaps a little dated but I loved it. It was such a warm and friendly place to be. We had loads of regular customers who felt like family as well as walkers and holidaymakers.

I paused halfway down the stairs to take in the scene below. Red and white lights twinkled on the tree and there were more fairy lights draped across the window ledges by the seating booths at the back of the café, overlooking the terrace. Miniature Christmas trees also stood on the window ledges and realistic-looking swags of holly and ivy with bright red berries were hooked across the top of the windows. It all looked so beautiful.

Wham's 'Last Christmas' was playing and I laughed as Angie and Mum failed abysmally to hit the higher notes near the end.

'Pick a note, any note!' I joked, descending the stairs. 'But not that one!'

'Cheeky!' Mum put her arm round Angie's waist and they caterwauled all the way to the end of the track.

Just as they finished, the door opened and Dad arrived with Willow, our pale golden retriever, who scampered over to say hello. She'd never been overly bothered by fireworks and the constant attention from the guests was the perfect distraction.

'Ho! Ho! Ho!' Dad boomed before crossing the café to hug and kiss Mum. My brother Isaac and his girlfriend Bex were right behind him, arms round each other as usual. The pair of them were so cute and cuddly together. Katie and Kyle – Isaac's best mate - were next, giggling as he produced a piece of fake mistletoe and was rewarded with a playful poke in the ribs.

A warm and fuzzy feeling enveloped me once more as hugs were exchanged. This was it. This was the start of Christmas – family and friends, decorations, food and drink, warmth, laughter – and I loved every single second of it. Even the dodgy singing.

Within ten minutes, nearly all the guests had arrived and The Starfish Café was buzzing with chatter and the clink of glasses. Angie's husband Martin was here and so was Katie's boyfriend Trey along with family, friends and neighbours. Willow was in her element, getting fussed over with scratches behind the ears and belly rubs.

'You've outdone yourselves this year,' Isaac said as we stood together in front of the tree, sipping from bottles of lager. 'There's just one thing that spoils it.'

'What's that?'

'That dodgy angel at the top of the tree.'

'Oi!' I gave him a playful shove. 'She's meant to look like me!' It had been Mum's mission in life to find a Christmas tree angel that looked like me. Last year she'd finally tracked one down in a Castle Street gift shop which she was convinced was my doppelganger, with her long, dark blonde hair, rosy cheeks and brown-green eyes.

'My point exactly,' Isaac deadpanned.

'Don't be so mean!' I shoved him again, but I knew he didn't mean it. My brother was eighteen months older than me and we were really close and always had been. I knew I was lucky to have that sort of relationship because neither Katie nor Craig got on with their siblings. Craig and his younger sister Avery had this weird competitive rivalry thing going, and Katie's older sister Serena was a spiteful bully who seemed to delight in causing conflict between Katie and her mum.

'I'll tell Mum on you,' I added.

'Ooh, I'm scared!'

'I hope you're not picking on your sister,' Bex said, joining us and trying to give Isaac a stern look; impossible when her eyes sparkled with love for him.

'As if I'd ever do that.' Isaac wrapped his arms round Bex and gave her a gentle kiss. At 6' 3" – an inch taller than Dad – he towered above her and they looked so cute when they were side by side. Bex had a choppy blonde bob, curvy figure, beautiful grey eyes and a girl-next-door innocence about her. My athletically built brother was also blond with piercing blue eyes. Katie said the pair of them would have stunning children and I had to agree. As well as looking great, they really were the most adorable couple together, always hugging each other, always laughing.

Kyle appeared by my side, whipped out his fake mistletoe and puckered his lips.

'In your dreams!' I said, laughing. 'But you can have a hug because I haven't seen you for weeks and I've missed you.'

'Hollie hugs are the best.'

I squealed as he grabbed me in a bear hug, lifted me off my feet and spun me round. 'Put me down, you daft muppet!'

I adored Kyle. We'd always got on well. He could act the fool sometimes but he was thoughtful, caring and a great friend to my brother. I wouldn't change him for the world. Bex would, though. She was pleasant enough towards him, but I sensed she tolerated rather than liked him, which was a shame when he was such an important person in Isaac's life.

The clinking of a knife against a glass drew our attention and we turned to where Mum was standing on the stairs.

'Thank you for joining us again for our annual Bonfire Night soiree,' Mum said, a big beam on her face as she scanned her eyes across the group. 'The fireworks will start shortly and I wanted to say a few words before they do. I know Craig isn't here yet and I'm really sorry to give the news without part of the family here, Hollie, but I can't keep it secret any longer. I had an appointment with my oncologist yesterday and I'm delighted to say…'

I grabbed Kyle's arm, my heart thumping.

'…I'm cancer-free! I've won the second and hopefully the last battle. So I'm going to be able to…'

But she didn't get to finish whatever she wanted to say because we all swamped her with hugs and kisses. Tears streamed down my cheeks as I flung my arms round my Mum.

'Best news ever!' I whispered.

Fireworks exploded outside and the café was lit by the colourful sparks. It felt as though the whole town was celebrating Mum's fabulous news, and quite rightly so.

* * *

'How amazing is your mum's news?' Katie asked, plonking herself down opposite me in one of the booths after the fireworks finished, her eyes glistening with tears.

'It's the greatest. I'm so relieved. It's like Christmas has come early.'

'She's such an inspiration.'

I glanced over at Mum, who was laughing with Angie. 'She is. Every single day.'

hed across the table and squeezed my hand as we
ɔack tears. I wasn't surprised she was as emotional as
me. Mum and Dad had welcomed her into our home like one of the
family and she'd found the love and warmth at Sandy Croft that
she'd never had in her own home. I hated how her mum and sister
frequently ganged up on her. She'd learned that it was pointless
trying to defend herself and it was easier to walk away to a place
where people cared.

I'd loved having her round so much and, for her, the added
bonus had been the chance to see my brother Isaac, on whom she
had an enormous crush. We used to lie in bed and fantasise about
them getting married and Katie becoming my sister-in-law. Isaac's
best mate Kyle was also a frequent visitor and Katie was convinced
that Kyle and I would fall madly in love and we'd marry too. The
four of us would go on holiday together, live on the same street, and
our children would be best friends. It sounded lovely but it was
never going to happen. I liked Kyle but only as a friend and, unfor-
tunately for Katie, Isaac made it clear that he viewed her like
another sister.

Four years ago, Isaac started seeing Bex and it could have been
awkward but it was obvious from the start how perfectly suited they
were. Katie wasn't the sort who'd be off with Bex just because her
feelings for my brother weren't reciprocated. By the time Isaac and
Bex moved in together last summer, Katie had long since got her
feelings under control. She'd recently started seeing Trey, a
colleague from the recruitment consultancy where she worked. It
was early days but they seemed well suited so I had high hopes for
them.

Craig finally arrived a little later, looking all handsome in his
suit. A warm and fuzzy feeling hugged me as I watched him work
the room with ease, smiling and exchanging warm greetings with
everyone he passed. He had an impressive ability to talk to anyone

from any age and background, which was probably why he was so good at his job.

I went to hug him after he made it through the throng, but he managed to dodge it, planting a chaste kiss on my cheek instead.

'I hadn't realised there'd be so many people here,' he said.

'Same as last year.'

'Really?' He frowned. 'Seems more.'

I wasn't going to be pulled into some petty bickering about guest lists when there was so much to celebrate. 'Guess what? Mum made a big announcement. She's been given the all-clear. I'm so relieved.'

'That's good news.'

Craig could never be accused of over-excitement, but I had expected a little more enthusiasm from him. His tone was what I'd have expected if I'd said: *We thought we'd run out of sausage rolls but found an emergency bag of frozen ones.*

'Good?' I challenged, eyebrows raised in disbelief. 'It's amazing!'

He looked shocked by my outburst. 'Keep your hair on! Good. Amazing. What's the difference?'

I stared at him for a moment and bit my lip. I was being unfair to him by expecting the same level of emotion I'd had from Katie. 'Nothing. Forget it.' I forced brightness into my voice. 'How was your meeting?'

'Yeah, all good.' He glanced round the room. 'I'm feeling conspicuous in a suit. I'll nip to the gents and change. See you in a bit.'

And then he was gone, leaving me with a familiar tinge of disappointment. I sank into another booth, frowning. Was it too much to expect a warm hug from my boyfriend under the circumstances? Craig didn't like public displays of affection. I understood that to some extent as I certainly wouldn't be comfortable with a long passionate kiss in front of everyone, but I saw no harm in a gentle kiss and a hug. Isaac and Bex did it all the time and it never made anyone feel awkward.

I fidgeted with the small gold wedding band I wore on a chain round my neck. It had been Granny's before her fingers swelled with arthritis and she'd had a larger one made, which Mum wore on her right hand.

'What's with the sad face?' Mum asked, coming over with Willow and slipping into the seat beside me.

'Craig's just arrived and I told him your news. I thought he might give me a hug.'

She quirked an eyebrow. 'Craig? In public?' She glanced out the window. 'Ooh, was that a pig flying past?'

I let go of the necklace. 'Am I over-reacting again?'

'No, Angel, but you are comparing your relationship again. There isn't a right or wrong way to behave and every couple finds what works for them.'

I followed her eyeline towards Isaac and Bex, who were out on the terrace with their arms round each other. He kissed her on the forehead and said something which made her laugh.

'Your brother and Bex are affectionate in public but it's what they're used to. They were both brought up in families that openly show affection. You told me Craig's parents aren't like that.'

'I've barely seen his parents together with his dad working abroad so often, but I can't say I've ever seen Craig hug his mum or Avery.'

'There you go, then! He's not used to being demonstrative in public. It doesn't mean he doesn't care about you; he just shows it differently. If it bothers you, you should talk to him about it. These things can seem small but they can soon eat away at a relationship.'

I smiled at her, feeling reassured as I always did by one of her pep talks. 'I'm fine. Just being silly. I'm a bit emotional because of your news. Thanks for listening.'

She hugged me to her side. 'Anytime, Angel. I'll always be here for you with a listening ear and a ready hug.'

I was definitely guilty of comparing my relationship but it was mainly because having a boyfriend was still new territory for me. At school and college, I'd been more focused on my studies than finding love, and working in The Starfish Café wasn't the ideal environment for meeting someone. It was predominantly frequented by older customers or families on a trip to the beach to see the seals. It was a destination café; not like a café in Whitsborough Bay's town centre where a lone businessman might drop in for a quick coffee or a meeting and lose his heart to one of the staff.

My love life – or lack of it – was an endless topic of fascination among our regulars and there were very few who hadn't at some point declared that they knew a 'nice young man' for me – a son, grandson, or great-grandson – and I'd perfected the art of smiling politely and changing the subject. Craig's grandparents had been no exception. Clifford and Doris Easton were the sweetest couple and had been regulars at the café for as long as I'd worked there, dropping by every Saturday morning for tea and cake. Doris often spoke of her 'wonderful grandson' and was convinced we'd make 'a fine young couple'. When Clifford passed away five years ago, we didn't see Doris for several weeks so were delighted when she returned, this time accompanied by Craig.

First impressions of Craig – purely based on looks – were positive. He was tall with light brown hair, warm hazel eyes and chiselled cheekbones. But for me, the personality was far more important.

Going to their table to take their order, I hugged Doris, welcomed her back and asked how she was holding up.

'I miss my Clifford every minute of every day but I will be forever grateful for the sixty-three happy years we spent together. And now I have a new cake companion. This is my wonderful grandson, Craig, who I was telling you about. Craig, this is Hollie Gabrielle Brooks. An angelic name for a sweet angel.'

'Aw, Doris, you'll make me cry!' I smiled at Craig. 'Your grandma is lovely, although I'm sure you already know that. Good to meet you at last.'

'And you. I thought it was time I checked this place out for myself. Grandma's always talking about how beautiful the cakes are.'

'And it's not only the cakes that are beautiful,' Doris declared, smiling warmly at me. 'Look at her, Craig! Isn't she a vision? It's a travesty that she's single.'

I didn't know where to put myself. My cheeks had to be the colour of beetroot.

'Grandma!' Craig cried.

'I've always said the two of you would make a fine young couple and I stand by that. So are you going to ask her out?'

Craig's jaw dropped open and he looked as mortified as I felt. 'Grandma! I'm sorry, Hollie. She promised she wouldn't do this.'

Doris crossed her arms and glared at him. 'I speak the truth.'

'Which is embarrassing Hollie and me,' he said through gritted teeth.

'Erm, do you know what you'd like to order or should I give you a bit longer?' I asked, desperate to make my escape.

'I might come over to the counter to look, if that's okay?'

'Of course.' Cringing, I scuttled back to the counter. Doris had just won the award for most embarrassing meddle ever. And now Craig was coming over and it was going to be so awkward.

'I'm sorry about Grandma,' he said. 'Since Granddad died, she's been so fixated on setting us up, convinced we'd be as happy as they were, and I told her I wouldn't bring her here until she promised to let it go.'

'It's fine. Lots of the customers try to do it although they're usually a bit more subtle. I don't know why they're all so convinced their grandsons would be interested in me.' My cheeks flushed again as I realised it might sound like I was fishing for a compliment.

He shuffled on the spot and ran a finger round his shirt collar. 'Actually, I *can* see why, but I'm seeing someone at the moment and—'

'You don't have to explain anything,' I said, holding my hands up to stop him. 'Do you know what you'd like?'

He placed his order, apologised once more, and returned to his table. My lasting memory should have been mortification at Doris's meddling, but all I could picture was the warmth in his eyes and the gentle smile on his lips when he'd said, 'Actually, I *can* see why.'

Craig and Doris became weekly visitors and, as happened with all regular customers, a friendship formed with Craig. Doris continued to meddle and it became a standing joke between us. Each Saturday, Craig came to the counter to check out the cakes but, as he always picked Victoria sponge or chocolate fudge cake, it felt like an excuse to chat to me alone. Even though I knew he was attached, my feelings towards him gradually deepened. He was definitely more than good looks. I loved how devoted he was to Doris, bringing her out every Saturday morning when there were probably a thousand other things he'd rather do, and I allowed myself to imagine that he accompanied her just to see me.

At the start of last year, we were devasted to hear the news that Doris had joined her beloved Clifford. For the next few Saturdays, I kept half an eye on the door, wondering if Craig might stop by on his own but he never did and I resigned myself to never seeing him again. My little fantasy had been exactly that. He was a customer being friendly. Nothing more.

Last June I was out for drinks with Katie and we bumped into Craig in The Old Theatre. He was out with a group of friends celebrating his birthday and we were invited to join them on their pub crawl, then on to a club. Craig was a bit drunk. He kept apologising for not visiting since Doris died and saying he'd missed the café and the cakes. Katie was convinced he was interested in me, especially when she discovered from one of his friends that his relationship was over, but I was so unused to male attention, I couldn't tell the difference between flirty, friendly and drunken gibberish.

As we piled out of the club, he pulled me to one side and said: 'It's not just the café and cakes I've missed. It's you too. I think my grandma might have been right about you and me.'

She had been. For someone who'd never made it past three dates, I was delighted to have made it to way past a year and it was great. Or it would be if I could stop comparing our relationship to other people's.

3

Bonfire Night, eight years ago

I loved my job as a charge nurse at Whitsborough Bay Hospital and had never doubted my career choice for a second. I loved the excitement of working in A&E, never knowing what I'd be dealing with from one hour to the next. Twelve-hour shifts didn't bother me. I'd have worked longer if I could because what I didn't love about my job was all the downtime between shifts. Last night, I came off the second of two twelve-hour day shifts and now I had three days off. What the hell was I meant to do with them?

Colleagues spent the time off shopping, catching up with friends, being with family or going on short breaks. I hated shopping, I didn't have any local friends and my only family was Nanna, so I frequently found myself with empty days and nights bleakly stretching out before me.

I wished I could lie in but I'd never been able to. It probably didn't help that Nanna, who I lived with in Lighthouse View – her three-bedroom three-storey townhouse at the top of Ashby Street in Whitsborough Bay's Old Town – was a creature of habit. She loved to be 'up with the lark' as she called it, clattering about in the kitchen as she made a pot of tea and porridge. As soon as she'd eaten, the vacuum cleaner would whirr into life and she'd turn her old 'wireless' up so she could sing along while she cleaned.

I'd learned that it was easiest to go for a run while she completed her cleaning frenzy. Nanna's many routines amused me until I realised I had several of my own, including running the same 2.4 mile circuit every single day. I always turned left out the door, ran down the street, crossed over to the harbour, stretched out by the railings, then ran south along the seafront.

This morning, being a Tuesday in early November, it was quiet. The shutters were pulled down on the shops and arcades, there weren't many vehicles about, and the only people were dog walkers, cyclists or runners like me.

Pounding my feet in time to my running playlist on my phone, I raced past the lifeboat station and along the wide pathway above South Bay's sandy beach. The Bay Pavilion – an entertainment complex with a theatre, restaurant, bar and function rooms – at the far end of South Bay was almost the halfway point. Turning there would be a two-mile circuit but I liked to push it a bit further, running through the covered walkway and as far as the site of the old lido, now filled in. There the path forked round a grassy circle which acted like a roundabout, sending me on the return route.

Every so often, Nanna got a bee in her bonnet and announced I needed to get out more because 'a young man like you should have more to life than work and a daily run'. She'd joke that she was sick of me being under her feet between shifts and I should get a hobby to fill my time. I'd thought about joining a sports team but quickly dismissed it. I'd never enjoyed team sports – wounded by being the friendless kid who got picked last and therefore was crap at them all. Gyms intimidated me but I'd taken up running in my late teens so, a year after graduating, I decided to challenge myself with long-distance running. By the time I'd built up my distance to a half-marathon, I was so bored with the endless tedium of pounding the pavements and having far too much time to think that I reduced it to back to 2.4 miles a day. And the empty hours stretched out ahead of me once more.

By the time I returned to Lighthouse View this morning, I still had no idea how I was going to spend the next three days.

'Leave it with me. I'm sure he'll say yes,' I heard Nanna say as I pushed open the front door. 'Oh! That's Jake home now. See you later, love.'

My eighty-five-year-old nanna stepped out of the kitchen and into the hall. At 5' 2" she was a full foot shorter than me, with a shock of unruly white hair that, no matter how carefully she styled it, always looked like someone had rubbed it with a balloon.

'What am I going to say yes to?' I asked, rubbing my sweaty face and neck with the hand towel she tossed at me.

'We've lost our lift for tonight. Hilda Beckwith's come down with a migraine.'

'So you want me to drive you and Irene into town?' I asked.

'Yes please, if you don't have other plans.' She raised her eyebrows at me knowingly.

'You know I don't.'

'In that case, we thought you might like to join us for the talk.'

'Thanks, but no thanks. I'm not interested in an evening of poetry.'

'Poetry's at the end of the month. Tonight is...' She paused and scrunched up her face. 'It's something you used to love.'

I stopped rubbing the towel and stiffened. 'Don't say photography.'

'It's photography.'

'Then I'll be your taxi, but no thanks to the ticket.' I set off up the stairs.

'Jake!'

'I'm going for a shower.' I tried to keep my voice gentle. It wasn't Nanna's fault.

'*Jake!*'

I hung my head as the hot water cascaded over my body a few minutes later, feeling ashamed that I'd be turning twenty-seven tomorrow but my older sister Larissa still had a hold over me.

Larissa had been twelve years old when I was born and I was never in doubt as to how much she hated me. Mum died from complications following childbirth so Larissa blamed me for that. She used to nip me, pull my hair, call me names, made snide comments, tell lies about me and generally made life awkward. She wouldn't have photos taken with me – even when I was a baby – so there wasn't a single family photo featuring us both, which hurt Dad because photography was one of his passions.

One of Larissa's many epic cruel moments came when I was eight. Dad bought a new camera and gave me his old one. That summer, between his shifts at the police station, the two of us took our cameras and explored Whitsborough Bay. It was an era before mobile phones or even digital photography so Dad had to send the films away to be developed. It was such a thrill when the photos arrived through the letterbox a week later. My first attempts weren't great – mainly shots of sky or pavement – but I could see an improvement as the summer progressed.

Dad bought me a big cork noticeboard and, by the end of the summer, it was covered with my favourite photos and I could have burst with pride as he pointed out what he loved about each of them.

Larissa had left home by this point and moved in with her boyfriend, Andrew Kent, but she still had a key and often dropped in. Supposedly it was to collect her post but I knew it was really to sneak into my bedroom and damage my things. I'd frequently find jigsaw pieces missing, pages ripped out of books, Lego constructions broken – all stuff that Dad said could have happened accidentally but which I knew were Larissa because I took good care of my belongings.

Then one day we arrived home to find every single photograph on my board had been defaced. She'd drawn marker pen moustaches and glasses on photos of people, put crosses through some photos, and scribbled all over others. What hurt the most were the ones on which she'd written insults: *crap, rubbish, disappointing, try harder, you're kidding, appalling, laughable.*

Larissa feigned innocence but Dad was having none of it this time. He'd been exceptionally patient with her through years of pettiness and awkwardness but it was as though the vandalism was the straw that broke the camel's back. I cowered in my bedroom with my hands over my ears as he yelled at her but she gave as good as she got and it went on for ages. The neighbours called the police and a patrol car turned up – awkward when Dad was a police sergeant. Larissa stormed out and they didn't speak for the next fortnight.

The photos went in the bin and I returned the camera to Dad. I could have ignored her scribbles but it was the note that I found under my pillow – the one I chose not to mention to Dad or Nanna at the time – that killed my newfound love for photography:

Do you have any idea how much of Dad's time and money you have just wasted with your pathetic little photography hobby? And for what? A monkey wearing a blindfold could have taken better photos. You are useless. Always have been. Always will be. You can't take photographs. You can't do anything and you will

*never amount to anything. The day you accept that, the world will
be a happier place.*

I still had the note tucked away in a box file in the back of my
wardrobe. I didn't need to look at it as those words were permanently etched in my mind but, every so often, I dug it out.

It took several years to get to the point where Larissa's taunts
had the opposite effect on me than she'd intended. Instead of
making me crumble, they drove me to success. I'd prove her wrong.
I *would* amount to something. Her words pushed me to achieve top
grades for my GCSEs and A levels, and a first-class degree. But I'd
never picked up a camera since. And I'd never told Nanna about the
note. Larissa's attitude had hurt her enough over the years and I
didn't need to add to it.

When I finished in the shower, I marched into my bedroom and
rummaged in the back of the wardrobe for that box file. Drawing
back my shoulders and holding my head high, I read the crumpled
note. Sod it!

'Nanna!' I called, running down the stairs in my towel. 'I've
changed my mind. I *will* join you tonight.'

'I think that's the right decision, love,' she said gently. 'Don't let
her win.'

* * *

'Ey, Violet, I'm not buying that Hilda Beckwith's story about a
migraine,' Irene announced to Nanna the moment she opened the
car door. 'I think she's got her fancy man round again.'

I caught Nanna's eye while Irene was distracted buckling herself
in. Eleven years Nanna's junior, Irene Trent had lived in Seafarer
Lodge next door all my life. She was kind-hearted, but she was an

eternal curtain-twitcher and consequently knew everyone and everything.

'Hi, Irene,' I said. 'All set?'

'Oh, hello, young Jake. Yes, good to go. You'll love it tonight. They're brilliant photographers. Been all over the world. Unbelievable photos.'

'Sounds good.' I pulled out of the space and headed down the hill towards the seafront.

'Where was I?' Irene said. 'Oh yes! So, there was this blue estate car parked there from four and she called not five minutes after that. Bit of a coincidence, don't you think? The same car was there two nights ago and her husband's only six months cold. Bit soon if you ask me…' And she was off, sharing the gospel according to Irene Trent about how long after a bereavement it was decent to move on.

Nanna and I sat in silence, smiling. Irene would run out of steam soon. She always did. Her own husband Derek had died twenty-five years ago. With no children and no extended family, I suspected she was lonely and that's what led to the tidal wave of information whenever we saw her. Sure enough, by the time I dropped them outside the library and went to park, Irene had drawn breath and it was Nanna's turn to speak.

Irene had been a good friend to us both over the years, along with another neighbour, Kay Summers, who lived in Seashell Cottage on a side street opposite Lighthouse View. Kay was younger still – turning sixty next year – but the three of them were single and always in and out of each other's houses for a cuppa and a chat. I suspected Kay would have joined them tonight but she currently travelling round the world. All right for some!

I found a parking space down a side street a few minutes away and, as I walked back to the library, I tried to recall how I'd felt the first time

I looked at one of the photos I'd taken and realised it was good. It was a picture of the red and white striped lighthouse on the small island off Starfish Point. In focus, in frame, central. I'd been elated when Dad hugged me and sang my praises. That particular shot had taken pride of place on my noticeboard. Larissa had scribbled one word on it: *shite.*

Would tonight's talk inspire me sufficiently to pick up a camera again? I doubted it. The speakers, Philip and Michael Heslington, were a father and son team of professional photographers from Whitsborough Bay. I wasn't sure if they'd be focusing on local photography or their worldwide travels, but I supposed looking at some decent photos wouldn't be a bad way to pass an hour. It wasn't like I had a better offer.

* * *

The event was in a large auditorium above the library. Nanna and Irene had secured seats a few rows from the front and waved me over. A few minutes later, the lights dimmed and a member of the library staff walked up to the podium to thank everyone for coming and introduce the evening's speakers.

Philip, who was maybe in his early sixties, took to the stage. 'It's great to have a full house. Michael and I weren't sure whether we'd get many takers with it being Bonfire Night so looking out at a sea of faces is a huge relief. As you've given up the opportunity to see the fireworks tonight, we thought we'd start by sharing some images we've taken of fireworks displays.'

Several photos of stunning displays appeared one after the other on the large screen behind him.

Michael, roughly in his early thirties, stepped up beside his dad. 'Dad and I have been all over the world and we've seen some spectacular fireworks displays on our travels. Any guesses where those photos were taken?'

Various glamorous locations were shouted out.

'Some great suggestions,' Michael said. 'We've taken photos in many of those places, but all the images you saw just now were taken in the same place: Whitsborough Bay.'

A gasp rippled round the room.

'This is a beautiful town surrounded by amazing countryside and home to more wildlife than you might imagine. Up and down the coast, there's so much versatility from sandy beaches to rugged cliffs to historic buildings. Our intention tonight is to show you that you don't have to jump on an aeroplane to take stunning photographs when you have it all right here on your doorstep.'

I don't think I moved a muscle for the next hour. Philip and Michael had me captivated. The photos were outstanding but what really hooked me was when they talked about the skill needed to be a good photographer, showing how different a photo could turn out if they changed their position or the camera settings. There was way more to photography than I'd appreciated and I was eager to learn more.

Larissa's voice was still in my head telling me I was useless but I could study. I could learn. I could prove her wrong. Again.

* * *

I threaded my arm through Nanna's as we shuffled out of our seats. For the last month or so, I'd noticed her being a little less steady on her feet. I knew better than to deliberately offer her my arm and wouldn't dare suggest she use a stick as it would earn me a jovial clip round the ear and an accusation of being a 'cheeky little blighter', but I was keeping my eye on her. She'd been blessed with good health and fitness until now, which was just as well because she hadn't been blessed with much else: her husband running off when their only son – my dad – was two, the death of my parents, and being saddled at the age of sixty-seven with an angry, confused nine-year-old.

'You were gripped, weren't you?' Nanna said, tightening her hold when she wobbled.

'I need to buy myself a camera.'

She patted my arm. 'Irene and I hoped you'd say that.'

Bonfire Night, seven years ago

'Don't think we'll be going out on the terrace this year,' Mum said, placing a tray of hot chocolates on the table of the nearest seating booth while Angie and I hung red and gold baubles on the Christmas tree in the café. 'Look at that rain.'

It had been raining steadily since mid-afternoon and the forecast suggested it would continue until the early hours, although there might be a couple of breaks. With any luck, one of those would be around seven when the display started.

'Do you think that means no fireworks?' Angie asked, looking hopeful.

'There's been torrential rain before and it hasn't stopped them,' Mum said. 'Sorry, Angie.'

'Storeroom for me again,' Angie joked.

I loved fireworks and Bonfire Night had to be one of my favourite nights of the year because it symbolised so much happiness: putting up the tree at the café which heralded the start of the Christmas celebrations, a lovely evening with family and friends and, since last year, Mum's remission from cancer. That deserved the brightest and loudest of fireworks.

'Tree's looking good,' Mum said, standing beside me. 'Especially our beautiful angel Hollie Gabrielle at the top.'

'Mum!' I protested. 'She doesn't look like me.'

'She does!'

'I think she does too,' Angie added. 'And so do the customers.'

'My cheeks aren't that pink.'

'They are when you get embarrassed,' Mum quipped.

'And when it's cold,' Angie added.

Mum laughed. 'And when you're excited.'

'And when you get too close to the oven or you've—'

'Okay, okay, I get it! I have rosy cheeks.'

'Which is why she looks just like you,' Mum said, hugging me to her side. 'My two special angels and both absolutely beautiful.'

'I think you need to find a Christmas elf that looks like Isaac.'

Mum laughed. 'Love it! I accept your challenge.' She stepped up to the tree and ran her fingers over one of the wooden decorations I'd made. 'These are gorgeous. My dad would be so thrilled. Another family tradition kept alive.'

I'd wood-turned a few Christmas trees, snowmen and bells – my first attempts at making Christmas decorations. A passion for working with wood had been passed down through Mum's family. It had started with my great grandfather, who used to whittle wood to create animals for my granddad when he was a child. He taught Granddad, who also developed a fondness for wood turning. He passed on his knowledge to Mum, but wood never captured her interest because she'd shared Granny's passion instead: baking. Granddad hoped that he'd have a grandchild one day who could act as his apprentice but it wasn't to be. He had a fatal heart attack a year after Isaac was born and Granny joined him when I was four. Granny had asked Mum to keep Granddad's hand-held tools and lathe and pass them to Isaac when he turned sixteen, hoping the passion for wood might skip a generation onto him. It didn't. It passed to me instead. Isaac loved the outdoors and spent most of his spare time mastering various watersports. If he was inside, his time was spent pursuing his other passion of maritime history. He had zero interest in being locked away in a shed with a lathe but I was fascinated by how a lump of wood could be transformed with skill and imagination, so Granddad's lathe and tools passed down to me and, at fourteen, I created my first of many bowls and was hooked.

'I really think you could sell these,' Mum said.

'Me too,' Angie agreed. 'And I'm first in the queue. Can I have a set for my tree please?'

'And I'll have a set for home,' Mum added. 'Let me know how much.'

I blushed – just like the angel on the tree – flattered by the compliments. 'I'll happily make you both a set, but I'm not charging.'

Angie shook her head. 'Then I don't want one. Don't sell yourself short, Hollie. What you've done here takes skill and talent.'

'I echo that,' Mum said. 'I'm so proud of you. I bet you'll find customers wanting some too. Will you think about it, Angel?'

'Maybe.' I gazed at my creations. I'd been proud of them too and had initially considered making extras to sell, but Craig had been so dismissive when I'd shown them to him that I'd swiftly buried that idea.

'What's it meant to be?' he'd asked, scowling at the piece of wood.

'A snowman.'

'Where's his face?'

'I haven't drawn it on yet.' I hadn't been sure whether I was going to add a face and buttons as I thought the top hat resting on two different-sized spheres made it obvious what it was. I hadn't mentioned that to Mum or Angie as I didn't want them to think badly of Craig. I'd asked for feedback and he was merely being honest. But Mum and Angie were always honest too and they loved them. I needed to believe in myself more when it came to my woodwork.

Mum added a couple more baubles to the tree and stepped back. 'I think we might have achieved full-on festive fabulousness. Hot chocolate time! Should be able to drink it before the first guests arrive.'

We sat in one of the window booths and sipped on our drinks, laughing at a dollop of cream on Angie's nose.

'One year in remission,' I said, raising my mug to Mum. 'And looking a picture of health.'

'Helped by my hair *finally* growing back.' She flicked her shoulder-length blonde hair to prove her point. It was thicker than before and curly, which she'd said was an unexpected silver lining.

We finished our drinks and I cleared the crates and boxes away as usual while Mum and Angie brought out the food. Before long the café was filled with laughter and chatter as we celebrated another Bonfire Night with the people we loved.

* * *

By 6.45 p.m., there was no sign of Katie or Craig. Craig had an appointment and, although he'd promised me he'd make it for the fireworks this year, I knew what these things were like for running over. It wasn't like Katie to be late, though. She was usually one of the first.

The door opened and I looked over expectantly but it was

Martin. I watched as he greeted Angie with a quick peck on the cheek. It was all very formal and awkward – like Craig behaved towards me in public – although I'd never noticed that about them before. I hoped everything was okay.

Following my conversation with Mum at last year's party, I'd decided not to make an issue of it with Craig because he wasn't a particularly tactile person even when we were alone. We were the classic case of opposites attract. I'd learned a few things from him about the importance of planning and I'd like to think he'd learned a little from me about being spontaneous and living in the moment. Although maybe that was more of a work in progress.

I'd have liked him to have been more supportive of my wood-working but I think it was that he didn't get it, being a practical rather than creative person. Although Bex was supportive of Isaac's hobby and she didn't 'get' that.

My brother and Kyle were fascinated by local maritime history but their absolute passion was smuggling, which had been rife on the North Yorkshire Coast during the eighteenth to mid-nineteenth centuries, including at Starfish Point. One wall of his bedroom was covered in cork tiles like a giant noticeboard and the cork was barely visible for maps, charts, photos and Post-it notes covered in questions as they attempted to solve the local mystery of Tingler's Treasure. Isaac and Kyle called it 'The Smuggler's Key'. There'd been no space to replicate the board at his and Bex's house so he kept it at Sandy Croft and regularly visited with Kyle. Bex never complained, although I sometimes wondered if it provided the perfect excuse not to have Kyle round their house. Whether that was the case or not, she was supportive of Isaac's hobby in a way that Craig wasn't supportive of mine.

I noticed a lull in the rain, providing an opportune moment to take the bin bags out. I'd only just raised the lid of the wheelie bin when the sound of Craig's raised voice drew me to a halt.

'Whatever you think you know, you're wrong.'

Frowning, I quietly lowered the lid.

'Really? So why don't I believe you?'

My stomach lurched at Katie's voice, also raised. Since when had the pair of them rowed like that? I placed the bin bags on the floor and crept along the front of the building in the direction of their voices.

'Because you don't want to believe me,' Craig responded.

'You can't treat people like that and get away with it.'

'I'm not doing anything to anyone.'

I jumped as Katie stormed round the corner, stopping when she came face to face with me, guilt written across her face.

I was about to ask what was going on but Craig shouted, 'And you needn't think...' He stopped mid-flow as he rounded the corner. 'Hollie! I didn't know you were there.'

'I heard voices. Why are you two arguing?'

They exchanged glances and Katie tucked her hair behind her ear, which she only ever did when she was nervous. 'It's nothing. Don't worry.'

'It didn't sound like nothing.'

'It *is* nothing,' Craig said, smiling at me. 'Avery's been whining about me at work yet again and has dragged Katie into it.'

I looked at Katie who shrugged and nodded. 'She was upset. You know what he's like with her.'

I did. Craig and Avery frequently clashed. Childhood bickering had escalated into competitiveness as adults. Both were career-driven and ambitious. Craig had initially been proud of his little sister for her career success and prided himself in having given her some helpful advice. That all changed when Avery recently announced that she had enough money saved to put a deposit down on her first home. Craig and I hadn't come close to that point.

I looked between Katie and Craig, shaking my head. 'You have to let it go, Craig!'

'She's three years younger than me.'

'What's age got to do with it? You're both brilliant at your jobs but you're on different career paths. Avery's happens to award bigger bonuses and you can't keep comparing yourself to other people.'

As I spoke the words, the double standards weren't lost on me. Despite Mum's pep talk last year, I was still comparing our relationship and it wasn't just affection in public or support with hobbies. Craig had proposed to me in June, or rather we'd got engaged in June as he hadn't actually popped the question.

We'd been out with his housemates for his twenty-ninth birthday and, while they were at the bar, he said, 'It's two years since we started seeing each other so we might as well make it official. I've got you this.' He plonked a navy-blue ring box on the table.

I flicked the lid open to reveal an enormous rectangular-cut diamond surrounded by smaller ones set in a gold diamond-encrusted band. 'Wow! It's...' *Ugly? Gaudy? Ostentatious? Not me at all?*

'Three months' salary,' he declared proudly. 'Put it on, then!'

I slipped the ring onto my finger, trying to get a grip on my emotions. The man I loved wanted to marry me, which was amazing and exciting and I should be tearing up with delight instead of disappointment. Craig wasn't romantic. I knew that about him. He wasn't the sort who'd whisk me away to Venice or Rome and get down on bended knee. This 'proposal' was practical, like him. We'd talked about getting married at some point so it was what I wanted, but I'd always imagined that he'd surprise me by doing something romantic, which would make the proposal all the more special because it was going against type.

'I nearly chose platinum but you always wear that gold necklace so I figured gold was your favourite.'

I automatically reached for the chain round my neck. If he'd ever asked, he'd have known that the necklace was for sentimental reasons only and I preferred silver. But it was sweet that he'd thought to match my necklace and it was perhaps romantic that he'd chosen our two-year anniversary on which to get engaged.

Over the weeks that followed, my disappointment was swallowed up by the excitement of wedding plans, setting a date for June the year after next.

Then Isaac shared his plan for New Year's Eve: an overnight stay in one of those clear domes in Iceland where he was going to propose to Bex under the Northern Lights. The two proposals were worlds apart and, for a moment, I had an insight into Craig's world, experiencing envy towards a sibling.

* * *

'Are you sure everything's okay?' I asked Katie once we were inside and Craig had disappeared to change out of his suit.

'Yeah, it's fine.' Katie's words didn't match her expression.

'When you pout like that, you look just like Serena.'

'Urgh!' She threw me a dazzling smile instead. 'Do I look like me now?'

'Much better.'

Serena was three years older than Katie but they could pass for twins with the same long dark hair, deep blue eyes and full red lips. They were no match in personality. Where Katie was warm and full of fun, Serena was cold and cruel. She made it clear she didn't like me, which was fine by me as the feeling was mutual.

Desperate to escape Serena's clutches, Katie had saved her salary like crazy and I couldn't have been happier for her the day I helped her move out last year into a house of her own. She'd barely spoken to her sister or her mum since and it was definitely their loss, not hers.

I glanced towards the door. 'Trey's just arrived so can we have a genuine smile from you now?'

Her eyes lit up as she saw him. 'Sorry. Thanks for cheering me up, as always.'

'What are best friends for?'

* * *

Craig and Katie put their differences aside and we had the usual fun and laughter-filled Bonfire Night event. The rain held off long enough to enjoy the fireworks from the terrace, but picked up again by eight.

As the evening drew to a close, I found myself seated round a table with Mum, Angie, Bex and Katie with mugs of coffee and tea.

'It's been another lovely Bonfire Night,' Mum said, smiling at us all. 'Thank you all for coming. I've made a big decision. After getting the kitchen refurbished at Sandy Croft, I've realised how shabby The Starfish Café is looking…'

'And dated!' Angie said, giving her a gentle nudge.

Mum pretended to look offended. 'What could you possibly mean? Are you suggesting that pine tables and a Swiss cuckoo clock are last season?'

'No! The season before that. Or maybe even the one before that.'

'I like the cuckoo clock,' Bex protested. 'It's cute.'

'Thank you!' Mum said, patting Bex's arm. 'At least one of you has good taste. And it's a very special cuckoo clock. Joe bought me that in Switzerland on our honeymoon. But I'm maybe thinking an alpine-themed café isn't quite the thing for North Yorkshire so it's time for a change.'

'What are you thinking, Mum?' I asked.

'Something fresh.'

'Knock it down and rebuild it in the shape of a starfish,' Katie suggested, giggling.

'That might be a bit extreme, but I do like the idea of still having a theme.'

'What about something nautical with starfish and seals and octopuses?' Bex frowned. 'Or is it octopi?'

'What about New England-themed?' I suggested, building on Bex's idea, immediately able to visualise how different and amazing the café would look. 'White walls and white furniture but blue, turquoise and even red accents on the seat covers, pictures and crockery.'

Nods of approval went round the table.

'Congratulations, Angel!' Mum grinned at me. 'You have just secured the job of chief designer and project manager. I love the New England idea.'

I gasped. 'But I know nothing about design.'

'You've got a better eye for detail and colour than me. I am, after all, responsible for the cuckoo clock.'

As more ideas were thrown into the mix for how to develop the New England theme, I could feel the excitement building. I gazed round the café, smiling. A refurbishment was exactly what it needed and it should help bring in some new customers who might have previously dismissed the café as dated. They'd hopefully become regulars and keep us running for decades to come.

'I can help you create some mood boards if you like,' Katie suggested. 'Like I did for my house.'

'Yes, please.'

'I love it!' Mum enthused. 'So it's out with the pine tables, plastic table cloths and the cuckoo clock and in with fresh clean lines and nautical colours. I can't wait to see it!'

* * *

'Can you manage another cuppa?' Mum asked when we arrived back at Sandy Croft later that evening while Dad went to drop Isaac and Bex home.

'I have tea sloshing round inside me, but I'll keep you company if you'd like one.'

Dad's surprise extravagant Christmas gift for Mum last year had been something she'd longed for: the family kitchen/diner of her dreams. He said it was also to celebrate the great news about her cancer. Work had started in the New Year and it was now my favourite room in the house. The fittings were modern – a cream double range oven and an American-style fridge-freezer – and the pale sage units were an on-trend colour but the style complimented the property's Victorian era. A large island unit housed a Belfast sink at one end and a breakfast bar at the other, and the dining table was in an extension with a vaulted ceiling and doors out onto the garden. My absolute favourite part was a snug with a real fire, a pair of two-seater sofas, and Willow's bed.

I stoked the fire while Mum made her drink and we settled on a sofa each. Willow was curled up in her dog bed asleep, no doubt exhausted after an evening of wandering round seeking attention at the café.

'Another successful Bonfire Night soiree,' Mum said, smiling at me. 'But the best part of the evening is always getting home and being with you. Although this could be our last year together. You and Craig might have your own home by this time next year. It'll soon just be your dad, me and Willow rattling round in this big old house.'

'You don't get rid of us that easily! I'm in no rush to move out and, even when I do, my workshop will still be here. Isaac keeps coming back to add another clue to "The Smuggler's Key" so we both have forever ties. And I couldn't imagine not being here every Christmas.'

'It warms my heart so much to hear you say that.' Tears sparkled in Mum's eyes and I rushed over to sit beside her and snuggle up close. 'Sandy Croft will always be your home and your dad and I will always be right here with endless hugs.'

If only that last part had been true.

5

JAKE

Bonfire Night, seven years ago

I stepped back from the magnetic whiteboard on the top floor at Lighthouse View and scrutinised the A4 photos I'd printed off using my brand new printer, an early birthday gift from Nanna. It wasn't my birthday until tomorrow but we never celebrated it on the day itself. Usually, we didn't celebrate it at all.

Inspired by Philip and Michael Heslington's talk last Bonfire Night, I'd picked up a second-hand camera and lenses and borrowed a few photography books from the library. I'd never appreciated how involved it was. I spent hours online watching vlogs from professional and amateur photographers, lapping up hints and tips about camera settings, exposures, lighting, and poring over reference books. I learned all about the 'blue hour' before sunrise and sunset, the 'golden hour' during these times and 'astronomical twilight' when the sky turned completely black. I studied the rules of composition – leading lines, rule of thirds, the golden ratio – and how to digitally develop pictures using post-processing software. I'd done what Nanna wanted – found a hobby – but I still managed to be under her feet!

'Trust you to pick a hobby that takes up so much space,' she'd said, shooing me, my camera and my books off the kitchen table at the start of the summer so she could prepare dinner. 'The spare bedroom needs a good clear-out. If you do that and create some space for the stuff I want to keep, you can have it as your photography studio.'

'Seriously?' The spare bedroom took up the whole of the top floor. With the staircase leading directly into the room and windows front and back, it was a brilliant space. When Dad died and I moved in with Nanna, I'd asked if I could have it as my bedroom but she wouldn't let me. Too much stuff to clear out. Needed the room in case Larissa ever wanted to stay. As if Larissa would ever stay in the same house as me!

'It might as well be used,' she said.

I threw my arms round her. 'You're the best of the best.'

'You won't be saying that when you start sorting through my stuff. It's become a dumping ground.'

There was a *lot* of junk up there, but six tip-runs later and a few days of labour and I had my studio set up. 'Studio' was perhaps an exaggeration as I wasn't interested in indoor photography so it wasn't like I had lights or backdrops set up in there. I had a large desk, a printer cabinet, shelves for my equipment and books, and an armchair.

'Knock, knock!'

I spun round to face a tall brunette coming up the last few stairs, her hands thrust into the pockets of a black puffer jacket.

'Cara! What are you doing here?'

'Nice to see you too, Jake.' She planted her hands on her hips, sarcasm dripping from every word.

'I thought we were meeting down the seafront.' There was no 'thought' about it; that had *definitely* been the arrangement. I never invited women to the house.

'We were but I got there early and didn't fancy hanging about in the rain so I thought I'd walk up and call for you. Okay?' The last word was accompanied with a glare and the tone indicated a statement of fact rather than a question.

Feeling an argument brewing – not the finest start to a first date – I swallowed down my discomfort at having her in my personal space and smiled. 'Looking forward to the fireworks?'

She smiled back. Disaster averted. 'Always. I love Bonfire Night.' She wandered towards me and glanced at the whiteboard. 'What are you doing?'

'Looking at some photos.'

'Did you take them?'

'Yeah. I've been studying photography for the past year. They're the first ones I've printed off.' I wanted to ask her what she thought but all I could hear in my head was Larissa's voice telling me everything I did was crap. I wasn't ready to hear that from a stranger.

Cara peered a little closer. 'What is it?'

My jaw tightened at the whine in her voice and I fought to keep my tone light. 'It's a piece of wood on the beach tangled in some fishing net.'

She curled up her lip and scrunched her forehead into the ugliest expression. 'Why would you want to take a photo of some old washed-up crap?'

I tensed. *Because it's interesting. Because it's full of colour and texture. Because it took hours of processing to get the light just right.* But I didn't say any of those things.

'Should we go? Don't want to miss the fireworks.' I pulled on my hoodie and headed down the stairs. It was going to be a long evening.

* * *

'Your nanna seems nice,' Cara said, linking her arm through mine as we hurried along the seafront towards The Lobster Pot opposite the harbour after the firework display ended. The rain had stopped before the fireworks started but more was forecast so we wanted to get inside before it hit.

'She's great.' I sighed inwardly, knowing exactly where this was going.

'And that's her house?'

'Yes.'

'How long have you lived there?'

'Most of my life.'

'Why do you still live with your Nanna?'

Translation: *You're in your late twenties. Why the hell haven't you left home?*

Fortunately, we'd reached the pub. I opened the door for her and we were hit with a blast of warmth and chatter. 'I'll get the drinks in. What are you having?'

As I leaned against the bar waiting for the server to pull my pint and pour a glass of red wine for Cara, I closed my eyes for a moment. This was why I didn't date. Too many questions. Too much intrusion. Cara seemed nice enough – bit bolshy perhaps – but I already knew I wouldn't see her again after tonight.

For the past few years, I'd frequented The Lobster Pot on a Monday evening. I knew how worried Nanna was about me never going out so it was my way of keeping her off my back. It was usually quiet so I could read the paper and drink a couple of pints until the crowd from the lifeboat station appeared after their training session. At that point, the clientele would quadruple and so would the noise but I'd usually read what I wanted to by then and would relax at the bar, listening to the laughter and banter and wondering what it felt like to be part of a team like that.

This week had been different. Cara was serving. I'd never seen her before and, for reasons unbeknown to me, I struck up a conversation. I discovered she was new to the area and had picked up a few casual bar shifts while she looked for a permanent job. She'd heard that Bonfire Night on South Bay was impressive but she didn't want to go alone so I stupidly offered to accompany her and invited her for a drink afterwards.

It wasn't Cara's fault she'd turned up at Lighthouse View earlier. I shouldn't have let my guard down and told her where I lived. I'd therefore been careful not to hold that against her, especially when she'd been trying to get out the rain. I'd tried not to let her comment about my photos get to me either because I knew Larissa had made me touchy but, my God, those endless questions! No stone was left unturned: *Why did you want to be a nurse? Why were you brought up by your nanna? What happened to your parents? Do you have siblings? Why were you in the pub on your own on Monday night?*

First dates were meant to be about getting to know each other, which logically meant questions, but she was full of the types of questions I didn't want to answer. Every time I steered the conversation away from family, she found her way back. What was wrong with mindless conversation about music and films?

'Can you please quit it with the interrogation?' I asked, unable to bear it any longer. I kept my tone light. I even gave her an apologetic smile. Didn't do me much good because the look she gave me was reminiscent of a Larissa special.

'What the fuck's your problem?'

'I don't have a problem, but when someone keeps steering you away from questions about their family, that's a big clue that they maybe don't want to talk about them.'

'And when someone keeps ignoring your questions but doesn't

have the decency to say *I'd prefer not to talk about my family*, that's a big clue that they're a fucking weirdo.' She stood up, necked back her drink, and pulled on her coat. 'No wonder you were on your own on Monday.'

That was a low blow but I wasn't going to fight back. 'I'm sorry it didn't work out.'

'I'm not. Lucky escape if you ask me. Where can I get a taxi?'

'There's usually a couple by the harbour. I'll show you.'

I left my half-drunk pint as I raced after her out of the pub. *Please let there be a taxi there.*

Thankfully there was. She refused to look at me as it pulled away. I couldn't blame her. I wasn't proud of how I'd handled it.

Cara's taxi disappeared into the distance. I checked the time on my phone – just past nine – and shoved my hands in my pockets. I didn't want to go home as Nanna would still be up and she'd have her own questions. I kicked aside a few burnt-out sparklers as I sauntered along the seafront, past the entrance to the Old Town. I leaned on the metal railings beyond the lifeboat station and looked up and down the beach below. The tide was out and there were still a few fires spread intermittently across the sand, some small with a couple of people standing by them and others much bigger with groups crowded round them, the return of the rain not putting them off. Private fireworks displays across town occasionally lit the sky, the bangs echoing out to sea.

It was a cold, wet evening but there was no wind so the dark sea beyond the fires was fairly calm. I shuddered and turned away. Enough.

One of Nanna's routines was bed at 10 p.m. so I continued along the seafront up to The Bay Pavilion, skirting round puddles and avoiding overflowing gutters. Guilt prodded me all the way. I should never have asked Cara out. When she'd smiled at me in the pub on Monday night, I should have politely smiled back and continued reading my paper. It had been wrong to chat to her and even worse to suggest a date, knowing how close we were to my birthday. Even if she hadn't asked me all those questions tonight, the outcome would probably have still been the same. I was always in a world of my own around my birthday. Distant. Grumpy. It was something to be endured rather than celebrated. A day to reflect and remember, although I often wished I could forget.

As I returned to Ashby Street a little later, I glanced back at the sea once more. It would be nineteen years tomorrow since Dad died. How had nearly two decades passed?

* * *

I hung my soggy coat and hat up by the door and kicked off my boots, frowning at the light coming from the kitchen.

'What are you still doing up?' I asked Nanna, feeling anxious about the break in her routine.

'I wanted to make sure you were okay.' She removed the pan of boiling milk from the hob and poured it into two mugs. We hadn't had hot milk for years.

'Why wouldn't I be?' I could hear the uncertainty in my voice.

She passed me a mug and sat at the kitchen table. 'You tell me, lovey.'

I sighed as I sat down beside her. 'It was a disaster, Nanna. Like a job interview. Question after question.'

'Oh dear. What did you do?'

'Kept trying to change the subject. She left just after nine in a huff. Told me I was a weirdo.'

'Oh, lovey, I'm sorry. I hope you know you're not.'

I shrugged. 'I can see why she'd think I am. I shouldn't have gone out with her. Not at this time of year.'

Nanna patted my hand. 'I was surprised when she turned up.'

'Not as surprised as me.'

'I guess you won't be seeing her again.'

'Definitely burned my bridges there.'

Nanna looked at me thoughtfully. 'You say it's the time of year, but—'

I knew where she was going as it wasn't the first time she'd suggested she was holding me back. 'Don't you worry about me. I'm in no rush to meet someone. I've got my hands full with you and Irene. Two demanding women in my life is quite enough.'

'It's not me! It's that Irene Trent. She's the trouble-maker.' Nanna squeezed my hand. 'You're a good lad, Jake, and I've been glad of your company over the years but don't ever close yourself off to love because you feel you need to look after me. I can manage on my own if you meet someone and want to move out.'

'Is this your way of telling me you've got a fancy man like Hilda Beckwith and you want me to move out so you can move him in?'

Nanna chuckled. 'Oh, yeah, I've got a host of suitors queuing up.'

We sat in companionable silence for several minutes, sipping on our drinks, until Nanna pushed back her chair. 'My bed's calling.'

She swayed and I reached out my arm to steady her. 'Did you slip a little something into yours when I wasn't looking?'

'Cheeky little blighter! I'm just tired.'

'Same here.' I faked a yawn. 'I might need you to help me up to my bed.'

Nanna didn't object when I held out my arm. We took each stair slowly and I felt her grip tighten. The years seemed to have caught up with her over the past twelve months and it terrified me. Without Nanna, I had nobody.

Saturday 25th June, five years ago

I walked down the stone-flagged aisle in the cool church, the most stunning lace wedding gown swishing from side to side. All round me, family and friends smiled. Some blew me kisses and others dabbed their eyes with tissues.

At the end of the aisle, Craig had his back to me and my heart leapt with love. Today was the day. Four years together and we were about to say 'I do' to a lifetime of happiness.

Only something felt wrong. My stomach lurched. The congregation looked confused as they glanced from me to the altar where... Oh my God! She was already there next to my fiancé! Tall. Long dark hair. She turned towards me and raised her eyebrows, a ghost of a smile on her full red lips as if to say, 'He's mine now!'

This was all wrong. It was my wedding day; not hers.

I looked up at Dad for reassurance. 'I'm sorry, Angel,' he said, his voice sad and distant. 'I never wanted to leave you.'

*I followed his eyeline to the front of the church. Craig had gone. She'd
gone. In their place were three coffins.*

*Heart thumping, I looked back at Dad only it wasn't him anymore. It
was the vicar looking down at me with watery eyes full of sympathy. He
patted my arm. 'I'm so sorry for your loss.'*

'Dad!' I cried. 'Dad!'

I sat upright in bed, my nightie drenched in sweat, my cheeks
damp, calling out for my dad. Another bad dream. I took several
shuddery gulps of air as my eyes adjusted to the early morning
gloom.

Drawing my legs up to my chest, I wrapped my arms round
them and sobbed. If only it was all a nightmare but it was based on
reality. I wouldn't be getting married tomorrow because *she'd* taken
Craig from me.

But that heartbreak was eclipsed by the devastation of losing
Dad and Isaac just after Christmas eighteen months ago and Mum
a year later. In the space of a year, how had my life gone from
having everything to having nothing?

* * *

'Oh my goodness! What time did you get here this morning?' Angie
cried, staring wide-eyed at the results of my epic baking frenzy.
Several batches of scones, two quiches, two pies, brownies, flapjacks
and cakes were spread across the kitchen worktops.

'Quarter past four. I woke up at two and there was no way I was
getting back to sleep so I thought I might as well come here and
crack on.' My attempt at sounding breezy didn't fool Angie.

'Another bad dream?'

I sighed. 'Every night this week.' I outlined the latest one.

'It's bound to feel strange,' Angie said, her voice full of
sympathy.

'Why, though? It makes no sense. It's not like I love Craig anymore.'

'But you did once and, despite what he did to you, it's going to be on your mind that today would have been your wedding day. And do you know why else I think you're struggling to sleep?'

'Hit me with it.' I'd welcome any insights as I couldn't fathom why the wedding (or lack of it) was preying on my mind so much when the truth was I was well shot of him. How he could have done what he did while I was going through hell was beyond me. His behaviour had been despicable. Hers, too.

'Because being with Craig, getting engaged and planning your wedding was from before. It was from happy times. And because even if you'd still been together, today would have been a difficult day for you.'

'I honestly don't know if I could have gone through with it. It wouldn't have been right without Mum, Dad and Isaac.'

'If you'd still loved Craig, you could have,' she said, her voice soft and gentle. 'You're the strongest person I know.'

'I don't feel very strong sometimes.' The words were quiet. Uncertain.

Angie drew me into a hug. 'I know. Neither do I. But we have each other, we have The Starfish Café, and we have our wonderful customers. And maybe a few unusual ones too.'

I laughed as I pulled away. 'Unusual? You couldn't possibly be referring to Ten Sugars or Mrs Sultana, could you?'

She winked at me. 'Among others. Time for a cuppa?'

'Yes please.'

I smiled to myself as Angie headed into the café to make us drinks. I don't know what I'd have done without her over the past eighteen months. She'd been my rock, I'd been hers, and the café had given us both meaning and focus. I was so relieved I hadn't listened to Craig.

When the cancer returned for the second time, Mum wanted to discuss the future of the café. She was determined to fight it but only wanted to return to work on a part-time basis which would mean promoting me to full-time manager and making Angie the assistant manager. However, she was conscious that I might not have chosen to work in the café if it hadn't been a family business so she'd had it valued and, if I wanted to pursue a different career, she'd sell up and give me a chunk of the proceeds to invest in re-training and a house deposit. I was so touched that she'd even consider selling her beloved café for me but The Starfish Café was in my blood and the idea of selling up made me feel queasy. I loved the café, the customers, the staff, and I loved baking. There was nothing I'd rather do. I also didn't feel ready to move out so I gratefully accepted the promotion.

When I told Craig about Mum's offer, he got really funny about it. He thought I should take the money and didn't seem to understand that the café meant more to me than a house deposit ever could.

It was a subject that cropped up every so often, especially after Avery moved into her first home. I lost track of how many times we paused by an estate agent's window while he gazed dreamily at the properties on display. He never said anything but I knew exactly what his exaggerated sigh meant: *we could have afforded that if it wasn't for you.* For me, selling up absolutely wasn't an option and I refused to get sucked into a debate about it.

* * *

'This is a rare treat indeed,' Angie whispered to me as I added clean cutlery to the drawer behind the counter later that morning. 'Ten Sugars is already here but look who else has just walked in.'

I turned towards the door to see a petite lady, maybe in her mid-eighties, with long white hair, unwinding a stripy hand-knitted scarf from round her neck. I'd never seen her without the scarf, even on the hottest of days. 'She doesn't usually do Saturdays.'

'Well, she has blessed us with her presence today.'
Mrs Sultana had been coming in for the past five months but nobody had managed to discover her real name or strike up a conversation about anything other than her order, and that could hardly be classed as a conversation because she always asked for the same three items.

She sat in the middle booth, scarf cuddled to her chest, and gazed out at the sea. 'I'll take her order,' I said to Angie.

'Morning!' I declared in my brightest voice when I reached her table. 'Gorgeous weather, isn't it?'

She looked up at me with watery grey eyes. 'Large pot of tea, fruit scone, flapjack, please.' Her voice was so soft, it always made me think of a gentle breeze whispering through the tall pine trees surrounding the café.

'Coming right up. You're sure you wouldn't prefer a plain scone?'

She'd already turned to look out the window once more and shook her head without glancing back at me.

I wondered if it was unfair to try to draw her into a conversation, but I never wanted her to think I treated her differently to other customers with whom I regularly chatted. It mustn't bother her for her to come back so often. Everyone was different. Not everybody liked to chat and I respected that. What I didn't understand was her insistence at having a fruit scone only to pick out all the sultanas, especially when there was a plain alternative. Each to their own.

I'd no sooner placed her order on a tray when an elderly man placed his empty mug on the counter. 'Another latte please, Hollie. Ten sugars. Same mug's fine.'

I smiled at him. 'I'll bring it over to you, Rodney.' I'd given up trying to explain that it was no problem to put his mug through the dishwasher but he got agitated if we gave him a fresh one. And how that man remained so slim and didn't have a mouth full of fillings was beyond me.

He returned to the booth next to Mrs Sultana's and I had a warm and fuzzy feeling as I gazed at two of our more 'unusual' customers. Mum had often talked about The Starfish Café as a community, which was another thing Craig had never understood. He reckoned it made no business sense to let someone like Ten Sugars hog a table for two hours and only consume two lattes. For Mum, Angie and me it wasn't about the money, although, if we were going to strip it down, two lattes twice a week for fifty weeks a year was far more profitable than a family visiting once and ordering a big meal. Even with the amount of sugar he consumed!

Mum had built a legacy around warmth and friendship and I was determined to keep that going. All were welcome, whether we knew them well or they remained an enigma. Who knew what was going on in Rodney Ten Sugars' life or Mrs Sultana's but, for whatever reason, they had both chosen The Starfish Café to be part of it and that was a privilege.

As I was heading back to the counter after delivering their orders, I saw a couple of my favourite customers, Betty and Tommy, getting out of their car. I placed the empty tray on the counter and opened the door for them.

'Morning, Tommy! Morning, Betty!'

'Morning, darling girl,' Tommy said, tipping his grey tweed trilby to me.

'Have you got any of those chocolate and orange scones left, my dear?' Betty asked, grasping my hand.

'Two days in a row, Betty?' I winked at her. 'I might have a couple put by just for you.' I had fruit, cheese and plain scones available every day plus a different daily special. I knew Betty could never resist a double dose of the chocolate and orange ones so always saved her a couple for the following day.

'You're so precious,' Betty gushed. 'Your mum would be so proud.'

In their late seventies, Betty and Tommy were the most wonderful couple. They came in for tea, scones and the occasional cheeky slice of cake around mid-morning every day except Sunday. Tommy was always dressed in a shirt, tie and his smart trilby hat, and Betty always looked stunning in a dress or two-piece. Mum had told me they'd been ballroom dancing champions in their younger days. They walked with such grace that I could easily picture them waltzing round a ballroom.

When I took their order over, Betty insisted I sit down. 'I have something for you. We know it would have been your wedding today and we wanted to give you something to say that we know your young man let you down but there are many people who care about you very much.'

She passed me something wrapped in lemon tissue paper. I carefully peeled back the tape to reveal a miniature crocheted teddy bear with pale pink flowers behind one of its ears, wearing a corn-flower blue dress with a cerise heart on it. I knew Betty loved to crochet but I'd never seen her creations before.

'Did you make this?' I asked, turning it over and marvelling at the craftmanship.

'Yes. It's my first miniature and I'm really pleased with how she turned out.'

'Betty, she's beautiful. Thank you. And thank you both for thinking of me. It's so kind of you.'

'You do so many nice things for other people so we thought it was time somebody did something nice for you.'

'I'll treasure her always.' She'd be a perfect addition to my bedroom shelf alongside framed photos of my parents and Isaac.

Betty and Tommy exchanged looks and he nodded to her as though encouraging her to add something.

'What's going on?' I asked.

'I made something else for the bear but I changed my mind.'

'I think she should have added it,' Tommy said.

'But I said it might upset you, Hollie.'

'She brought them with us so it's your choice. Show her, Betty.'

Betty rummaged in her bag and took out a pair of tiny sparkly crocheted angel wings. 'I've got some thread. I can add them on now if you like them but it was your mum's thing for you and... I told you it would make her cry, Tommy!'

I wiped at my eyes. 'Sorry. They're not upset tears. It's a beautiful idea.' I held the wings against the back of the bear. 'I'd like her to have angel wings, please.'

'I told you she'd be all right with it,' Tommy said. 'Our Hollie's a strong young lady.'

That was the second time today someone had called me strong.

After the lunchtime rush, Avril, our waitress took her break, carrying a toasted panini across to a two-seater booth overlooking the terrace. In her late forties, Avril had been with us for twelve years. She couldn't bake if her life depended on it but she was brilliant with the customers, good fun and extremely reliable.

She'd only been seated five minutes when there was an almighty crack and she leapt up. My stomach sank at the thought of yet another repair as I rushed over.

'Are you all right, Avril?'

She smiled and nodded. 'I think the seat might be hinting that I didn't lose my Christmas pounds.' She lifted the seat cushion, revealing a long crack in the wood beneath and a gap where a chunk had splintered off.

'You definitely didn't hurt yourself?'

'No. I'm fine. But I might sit the other side to finish my lunch.'

'I'm so sorry.' Tears rushed to my eyes. Everyone might think I was being strong but I wasn't facing up to things, the biggest one being the state of the café. The place was falling apart. There'd been several repairs to the booths already, I'd had someone in to fix the oven last week and the plumbing in the toilets also needed attention.

'Hey, it's not your fault.' Avril stroked my arm. 'I'm not hurt, it didn't happen to a customer, and it can soon be fixed.'

I nodded. 'Thanks. I'll prepare a *do not use* sign for when you've finished.'

* * *

I'd just finished tidying in the kitchen at the end of the day when Angie poked her head round the door.

'There's a large cappuccino out here with your name on it,' she said.

'What for?'

'I think we need to have a little heart-to-heart.'

I joined her in one of the window booths and gazed outside for a moment, taking in the stunning vista. Starfish Point is home to a colony of roughly 200 grey seals and smaller common seals. The main colony resides on Starfish Arc – a curved formation of flat rocks roughly 120 metres (the length of a football pitch) from the beach – which can clearly be seen from the café and the terrace. Visitors can usually find at least a dozen lounging on the sand or rocks on the beach below.

Behind Starfish Arc is Starfish Point Lighthouse – a beautiful red and white striped lighthouse warning boats of the dangerous rocks along our part of the coast. There was something about that view of the sea, seals, and lighthouse that made my spirits soar.

I turned back to Angie. 'I know what you're going to say. The little fixes aren't enough.'

'So what's stopping you from refurbishing it?'

I glanced round to the cuckoo clock on the wall as it gave one chime to indicate half past five. 'This was Mum's vision. She loved this place so much. It doesn't feel right destroying it when I've already lost nearly everything.'

'But it's not her café anymore,' Angie said gently. 'It's yours. And you know what else is yours? The memories of her. You could flatten this place and rebuild it in the shape of a starfish and you'd *still* be able to picture your mum and hear her voice and her gorgeous laugh. She's in here.' She tapped her finger against her temple. 'And in here.' She patted her heart. 'She's in the heritage, the recipes, the customers, the staff, and she's in you. She's in me too.'

Her voice cracked and she blinked back tears, reminding me how painful her loss had been too after fifty years of friendship.

'We all love this place,' she continued. 'But your mum was ready for a change. She thought the New England theme was brilliant and she loved the mood boards you and Katie made. You already have her approval. But if you've changed your mind and want to go for a different look, she'd have approved of that too because she believed in you and so do I. Make this *your* café. If I know Heather, she's looking down on us right now, rolling her eyes and wondering why we're still haunted by that crazy cuckoo.'

I wiped my eyes as I laughed at the thought. 'Thanks, Angie. I needed to hear that. I'm not sure how I'd have got through any of this without you.'

She squeezed my hand across the table. 'I'll always be here for you. So what do you think? New England or something else?'

I shrugged. 'New England. It's what Mum wanted.'

'But is it what *you* want? Your mum loved her traditions but she was never averse to change. Don't forget she knocked down Norma's Nook and rebuilt it as The Starfish Café. She didn't see that as destroying what your Granny started. It was all about taking her mum's legacy and making it bigger and better. She couldn't wait to get in that bulldozer. In her element she was that day.'

'Mum actually bulldozed Granny's café?'

Angie frowned. 'You don't know that story?'

'I thought it was a joke. I didn't realise she *literally* drove the bulldozer.'

'I've got photos somewhere. I'll dig them out although some of them are a bit blurred. She persuaded the builders to let her have the first swipe at the building and then refused to get out of the cab until she'd flattened the whole thing. I was laughing so much; I couldn't hold the camera straight.'

'I'd love to see those. That's such a Mum thing to do.'

'The stories I could tell you!' Angie chuckled. 'For another time over a bottle of wine. Returning to your plans for this place, is the timing right for you now? I'd normally say that only you can answer that but I think the café's already answering it for you.' She swept her arm round the building.

I knew it was a false economy and it was time for me to accept that I couldn't change the past so I needed to stop living in it. Or at least I did as far as the café was concerned. Not so easy when it came to everything else.

'I'll get in touch with that builder who did the kitchen at Sandy Croft. We can close after the summer and do a refurb.'

'No bulldozers for you then?' Her eyes twinkled with mischief.

'No bulldozers. But I am going to stick to the New England theme. It was my idea anyway and it feels less of a radical change knowing it had Mum's approval.'

'That's a good decision. Just promise me that cuckoo clock won't reappear.'

I laughed. 'I promise.'

'Should I let you into a little secret? Your mum never liked it.'

'You're kidding!'

She shook her head. 'She loved it because your dad bought it for her on their honeymoon so it had sentimental value, but the cuckoo drove her mad.'

'She never breathed a word.'

'Because she loved your dad so much and the clock reminded her of him.'

I gazed at the wooden clock, stunned at her revelation, but it was exactly the sort of thing Mum would do. Would I ever find a love like theirs one day? After what happened with Craig, there was no way I'd ever settle for something that wasn't quite right, thinking that's how it had to be. It had to be all or nothing.

* * *

Returning to Sandy Croft feeling inspired by Angie's pep talk, I went up to the top floor and into my old bedroom. The mood boards Katie and I had created were stacked together in a corner. I propped them against the wall in a row and stepped back, my mind swirling with laughter-filled evenings as we'd added paint colours, material swatches and pictures ripped from magazines or printed from the Internet. I pictured how Mum's eyes had shone with excitement as we walked her through our vision. It was the right thing to do. She'd love the changes. But would the customers? I shook my head as I thought of Mum's mantra when she originally knocked down Norma's Nook to make way for The Starfish Café: *If I build it, they will come.* I wasn't going to rebuild anything but I was going to recreate. And they *would* come. They'd come for the food, the view, the memories of Mum and for the legacy she'd left behind about all being welcomed and made to feel part of the family.

I sat cross-legged on the floor in front of the boards, excitement welling inside me. As part of the refurbishment, I could do something with the upstairs. Mum had originally used the first floor for overflow seating in the busy summer months, but when she'd later added the substantial outside terrace, the extra indoors space hadn't been needed. It had since become a dumping ground but I could make use of it. I'd apply for a drinks licence and run private functions and parties. The double-height space was exceptional and all those windows revealed an amazing view, which should be enjoyed.

I thought about the photographs Angie said she had of Mum bulldozing Norma's Nook. I'd make a frame for those, put Mum's mantra in the middle, and hang it on the wall, showing the evolution from prefab to The Starfish Café versions one and two. Granny and Mum had created their visions and now it was my turn and, for the first time since I lost Mum late last year, I felt excited about the future.

8

JAKE

Saturday 25th June, five years ago

As I waited in the first-floor corridor for my appointment with Mr
Grundy of Grundy & Miggs Solicitors, a nervous tic caused my
right leg to bounce up and down, tapping the heel of my best shoes
on the parquet flooring. The sound echoed down the corridor.

A middle-aged woman on a chair further along the corridor
repeatedly glanced up from her magazine to send a filthy look and
a sigh in my direction. The look didn't bother me. I'd spent a childhood on the receiving end of withering looks from Larissa and
corridor-lady wasn't a patch on her. The phrase 'if looks could kill'
was coined for my sister. What I didn't appreciate was the passive
aggression. Not today. Not when I was about to receive the news
that I was going to be homeless.

The only positive – and I really was scrabbling around for one –
was that Mr Grundy had arranged to see Larissa and me separately.
I'm not sure I could have stomached sitting beside her, seeing the

smug expression on her face when Nanna's solicitor confirmed that she was the new owner of Lighthouse View.

While I didn't relish the idea of being homeless, the thing that wound me up most was that, unlike me, Larissa didn't care about Nanna or Lighthouse View. I'd hoped she'd prove me wrong and turn up to the funeral. She hadn't. But she was more than happy to turn up for the will-reading. It summed up my sister perfectly: selfish, self-centred and heartless.

I wasn't going to kick up a fuss when I heard Nanna's last wishes. I was already prepared for the worst.

'There are some surprises in my will,' Nanna had told me as I sat beside her in hospital after her first stroke in February.

'Don't talk like that. You're going to be fine.'

'Jake, lovey, I'm eighty-seven and I'm weary... Not long left for this world... Have to warn you what to expect.' The stroke had slowed and slurred her speech and I could see the frustration in her eyes as she struggled to force the words out.

'Your sister... So many years apart 'cause I chose you... Had to do the right thing by her.'

'Don't try to talk, Nanna.'

'Need to. Lighthouse View. Had to be fair. Don't think badly of me. Your sister...'

She drifted off to sleep but I'd heard enough. She wanted to make amends with Larissa for choosing me all those years ago and the only way she knew how to do that was by leaving the house to my sister. It made sense and I could never think badly of the woman who'd tried to be my mum, dad and four grandparents all rolled into one.

A series of mini-strokes followed before a severe one took her a fortnight ago, aged eighty-eight. Preparing for the inevitable, I packed up my clobber – not that I'd accumulated much – and stored it in one of Irene's spare bedrooms. She'd offered me her other room temporarily but I couldn't stay there with Larissa lording it in Lighthouse View. Not that I anticipated my sister staying for long. I reckoned a week maximum to strip the place of anything she thought would fetch a price and to get the house on the market. I couldn't afford to buy it from her and, even if I could, she'd never have sold it to me. She was the sort who'd rather take a ridiculously low offer than show any compassion towards me. I'd look for somewhere to rent and start over.

A door opened and corridor-lady headed into her appointment. Just as well because, with the time ticking ever closer to my slot, both legs had started bouncing and she'd tutted loudly and cleared her throat several times.

'Jake MacLeod? I'm Mr Grundy. Come in.'

Stomach churning, I stood up and shook hands with a short sturdy man – possibly mid-sixties – with receding grey hair. I followed him into a small office with wall-to-wall bookshelves and sat down on one of the chairs opposite a gleaming mahogany desk. An official-looking document was positioned in front of him and a brown glasses case rested on top of it. Mr Grundy removed the glasses, placed them on the end of his nose, then steepled his hands under his chin while surveying me.

'It's a very sorry state of affairs,' he said eventually, pushing his glasses up his nose and straightening up.

'Nanna dying?'

'No. Well, yes, that's very sad. My condolences. I mean this.' He tapped the document several times with his middle finger. 'Ms MacLeod discussed the contents of her will with you?'

'No. She said there'd be some surprises. I think she might have left everything to my sister.'

He peered at me over his glasses but I had no idea what that look meant.

'Best get on with it, then.' He opened up the document and

spieled off the sort of legal jargon I'd heard on TV shows about last will and testament and being of sound mind and so on. My leg started twitching again. I just wanted him to spit it out so I could get home, remove the last of my belongings, and move on with my life.

'Ms Violet MacLeod has requested that I read out this letter to you before I read her will. The letter is directed to your sister, Mrs Larissa Kent, but she wanted you to hear it too.'

I nodded, my heart racing in fear. *What will be will be. You'll cope.* Mr Gundy cleared his throat and began reading the letter:

Life is all about choices. Some choices are easy and feel right, some are difficult but are ultimately for the best, and others cause too much pain to be right. You've always loudly proclaimed, "You know your choice" and I do. As I write this, my last will and testament, I have two options. I can choose to continue to provide a home for a scared and lost boy who grew into the kindest, most thoughtful and caring man, devoting himself to saving lives, and who makes me so very proud every day. Or I can choose to support an angry, bitter woman who seems to hate the world and everything in it, including me, and has no qualms in repeatedly telling me why she wants nothing to do with me.

My stomach lurched. This didn't sound like it was going to go in Larissa's favour after all. *Best not jump the gun. Listen. Concentrate.*

If you want nothing to do with me, surely it follows that you want nothing from me. Although it breaks my heart to do this, the choice over what to do with my estate is not a difficult one. There is only one thing I can do. This could have been so different. A family should be united at times of tragedy, not divided by it. You weren't the only one in pain but the difference between Jake and you is that you chose to let it consume you and he chose to channel it into good so my final choice – the one that

I thought might be difficult but turns out to be both easy and right – is
that your brother Jake is the sole beneficiary of my estate.

I stared at Mr Grundy, mouth open, scarcely able to take it in, a jumble of emotions flowing through me. Being sole beneficiary was not what I'd expected. The words about me were touching, the fact she'd stood up to my bullying big sister made me want to punch my fist in the air and cheer, but to disinherit Larissa? Nanna said to expect surprises but she'd shocked the hell out of me with this one. When she asked me to forgive her for her decisions, I had very wrongly assumed she was going to make peace with Larissa by giving her Lighthouse View; not that she was going to teach her a difficult life-lesson.

I have requested that a representative from Grundy & Miggs attend my
funeral, If they witness you, Larissa, attending then you will receive
£25,000. I'd love to be wrong about you but I'm almost certain you won't
bother and, in that case, the money will go to the RNLI; a worthy cause
close to my heart and to Jake's.

My stomach tensed. Larissa hadn't been at the funeral. She'd had her chance of walking away with something and she'd blown that too. She was going to be so pissed off.

'She won't accept that decision,' I muttered. There could be years of wrangling ahead. Losing Nanna had been hard enough. I couldn't face a lengthy legal fight against her final wishes.

'She has no choice.' Mr Grundy didn't look too impressed at the interruption. 'I'll continue, should I?'

'Yes. Sorry.'

Please know that it is not worth your while trying to contest any part of
this will. Grundy & Miggs have the original cards and letters you

returned to me with your catchphrase scribbled across them. They also
have all the poison pen letters you wrote to me and your brother. No
court is going to award you anything when they see what you really
thought of us both. And if you continue your campaign of hate against
your brother, there is already a case opened up with the police and Mr
Grundy will have no hesitation in providing them with twenty years'
worth of evidence.

Mr Grundy lay down his papers, removed his glasses and sighed. 'As I said, it's a sad state of affairs.'

My head was reeling. 'Larissa wrote hate mail?'

'A lot of it.'

'What did she say? Can I read the letters?'

'I wouldn't encourage it.'

'Have you read them?'

'Some of them and it was clear that your sister is how Ms MacLeod described her: angry, bitter and consumed by hate. I can't stop you reading the ones addressed to you, but my advice is that there's nothing to gain from doing so and much to lose.'

'Did Nanna say anything about it?'

'That she would strongly urge you *not* to read them. She would prefer they remain here in safe storage.' He put his glasses back on, the subject of the letters evidently closed as he continued to read the official will, explain exactly what I'd inherited, and the process going forwards. The words barely registered with me. All I could think about was Nanna hiding Larissa's hate mail for two decades yet still somehow finding the strength to keep writing to her and hoping there could be a family reconciliation.

In a daze I signed documents, scarcely able to take in what Nanna had hidden from me. Throughout my life and right until the end, she'd remained my protector when it could so easily have gone the other way, especially after the way I'd initially behaved after Dad died.

Mr Grundy stood up and thrust out his hand. Meeting obviously over, I stood up and shook it.

'I'm seeing your sister in ten minutes. If she's early, she might be outside. Forewarned is forearmed.'

As I thanked him and left his office, I couldn't decide whether his worried expression was concern for me or himself.

A woman was seated in the chair I'd occupied previously, scowling at something on her phone. I paused for a moment, wondering if it could be Larissa, but she had bobbed grey wavy hair and a mature face – far too old to be my forty-two-year-old sister.

The woman looked up and our eyes locked. Her scowl deepened, her jaw tightened, and her body tensed. Nothing about her seemed familiar but, with that reaction towards me, who else could it be?

'Larissa?' It was barely a whisper.

She tossed her phone into the bag by her feet, folded her arms and narrowed her eyes at me. 'Ah! How delightful! It's the killer.'

My stomach did a somersault at her cutting tone. 'That's not fair.'

'Fair?' She jumped to her feet and jabbed her finger towards me. 'You want to talk about fair? After what you did to our parents?'

I cringed at the volume and shrill pitch of her voice; the sound that had chilled me to the core during childhood. 'You know it wasn't my fault.'

'It was *completely* your fault and you're delusional if you can't accept that. And do you know what else you are? Useless. A useless, lazy, pathetic little boy who has spent the last twenty-odd years sponging off an old lady. I bet you don't even have qualifications or a job.'

I wasn't having that. 'I have both, including a first-class degree.'

'In what? Being a useless twat?'

'In nursing.'

'Nursing? You girl!'

It wasn't the first time I'd experienced archaic attitudes that nursing was only for women and it astonished me all the more when that viewpoint came from a woman. I was about to rise to it but it didn't dignify a response.

'You know what, Larissa? You're not worth it.' I started towards the stairs.

'And neither are you! You should *never* have been born. Nobody wanted you. Everyone hates you, you useless fu—'

'Mrs Kent. You can come in now.' Mr Grundy had obviously heard the raised voices and realised an intervention was needed.

Shooting one of her special withering looks in my direction, Larissa snatched up her bag and coat and stormed into Mr Grundy's office. He widened his eyes at me before closing the door behind him. I wasn't sure whether that was for my benefit or his. I didn't envy him Larissa's wrath when he delivered the news about her disinheritance.

I ran down the stairs and out into the sunshine, where I leaned against the wall and took in deep gulps of air. That was it. It was over. I had a house and a small fortune but I'd have traded it all to have my parents and Nanna instead. What was the point in all those things without a family?

* * *

I drove back to Lighthouse View, my head in a spin. Despite the threat of police action, would Larissa walk away? From our encounter just now, she clearly hadn't moved on and twenty years of hate mail was further evidence of it. I wished I'd known about that, but I wasn't surprised Nanna hadn't shared. Protecting me as always, doing whatever she could to appease my guilt.

One thing now made so much more sense: the post box. She'd had the letterbox at Lighthouse View blocked up shortly after Dad died and a lockable metal post box installed on the wall by the door. She was obsessive about being the only one allowed to open it, even wearing the key on a chain round her neck.

When I was eighteen, in the summer that I finished college, I thought I'd discovered the reason behind it. Nanna was wiped out for a week after a minor operation and I took a few days off my summer bar job to look after her. The postman knocked on the door one day and handed me a bundle of letters, telling me the post box was full. Nestled among the bills was an envelope addressed to Larissa in Nanna's curly script, returned to sender. Scribbled across the back in thick red marker pen capitals were the words: YOU KNOW YOUR CHOICE. I could feel the anger emanating from each stroke of my sister's pen.

'What choice is this, Nanna?' I asked holding up the envelope.

She sighed. 'My head's too fuzzy to make something up. I suppose you're old enough to know the truth now. Sit down, lovey.'

I perched on the edge of her bed, waiting.

'Remember the day after the funeral when Larissa came round and Irene took you for an ice cream?'

I remembered it well. Nanna had sent me next door with a fiver and a verbal message for Irene: *Larissa's here. Nanna says can you take me down to the seafront for the biggest ice cream ever?* When we returned an hour later, Larissa was gone and Nanna was in the kitchen chopping vegetables. Her cheeks were wet and I asked if she'd been crying. She said she'd been chopping onions but the onions remained by the chopping board, still in their skins.

'While you were out, Larissa gave me an ultimatum.'

'What sort of ultimatum?'

'Her or you.'

'She did what?' Every time I thought my sister couldn't sink lower, she somehow managed it. What sort of choice was that? I'd still been a young child then but she'd already left home and moved in with Andrew. 'What did she think you were going to do? Place me in care so you could enjoy the occasional Sunday lunch with your angry granddaughter?'

'I don't know what she expected. I tried to reason with her but you know Larissa. There's no reasoning with her about anything.'

'So what's in the envelope?'

'I contact her every couple of months. Letters, cards, poems, photos of her and me together when she was little. Anything I can think of to reunite our fractured family.'

I glanced at the letter, re-sealed with sticky tape. 'She opens them.'

'Yes, but presumably it's just to see whether I've made my choice and picked her. Then she sends them back with the same message.'

'I'm really sorry, Nanna.'

'Jake, lovey, none of this is your doing. Don't forget what we discussed about her from when she was a child. She didn't suddenly change when you were born.'

As part of helping me cope with life after Dad – which included acknowledging that I wasn't to blame for everything – Nanna had confided in me that Larissa had been a difficult child. Moody, argumentative and demanding, she'd clashed with everyone – our parents, her teachers, her friends – and nobody knew why. Dad had known a child psychologist and sought her input but she could find no clinical diagnosis for my sister. My parents had tried every technique they could think of to get through to her from spoiling her to trying to reason with her to bribery and everything in between but nothing seemed to work. My birth provided a focal point for her anger.

I hated that Nanna had been trying unsuccessfully for nine years to make a difference while at the same time being full of admiration for her determination and resilience with every knockback.

'Will you stop writing to her?' I asked Nanna.

'No, lovey. It's part of my routine now.'

Her eyes started to droop so I left her to rest. The younger me would have added 'making Nanna sever ties with her only grand-daughter because of me' to my long list of things to feel guilty about but I'd found a fresh perspective on the tragedy over the last few years. It had taken the patience of a saint on Nanna's part and years of counselling, but I'd finally accepted that I couldn't spend the rest of my life blaming myself for what happened to either of my parents. The best thing I could possibly do was live life to the full and make them proud of me. I studied hard at school and had decided to commit my life to helping others. I couldn't wait to begin my nursing studies that September. It wasn't my fault that Larissa was consumed with hatred instead; that was her decision and nobody had forced her to make it.

But now I knew that there'd been another reason for the post box. Poison pen letters were absolutely Larissa's style. If what she'd written was anything like the note she'd left under my pillow the day she destroyed my photographs, I wasn't surprised Nanna hadn't told me about them, protecting me as always right until the end. What a remarkable woman.

Bonfire Night, present day

'That's me finished in the kitchen, Hollie,' Angie called, bursting through the two-way door between the kitchen and the café.

I looked up from the opposite end of the room, where I was teasing out the branches on a section of artificial Christmas tree. 'Thanks, Angie.'

She pulled on her waterproof jacket and made a beeline for me between the serving counter and a row of white wooden tables and chairs.

'Are you *sure* you're okay doing that on your own? I've taken some paracetamol. I'm sure they'll kick in soon.'

'Thanks, but you've been fighting that cold all day so you need to get home and rest. I can manage.'

She must have been feeling even more rough than she'd let on because she didn't protest further, instead held her arms out for a hug. She was the same height as me – 5' 8" – but curvier, like Mum had been before the third and final bout of cancer reduced her to skin and bones. If I closed my eyes when I hugged Angie, I could imagine I was holding Mum. What I wouldn't give to be able to do that again.

'I hate that Christmas is such a tough time of year for you,' Angie whispered, squeezing me tightly.

'But good for business.' I knew that my voice sounded overly bright.

Angie stepped back, hands on my forearms, and gave me her concerned surrogate mother look: sad eyes, slight tilt of head. 'Don't stay too late, will you?'

'A couple of hours then straight home.'

'And you promise to eat something?'

I rolled my eyes at her in response.

She squeezed my arms and sighed. 'Every day you look more and more like your mum. She'd be so proud of you, you know.'

I smiled and nodded. A couple of years back, a statement like that would have had me sobbing but now I found it comforting. I liked that we could talk about Mum. It helped me and I knew it helped Angie too.

I followed her into the large entrance porch. As soon as we stepped out of the comforting warmth of the café, goose bumps pricked my bare arms and I rubbed them for warmth.

'Crikey, it's cold.' Angie zipped up her coat.

'I reckon we'll have frost overnight.'

'You could be right.' She paused with her hand on the outer door handle and gave me that look again. 'If you need me, I'll be hiding behind the sofa with Felix and Pixie.' She shuddered. 'Why do fireworks have to be so loud? I *hate* them.'

An image popped into my head of Angie and her cats squashed

behind her sofa and I smiled at her. 'Thank you, but I'll be just fine. It has been nearly six years, after all.'

'It doesn't mean it doesn't still hurt.'

Our eyes locked in collective understanding.

'Go on,' I said. 'Get yourself home and hope your neighbours don't set off any rockets or you'll be the one calling me needing hugs.'

Angie laughed. 'I look forward to seeing the café in its—'

'Full-on festive fabulousness,' we chorused together.

Angie dashed towards her car and I shivered and swiftly closed the door behind her. Locking it, my thoughts turned to Mum. Angie was right. It did still hurt and likely always would, but dwelling on it didn't change it and it certainly didn't get the Christmas decorations put up which, as per tradition, had to be my task for this evening. It was usually emotional, but it was a tradition I wanted to keep alive. There'd been no way I could continue with the Bonfire Night soiree. Not without my family.

I selected a Christmas album to get me in the mood. Christmas was an emotional time but I couldn't ignore it and a jingle of sleigh bells and Mariah Carey's cheerful warbling soon transported me back to happy times when the whole family had been together.

* * *

I tweaked the positions of a couple of tree ornaments then stepped back to admire my handiwork. This year, the decorations were white and blue in keeping with the New England-themed décor. Among the shop-bought baubles hung hand-crafted felt and material beach huts I'd bought from Yorkshire's Best – the gallery and locally-made craft store on Castle Street in town. Blue and turquoise glass seahorses reflected the light from the white fairy lights, casting fragments of colour to dance upon the white walls. Pride of place went to my own creations: wooden boats with assorted blue and white fabric sails, colourful clay starfish, and clear baubles filled with shells.

Tradition dictated that, within a week, I needed to put up the tree at home too. Mum had believed that 'full-on festive fabulousness' at home helped maintain the Christmas vibe needed for the customers. She'd made me promise to still celebrate Christmas outside of work and I'd kept that promise. Sort of. I put the tree up each year, added a few token decorations, set the fairy lights on a timer... then closed the door and avoided the lounge until it was over and I could pack it all away for another year.

A couple of weeks after I set her the challenge, Mum had found an Isaac elf – tall, blond and blue-eyed. He sat near the top of the tree by the Hollie Gabrielle angel. As I glanced up at them both, I reached for the necklace to which I'd added Mum's wedding ring, and I had a sudden overpowering sensation of Mum standing behind me, her hand resting on my shoulder.

'Mum?' My hand closed round the pair of wedding rings and a feeling of warmth and peace flowed through me as tears trickled down my cheeks. I didn't believe in ghosts or spirits but occasionally, when I was alone in the café, I felt Mum's presence and it gave me strength.

I fished a tissue out of my jeans pocket and wiped my cheeks. *That's enough. You have more work to do.*

I'd earned myself a break first so, with Angie's words about eating ringing in my ears, I made a sandwich and a mug of hot chocolate and took them to one of the booths overlooking the decked terrace and the sea below. I'd left the terrace lights switched on but had dimmed the lights inside the café to indicate that we were closed. Not that anyone was about at this time of night as we were in a secluded spot off the main road between Whitsborough Bay and Fellingthorpe. We were only open on an evening if there was a private function upstairs and, although I'd run a few of those after the refurbishment, my heart hadn't been in it. It was on my task list for the next year to promote the café for parties. But it had also been on my task list the past two years.

I cleared away my dishes then continued decorating, placing driftwood trees adorned with shell decorations in the windows, adding a seaside-themed wreath on the inner porch door and replacing some of the beach-themed pictures on the walls with more Christmassy ones, although they were all still in keeping with the seaside theme. My favourite was a Christmas tree I'd made from clay starfish painted shades of cream and blue; simple yet effective.

While I worked, the café lit up intermittently as fireworks exploded above the sea from the 7 p.m. South Bay display. I did my best to keep my back to the window. I wasn't such a fan of fireworks anymore. Without my family, they didn't fill me with excitement.

By 7.45 p.m. I'd finished decorating. I needed to take the boxes to the storage room upstairs then I could head home and have a long soak in the bath before bedtime.

Taking one last look round the café, I wondered for the umpteenth time what Mum would have made of the changes. She'd wanted something 'fresh' and this certainly achieved that. It seemed so much bigger and brighter with the wooden cladding gone. The pine tables and chairs had been replaced with white ones and the display counter was made from whitewashed tongue and groove with glass display cabinets. Breaking up the white were gorgeous blues, teals and turquoises in the upholstery, blinds, pictures and crockery.

I studied the driftwood framed collage hung on the wall beside the kitchen door. The photos of Mum in the bulldozer made me smile every time I looked at them. Even from a distance, it was obvious she was laughing.

'I wish you were still here, Mum, to see how it looks now.' I lightly ran my fingers down the glass. 'I wish you all were. I miss you so much.'

10

Bonfire Night, present day

It was ten past six when I pulled into the car park outside The Starfish Café. There was only one other car parked close to the café, which presumably belonged to the owner, although the café was closed, with the lights dimmed.

I'd expected more cars so either I was the only one to think of taking photos from Starfish Point or I happened to be the earliest.

As soon as I opened the door, the heat was sucked from the car and the cold hit me. It felt a hell of a lot colder here than back at home. Not that it mattered. I was used to being out in all weathers and had several layers on under my waterproof. I pulled on my hat and secured a head torch over it.

Loading my camera bag onto my back and grabbing my tripod, I locked the car and strode diagonally across the car park towards the steps to the right of the café, which ran down to the beach.

I glanced through the café windows and saw a Christmas tree

with twinkling white lights. Bit early for Christmas. Movement by the tree caught my eye. A woman with her head lowered appeared to be wiping her eyes as though she was crying and I paused, captivated for a moment, wondering why she was all alone crying at a Christmas tree. She straightened up and moved away so I continued my descent. None of my business.

Ten minutes later, I reached the beach. I'd done a recce last week to find the best spot; the first time I'd been to Starfish Point since I was a kid. The plan was to get photos of the fireworks with Whitsborough Bay Castle and harbour as a backdrop. There were plenty of vantage points further up the coast but I'd visited a couple over the years and they'd been heaving. Each year, I'd got there early and set up my tripod, only to have some numpty brandishing a phone standing right in shot as they filmed the display. I was a placid person but stuff like that wound me up. Why couldn't people be more considerate of others?

The pebbles clinked underfoot as I stepped onto the beach, followed soon after by the crunch of shingle then the shush of the sand. I'd chosen a spot towards the north end of the beach next to a large flat-topped boulder. I'd have an uninterrupted view up the coast and could have my backpack open on the boulder for easy access. Hopefully there wouldn't be a seal lounging on it or I'd have to re-think. I might come back to photograph the seals another day, but I was there tonight purely for the fireworks.

Fortunately there didn't appear to be any seals around so I set my tripod up with my telephoto lens and took a few shots of the harbour and the castle, intermittently adjusting my settings and repositioning the tripod.

To my right was the lighthouse on Starfish Isle. I looked across at it, silhouetted on the island, the light rotating and sending a beam across the sea. I'd been so proud of the photo I'd taken of it. It hadn't been 'shite' like Larissa claimed. When I came back to photograph the seals, I'd take photos of the lighthouse too, print one off, and give it pride of place on my studio wall.

I thought I heard footsteps on the pebbles and whipped round but there was nobody there. Must have imagined it.

At seven on the dot there was an almighty boom and the sky lit up with a burst of red sparks. Bangs echoed across the calm sea, bouncing off the cliffs, as explosions illuminated the night sky.

I'd only taken three shots when, out of the corner of my left eye, I saw something shoot past me. Shocked, I stepped back and scrambled to regain my footing as my heel caught a rock. What the hell was that? No way could a seal move that fast. I peered into the darkness, stars swimming in front of my eyes as they adjusted from the brightness of the fireworks, but all I could see were the dark shapes of the rocks.

I was beginning to think I'd imagined it when there was a lull in the explosions and I heard frantic barking. I glanced behind me but there was no sign of any owner. Dogs were meant to be on leads so they didn't distress the seals, so it had to be lost and was likely half scared to death.

Following the direction of the barks, I found a small brown dog quivering between two large rocks. I was no expert on breeds but I recognised this one as a shih tzu. Nanna's favourite joke sprung to mind: *When I was a little girl, my parents took me to a zoo. I was really excited about seeing the lions, elephants and bears but all they had was one cage containing one small dog. It was a shih tzu.* The first few times she'd tried to tell me it, she'd been laughing so hard in anticipation of the punchline that she'd been unable to get her words out. Then she got the punchline wrong, which made her laugh even more. Whenever I thought about Nanna, it was to picture her laughing and joking like that. Not sure how she'd managed that after everything she'd been through.

I bent down in front of the dog. 'Hi there. Are you lost?' I wasn't used to being round animals, having never had pets as a kid, but I did love dogs and hoped this one would feel that vibe as I slowly reached one hand towards it, wondering how I was going to grab it when it wasn't wearing a collar. It stopped barking and sniffed so I reached forward with the other hand and shuffled closer. I was about to grab it when the steady pop of fireworks gave way to what sounded like a thunderclap. With a yelp, the dog sprinted through my parted legs and raced off towards the other end of the beach.

I swore as I leapt up and turned round, my eyes scanning Starfish Point, the dog's dark fur making it almost impossible to spot it in the darkness. I glanced up at the fireworks and at my camera and sighed. Maybe next year. There was no way I could leave that dog for a moment longer.

For the next fifteen minutes or so, I ran up and down the beach, my feet getting steadily wetter as I stumbled through the rockpools. Every time the dog stopped and let me approach, an extra loud firework spooked it and it took off again. Not that I could blame it.

I'd had to bend over with my hands on my thighs catching my breath on several occasions, which was ridiculous. Here was me thinking I was fit!

Fortunately the dog eventually ran out of steam too. I was catching my breath again when it slumped onto the sand in front of me and looked up as if to say: *Okay, you win. I submit. I'm scared, cold and knackered. Help me!*

It made no attempt to fight me when I picked it up and it pressed its body against mine. It was wet and covered in sand and I could feel it trembling.

'It's all right. You're safe now.'

I wanted to make sure it hadn't been injured but a quick inspection under the light of my head torch revealed no obvious cuts. The shih tzu was a boy and, despite the lack of collar, he didn't strike me as a stray. Too clean. Presumably he'd somehow got lost, perhaps escaped from a garden, although he had to have travelled some distance as there were no houses nearby.

'I'll grab my stuff, take you home and see if we can track down an owner for you.'

The next challenge was how to pack away my equipment while holding the dog.

'If I put you down, do you promise not to run off again? Sit!' He obediently sat down.

'Good dog! Lie!' He did that too. Impressive.

'You're well trained, aren't you?' I removed a couple of layers and placed them over him for warmth. 'Stay!'

He'd obviously decided he was safer with me than fending for himself because he didn't attempt to move while I packed up my kit, stuffed my discarded layers and hat into the top of my backpack, pulled on my waterproof and hoisted the pack onto my back.

Picking him up and tucking him under my right arm with my tripod in my left hand, I took the steps back up to the car park and hoped he wouldn't try to wriggle loose as I couldn't face a repeat of earlier.

11

I placed the final box on the shelving unit in the storeroom upstairs and rolled my stiff shoulders. Time to go home for a bath. I could almost smell the lavender bubbles and feel the steam on my face.

As I reached the bottom of the stairs, a loud rap on the door made me jump. Heart thumping, I edged along the serving counter, jumping again at another knock.

'Hello?' called a man, his voice muffled. 'Anyone there?'

I tentatively approached the door and shouted, 'We're closed.' My voice came out strong and confident, despite feeling apprehensive about an unexpected night-time visitor.

Through the glass, I could see a tall dark-haired man cuddling to his chest what looked like a brown shih tzu. He said something else but I couldn't make it out. I opened the inner door.

The man smiled and waved. 'Sorry to bother you. I saw the lights and wondered if this was your dog. I think he's lost.' His breath hung in the air as he spoke.

Serving thousands of strangers at the café over the years, I considered myself to be an excellent judge of character and my gut feeling about the man who appeared to be about the same age as me – mid-thirties – was that he posed no threat. He had a kind face, a wide, friendly smile, and I could tell by the way he was holding and stroking the dog that he loved animals.

Relaxing, I flicked on the full set of café lights then unlocked the outer door. 'I'm sorry but he's not mine.'

Fireworks exploded overhead and the dog whimpered and tried to burrow into the man's coat.

'Aw, poor thing's terrified,' I said. 'Do you want to come inside until the fireworks stop?'

The dog yelped at another explosion and attempted to leap out of the man's arms. 'Yes, please, before he escapes again.'

He wiped his feet on the mat, instantly going up in my estimation.

'I'm Jake. And I have no idea who this is. There's no collar. He's a boy. That's all I have.'

'I'm Hollie and that looks like one scared little pooch.' I let the dog sniff my fingers before I stroked him. 'Imagine being lost in the dark on Bonfire Night of all nights. No wonder he's shaking. Give me a second, Mr Shih Tzu, and we'll see what we have for you behind the counter.'

Jake followed me into the café but waited near the door, cuddling the dog and whispering reassurances to him while I filled a dog bowl with water.

'I love what you've done with this place,' Jake said, looking round. 'I haven't been in here since I was a kid.'

'Then you've missed out on the best coffee, scones and cake with the most spectacular view in Whitsborough Bay.' I placed the dog bowl on the floor beside them before going back behind the counter.

Jake lowered the dog, who eagerly lapped up the water. 'He's probably been drinking seawater out of the rock pools.'

'Is that where you found him? On the beach?' I removed a handful of dog biscuits from a storage jar.

'Yeah. I was down there trying to take photos of the fireworks and he ran past me and hid between some rocks. There was nobody else around so I thought I'd better take him with me.'

'Were there any seals on the beach?'

'None that I could see.'

'That's a relief. It's pups season for the grey seals.' I'd never ban dogs from the beach, but I asked that they be kept on leads, especially around pups season as mother seals distressed by dogs could abandon their pups.

Joining Jake by the door, I held up a biscuit to the little dog. 'Sit!' He did. 'Paw?' He obediently lifted a paw and handed it to me to shake gently before I gave him his first treat. 'Looks like he's well trained so I don't imagine he's a stray.' I fed him another biscuit, fussing him all the while.

'He seems to like you,' Jake said. 'You're a dog lover?'

I straightened up and nodded. 'We've always had dogs in our family, usually retrievers or Labradors. I don't have one at the moment but we're a dog-friendly café so I'm never short of four-legged friends to fuss over. You?'

'I've always wanted a dog but I lived with my nanna and she was more of a cat person, not that we had one of those either.'

I picked up the shih tzu and ruffled his ears. He had the most adorable face like a teddy bear. His tipped fur was light brown with darker chocolate-coloured patches on either side, his tail, his ears and his muzzle.

'He's a gorgeous-looking dog. I'm sure someone's going to be very anxious right now. What's your plan?'

Jake shrugged. 'Take him home and put something on social media to see if I can find his owner and, if not, get in touch with the

RSPCA or a vet tomorrow. I've never found a dog before so I'm not sure what I'm meant to do.'

'All dogs have to be microchipped by law so, unless he's a stray, a vet will be able to help track down his owner.' I gave the dog a kiss on the top of his head then put him down on the floor. He looked up at me, head cocked on one side, as if to say: *What did you put me down for? I was enjoying my cuddle.*

Offering him one more biscuit, I pulled my phone out of my pocket. 'We've got thousands of followers on social media. Do you want me to post something?'

'That would be great.'

The shih tzu stayed still while I took a few photos on my phone from different angles. Evidently realising he wasn't going to be picked up again, he went to explore the café, sniffing at the furniture.

'Do you want a tea or coffee to warm you up?' I asked. 'The machines are off but I can soon boil the kettle.'

'Were you about to have one?'

'I was. I've just finished putting the Christmas decorations up and I've earned myself a drink.' I'm not sure why I felt the need to point to the tree. He could hardly have missed it. And I'm not sure why I said I was staying for a drink when a bath back at Sandy Croft was calling me. I looked down at the dog. It was because of him. I wanted to get him warmed up and relaxed and to get the appeal out.

'In that case, I'd love a black coffee. Thanks.'

Jake chose a seat while I made the drinks. When I returned, he was sitting in one of the window booths with the dog nestled in his arms like a baby, tickling his belly.

'You two look adorable together,' I said, placing the mugs down on the table. 'Let me put the appeal out now. I'll tag you in and ask people to contact you if they know the owner.' I typed in a message on the café's Facebook feed and added several photos then shared it on our other social media accounts. 'All done! What will you do if his owner doesn't come forward? Will you keep him?'

Jake shook his head. 'I'd love to but I'm not sure I can. I live on my own and I work shifts. It wouldn't be fair on the dog.'

His admission that he lived alone stirred butterflies in my stomach. I hadn't felt that sensation for years and had no idea why I was feeling it now. 'What do you do? I'm guessing not a full-time photographer if you work shifts.'

'I wish! No, that's a hobby. I'm a charge nurse on A&E.'

Those butterflies stirred again. Caring for animals and people? 'That's a bit different to photography. I bet that's stressful.'

He smiled. 'It can be, which is one of the reasons why I love photography – switching off and doing something different – but it's rewarding too.'

'I can imagine.'

There was a moment's silence as we held each other's gaze. His eyes were mesmerising – blue with flecks of hazel and a band of hazel round the iris and they sparkled every time he smiled. And he smiled a lot. His dark wavy hair was ruffled and there was a line of three faint scars across his left cheekbone. I wanted to reach out and stroke my fingers over them and ask what had caused them. Completely inappropriate for someone I'd only just met.

'I bet you've seen a few interesting injuries in your time,' I said.

He grinned. 'You bet! I've lost count of the number of items I've had to retrieve something from out of ears, up noses, or up the rectum...'

With the dog curled up on Jake's lap, we laughed as he regaled me with various gruesome stories. I told him about some of the more unusual requests we'd had from customers over the years and some of the things that had been left behind including enough umbrellas to open my own shop, several sets of false teeth, and the time a family left their baby sleeping in the highchair although they did thankfully realise they'd forgotten her as soon as they got to their car.

'The general public, eh?' Jake said, rolling his eyes. He glanced down at his phone. 'It's never ten o'clock already.'

I yawned and stretched my arms. 'Time flies when you're having fun. Let me see if we've had any responses.' I scanned down the comments. 'Stacks of shares and likes but no positive ID yet. Hopefully tomorrow.'

Jake gently lifted the dog up. 'We'd better get going. Looks like you're staying with me tonight, buddy.'

I followed them over to the door.

'Bye, Hollie, and thanks for your help.'

'Pleasure. He's such a cutie. Hopefully the appeal will find his owner and there'll be a happy ending. Keep an eye on the posts. I'll do the same and message you if I spot anything, but definitely check with a vet tomorrow as, if he's chipped, that should track down the owner.'

I gave the dog another stroke then waved to Jake as he headed towards his car. I locked the door and returned to the café to collect my belongings and switch off the lights. A happy ending. I hoped so. At this time of year, I was always extra eager to grasp at the happy things.

12

'She was helpful, wasn't she?' I said to the shih tzu as we stopped by the car and looked back. I couldn't see Hollie inside and the lights on the tree had gone out so she probably wouldn't be far behind us. The outside of the café looked vaguely familiar from childhood but the interior had changed beyond all recognition. I seemed to remember there being a cuckoo clock before.

Opening the back door of my car, I hesitated. No lead. No collar. Not very safe. Crap.

'If I put you on the back seat, will you promise to sit still?'

He looked up at me, head cocked to one side.

'I'll take that as a yes. You don't get travel sick, do you? Should we cover the seat in case? I've got Nanna's old picnic blanket in the boot. Stay!'

'Hopefully I won't have to do any emergency stops,' I told him, spreading the blanket across the seat moments later. 'And it's not far, although we'd better go via the supermarket and get you some food, hadn't we?'

The shih tzu whimpered as the occasional firework exploded

while we drove towards Whitsborough Bay, but he remained lying down on the blanket.

* * *

Forty minutes later, clutching the dog and the blanket under one arm, a couple of paper carrier bags in my other hand, with my camera equipment loaded onto my back, I unlocked the door to Lighthouse View.

'This is your temporary home,' I said, lowering him to the floor once I'd closed the door. 'Let's get you some food and water.'

He must have been ravenous because he seemed to inhale the food. After he'd eaten, I leaned against the kitchen worktop and scrolled through Facebook while he explored the kitchen. Still no positive ID.

I set the log burner away in the lounge and, stomach rumbling, returned to the kitchen to boil some spaghetti and heat up a pan of leftover bolognaise. The dog followed me every step of the way.

When I took my bowl into the lounge and plonked down on the sofa, he made no attempt to jump up but looked up at me as though asking for permission to join me. I patted the sofa cushion. 'It's okay, buddy. You can come up.'

He immediately leapt up and pressed himself against my leg.

'It won't be long before we find your owner,' I told him, flicking the TV on. 'I'm sure of it.'

It didn't take him long to drift off to sleep and I found the gentle sound of his steady breathing comforting. His legs twitched and he whimpered occasionally as though his dreams were taking him back to his ordeal on the beach and I felt that same rush of compassion for him that I felt for many of my patients at hospital.

'You're safe now, buddy,' I whispered, stroking his back, enjoying some company for once.

As the evening wore on, I intermittently checked social media. More shares, more comments, but still no owner. I flicked through the rest of the café's feed. The profile picture was the starfish logo and the cover image showed the interior. Regular postings all related to the business – photos of the food, the view, the opening hours, special offers. No photos of Hollie. I searched on her name and several results appeared but none of the women had long dark blonde hair and brown eyes. I tried 'Hollie Brooks Whitsborough Bay' to narrow it down. No results. I shook my head and put my phone down. What was I doing? Since when had I turned into a stalker? But I felt drawn to her. We'd laughed and chatted for nearly two hours and I'd never once felt uncomfortable. None of her questions had been intrusive. I'd never felt so relaxed around a stranger.

I tried to focus on the TV but kept picturing Hollie standing by the Christmas tree crying and wondered why. Whatever it was had passed while I'd been down on the beach as she'd seemed bright and cheerful when I met her.

By 11.30 p.m., I was shattered. The fireworks had stopped and the shih tzu was in a deep sleep. I didn't want to wake him up but I needed to let him into the garden to pee before I went to bed. Hopefully he'd settle downstairs without a basket or crate to sleep in. I didn't object to the idea of him sleeping on my bed but I didn't dare risk it. I wasn't used to company and he was only little. I might roll over and squash him.

I picked up my phone for one more check of Facebook. Scrolling down the comments on the café's feed, my heart leapt as the same name kept cropping up:

I think he belongs to someone on my street – Margaret Hamilton.

I recognise him. He's Margaret Hamilton's dog.

He's definitely Margaret Hamilton's dog but she's gone into a nursing home, hasn't she?

Margaret Hamilton went into a nursing home a couple of months ago but her daughter is looking after the dog. I don't know her name. Christine? Claire?

Carole Jessop, isn't this your mum's dog? He was found this evening at Starfish Point.

The last person was tagged in. Might as well get straight onto it. I clicked onto Carole's Facebook profile and sent her a message:

✉ Hi Carole,
I found a brown shih tzu on the beach at
Starfish Point below The Starfish Café this
evening. The owner of the café put out an
appeal. Several people have said he's yours. If
he is, he's safe and well and staying with me in
the Old Town in Whitsborough Bay. Can you
collect him tomorrow? If he's not yours, please
can you let me know asap?
Thanks
Jake

I let the dog into the back garden where he sniffed round a bit then cocked his leg against a shrub. Back inside, I placed the blanket from the car on one end of the sofa and told him he could jump up. He curled up against a couple of cushions.

'Looks like we've tracked down your owner so you'll be reunited tomorrow.' I scratched behind his ears. 'You stay here and I'll see you in the morning.'

I left the lounge door open and half-expected the dog to follow me up the stairs, but he stayed where he was.

As I bent over to put my phone on to charge beside my bed, a message pinged through from Carole Jessop:

✉ From Carole
Mr Pickles is my mum's dog but she's in a care home so he's staying with me. He slipped his lead this afternoon when I was walking him. We have plans tomorrow so can't collect him during the day. We might be able to make 7pm at a push. What's your address?
Carole

I frowned as I re-read the message several times, shaking my head. How odd. If I'd owned a nice dog like Mr Pickles – not that I'd ever name a dog that – I'd have been gutted about losing him, thrilled he'd been found, and would have gone out my way to collect him that evening. Where was the gratitude? Where was the relief?

✉ From Jake
It's Lighthouse View on the right near the top of Ashby Street in the Old Town. See you at 7pm tomorrow. Shout if you need any directions.
Jake

As I switched off my phone and put it on to charge, I felt uneasy. Slipped his lead? If he'd done that, he'd still have had his collar on. I sighed. It was late and I was probably reading too much into one short message. It would be fine. Mr Pickles would be reunited with his owner tomorrow. That wasn't a bad thing. Or was it?

13

'You've outdone yourself this year.' Angie, looking and sounding much brighter, stood next to me by the Christmas tree on Saturday morning, smiling as she ran her fingers down the sail of one of the driftwood sailing boats. 'You've just made your first sale. I'll take three.'

'Thank you. They're hanging up by the till so you get first pick.'

'I'm so impressed with what you do, honey. Most of us would look at a lump of wood and see a lump of wood, but you see its possibilities. You give it new life.'

I made my way behind the counter, glowing from Angie's compliments while she selected her boats. I'm not sure what I'd have done with myself over the past six years if it hadn't been for my workshop. I still occasionally turned wood but driftwood had become my absolute passion. Repurposing the pieces I found washed up on the Yorkshire coast gave me such a thrill.

When I finally refurbished the café five years ago, I used driftwood for the coat hooks and the frames round the mirrors in the toilets. Customers often asked where I'd bought them so I started taking commissions. Under the brand of Hollie's Wood, a steady business built with the profits donated across three charities close to my heart.

Mum and Angie had been right about customers wanting those first wood-turned Christmas tree decorations I'd created and, each year since, I'd come up with a new idea and made enough extra stock to sell to admiring customers. I loved having the distraction of a project and something happy to focus on at this time of year.

'I've chosen,' Angie said, holding up three boats. 'You must have spent hours making all these.'

'I enjoyed it.' I steeled myself for what I knew was coming next.

'I wish you'd get out more. Find yourself a new boyfriend. A nice one this time.'

'You sound just like Mum when you say that.'

'I can't help it. There was a reason we were best friends all our lives. I know what she'd have said and done in every situation and I know she'd have been worried about you. Like I am.'

'You don't need to be.' A buzzer sounded from the kitchen, giving me an excuse to escape. 'Fruit scones are ready.'

Angie followed me. 'Don't change the subject.'

'I'm not, but I don't think the customers will appreciate burnt offerings.'

As I lifted the tray out of the oven, she hovered in the doorway.

'Honestly, Angie, I'm happy on my own,' I said as I placed the scones onto metal cooling trays. 'I've got this place and I've got my wood. That's all I need.'

'Are you trying to convince me or yourself?'

I finished with the scones and turned round. 'Okay. I'll admit it. Sometimes it *would* be nice to have someone to go home to but, every time I weaken, I think about what Craig did.'

'Not all men are like Craig.'

I placed the empty baking tray into the large stainless-steel sink.

'I know, but he let me down during the toughest time of my life and I don't know if I can trust anyone else not to do the same.'

Angie's downcast expression made me laugh. 'I'm not saying I'll *never* have a relationship again. Just don't rush out and buy a hat. Now get your coat off and earn your keep.'

'Yes, Chef,' she joked. She slipped off her waterproof and hung it up in the small cloakroom next to the pantry.

I knew that Angie was only looking out for me and I'd always appreciated her stepping so easily into the surrogate mum role, but I didn't like discussing my love life – or lack of it. It made me think about Craig and thinking about him made me angry, which got me thinking about all the other injustices in my past and I absolutely couldn't go down that path again. No way. It had taken me years of professional help to get to where I was today and I was *not* prepared to take a step back.

While I pressed the cutter into the cheese scone mixture, Angie pulled on her apron and started cutting up a tray of flapjack.

'How was last night?' I asked, keen to change the subject. 'Did Felix and Pixie protect you from the nasty fireworks?'

She shuddered. 'It was awful. I'm not sure who was most scared. Probably me!' She laughed lightly, then her expression darkened. 'Second Bonfire Night without Martin. He was brilliant at keeping us all distracted.'

I put the cutter down and leaned back against the worktop. 'You really miss him, don't you?'

'How could I not? We were together for nearly thirty-six years.' Her tone was wistful, like it usually was when Martin was mentioned.

'Then pick up the phone and talk to him. Arrange to meet for a drink or go for a walk together. Anything!'

'What if I do that and he asks me for a divorce?'

'If he wanted a divorce, he's had plenty of time to ask for one.

Maybe he's feeling the same way as you. Maybe he wants to come home and go back to being a normal married couple.'

Angie sighed. 'I doubt it. Being a normal married couple was what split us up in the first place, remember?'

I did remember. I'd arrived for work one January morning nearly two years ago to find Angie leaning over the steering wheel in her car, sobbing. With my arm tightly round her, I ushered her inside and listened while a teary story spilled out. They'd fallen into a rut and drifted apart. Martin had found excitement and passion again with another woman and had left Angie to move in with her, but Angie had also turned to someone else.

I wouldn't have expected it from either of them. They'd seemed so solid together but, when I thought about it more, I could recall so many times over the past five or six years when they'd seemed cold and distant – such a contrast to my parents, who were always warm and affectionate towards each other.

'Do you regret it?' I asked.

Angie moved the flapjack aside, grabbed a fresh knife and started on the millionaire's shortbread. 'Now there's a question! Do I regret it? I *don't* regret that it ended when it did. We were angry with each other for the rut we were in and it needed to end before it turned nasty. But I *do* regret that we got into the rut in the first place. We shouldn't have let it happen. We should have talked about it and changed things before it was too late.'

'Can't you talk about it now and start afresh?'

She rolled her eyes at me. 'For someone who doesn't like to talk about her own love life, you suddenly seem very interested in mine.'

I grimaced. 'Sorry. It's just that you sounded so sad just now when you talked about him not being there for you last night.'

'What's done is done.'

Her voice was a little too cheerful and I wasn't convinced by her words either. If it was absolutely irrevocably over, surely one of them would have filed for a divorce. Within eight months of separating, both the relationships had ended and neither Angie nor Martin had seen anyone else since, although they hadn't seen each other either, keeping in touch intermittently by text instead.

She was right about me not liking the interference, so I had no right to push her further. Not at the moment, anyway. I picked up a ramekin of egg yolk mixed with milk and brushed the top of the scones.

'I don't suppose you saw my post on Facebook last night about the lost dog?' I asked.

'No. Lost here?'

I told her about Jake and the shih tzu while I finished the cheese scones, popped them in the oven and started making some cherry ones.

'He messaged me first thing to say the owner's been found and they're picking him up tonight. They must be beside themselves with relief.' I smiled as I pictured him. 'He's such a gorgeous dog. Lovely temperament and well trained too. Don't you think shih tzus have such lovely faces, like little teddy bears?'

'Sounds like someone's getting broody for another dog.'

I shook my head. 'Don't say that. I couldn't. It wouldn't be fair when I'm here all day most days.'

'So bring the dog to work like your mum did with Willow. She was good as gold and the customers loved her.'

I pondered on it while I cut up the cherries. It would be lovely to have a dog for company again and bringing one to work with me was possible, as Mum had shown. I visualised where I could put a dog bed and tears unexpectedly rushed to my eyes as I pictured our family dogs over the years. I blinked them back. 'Maybe one day,' I offered feebly. 'Would you mind nipping upstairs for some more napkins? The cupboard's nearly empty.'

It was the truth but it was also an excuse to have a moment alone. As soon as Angie left the kitchen, I gripped the worktop with both hands, dipped my head and took a couple of deep breaths as I fought the emotions swirling inside me.

Most of the time, I coped. There were obvious challenging days like birthdays, anniversaries and Christmas, but I knew they were coming and could psych myself up. There were traditions I'd continued like putting up the Christmas tree in the café last night and, again, I could be prepared for them. But occasionally something cropped up that blindsided me and today it was dogs.

When Willow crossed the rainbow bridge four months after I lost Mum, it nearly broke me. She'd been fourteen and had already lived longer than the life expectancy for the breed so I'd known I wouldn't have long left with her but every day was precious. Willow gave me a reason to get out of bed each day and remember to breathe when, in the space of a year, we'd gone from being a family of five to three to two.

An alarm on my phone pulled me from my memories. It sounded at 9.55 a.m. each day to give me a five-minute warning of opening time as it was too easy to lose track when I was baking or deep in thought. I inhaled deeply and shook my arms to release the tension. *Smile. Sparkle. You've got this.*

'All set?' I asked Angie as I passed the serving counter.

She looked up from the packet of napkins she was unwrapping and smiled. 'All set.'

I turned round the 'closed' sign, unlocked the outer door and took a deep breath of cold sea air. As predicted, there'd been a heavy frost overnight, which now covered the car park, clung to fallen leaves, and embraced the tree branches. It wasn't slippery so there was no need to spread any grit. The frost would melt away as soon as the winter sun peeked through the gaps in the trees surrounding the car park.

The only cars were mine and Angie's, as was usually the case first thing out of season. I watched a couple of starlings squabbling over the fat balls hanging from one of the frost-covered branches and smiled at a grey squirrel scampering up the wide trunk of a Scots pine. There was something so magical about standing outside the café before the customers arrived, listening to the whispering of the pine trees, the song of birds, the shuffling of the wildlife, and the tumble of the waves below. I was so lucky to own The Starfish Café and spend my days doing what I loved in this stunning location which was so blessed by nature. But I'd give it all up in a heartbeat, if only...

I shook my head and closed the door. I could clearly hear Mum's voice in my head: *There's always somebody having a tougher time than you. Be grateful for the small things and keep dancing in the rain.*

'You've got this,' I whispered. 'Keep dancing.'

I'd expected to be woken in the early hours but I didn't hear a peep from Mr Pickles all night. When I went downstairs, he was waiting in the lounge doorway, tail wagging frantically.

'Good morning, Mr Pickles.'

He followed me through the kitchen into the garden, and I left the door ajar while I put the kettle on.

'We found your owner,' I said when he ventured back inside. 'But you're not going home until tonight, buddy, so you'll have to put up with me for the day. Is that okay?' He looked up at me, tail wagging, and I had that same sense of unease from last night. He was a good dog. Why hadn't Carole Jessop rushed to get him back?

'We need to walk into town first thing to buy some flowers, then we're off to the cemetery in the car, but we'll go for a run along the beach after that. Would you like that?'

I'd found a ball abandoned in the front garden a couple of years ago and it had seemed a waste to throw it out. Where had I put it? My eyes rested on the shelves above the kitchen table and I lifted down a glass bowl from the top one. Yes! Ball! I removed it and placed it on the table and was about to put the bowl back when I clocked what else was inside. I picked it out and turned it over in my hands. That brought back memories.

Mr Pickles barked at me, bringing me back to the present. 'Are you hungry?' I presumed dogs ate each morning and evening – maybe I'd better Google that later – so I put the item down on the side while I dished up some food for him and replenished the plastic container I'd used as a water bowl.

'It's good you're here today,' I said, watching the dog tucking into his breakfast. I retrieved the item I'd removed from the bowl and slid down against the unit to sit on the quarry tiles next to him. 'November the sixth is always the toughest day of the year. I might need your support, buddy.' I stroked the dog's back and behind his ears. 'Might not be so tough with you here.'

Opening out my hand, I stared at the part-built Rubik's Cube. I glanced towards the bowl containing the missing pieces, then looked upwards.

'Did you send Mr Pickles to me, Nanna? If you did, thank you.' I held up the cube. 'I promise I'll fix this one day. I just need a little more time.'

* * *

I borrowed an old dog lead from Irene and walked into town with Mr Pickles to pick up some flowers. Nanna's friend Kay used to run Seaside Blooms on Castle Street so Nanna and I had always bought our flowers for the cemetery from there. Her niece Sarah took over when Kay went on her worldwide travels.

As soon as I pushed open the door to Seaside Blooms, Sarah looked up and smiled.

'Hey, Jake, how are you?'

'Bearing up. I swear the anniversary never gets any easier.'

'But does it get any harder?'

'No.'

'Then hang onto that positive.'

'I'll try to.'

'I saw your post on Facebook.' She crouched down beside me and stroked Mr Pickles. 'Aren't you a beauty? Did you find the owner?'

'Yes, but she can't come to collect him until tonight so Mr Pickles...' we exchanged knowing looks over his name, 'is keeping me company at the cemetery in exchange for a run on the beach later. I've got a ball.'

'Sounds like you're going to have great fun, Mr Pickles.' Sarah straightened up. 'Am I allowed to wish you a happy birthday?'

I grimaced. 'You can if you want, but I tend to avoid it altogether. It's easier that way. Saves awkward questions.'

She nodded. 'Makes sense. My Auntie Kay sends her love, by the way.'

'Cheers. How's she getting on? Still doing the photography?' During her travels, Kay had developed an interest in photography and met Philip Heslington – the man who'd inspired me to take it up – through wanting to pursue it further once she got back. They'd since married but I'd not seen much of her since she moved out of Seashell Cottage, which was now home to Sarah's brother Ben and his wife Clare.

'She's got such an eye for it. I keep winding Philip up that she's better than him. They're off to the States tomorrow on a photography tour round the national parks. You'll have to watch out for the photos on Facebook.'

'Will do. I'm very envious.'

'Do you want yellow flowers again?' Sarah asked.

'Please.' Yellow had been Mum's favourite colour so it was what we'd always bought.

Mr Pickles and I stepped to one side while Sarah selected the flowers. My eyes fell on a display carousel of greetings cards. The ones facing me were all for birthdays. What must it feel like to celebrate a birthday like a normal person? To feel excited? To have presents, balloons and a cake each year?

As a young child, all I ever wanted to do was to spend the day with Dad. It was too hard for him, though. He needed to spend the day grieving. Nanna used to tell me that the baddies didn't stop being bad just because it was my birthday, so Dad still had to work and that was why I needed to spend the day with her. She pulled out all the stops to try to make my birthday fun. She'd decorate Lighthouse View with balloons and streamers, bake a cake and spoil me with presents but the only present I really wanted was the one thing I couldn't have: my parents.

After we lost Dad and I moved into Lighthouse View permanently, even Nanna – usually a bubbly optimist – struggled to act jolly and to celebrate my birthday, and who could blame her?

'Are these all right for you?' Sarah held out some flowers.

'Perfect. Thanks.' They were yellow. That was all that mattered.

After she'd wrapped them and taken payment, she bent down and stroked Mr Pickles. 'You look after Jake for me. Good boy.' She straightened up and gave me a gentle smile. 'I hope it's okay at the cemetery.'

'Thanks. It'll be...' I shrugged. It was what it was. 'See you later.'

* * *

Thirty-five years old today. Thirty-five years since Mum died. Twenty-six since Dad followed. Five years of going to the cemetery without Nanna. Grim.

'This next bit won't be fun, buddy,' I warned Mr Pickles as I let him out of the car at the cemetery. 'But I promise the beach afterwards will be. For you, anyway.'

Nanna once told me that Mum had wanted to be cremated but Dad chose a burial, wanting a place he could go and talk to her. He'd been buried in the same plot. I hated visiting the cemetery. I didn't feel close to them there but felt obligated to visit. Nanna felt the same and had chosen cremation, instructing me to scatter her ashes from the ruined keep at Whitsborough Bay Castle. It had been no mean feat doing that when nobody was looking!

The winter sun hadn't yet melted the frost so my feet crunched as I walked along the path and over the grass to the grave. I removed the dead flowers from the black vase beside the joint headstone, added the new bunch, and stepped back. After all these years, I still didn't know what to say. I much preferred wandering round the castle grounds than staring at a chunk of granite.

'I found a dog,' I said eventually, my voice hushed. 'This is him. Mr Pickles. His owner's collecting him tonight. Erm... I'm still at the hospital. Still single and...' An image of Hollie appeared in my head and my stomach did a backflip. Not sure what that was all about. 'Yeah, so, still single and still doing the photography. Irene sends her love. Erm... That's it, I suppose.' I grimaced. How many times could I use the word 'still'?

Mr Pickles pressed his body against my leg and looked up at me. I picked him up and buried my head in his fur. Just what I needed. We stood there for a few minutes more, then I picked up the dead flowers and the packaging, deposited them in a nearby bin and returned to the car. Done for another year.

* * *

I drove to North Bay. The sky was brighter down there and the frost had gone.

'Come on, Mr Pickles,' I said, letting him out the back. 'Time to chase a ball.'

He wagged his tail vigorously and I could already feel my spirits lifting as we crossed the road and made our way down to the beach.

'Ready?' I tossed the ball and smiled as he scampered after it and came to a skidding halt before racing back to me and dropping it by my feet. 'Was that fun?'

I felt steadily brighter as we ran along the sand chasing after the ball. Mr Pickles raced in and out of the rock pools and, when we reached the southern end of the beach, we turned and ran back along the shoreline. It was chilly but invigorating, turning my nose and cheeks numb with cold and making my eyes stream.

'Do you know what?' I said to him as we sat on the sea wall a little later, catching our breath. 'This is only the second time I've been down to the seafront on my birthday since I turned nine.' It also struck me it was the first time I'd laughed on my birthday since then. Who'd have thought a dog would help me put aside my twenty-six-year-old birthday demons?

I lifted him down from the wall. 'There's somewhere I want to show you.'

When we reached the old slipway, I picked him up and cuddled him against my chest as I looked out at the steady rise and fall of the waves. 'It's choppy today, but you should have seen it twenty-six years ago. The waves were huge.'

And so was the impact of what happened that day.

15

Twenty-six years ago

'Nanna, please can you talk to Dad?' I tugged on her sleeve as she mashed the potato for Sunday lunch at Lighthouse View the day before my ninth birthday.

'Jake! We've talked about this before. Your dad has to work. He has to catch the baddies.'

'But I never see him on my birthday. Please.'

She shook her head. 'I've said no and that's my final word on the matter. I don't want to hear another peep out of you, young man.'

'But it's not fair.' I slumped down onto the dining chair with my head resting in my hands.

She stopped mashing and ruffled my hair. 'I know, lovey. It's hard but I promise you'll understand one day.'

I scowled. 'He always spends Larissa's birthday with her.'

She ruffled my hair again but didn't speak. I didn't like it when she looked sad like that so I didn't say anything else but it really wasn't fair. Larissa made such a fuss about Dad having a day off from arresting baddies and taking her out on her birthday. I knew he didn't work on my birthday because he didn't have his police uniform on when I left for school and he was home when I got back. Larissa said it was because he loved her and hated me, but she was lying. Larissa lied a lot.

After lunch, I played in the garden but it was boring on my own. Most of the other kids at school had brothers or sisters or both and they played together but I only had horrible Larissa. She was old and mean and I didn't ever want to play with her.

I wanted a puppy or a kitten to play with but Dad said they were too much work. I'd asked Santa Claus for one the last two years but he must have got confused because he left me a soft toy cat in my stocking one year and a soft toy dog the next. Larissa told me it was because Santa Claus didn't exist and the presents were from Dad. She also said that, if Santa had existed, my stocking would have been full of coal because I'd have been at the top of his naughty list because I killed Mum. She wasn't allowed to say that. It made Dad very angry but it never stopped her. Larissa said and did whatever she liked. I wished Dad would put her in jail with the baddies.

I didn't love the toy dog and cat as much as I loved Binky, my soft penguin. I took him everywhere. Larissa called me a baby and said I was too old for cuddly toys. She said she was embarrassed to be seen out with me and Binky, but she didn't like being out with me even if Binky wasn't there, so I didn't listen to her.

Nanna's garden wasn't very big. I wanted to play hide and seek with Binky but there weren't any good places to hide. It was just grass and flowers. Over the garden wall I saw two older children walking past with fishing nets.

I had my hand on the back door handle and was about to step into the kitchen to ask Nanna if we could go down to the river to play when I heard loud voices through the open window.

'It's not right, Bobby,' Nanna shouted. 'He's only a bairn.'

'I know that, but it's too bloody difficult,' Dad responded, his voice loud too. If he hadn't been shouting, I might have giggled at the use of the naughty word. Dad never swore unless it was at Larissa when she said I was a killer.

'You don't think it's hard for him? Or me? Or Larissa? Tomorrow's difficult for everyone, but you and Michelle knew the risks. You were told time and time again not to try for another baby but—'

'Stop throwing that back at me, Mum! I know now that I should have put my foot down but I didn't know it then. It's what we both wanted and the thing with risks is sometimes they work out for the best. We weren't to know that this one wouldn't.'

Nanna's voice softened. 'I understand how you feel. Hindsight's a great thing. But you both took that risk and, even though it didn't work out for poor Michelle, you got what you wanted. You have a son and he's a wonderful little boy. You know what little boys like? They like birthdays. Can't you do something with him just this once? It's too late to organise a party but he won't mind that. All he wants is to spend some time on his birthday with his father. Can't you at least grant your son that one tiny birthday wish?'

I didn't hear Dad's answer because the phone rang. I clung onto Binky and scooted back down the garden, where I sat cross-legged picking blades of grass until I was called inside by Nanna a bit later.

She put a beaker of blackcurrant juice down on the table beside a plain digestive biscuit. 'Your dad has something to say to you.'

She glared at Dad and he cleared his throat. 'Erm, it's...' Nanna prodded him in the side. 'It's about your birthday tomorrow. I thought we could do something after school. Would you like that?'

I could have burst with excitement. 'Yes, please!'

'What would you like to do?'

I grinned at him and Nanna. 'Can we go down to the beach?'

'The beach?' Dad raised his eyebrows. 'It's November.'

'But I like the beach and we haven't been for ages. We could get an ice cream.'

'In November?'

'I have ice cream with my Christmas pudding in December.'

Dad smiled. 'That's good logic, son. Okay. We'll go down to the beach after school tomorrow and we'll get an ice cream.'

'You won't invite Larissa, will you?' I asked warily.

'It'll just be the two of us so don't go inviting any of your school-friends.'

'I won't.' I didn't really have any friends anyway. 'But can Binky come?'

'Just the three of us, then. You, me and Binky.'

I jumped out of my chair and hugged him. I didn't care if it was cold or wet. I was spending my birthday with Dad and Binky and that was all I needed or wanted.

* * *

I was so excited at school all day, I couldn't concentrate. My teacher, Miss Lemmings, kept telling me off but I didn't mind. It was my birthday and I was going to the beach with Dad. Miss Lemmings said she didn't care about my birthday plans and I needed to do my sums. I didn't like her. She said I couldn't go out at afternoon play-time but it started raining so they rang the handbell for indoor play anyway.

I hoped the rain wouldn't change our plans. I liked the rain. I had a red waterproof coat and some navy wellie boots and Dad had a waterproof coat too but his was a boring green colour.

Dad was waiting for me outside the classroom when the bell went at three o'clock.

'I've got some bad news,' he said as we set off across the playground and my heart sank. We weren't going.

'The tide's going to be in so we won't be able to go onto the beach.'

'But we can still go to the seaside and get an ice cream?' I asked eagerly.

'We can still do that but you can't dawdle and you'll need to get changed in lightning-quick speed when we get home. It'll be dark even earlier than usual because of the rain.'

'I can run home,' I cried, dodging round the people in the playground.

We only lived a short walk from my primary school but the journey was extra quick, racing Dad home. I ran upstairs, pulling off my school jumper as I went. I threw my uniform on the bed and pulled on my jeans, T-shirt, a sweater and a thick pair of socks and, with Binky tucked under my arm, raced back downstairs for my wellies and waterproof.

'Ready!' I announced, bursting into the living room with my arms thrust wide.

Dad was seated in his favourite armchair with his head in his hands but he looked up and smiled. 'That was unbelievably quick. Why can't you do that at bedtime?'

'There's no ice cream at bedtime.'

He laughed at that. 'Come on. Let's get going. Your nanna's going to come round for tea and she's made a birthday cake so you can only have a small ice cream.'

'Can I have a flake and strawberry sauce?'

'I suppose so. Kind of defeats the object of only having a small ice cream.'

'But it's my birthday.'

He nodded slowly. 'Yes, it is. Happy birthday, son.'

* * *

'I thought we'd be going to Nanna's beach,' I said as Dad pulled into one of the parking spaces on North Bay seafront.

'This one's closer to us, which means we get there quicker. Remember what I said about it getting dark earlier.'

'Okay.'

'You always go down to South Bay with Nanna so I thought this would make a change, especially when we can't go onto the beach because of the high tide. We can sit on the wall and watch the sea from there.'

I pushed open the car door and reached for Binky.

'Would Binky not prefer to stay warm and dry in the car?' Dad asked.

'It's his birthday too so he wants to come with us.' Nanna had bought him for me for my sixth birthday after I'd fallen in love with the penguins at the Sea Rescue Sanctuary that summer. Despite Larissa being eighteen at the time, she'd thrown an epic strop in the gift shop after I'd made my penguin selection. She grabbed Nanna's handbag and stormed out, leaving Nanna with no means to pay and no choice but to leave. I loved that she'd gone back without me knowing and bought Binky ready for my birthday, although of course Larissa had sulked about that, saying Nanna spoilt me. Nanna spoilt my sister too but Larissa always moaned about the gifts she was given. Nothing seemed to make her happy.

I held onto one of Binky's flippers as we crossed the road to the sea. There weren't many cars or people around. The rain had got heavier since leaving school and the sky was dark grey. The tide was right in and the waves crashing against the sea wall showered us with salty spray.

'The sea wall's a bit wet,' Dad said. 'I don't fancy sitting on it and getting a soggy bottom. Do you?'

'Can we go down the slipway?' I asked, already taking a couple of paces in that direction.

When Dad followed me, I set off running. 'Don't go right down,' he called after me.

'I won't.'

I could see a man with a big brown dog hurrying towards us. I wondered whether to stay on the path so I could pet the dog but I thought Dad might decide it was too dark and wet to stay any longer so I didn't stop.

The smell of seaweed became stronger as I reached the slipway. Because the tide was in, only the top section was out of the water. The bottom part was submerged and waves were crashing against the middle section, splatting white foam against the wall.

'Be careful!' yelled Dad.

I turned my head. The man with the big brown dog had stopped to talk to him.

'We're fine, aren't we, Binky?' I said, clutching my damp penguin's flipper in my right hand as we took a few paces down the slipway. Spray pelted my wellies and jeans and my feet skidded on the algae.

'Jake!' Dad called. 'Get back up here right now.'

I spun round but he'd resumed his conversation with the man. The dog was sitting down watching me and I hesitated. It was cold and, now that my jeans were wet, I wasn't enjoying this as much as I'd expected. Maybe I should do what Dad said, pet the dog, get my ice cream and go home for tea and birthday cake.

But that split second of hesitation was about to completely change my world.

'Binky!' I screamed as an enormous wave crashed over my head, drenching me and dragging my beloved penguin from my grasp and into the sea.

'No!' Dad yelled.

I crouched down on the slipway, my heart racing as Binky bobbed in the waves below. I could reach him. I just needed to stretch over.

'Leave it!'

'Dad!' I shrieked as another wave crashed over me and pulled me into the icy water. Salt water filled my mouth and stung my eyes as I flailed with my arms. I was pulled back by the current then thrown forward. I was on the surface, coughing and gasping for air. Dad was on the slipway, yelling my name.

'Help!'

And then I was dragged below the water again. My hand brushed against something. Binky?

* * *

I could hear shouts. A dog was barking. Someone was crying. Something or someone was pressing on my chest and I was going to be sick. I spewed up a mouthful of salty water and coughed.

'He's back,' a man said. I felt too tired, too shaky to turn to face him.

'Can you hear me, Jake?' A woman in a fluorescent yellow jacket peered over me. It was dark and there were flashing blue lights behind her.

'Dad?'

'We need to get you to hospital, Jake. We're going to lift you onto a stretcher and take you in an ambulance.'

'Dad?'

But the woman had already moved away. I closed my eyes as fear gripped me. Where was Dad? Why wasn't he with me?

My memories of what happened next were in flashes of sound and movement: the sensation of the stretcher being raised up then bumping over the pavement, someone tugging off my soggy clothes, the softness of blankets and the crinkle of a silver thing that looked like a giant sheet of the foil Nanna used when she cooked a chicken for Sunday lunch.

When I opened my eyes again I was in a bed, but it wasn't mine. Nanna was next to me, her head lowered, a handkerchief clutched between her hands.

'Nanna?'

Her head shot up. 'Jake! Oh, thank goodness. I've been so worried about you.'

I ran my tongue over my dry, cracked lips.

'Would you like some water?' Nanna pressed a button and the top of my bed lifted up before she pressed a plastic cup of water against my mouth. I took a few sips, then rested back against the pillows.

'Dad?'

Her bottom lip wobbled and her eyes filled with tears. 'We don't know. They're out looking for him.'

'Who?'

'The people on the lifeboats.'

'He fell in the sea like me?'

'Yes, lovey, he fell in the sea like you.'

'It was freezing. I hope they find him soon.'

'So do I.'

* * *

The people on the lifeboats did find him but they couldn't save him. I screamed when the doctor told me. I called her a liar and begged Nanna to take me to him. They gave me something to help me sleep. I didn't want to sleep. I wanted my dad.

When they discharged me from hospital, Nanna took me back to Lighthouse View. She settled me in bed with a mug of warm blackcurrant beside me and the soft dog and cat Santa had delivered. They hadn't found Binky. I wanted my penguin, too.

There was a bang on the front door. 'I'll just see who that is,' Nanna said, pulling the duvet up to my chin.

Moments later, I heard Larissa shouting and Nanna's protests as my sister thundered up the stairs, screaming: 'Where's that killer?'

She stormed towards me and I think she would have beaten me up if Nanna hadn't shouted, 'You lay a finger on him and I'll have you arrested.' Her tone shocked me. Larissa had done so many horrible things to me and Nanna had told her off plenty of times but she'd never shouted before. I hadn't known her voice could be so loud.

Even Larissa seemed stunned for a moment, staring at her with her mouth wide open. Then she shouted back. 'Fine! And they can arrest *him* while they're here.'

'It was an accident.'

'Which wouldn't have happened if he hadn't been so stupid. I know *exactly* what happened. Andrew's uncle was there with his dog. He stopped to talk to Dad and that stupid idiot there was playing on the slipway. Dad told him to come back but he had to do what he wanted as usual. Next minute he's in the water trying to retrieve his stupid fucking penguin.'

'Larissa! That's enough!'

Spit had flown from Larissa's mouth as she shouted. She scared me.

'You're a demon!' she cried, lunging at me again. 'I wish it was you who'd drowned.'

Nanna's cheeks were red as she grabbed Larissa's arm and yanked her towards the door. 'Get out! Now!' She lowered her voice. 'We'll talk later.'

'I don't want to talk. I want my parents back but he killed them both.'

My sister gave me one last murderous look. 'I hate you.'

I gulped and sank down under the duvet, shaking, feeling the full force of that hatred. I jumped as the front door slammed moments later.

'She didn't mean it,' Nanna said, her voice gentle and reassuring as she returned to the bedroom. 'She's upset about losing your dad. We all are.'

I peeked over the duvet. 'Was it my fault, Nanna?' I asked tentatively.

'Of course not, lovey.' She sat on the edge of the bed and stroked my fringe back from my face. 'It was just one of those tragic accidents where lots of different factors came together, but nobody was to blame.'

'But I was the one who wanted to go to the beach.'

'And I was the one who insisted your dad do something on your birthday, and your dad was the one who took you down to the seafront when it was stormy. Andrew's uncle distracted your dad while you were on the slipway.'

'And Binky fell in the sea and needed rescuing.'

She gave me a gentle smile. 'That's right. So, as you can see, no one person can possibly be blamed for what happened. Just a chain of events.'

'But Larissa blames me.'

Nanna released the biggest sigh ever and slowly shook her head. 'Larissa is a very challenging and complex young woman.'

I didn't know what that meant, and I didn't want to. Nanna left me while she went to prepare some lunch. I looked across at the rain battering the window and shuddered as I relived what had happened. I doubted I'd ever forget the fear as I reached for Binky, the shock of the cold when I fell in the sea, or the feeling of guilt clawing at me now because Larissa was right. I *had* killed our parents.

Nanna was trying to help when she said it was nobody's fault but everything she mentioned could be traced back to me. I'd been the one who begged her to make Dad spend the day with me, I was the one who'd asked to go to the beach, I was the one who'd taken Binky with me when Dad suggested leaving him in the car, I was the one who'd run down the slipway and ignored Dad's repeated demands for me to return. And I was the one who'd fallen in and made Dad follow.

I was only nine years old but I already wished I was dead. My big sister wished I'd been the one who'd drowned, and so did I.

16

Present day

'You've been great company today, buddy,' I told Mr Pickles early that evening as I made a coffee back at Lighthouse View. 'I'm going to miss you.' I'd heard colleagues and patients talking about dogs bringing joy to their lives and, after only one day, I had some insight into what they meant. Mr Pickles had provided an unexpected lift on what was normally the crappiest of days.

I glanced at the clock: 6.50 p.m. 'How about we let you in the back garden so you're good to go when your owner gets here?'

He obediently trotted to the back door, which I left ajar so he could explore the lawn and flower beds for the last time. When he returned to the kitchen, he stopped dead, pricked up his ears, then barked as he raced past me and down the hall.

'Is she here?' I asked, striding after him.

There was a stained-glass panel on the door – a red and white striped lighthouse with a sailing boat either side – and my vision through it was clear.

'There's nobody there, buddy.'

He jumped up and down, barking. Maybe she was on the path outside, searching for the right house. Most of the houses had names rather than numbers so it could be confusing for someone unfamiliar with the Old Town. I opened the door and peered into the dark street but it was deserted.

'Sorry, bud. She's not here yet, but it's not quite sev—' Another bark stopped me mid-word and I looked down to see Mr Pickles circling round a couple of bin bags and a bag for life dumped in front of the bay window. That uneasy feeling was back. I stepped outside, peered in the bag, and my stomach lurched as I clocked a packet of dog biscuits, a couple of bowls and a lead.

'Shit,' I muttered, grinding my teeth together. 'Don't say she's...' Mr Pickles looked up at me with his dark eyes and it was as though he knew.

My phone beeped and I fished it out of my pocket.

Jake

I've left three bags in your front garden containing the dog's papers and belongings. We can't look after him. He belongs to my mother but she has dementia and has gone into a care home. My husband and I have enough stress in our lives running round after her without having the added inconvenience of a stupid mutt.

You can keep him or you can re-home him but, seeing as you're the one who found him, he's your responsibility now. I relinquish ownership to you. There's no point trying to debate this with me as I won't respond to any messages you send.

Who *were* these people? I looked down at the little dog, stunned at what I'd read. From what I'd seen so far, Mr Pickles was an obedient, affectionate animal. Why would anyone want rid of him like that?

'Come on, buddy. Back in the house. You're staying with me for a bit longer.'

He followed me into the kitchen, where I placed the bags on the pine table. I ripped open the first bin bag and removed a dog bed, a couple of blankets and some towels. Mr Pickles jumped up and down and turned in a circle, clearly excited at seeing – or perhaps smelling – his belongings. I placed the bed on the floor and he immediately settled in it, watching me.

The second bin bag was full of dog clothes from practical water-proof coats to knitted jumpers, hoodies and Christmas costumes. I lifted out an elf outfit and a striped hat with a bell on it.

'Oh, God, they didn't seriously dress you up in this, did they?'

I held the outfit out towards him, curling my lip, but Mr Pickles wagged his tail.

'You like it? Each to their own, buddy. But I'll stick with the waterproofs.'

As well as the lead, bowls and dog biscuits, the bag contained some packets of wet food, a few books about shih tzus, some toys, and a pink box file. I picked up a small blue teddy and showed it to him. His tail wagged vigorously and he seemed pleased to be reunited with his bear, taking it gently between his teeth.

I took the file through to the lounge. Mr Pickles followed me and lay on the rug in front of the log burner, playing with his teddy. My eyes widened as I rifled through the file's contents. It appeared that Mr Pickles was the shih tzu's shortened name and his full moniker was Mr Piccalilli Marmaduke Fluffington the Third. Poor thing. And he was a pedigree. Six years old. He'd won several competitions including Crufts: best in breed twice, going on to win best in group the second time.

'Check you out with all your awards,' I said.

I finished flicking through the paperwork. Dodgy outfits and name choice aside, it was obvious that Margaret Hamilton had loved Mr Pickles but that devotion hadn't passed down to her daughter. Carole had to have dumped him in the car park at The Starfish Café and he'd found his way down to the beach. It made my blood boil but how else would he have ended up there? It made sod all sense either. A well trained healthy dog like that could easily have been rehomed. Add in his pedigree and award credentials, there'd have been a queue of people desperate to take him – probably for good money – yet she'd chosen to remove his collar and dump him. He could have drowned or, if he'd run the other way, he could have been killed on the road. With so many options open to her, why the hell had she taken the cruellest one? On Bonfire Night of all nights, too. I remembered what Hollie had said about the seal pups, so she'd placed them at risk too. She reminded me of Larissa: angry and selfish.

He was safe with me. He'd been no trouble so far but what would happen when I was back on shifts? I also had another big commitment, which might only tie me up for a Monday evening now but would soon need flexibility.

I patted the sofa beside me and Mr Pickles jumped up. 'You can stay here again tonight, buddy. We've got your bed now so you'll be more comfortable. And then we'll have to think about what's best for you. Maybe we can go back to The Starfish Café and ask Hollie's advice. She seemed to know about dogs.'

I pictured Hollie being all attentive to Mr Pickles and how eager she'd been to help. As the dog cuddled up closer, I wasn't sure whether the warm glow I felt was from the comfort of my new companion or the prospect of seeing Hollie again. I'd noticed on the Facebook page that The Starfish Café was closed on a Monday out of season and Hollie had mentioned she didn't work on Sundays.

'We'll go back on Tuesday,' I decided. And Tuesday couldn't come soon enough.

17

HOLLIE

I woke up to my alarm early on Sunday morning, shoved back the duvet and wandered over to the large window to the side of my bedroom, grabbing my furry robe on the way to protect me from the morning chill.

Pulling back the curtains, I gazed out towards the sea. Sunrise wouldn't be for another forty-five minutes but the sky was already lightening. A ribbon of orange nestled under deep petrol blue. It was going to be another beautiful one.

The street was deserted, not even a lone dog walker. I used to love early morning walks with Willow, enjoying the peace and quiet while most people were still in their beds.

I missed having a dog in the house, hearing the gentle sound of paws tapping along the Victorian tiles in the hallway or on the stripped floorboards, and the frantic scampering to regain control after they'd bounded up the stairs too quickly.

Those weren't the only sounds I longed to hear again. I missed the chatter and clink of teaspoons in the kitchen as everyone got ready for the day ahead. I missed the laughter, the hugs, the company.

My grief counsellor Erica had explored the idea of me moving but I couldn't bear the thought of leaving my family home. I loved Sandy Croft so much. We all had. It was brimming with happy memories and moving would not take away the sense of loss. If anything, it would exacerbate it. And if I did move, what were the chances of me finding a property that was a smaller size for me but which still had a double garage to accommodate my workshop? It wasn't an option. Besides, being in our family home helped me feel that little bit closer to them all so that was where I was staying, even if a three-storey five-bedroom Victorian property was way too big for one person whose only company was her memories.

* * *

Twenty minutes later, I sat on the stone steps which led down to the beach. Nothing could quite beat watching the sun gradually rise behind Whitsborough Bay lighthouse a little further along the coast at the far end of South Bay beach, especially on a crisp day like today. The petrol blue sky gave way to deep lilac and strands of gold perforated the orange. Nature's canvas at its most beautiful.

If I could paint well, I'd love to recreate this but my artistic skills had their limitations and I couldn't even begin to do this scene justice. As a photographer, Jake would be able to capture the magic. I frowned. Why had he popped into my mind? He kept doing that. That gorgeous little dog would have been collected last night. I bet the owner was so relieved to have him back. I'd have been frantic if one of our dogs had gone missing.

The colours over the sea changed with each passing minute. What a beautiful place to have right on my doorstep – only a six-minute walk down the zig-zagged cliff path.

Isaac and I had loved coming down here as kids. There was so much variety on this section of beach – golden sands, rock pools, a cove full of pebbles and shells, and several boulders to clamber across – yet it was never as busy as Whitsborough Bay's North Bay and main South Bay beaches.

A lone silhouetted figure headed towards the shore with a board tucked under their arm. There wasn't any swell and North Bay was generally favoured for surfing so I suspected they were going paddleboarding. Isaac and I had tried it when I was ten and he'd just turned twelve. He'd taken to it immediately – hardly surprising as he'd attended summer surf school since he was six – but I'd never managed to get my balance, so I'd stuck to bodyboarding. I liked splashing about in the water and I was a strong swimmer, but Isaac had been the water baby in our family, just like Dad. The rock pools were more my cup of tea. I'd spent many a happy hour searching in them, usually accompanied by the family dog, while Isaac was in the sea.

The figure entered the water and I'd guessed correctly. He was upright instantly, paddling along the shore just like my brother. Sipping the remnants of my coffee, I watched them for a few minutes then stood up and wiped the sand off my jeans and jacket. It was time to go beachcombing before too many memories took hold and made me melancholy.

* * *

A couple of hours later, I stretched out and took a few deep gulps of sea air then picked up my bags. I had a good haul of sea glass – chunks of glass bottles tossed by waves, sand and stone to become small polished colourful pieces – as well as shells and driftwood.

I didn't usually find substantial pieces of driftwood down here unless there'd been a storm but there'd been a few good-sized ones this morning. Some pieces were partially burnt so I suspected they'd been swept into the sea then ashore again from the small fires people lit along the beach on Bonfire Night.

It was quarter to ten as I made my way across the beach towards the steps by the covered walkway. There were several people out for a walk now, many of them accompanied by dogs. All our dogs had loved the beach, chasing a ball, digging in the sand, or paddling in the sea. Willow had never been fond of going in the sea but she'd loved the rock pools.

After Mum died, I went down to the beach every Sunday with my faithful companion by my side. She trotted down there with enthusiasm but I started to notice that the journey back up the cliff was taking its toll. She walked more slowly. She stopped intermittently. I didn't want to think about her age. I couldn't bear to imagine her leaving me, too.

We stopped going down to the beach, sticking to the wide esplanade round the corner from Sandy Croft. Then, one April day almost exactly four months after Mum died, we set off on our usual Sunday jaunt and Willow tugged on the lead as we passed the entrance to the cliff path.

'Not down there,' I told her. 'You know the walk back up is too much.'

She tugged again, with more strength than I'd felt in months.

'Okay, then. You win. But we're coming back up in the cliff lift and I'll be taking the fare out of your pocket money.'

It felt like old times down on the beach. She sent ripples across the still pools and raced in circles. She leapt into others. It was as though the clocks had been turned back and she was reliving her youth with the same vigour she'd had back then.

We caught the cliff lift up to the esplanade and took the short walk back to Sandy Croft. I left her lapping up her water in the kitchen while I changed into a fresh pair of jeans. By the time I returned downstairs, she'd gone. I slumped to the floor, cradled her against me and loud, painful howls poured from me. My next-door neighbour must have heard and alerted Angie at the café. She turned up with Martin and they took care of things for me.

I've often wondered if Willow had known it was her time. Had she thrown every last ounce of energy she'd had into one final magical day together? Thankfully, the end hadn't been painful. Or at least not for her.

I brushed the sudden tears away with my gloved hands. Jake and the lost shih tzu had stirred up thoughts of having a dog again. Having dogs had been a whole family experience. I loved keeping some traditions going but could I have a dog on my own? I paused and watched a couple of spaniels chasing each other up and down the beach and smiled to myself. Dogs were such amazing company and I'd been on my own for so long. Maybe it was time to share my life with a four-legged friend once more.

18

Six years ago

I'd never blamed myself for Mum's death, no matter what accusations Larissa hurled at me. Dad didn't talk much about Mum but sometimes I caught him looking at me, a distant expression in his eyes. When I asked him if he was okay, he'd smile and tell me he was thinking how lucky he was to have me. Then he'd mutter something about how much Mum had loved and wanted me before making a swift exit.

I hadn't known they'd been advised against a second baby until I overheard Nanna and Dad arguing the day before my ninth birthday. When I started counselling, I questioned Nanna more about it. She told me she'd have loved to have a brother or sister for Dad but Granddad, a violent man, took off when he was two and Nanna couldn't face another relationship after that so Dad had remained an only child. By contrast, Mum had been the youngest of five and loved being part of a big family so my parents wanted siblings for

Larissa. It was therefore their joint decision – against medical advice – to have me.

Nanna later told me that Dad carried guilt but not blame. My parents had discussed it at length and Mum had made him promise that, if the risk didn't pay off, he'd never blame himself or hold me accountable. Shame she hadn't had that conversation with my sister.

I did, however, 100 per cent blame myself for what happened to Dad. For the next couple of years, I put Nanna through hell. I played up at school, got into fights and stomped about in a rage. After I was excluded from school, she tried to teach me at home but I was too tired and distracted to learn. Nightmares about drowning plagued me for months afterwards, depriving us both of sleep. Sometimes I could see Dad's face as he sank into the water beside me. Sometimes I could see Binky. Other times I was all alone.

I was full of attitude towards Nanna and Irene and even took it out on Uncle Adrian and Auntie Maggs. Uncle Adrian had been Dad's best mate since they joined the police together and Auntie Maggs and Mum had been good friends. Auntie Maggs sometimes babysat while Dad and Uncle Adrian were on shift. I loved those nights because she'd tell me all about Mum; something Dad rarely did. When she read a bedtime story and kissed me goodnight, I had a glimpse into what it might be like to have a mum.

Larissa repeatedly told me I was stupid for calling them auntie and uncle when they weren't blood relations, but I knew Auntie Maggs loved it. They had no children and no nephews or nieces so I was like their family.

After Dad died and I fell apart, I struggled with my relationship with them. Sometimes I'd accuse them of trying to replace my parents and tell them I hated them. Other times I'd beg them to adopt me then bang my fists against the wall until they bled when they said they couldn't do that because I already had a loving home with Nanna. They tried to stay in my life but, as my behaviour deteriorated, Nanna had to ask them to stop coming which was probably a relief to them.

When I started senior school, Nanna finally managed to access professional help and my feelings of guilt and self-loathing were the focus of most of my counselling sessions. It didn't matter how many times we explored the concept of an accident; I still absorbed all the blame and it was too much for me, making me lash out at the people I loved.

I hadn't paused to think about the impact my behaviour had on others and how much they might be hurting too but we explored it over a series of sessions, and I realised how much Nanna had lost but how she never complained or lashed out. She'd lost her son and daughter in law, her granddaughter refused to be in her life, and I kept pushing her away so she'd effectively lost me too. I thought about all the cruel things Larissa had said about how useless I was and resolved to get my life together for Nanna's sake and to prove her wrong.

At school, I discovered a passion for biology. A school careers adviser asked if I'd considered nursing. I thought about the two paramedics who'd worked on me after I was pulled from the sea and how they'd saved my life. I could do that. I volunteered for St John's Ambulance while I was still at school and eagerly lapped up the first aid knowledge. Helping others gave me a buzz and my St John's leader often praised me for how calm and reassuring I was when responding to an accident.

Nanna never stopped smiling the day I graduated with my nursing degree, although her eyes clouded with tears when she told me how proud Mum and Dad would have been.

Over the next few years, I threw myself into nursing and loved it. I wouldn't say I made friends at work – it's hard to do that when you keep everyone at arm's length – but I didn't feel like the weirdo or the outsider. And I genuinely felt I was making a difference.

My twenty-ninth birthday arrived, signalling a whopping twenty years since we lost Dad. He'd been out of my life more than twice as long as he'd been in it and that felt strange. In all that time, I'd never returned to the slipway. Nanna and I visited the cemetery together and laid flowers every year but the twenty-year anniversary felt significant. It was time to visit the place where it happened.

Large cement boulders blocked off the slipway and two large signs warned of the danger. There'd been another fatality four years after Dad but it had taken a third tragedy before the boulders and signs materialised. An entire family of five and their dog – visitors to the area – were swept into the sea seven years ago and only the dad came out alive. How would you even begin to pick up the pieces after that?

'How does it feel, being back here?' Nanna asked, leaning against the sea wall after placing a bunch of yellow flowers on top of the middle boulder.

'I don't know. I thought I'd be nervous.' I moved beside her and rested my arms on the wall. It was low tide so there was a stretch of beach below and several rock pools.

'It was a long time ago and you were just a bairn.'

'I can still only remember fragments of that night. Looking at the sea now, it's hard to believe it was even possible.' There was only the slightest of ripples on the water and the sky was the palest blue, fading to grey then white on the horizon. Such a contrast to that night. 'Why couldn't it have been like this?'

'The sea has many personalities and you caught her on a bad day. We can't go down the blame path again. It won't change what happened. The important thing is we learn from it and we try to protect others from the same fate.'

'I wonder how many lives these boulders and signs have saved.'

'A good few, I'd have thought. And those wonderful RNLI volunteers rushing to rescue those in trouble will have saved hundreds of others.'

'I'll never understand how a service that valuable is run mainly by volunteers.'

Nanna sighed. 'Don't get me started on that one. Let's just be grateful that there are men and women out there willing to risk their own lives to save others. Ordinary people doing extraordinary things.'

Nanna shivered suddenly and pulled her coat more tightly round her. 'That blue sky's deceptive. There's a definite nip in the air. I might go and sit in the car.'

I handed her my car keys. 'I won't be long.'

Resting my arms on the wall once more, I reflected on what she'd just said. I'd taken swimming lessons as a child and had been a good, fast swimmer but, when I found myself yanked fully clothed into the icy cold North Sea, I panicked. I had no idea what to do or how to save myself. All the swimming badges and gala wins meant nothing because nobody had taught me what now seemed so obvious: don't play with the sea because you're likely to lose.

Nanna had suggested I return to swimming lessons immediately, going on about getting back on the horse after a fall. I wasn't ready but she kept coaxing me, so I reluctantly returned to the pool a year later, had a panic attack in the shallow end, fainted and slipped under the water. I never visited the pool again and wouldn't even paddle at the shore on a calm summer's day. That needed to change.

I turned my gaze to the giant rusted steel sculpture of Stanley Moffatt sitting on an oversized bench a few metres away, looking out towards the sea. Moffatt had been a local fisherman in the 1950s and a great supporter of the RNLI – the Royal National Lifeboat Institution – after they saved his life when his fishing boat capsized.

When he died, he left them a substantial sum, enabling them to buy a lifeboat named after him. An elderly resident had commissioned the sculpture and donated it to the town. I wasn't sure if placing him near the slipway had been deliberate, but I liked the idea that someone so connected to the sea and the RNLI was immortalised there.

'I've come to a big decision,' I announced, clambering back into the car beside Nanna.

'That sounds ominous. Should I be worried?'

'No. It's something you wanted me to do twenty years ago. I'm going to return to the pool. I need to overcome my fear of water.'

She grabbed my arm. 'Oh, Jake! That's wonderful news. I know you can do it.'

'That's not the *big* part of the big decision. When I've conquered my fear I'm going to volunteer with the RNLI. I want to help educate people in the dangers of the sea and I want to help save those who get into trouble.'

Nanna stared at me for a moment, tears glistening in her eyes. 'I didn't think it was possible to be more proud of you than I was the day you got your degree, but I think I might just be the most proud I've ever been right now.'

She hugged me tightly and something inside told me that I'd finally redeemed myself for everything I'd put her through. And I might just have forgiven myself, too.

Present day

Monday night training sessions with the RNLI typically alternated between shore-based and at-sea activities and tonight was the latter. Sometimes it would be skills practice and sometimes there'd be a scenario given to add more realism.

I left Mr Pickles with Irene and wandered down to the seafront to the lifeboat station.

'We've got a scenario for tonight,' Chief – a huge, ginger bearded lumberjack sort of a man – advised the gathered crew. 'It'll test us on an incoming tide, in the dark, care needed around local wildlife and use of the spinal board. The coastguard's taken a call. The casualty's a woman aged thirty-two. She's taken a bad tumble down the steps at Starfish Point and there's a concern for neck and spinal injuries. The tide's coming in. She's with her husband, their three-year-old daughter and the family shih tzu so we're talking a small dog for those who don't know their breeds. The fall was caused by her tripping over the dog so there's a suggestion of an injured animal, too. What else do we find at Starfish Point?'

'Seals,' several crew members called.

'Exactly. So lots going on. Let's go!'

I had butterflies in my stomach as we exited the training room. Weird. My first few training sessions when I joined the RNLI as a trainee last year had been nerve-wracking – hardly surprising for someone who'd spent four years overcoming an extreme fear of water – but there was no reason for nerves tonight.

As we bounced over the waves in the D class ILB – the inshore lifeboat – heading south towards Starfish Point, Chief relayed further details as though they'd come in from the coastguard, simu-lating a live shout. Chief mentioned the shih tzu and the butterflies stirred again as an image of Hollie stroking Mr Pickles came to mind. I was still stunned I'd spent over two hours chatting to her at the café on Friday night. That was so unlike me.

I'd messaged her on Saturday about Carole's plans to collect the dog that evening but I hadn't let her know how that had panned out. I'd tell her face to face when I sought her advice on looking after a dog. The thought of seeing her again sent a ripple of excite-ment through me. That had never happened before.

Training went well and we piled round to The Lobster Pot after-wards. The pub still reminded me of that disastrous date with Cara a whopping seven years ago. I'd had to avoid it for a couple of months until Irene – who knew everything happening locally – told me that Cara had moved out of the area and it was safe to return.

'Cough up,' Chief said, holding out his hand. We each handed over a tenner and placed our drinks order. It was a fair system and the build-up of change went towards a Christmas meal out.

'Good work tonight, Mouse,' Chief said, handing me my pint. Everyone on the crew had a nickname and it was one of the many things that gave a sense of belonging. Some nicknames were obvious immediately and others took longer. Mine was because I'd been quiet as a mouse for my first month or so. Other nicknames included Jaffa who was always eating oranges, Simba who had six cats, Bart who had an obsession with *The Simpsons* and Belle who hosted kids' parties dressed as a Disney princess. I hardly knew anyone's real name.

'Cheers, Chief. It was a good scenario.'

'We should get your final assessment in before Christmas. I'm still waiting on a date but I'm hoping this month rather than December.'

'That'd be great.'

'It'll probably be a Saturday so text me later with any Saturdays you're on shift and I'll make sure it doesn't clash. And don't look so worried. You'll ace it.'

I took my pint over to the tables the others had pushed together.

'You all right?' Jaffa asked. He was the mechanic at the station – one of only two roles, along with Chief, our coxswain, to be full-time and paid – and usually took the trainees under his wing.

'Yeah. Chief's just said my final assessment should be soon.'

'You'll be sweet, mate. You know your stuff. You're calm. It's a formality. You've got this. Chief's asked Simba and me to be your crew. We've got your back, always.'

And I knew they did. When I'd made the decision to overcome my fear of water so I could volunteer with the RNLI, I'd been focused on saving lives and giving something back to those who'd tried to help my dad. I'd never expected it to change me, give me purpose and meaning, and bring me something that had evaded me for most of my life: real, genuine friendships. My life was in the hands of the crew and vice versa, and that was a safe place to be.

At lunchtime on Tuesday, I was in the kitchen mixing up a batch of coleslaw when Avril poked her head round the door.

'Hollie, there's a man here to see you.'

'Who is it?'

'I didn't ask his name.' She gave me a cheeky wink. 'But he's what my daughter would call lush.'

I smiled at her adjective. 'I'm nearly done with this, so I'll be out in a minute. Thanks.'

I was expecting a visit from a rep later to discuss an upgrade for the coffee machine, but I'd met him before and 'lush' was not how I'd describe him.

When I emerged from the kitchen to see Jake cuddling the lost shih tzu, my heart leapt. Lush? Definitely.

'Sorry for dropping in during a lunchtime,' he said, glancing round the heaving café as he approached me. 'I thought I'd update you on Mr Pickles.'

'Mr Pickles? Is that really his name?'

Jake grimaced. 'You think Mr Pickles is bad? His full name is Mr Piccalilli Marmaduke Fluffington the Third.'

I had no idea how to respond to that. That was surely bordering on animal cruelty.

'Yeah,' Jake said, correctly interpreting my silence as shock. 'I know.'

I took hold of Mr Pickles and gave him a cuddle. 'How come you've still got him? I thought his owner was collecting him on Saturday night.'

'She didn't turn up. Well, she did, but only to dump his stuff on the doorstep and do a runner.'

'No! Why would she do that?' I stroked the dog as Jake told me about Carole Jessop's message and his suspicions that Mr Pickles had been deliberately dumped.

'Then why respond to the appeal?' I asked, shaking my head in disgust.

'I don't think she had much choice. Several people had recognised the dog and tagged her in so I presume she was trying to save face.'

'Sorry to interrupt,' Angie said. 'The coffee machine rep's here.'

'I knew he'd do that to me.' I rolled my eyes at her. 'I *specifically* told him to come at the end of the day.'

'I'll make him a drink and tell him he'll have to wait until you're free.'

'I can see you're busy,' Jake said, reaching for the dog when Angie left us. 'I had no idea this place would get so packed.' He winced. 'I'll just take my size twelves out of that hole, shall I? I didn't mean it like that. It's just with it being November, freezing, out of town...' He shook his head again. 'I'm not making it any better, am I?'

I gave him a warm smile to show he hadn't offended me. 'People thought my mum was mad when she opened it all year round, but she proved the sceptics wrong. It's heaving during tourist season but we do a steady trade all year, helped by the popularity of the seals. You should stay and have something to eat. Might convert you into a regular.' I looked round the full café. A calm sunny day like today always increased custom. 'You'd have to wait for a table, though, and it could be twenty or thirty minutes.'

'I might struggle with that. Mr Pickles is getting checked over by a vet this afternoon, so we'd better head off and let you get on.'

'What's the plan? Are you keeping him?'

He shrugged. 'I don't know. I'm not sure I can. You said you'd had dogs before so I was going to ask your advice but...' He glanced round again.

'If you don't have plans for after you've been to the vet, you could always come back. We shut at four at this time of year, but it's usually fairly quiet for the last hour. We should be able to chat then.'

His eyes widened as Avril passed by with a customer order. 'Those scones look good.'

'They are. Family recipe handed down from my granny.'

'I'll make sure we get back this afternoon.'

'Brilliant. I'll await your return with bated breath.'

'Will you?' Jake's eyes sparkled as he smiled at me. Was he flirting? No. We barely knew each other.

'Of course,' I said, trying to sound casual. 'I'm dying to know whether Mr Pickles' forever home could be with you.' But, as I said it, I was aware that I really *would* await Jake's return with bated breath. I knew hardly anything about him, but I found myself wanting to know everything. And, since splitting up with Craig, that was a first.

'Are you all right?' Angie asked after Jake left. 'You look a bit flushed.'

I pulled at my T-shirt and fanned myself. 'It's a bit warm in here today, don't you think?'

She gave me a knowing look. 'Hmm. Couldn't possibly be anything to do with the young man who just left?'

'I've no idea what you mean.' I tried and failed to feign innocence. It had *everything* to do with him. Heart racing. Palms sweating. I knew I'd spend the afternoon counting down the hours until he reappeared.

The veterinary practice nearest to me turned out to be the one where Mr Pickles was already registered. The receptionist had recognised the dog's name and the vet didn't seem surprised when I explained how I'd come to be his new owner. Her tense jaw, dark eyes, and pursed lips told me exactly what she thought of Carole Jessop, even if she was too professional to vocalise it.

'Mrs Hamilton idolised this little chap,' she said as she conducted her checks. 'We've looked after him since birth and the two generations before him. It was sad how quickly she deterio-rated. Dementia's such a cruel illness.' She sighed. 'Anyway, I'm relieved you found him. He's a gorgeous dog and I hate to think what could have happened. You're right to have brought him in to be checked over but it doesn't look like he's come to any harm.'

'Thank you. He stayed with me the past four nights and he's been no bother but I wasn't sure what I should do next. Carole Jessop says he's mine now but I've got no connection to the family. It's pure coincidence I found him. Am I allowed to keep him, just like that?'

'Do you want to keep him?'

'I don't know. It's been great, but a few nights versus long-term... I've got lots of thinking to do.'

'I'm glad to hear you're not rushing into anything. You're absolutely right that enjoying a dog's company for a few days and being there for them for a lifetime are two very different things. A dog is a massive commitment. They need attention and plenty of exercise, even a small dog like Mr Pickles. You can pick up some leaflets in reception about what looking after him would entail and there's plenty of helpful information online. The bonus with Mr Pickles is that the hard work is done. He's extremely well trained, as you've no doubt noticed.'

'Do I need to phone the police or the RSPCA about him being abandoned?'

'Neither. Mr Pickles has come to no harm and he's safe with you so, no matter what you might think about the circumstances in which you found him, you're going to have to let that one go. Mrs Jessop is out of the picture now and the important thing is securing a loving home for Mr Pickles for the future. You've got it in writing that Mrs Jessop has given the dog to you so to all intents and purposes, he *is* yours. We'll get the paperwork changed into your name and the dog warden needs to be kept in the loop. Reception can give you his number and he can talk to you about what you want to do next.'

* * *

I rang the dog warden after lunch. It seemed I'd done everything right so far and it was all fairly straightforward.

'We'll go for a walk then drive back to The Starfish Café,' I told Mr Pickles.

Outside the house, I automatically turned left to head down to the seafront but stopped after a few paces. 'Fancy a walk along the river?' I haven't done that for years.'

The River Abbleby runs down to the harbour between the Old Town and Whitsborough Bay Castle. Despite the river only being a couple of minutes' walk from Lighthouse View, I couldn't remember the last time I'd ventured down there. Probably not since we lost Dad.

Moments later, I stopped and looked around. A wide cobbled footpath ran either side of the river in front of pastel-painted houses. There were a handful of shops and a café, none of which I remembered being there before. Behind the houses on the opposite side, a grassy bank rose up towards the castle wall. I used to clamber up it and roly-poly back down when I was a kid. I smiled at the memory of grass stains on my clothes, mud on my knees and lots of laughter. When Larissa wasn't around, that's how it had been before Dad died.

I set off up the path to the left, heading away from the sea, more memories surfacing. I remembered sitting on the riverbank with Dad and Nanna, a bright orange fishing net dipped into the water and a yellow bucket beside me. I never caught anything, but it was fun trying.

When we reached the end of the houses, the cobbles gave way to gravel and the path was lined by trees and shrubs. I'd run the same circuit along the seafront on my own for years, but I'd never considered going for a walk instead. We passed other dog walkers and everyone smiled and said 'hello'. A few people stopped to stroke Mr Pickles and I felt an unfamiliar swell of pride when they raved about what a lovely dog he was.

'What are you doing to me?' I asked him as we clambered into the car when we returned to Lighthouse View after our walk. 'Only four days and I'm already feeling proud of you. Do all dogs do this to their owners or is it just you?' He wagged his tail at me before settling down on the back seat.

Although it was cold, the blue sky and sunshine had drawn people outside and the seafront was nearly as busy as at the height of season, the only difference being that most visitors were wrapped in their winter coats.

We turned off the seafront, having bypassed the town, and stopped at the T-junction by Pavilion Bridge. The traffic lights had turned to red as we approached so I pulled on the handbrake and gazed ahead at a few pedestrians crossing the road weighed down by bags of shopping while others headed in the other direction towards the shops.

A cyclist suddenly shot past me, making me jump, and raced straight through the red lights. He veered across both lanes of traffic on the main road and my hands tensed on the steering wheel as he narrowly avoided a car. As he mounted the pavement at the other side, my stomach lurched. It was one of those moments where I could see exactly what was about to happen yet was powerless to do anything about it. An elderly man was walking towards the bridge in the exact path of the cyclist and the cyclist had his head down, going hell for leather and...

'No!' I cried as they collided and man, cyclist and bike were tossed in the air.

I had to help. A lane of parking spaces ran alongside the road I was on and the top few spaces were empty. Ignoring the frustrated honk on the horn from the car behind, I pressed my hazards and did a speedy reverse into the parking lane.

'Stay here,' I instructed Mr Pickles as I leapt out of the car, grabbed my first aid kit from the boot and sprinted across the road.

The cyclist was sitting upright, swearing loudly as he scowled at the tangled frame of his bike next to him on the pavement. He could move and he was speaking so I was more concerned about the elderly man, face down on the pavement, blood trickling from his forehead, silent. Several other people had stopped and a few bystanders were filming the carnage. What was wrong with people?

'Don't move him!' I called to a middle-aged couple crouched over the man, attempting to pull him to a sitting position. 'I'm a nurse. Can one of you call an ambulance?' Even if the man was conscious and claimed to feel okay, he'd had a hell of a shock and a collision at that speed could have caused some internal damage. I didn't want to move him and exacerbate anything.

The woman took out her phone and made the call while I knelt down next to the casualty. 'My name's Jake and I'm a nurse. Can you hear me?'

His eyes flickered and he moaned.

'Can you tell me your name and age?'

'Geoffrey. Eighty-seven.' The words were husky and whispered.

The woman on the phone relayed the information to the emergency operator while I carried out some initial assessments on Geoffrey.

I needed to keep him as warm and comfortable as possible until the ambulance arrived. I swiftly removed my jacket and was about to drape it over him when a woman passed me a picnic blanket.

'This was in my car,' she said.

'Thanks. That's really helpful. Can you put it over him?'

She lay it across Geoffrey and I added my jacket on top for extra warmth, all the while talking to him and hoping for a response.

The woman who called the ambulance gave me her scarf to place under his head. 'He'd better not get any blood on it,' she muttered as she handed it over. If I hadn't known what a difference it would make to his comfort, I'd have flung it straight back at her.

Out of the corner of my eye, I spotted the cyclist picking up his buckled bike and issuing a further barrage of expletives. I had no sympathy about the damaged bike. It served him right as he'd been bang out of order with his reckless speed across the road and on the pavement. However, I still had a duty of care towards the cyclist.

'Hey! Don't you want checking out?' I called as he limped up the hill, dragging his bike along on one wheel.

He turned round, scowling. 'Like you care,' he shouted.

'I'm a nurse. Did you hit your head?' He hadn't been wearing a helmet.

'Need to get to the chemist.'

'But you could have a concussion.'

He stuck one finger up at me and continued limping. There was clearly nothing I could say to convince him to get checked over. He could walk and talk and therefore my priority had to be with Geoffrey.

It never ceased to amaze me how fascinated the general public were with accidents. A crowd had gathered round us and most people had phones out, taking photos or filming it. I had to politely ask them to step back and give us space on several occasions.

The ambulance arrived, followed by a first responder and, after a quick handover, I relinquished responsibility over Geoffrey to the two paramedics. It wasn't looking good. His blood pressure was weak and he kept dipping in and out of consciousness. I hoped he'd be able to pull through.

As I waited for a gap in the traffic, I checked my phone. There was still time to get to The Starfish Café before it closed. I looked up again and noticed a young woman staring out of her car window at the ambulance, clearly oblivious to the three cars ahead of her, stationary at the lights. I winced at the sickening crunch of metal against metal as her car slammed into the back of a taxi, which slammed into the car in front, which hit the one in front of that. An all too familiar case of being too busy rubber-necking at an accident and causing another one. So much for getting to the café.

Some of the cars had passengers so there were seven potential whiplash cases, a nosebleed, a suspected fractured wrist, and a panic attack from the woman who'd caused the accident. It was just as well that first responder had arrived so I wasn't on my own trying to deal with seven casualties until more help arrived.

22

'Should I lock up?' Angie called down the café late that afternoon.

'Yes, please.' I pressed a button on the till to run off the day's sales report, a sigh escaping from my lips.

'Something must have come up,' she said, joining me behind the counter. 'Or I'm sure he'd have returned.'

I was going to ask 'Who?' but there was no point playing the innocent. Angie missed nothing.

'I wanted to see Mr Pickles again,' I said, folding up the report. 'That's all.'

She nudged me playfully. 'I might be daft, but I'm not stupid.'

Yes, definitely no point playing the innocent at all. 'I'll admit he's easy on the eye and he seems pretty decent but I know nothing about him. He could be happily married with five kids for all I know.' Although he had said on Friday night that he lived alone so I knew that wasn't the case. I wasn't going to give Angie that titbit.

'Wedding band?'

'No.'

Angie gave me a knowing look.

'Angie! Don't read anything into me noticing that. I could clearly see his ring finger when he was holding the dog. If he's not married, it doesn't mean he's not engaged or in a relationship. Not that it makes any difference because, as I've told you a million times, I'm not interested in seeing anyone right now.'

'But if you were, Jake would be in the running.'

I lifted the money tray out of the till, shaking my head at her. 'I'm not having this conversation. I'm going to count the money.'

It took me three attempts to get the till to balance and it was all Angie's fault. She was right. If I was interested, Jake would definitely be in the running. The only one on the list, actually. Which was unexpected because, since Craig, I hadn't felt drawn to anyone. Not even the tiniest spark.

I shook my head and tried to dislodge all thoughts of Jake as I sorted the float for the café's hidden safe and the rest to take home for banking.

'I bet he'll come in tomorrow,' Angie said as we prepared to leave a little later.

'You're never still on about Jake?'

She did a zipping motion across her mouth. 'Sorry. I'm pushing too much. I just want you to be happy again.'

'I *am* happy.'

'Hollie!'

'I'm getting there. The thing is, we both know that a man – even a gorgeous, amazing, sweep-me-off-my-feet future-husband-material one – is not going to magically make the sadness go away.' The moment I said the word 'sadness', a familiar wave of it engulfed me and tears pricked my eyes. I hoped I'd manage to finish what I wanted to say to put a lid on the subject before my voice cracked. She meant well and I loved her for it, but I couldn't keep having this conversation.

'Yes, there's a void in my life and my heart is broken but that's not because of Craig. Another man isn't going to be able to fill it and, even if I thought they could, I'm not ready to trust anyone again and to let them know my tragic tale. I'm all right with not being ready, though. Really, I am.'

'I'm sorry. It's just that you lit up when you were talking to Jake earlier and...' She paused and shook her head. 'I'll stop. I do understand.'

'Thank you. Jake seems nice and Mr Pickles is adorable. Maybe we can be friends but that's all I've got right now. The only thing that can heal the pain is time, patience and a heck of a lot of strength on my part and, until I'm a bit further down the road with that, a relationship isn't a good idea. Especially at this time of year. It's not never. It's just not now.'

Angie drew me into a hug and I have no idea how I managed to stop the tears from falling. Everyone kept saying how strong I was and how amazingly I'd coped but there were moments like this when I didn't feel as though I'd moved forward at all or that the pain would ever ease, but I kept hoping for a brighter future. I kept dancing in the rain.

I pulled into the car park at The Starfish Café and stopped, cursing under my breath. The café was in complete darkness and the car park empty. I'd known it would be – it was already past five after all – but I had to try.

Mr Pickles – now wearing a seatbelt harness, which had been among his belongings – put his paws up at the window, his tail wagging.

'She's not here. Sorry, buddy.' I looked into the darkness again and sighed. 'Okay. Let's go. Sit down.'

He did as instructed and dipped his head onto his paws, looking mournful.

'I know. I'm disappointed, too.'

I turned the car round and pulled back onto the road, frowning. Why was I disappointed? That made no sense. I barely knew her.

'I'll message her when we get home. Don't let me forget. It's important.' It might have only been a casual arrangement to drop by, but I'd said I would and I didn't want her thinking I was unreliable.

I started composing the message in my head. I needed to sound apologetic but not over the top. Casual rather than desperate. Maybe I could pose the question about keeping Mr Pickles and suggest a drink to talk it over. No. Too much, too soon. I didn't want to be the manipulative guy who used a dog to engineer a date.

A date? Where that that come from? Turning up the music, I shook my head. Why was I getting worked up about this? It was just a message. It meant nothing because Hollie meant nothing to me. We weren't even friends. She was just a friendly café owner who'd helped me when I found a lost dog and she was potentially someone I could turn to for some dog-related advice. Nothing more. Because anything more than that was too complicated.

I felt out of sorts as I drove home. Angie was right about me being disappointed by Jake's no-show and I couldn't keep kidding myself that it was only because I'd been looking forward to seeing Mr Pickles again. I'd wanted to see Jake. All afternoon, I'd been watching the door, feeling a little deflated each time it opened and it wasn't him. It wasn't because he was 'lush', either. Talking to him on Friday night had been so easy. Midnight could have come and gone and I wouldn't have noticed.

When Katie started seeing Trey, she'd talked about them sitting up all night chatting and I didn't get why her eyes sparkled and she got all gushy about it until now. I'd never had that with Craig – that desire to find out everything about him and tell him everything about me – but I felt that with Jake. Well, tell him *almost* everything. I knew it wasn't good to bottle up what had happened to Dad and Isaac but I couldn't help it. I could talk about Mum but it still hurt far too much to talk about them.

Back at Sandy Croft I changed into some fluffy PJs then headed straight for the freezer, seeking comfort in a tub of salted caramel ice cream. I plonked myself in front of the fire in the kitchen and shovelled it in, barely tasting it, while half-heartedly scrolling through Facebook on my phone.

I was about halfway down the tub when my heart leapt and I nearly dropped my spoon. Jake! There he was on a community page: the hero of the hour attending to two separate accidents. No wonder he hadn't made it back to the café.

Putting the tub aside, I smiled as I enlarged the photos then clicked onto a video showing the aftermath of a multi-vehicle pile-up. Even though tending to injuries was day-job stuff for him, I still marvelled at how calm and organised he appeared to be; a good man to have around in a crisis.

Feeling warm and fuzzy, I replaced the lid on the ice cream, returned it to the freezer and sat in front of the fire once more, searching for any coverage of the accidents in the local online news.

An hour later, a message pinged through:

✉ From Jake
Really sorry Mr Pickles and I didn't make it back to the café. We were actually on our way but stopped to help at an accident. I say 'we', but Mr Pickles's first aid certificate has lapsed so he wasn't a great help. He attempted CPR but the casualties weren't too enamoured by his doggy breath and slobber. Odd that.
I'm seriously craving scones and don't think the ones the corner shop sells are going to cut it. The best before date of five years' time rings alarm bells!
My next-door neighbour is going to look after Mr Pickles while I'm on shift this week which is great news and buys me thinking time. We'll come

in to see you on Saturday if that's okay. Will
avoid the lunchtime rush this time!
Hope you have a great week and look forward to
seeing you soon

Reading his message made me laugh out loud and left me with
another warm glow. I loved how he'd downplayed his part when he
could have easily acted the hero. I'd seen the photos and the videos.
I knew there'd been two accidents and multiple casualties.

⊠ To Jake
Thanks for letting me know. Just been reading
about it on social media. Talk about being in
the right place at the right time! Hope that
man's going to be OK and hope Mr Pickles isn't
hurt by the rejection. Look forward to seeing
you both on Saturday and I promise my scones are
fresh! Have a great week

I felt so lifted by Jake's message that I hauled the Christmas tree
out of the attic and put it up in the lounge. I still put the lights on a
timer but I added a few more baubles than usual and even spread a
festive garland across the mantlepiece.

I hoped Jake would keep Mr Pickles but I could completely
understand his reservations when working shifts. Perhaps his
neighbour could nip in to feed the dog and take him out for a walk
so that he wasn't home alone all day while Jake was working.

I pictured the little shih tzu's adorable face and how it felt to
cuddle him and could imagine him curled up in a bed in the café,
racing along the beach, and running round the house. Next
moment, I imagined Jake with him too and shook my head to try
and dislodge that thought. I was still in two minds about getting a

dog, but I definitely didn't need a man in my life. Even if he was a particularly attractive and caring man who'd actually messaged me to apologise for not returning earlier.

He couldn't be more different to Craig, who'd always taken every opportunity to big himself up, not that I'd realised it at the time. Love's blind, after all. If it had ever been love with Craig. Sometimes I wondered.

Seven years ago

The accident the day after Boxing Day instantly killed Isaac, and Dad slipped away the following day, having never regained consciousness. The last few days of that year passed Mum and me by in a painful blur of shock and confusion, anger and tears. The house filled with cards, flowers, and casserole dishes. We felt and appreciated the love and care from well-wishers but were unable to find the strength to read the words, sniff the blooms, or eat the food.

The soundless television illuminated the lounge while the fairy lights on the Christmas tree remained unplugged. Martin and Craig took the tree down; too painful a reminder of how happy we'd been only days earlier.

During that first week, many hours slipped by lying on my bed or sitting at my workbench staring into space, my mind still, my body drained. Others passed in a frenzy of activity. In the same way that clobbering a punchbag might release tension for some, sanding, drilling and grinding helped alleviate my anger. I wasn't trying to make anything – my creative well completely dry – but the noise of the machinery muted the screaming in my head.

Sometimes I curled up next to Mum on the sofa or her bed and we cried together. Sometimes we were silent. What was there to say? It was too early to reminisce. Too early to smile and laugh about happy days. They hadn't been ill. They hadn't been old. It was a senseless waste of two lives and it should never have happened.

Craig was a Godsend and exactly what Mum, Bex and I needed. He'd booked the time off work until after the New Year anyway, so he pretty much took up residence at Sandy Croft. While Martin, a funeral director, focused on the funeral arrangements, Craig assumed responsibility for the wake. He booked the venue, organised the catering and placed the obituary with the local newspaper.

Mum had wanted to make the exceptionally difficult phone calls to friends and family but only managed half a sentence to the first person before breaking down. Craig eased the phone from her hand and took over. I tried the second person but fared no better. I felt such a rush of love for my fiancé as he rescued me too. Between them, Craig and Angie passed on the tragic news then made contact again once the funeral plans were confirmed.

Angie kept us in a constant supply of tea or coffee, insisted we ate even when we didn't want to, put on a couple of loads of washing, and kept the house clean.

Craig gave his support with the paperwork and it was a shock to discover how much there was to sort out: bank accounts, credit cards, life assurance policies, pensions, the car, the house.

There was the business to deal with too. Dad and Isaac had a partnership – J & I Brooks Electricians – so there were clients to contact and more paperwork to manage.

Craig dealt with what he could before the death certificates were issued and assured Mum and Bex that he'd continue to help after he returned to work in the New Year. It was a relief to have someone who knew what they were doing to alleviate unnecessary stress and hassle at such a difficult time.

Everyone was generous with their time and we appreciated it, but it could feel stifling. Mum and I took it in turns to walk Willow, eager to escape for an hour or so.

We discussed keeping The Starfish Café closed until after the funeral but knew Dad and Isaac wouldn't have approved. They'd both had a pragmatic 'life must go on' philosophy. Angie opened up as usual after the New Year, placing a sign on the door warning that we'd be closed on the day of the funeral out of respect. Customers brought in condolence cards and flowers. With the house already looking like a florist's, Martin distributed the flowers to local care homes and Angie amended the sign to encourage charitable donations in lieu of flowers.

The Sunday before Dad and Isaac's funeral, Craig joined us for lunch, cooked by Angie. I watched Mum absently push a roast potato round her plate while I tried to force down the child-sized portion Angie had dished up. Craig downed his meal with gusto and shifted two portions of dessert.

Over coffee, he went through some more paperwork with Mum at the kitchen table while I sat in front of the fire stroking Willow.

'I need to head into town,' he announced when they'd finished what they were doing. 'I need a new shirt for the funeral.'

It was time for Willow's walk so I decided to accompany him.

'Nearly there with the paperwork,' he said as we ambled along the esplanade.

I linked my arm through his and snuggled against his side. 'I can't thank you enough. You've gone over and above with what you've done for Mum and Bex and we're all so grateful.'

'You're welcome. It was the least I could do.'

'I had no idea there'd be so much to sort.'

'Most people don't. It can be quite a shock.'

'How do you manage to stay so calm and organised at a time like this?' I asked, feeling so full of admiration and love for him for being so supportive during our darkest days. He wasn't the most tactile of partners but there'd been a ready supply of hugs from Mum, Angie and Katie and I'd appreciated Craig stepping up and being the strong, focused one when I was too emotional to think straight.

'I do this sort of thing every week so it's second nature to me,' he responded. 'Of course, it helps when you're not emotionally attached to the deceased.'

My stomach did a nervous somersault. Had he just implied he wasn't 'emotionally attached' to Dad or Isaac? How could that be? Craig and I had been together for over two and a half years and engaged for nearly seven months. He'd asked Dad's permission to propose to me. He'd spent loads of time at our house and had attended several family events. I needed to check what he meant or it would niggle at me.

'Then it's extra amazing that you can be so calm when you are.' I could hear the hope in my voice. I badly wanted to have misunderstood.

'But I'm not.' He stopped walking and frowned at me. 'They're *your* family, Hollie, not mine.'

I withdrew my arm from his and stepped back. 'I thought you liked them.'

'They were all right, but it's not like we were the best of mates.'

'So you're not upset that they're gone?' My voice sounded high and distant.

'Of course I am!'

I could have wept with relief. I *had* misunderstood.

And then he hammered another nail in the coffin. 'Because

you're upset and I hate seeing you cry. You know I'm no good round tears.'

I couldn't move, struggling to process what I'd just heard. He didn't care about my family? He wasn't upset? The lasting impact on him was that he didn't like to deal with me crying?

He tugged on my sleeve. 'Come on or the shops will be shut.'

Mouth open, I stared at him, feeling nauseous. He had no idea what he'd just said or the impact of it on me. In the crudest terms, he'd told me he didn't care that they were dead. What was I supposed to do with that? How could he say that to me at a time like this? Where was his empathy? I felt anger welling inside me. I didn't want an argument but there was no way of avoiding one if I stayed in his presence.

'Actually, I've got a headache. I don't think this cold weather's helping. I'm going to head home with Willow.'

'Suit yourself.' He kissed me on the cheek and set off again, his hands thrust into his jacket pockets, strolling along as though he hadn't a care in the world. And clearly he hadn't.

At that precise moment, I didn't love him at all. I actually hated him. And I didn't know what to do with that, either.

* * *

I paced up and down in my bedroom while Craig was in town, working myself into a rage as I kept replaying the conversation.

When I spotted him walking back towards the house a little later, a carrier bag in his hand, that feeling of nausea returned. I had no idea what to say to him. Should I give him the benefit of the doubt and ask him to explain himself again or let rip with what I thought of him?

He glanced up at the window and waved at me. I couldn't bring myself to raise my hand in greeting. He pointed to the bag, gave me a thumbs up, pointed to his car then nodded his head towards town. He was going to head straight home. Good. I gave him a thumbs up in return, although I really wanted to give him an entirely different gesture.

As soon as he drove away, I rang Katie. I needed someone to help me make sense all this before I said or did anything rash.

* * *

'I can't believe he said that,' Katie said, squeezing my hand as we sat on the edge of my bed. 'No wonder you're fuming.'

'You don't think I'm over-reacting?'

She shook her head. 'Even if he thought it, it was completely inappropriate to share it. What a tosser! And how could he make out he doesn't care about Joe and Isaac? They were lovely men and if he didn't feel like he was good mates with them, that was on him, not them. They'll have tried hard.'

I felt the passion in her every word. My family had been Katie's family and losing them had been devastating for her, too.

'They didn't have much in common with him but they definitely *did* try,' I agreed. 'I could have sworn he really liked them.'

'Yeah, well, that's because Craig lets people see what he wants them to see.'

I narrowed my eyes at her, my curiosity piqued. 'What do you mean by that?'

She sighed and looked as though she was about to share something but then she shrugged. 'Nothing. You know what he's like, all smiles and compliments while he works a room. He's a good salesman.'

'You're saying he faked liking Dad and Isaac?'

'I think he fakes a lot of things.'

I bit my lip as I grappled for the meaning behind her words. 'Like his relationship with me?'

'I didn't say that, Hollie,' she said, gently.

'But you think it?'

She lowered her eyes. 'I think you and Craig are like chalk and cheese. You're kind and generous and wear your heart on your sleeve and he's Mr Practical, all detached and pragmatic. It's not his fault. It's what he's used to. His whole family are like that. It's why he's so good at his job and why Avery's brilliant at hers. They all have an emotional off switch and you, my lovely friend, don't. Those differences between you haven't been so noticeable while life has treated you well but disaster has just struck and you've both defaulted to type. And Craig's type is absolutely what you need when dealing with death certificates, insurance claims and bank accounts. That help is invaluable. But would you rather have that or someone to hold you tight, dry your tears, and reminisce about the happy times?'

She'd nailed it! Craig had been round all the time but he hadn't stayed over since it happened. Hugs had been quick and awkward and usually because I'd launched myself at him. I'd been fully aware of our differences all along and had convinced myself they were why we worked, but since the accident I'd felt like they'd created a wall between us that I'd been unable to penetrate.

I slumped forward with my head in my hands. 'Oh, God, Katie! What should I do?'

She rubbed my back. 'You know I can't make that decision for you.'

'But you think I should end it?'

'Do *you* think you should end it?'

I straightened up. 'I wanted to earlier, but I've calmed down a bit and, truth is, I don't think I can cope with losing someone else right now.' My voice cracked and the tears started to flow.

Katie put her arm round me and I rested my head against her shoulder. 'Then don't end it. Get through the funeral, let things settle a bit, then see how you feel.'

'What would you do if you were me?'

'I'd dump the stupid twat.'

'Katie!' I cried, sitting up, shocked at the blunt delivery. 'Are you being serious?'

'Deadly serious.' Her shoulders slumped. 'Look, I didn't want to say this because I didn't want to upset you but Craig's already done that spectacularly so I might as well. I've spent a lot of time here since the accident, yeah? Every time I've got home, Trey's had a bath run for me and a meal cooking. He's mopped up my tears, he's listened to me talking endlessly about your family, and he's encouraged me to talk about Isaac. He knows your brother was the first man I loved so that couldn't have been easy for him, but he was there for me. And do you know what he did? He got my favourite photo of me with your Dad and Isaac enlarged and framed.'

I smiled through my tears, thrilled for her that she'd found someone so caring. 'That's so sweet of him. He's a keeper.'

'I know, but that's not why I'm telling you this. What has Craig done for you? And don't say organised the wake and completed the paperwork. That's day-job stuff for him. What has he done for *you*?'

She paused and raised her eyebrows at me and that feeling of nausea was back. The truth was he'd done nothing for me. Willow had been more comfort than my fiancé.

Katie sighed. 'That silence speaks volumes. My worry is that you're settling for a practical financial adviser when what you've always dreamed of is a romantic knight on a fiery steed. If you really, truly love each other, the differences wouldn't matter but, if you're brutally honest with yourself, I think they've mattered for a long time and you haven't wanted to admit it.'

She stood up. 'I've got to get home 'cause I've got a Skype scheduled with my dad but think about it, won't you? Don't rush into anything. We can talk more later.'

I nodded, forcing down the lump in my throat.

Katie grabbed me and hugged me tightly. 'I don't think he's right for you, but what I think doesn't matter. The question is whether you think he's right for you, or are you settling for second best?'

26

The day before the funeral I took Willow for a walk along the esplanade and sat on one of the benches overlooking South Bay. It was a cold and blustery Wednesday but I'd come out prepared in several layers, a quilted jacket that hugged me like a duvet, a warm scarf, and a fleece-lined hat.

'It's the funeral tomorrow,' I said, stroking Willow's head as she sat by my feet, bundled up in a fleecy coat. 'I keep expecting them to walk through the door. You do too, don't you?' Every time she heard a car pull onto the drive or footsteps approaching the house, she padded to the kitchen door, tail wagging in anticipation. It tore me apart seeing her tail droop between her legs when it wasn't them. It would never be them again. How do you explain that to an animal?

Willow stretched out across the pavement and I sat back against the wooden bench, my eyes scanning the scene below. Angry waves snatched at the deserted beach, spitting spray over the railings, while ominous grey clouds threatened rain. More of the same was predicted for tomorrow.

I chewed on my lip. Tomorrow. I wanted to get it over with but dreaded its arrival in equal measure. It was hard to believe that the approaching weekend would signal three weeks since that fatal stormy night. How had so much time passed when it felt like only yesterday that we'd been celebrating my Christmas Eve birthday, then Christmas Day as a family?

Aching for the buzz and the routine of the café, I'd gone in for a shift on Saturday but it was harder than I'd anticipated with the sympathetic glances, hugs and pats of my hand. Being out of season, it hadn't been busy enough to give me the distraction I'd longed for, so I hadn't returned since.

On Friday, routine would be restored but I knew my life would never be 'normal' again. Neither would Mum's or Bex's or the lives of the many other people who'd loved Dad and Isaac.

I still wasn't over the shock from Sunday that Craig didn't fall into that bracket. I hadn't been able to sleep on Sunday night, replaying what he'd said and my conversation afterwards with Katie. She'd never voiced anything negative about Craig or my relationship before but why would she? I'd never given her reason to. I'd told her about the unromantic engagement but I'd presented it in a light-hearted way as though I hadn't been bothered. We'd even laughed together about the ring and joked that I'd need a matching gold necklace and bracelet on my wedding day and that, as bridesmaid, she'd need to wear coordinating bling.

I'd loved it that Katie and Craig got on. Or at least they had until that argument on Bonfire Night. They hadn't crossed paths again until Christmas Day and they'd been friendly, but I had seen them exchanging looks and frowns. Was there more to that than either of them were letting on?

I slumped forward on the bench and released a long sigh. I definitely couldn't deal with this right now with the funeral so imminent. That was enough emotional turmoil for the moment.

* * *

We were about an hour into the wake when it all became too over-whelming. Mum, Angie, Bex, Craig and I had travelled together in a sleek black limousine, headed straight into the service, then retreated to the limo immediately after, but now I had to speak to people and I knew I needed to be strong when the reality was that I felt far from it.

Retreating to a cubicle in the pub toilets, I sat down on the lid, relishing ten minutes away from the well-meant platitudes, hugs, and sympathetic gazes. I closed my eyes for a moment, trying to empty my head of all thoughts and emotions.

The toilets in the other two cubicles were flushed in quick succession, followed by the sound of doors unlocking.

'Why do we always bump into each other in the toilets?' I recognised Angie's voice.

The laugh in response sounded familiar and I realised it was Dad's cousin, Josephine, a regular visitor to the café. 'How are they both holding up?' she asked.

'As well as can be expected. It's so tragic.'

'Must have been difficult organising this, especially over the festive period,' Josephine said.

'We all helped where we could. Martin sorted the funeral, obvi-ously, and Hollie's fiancé Craig sorted out the wake and the paper-work. I'm sure he'll point that out if you speak to him later.'

I sat forward, frowning. It was a passing comment and certainly not said or meant in a vindictive way – Angie wasn't like that – but it weighed on my mind when I returned to the pub lounge a little later.

Craig was talking to Josephine's parents – my Great-Aunt Mary and Great-Uncle Clive. I hovered nearby and caught part of their conversation.

'...don't know what they'd both have done without my help. I

arranged the venue and food here and I've been helping Heather
with the paperwork for home and for the business.'

'That's very good of you,' Great-Aunt Mary gushed, patting
his arm.

'It needed several hours of work but it's the least I can do at a
difficult time like this.'

'You're a good lad.' It was Great-Uncle Clive's turn to gush. 'Well
done, son.'

'I'm doing the same for Bex, too. It's no big deal. Just a few long
evenings and weekends.'

I overheard a similar conversation at least four more times. How
had I not noticed it before? It was natural to enjoy praise and it was
part of my job to seek feedback at work, but this wasn't a café. This
was my fiancé helping us out during a time of crisis, but he was
actively seeking adulation from our friends and relatives. Wasn't it
enough that we'd thanked him ourselves many times?

Now that I'd noticed it, I recalled many times he'd done something similar. The man was obsessed with being thanked and
praised and it wasn't a particularly attractive quality. And there
were several other unattractive traits that also sprung to mind. With
Katie's views on the differences between us ringing in my ears, I
downed my glass of wine in one and grabbed another from the bar.
I gazed down at my engagement ring, then glanced across at Katie
talking to Bex. She'd been spot on with her description of our relationship. I'd been annoyed with myself for comparing our relationship to Isaac and Bex's. Even Mum had said I shouldn't do that
because every relationship was different and she was right. It was
unhealthy to compare. But what it had revealed to me was something I hadn't wanted to admit: I *did* want the romantic knight on
the fiery steed. I wanted the hugs, the tenderness, the passion, the
warmth and I didn't get any of that from Craig. I loved him but that

wasn't enough if I didn't feel loved by him. Could he change? And, if he could, did I even want him to?

* * *

'I'm so ready for this,' Mum said, handing me a mug of tea back at Sandy Croft that evening.

'Me too.' I kicked off my stilettos, released the clip from my hair, and curled up on one of the sofas in front of the fire in the kitchen. Willow rested her head on my knee and I stroked her soft ears. 'How are you feeling, Mum?'

'Like it's happening to someone else and I'm on the outside looking in.'

'I know what you mean. I still can't believe they're gone.'

We both stared into the flames, sipping on our drinks, lost in our thoughts.

'Do you know why your dad and I had such a strong marriage?' Mum asked after a while.

'Because you loved each other?'

She smiled. 'We did. So very much. But that's not the reason our marriage was strong. People can still be in love but not like each other very much and sometimes they can like each other but not be in love.'

She paused and held my gaze. Was that last comment directed at me? Which camp did she think I fell into? I didn't react.

'What made our marriage strong is that we made each other laugh every day. No matter how tough things got, we found a moment to share some humour.'

I pictured them giggling together. If Mum was having a bad day, Dad could soon have her laughing and vice versa. Dad had been Mum's rock, supporting her through two bouts of cancer with positivity and good humour. It had been inspiring and I'm convinced it was instrumental in her recovery.

'Does Craig make you laugh, Angel?'

'Sometimes.'

'When was the last time?'

I couldn't remember. A good sense of humour wasn't one of his traits. 'It's been a tough few weeks.'

'The absolute worst, but what about before the accident?'

I shrugged.

'I like Craig. I *like* him a lot.' She placed a strong emphasis on the word 'like'. 'And the problem is, I think you do too.' She held my gaze, her eyebrows quirked. 'You and Craig started as friends and sometimes that's the best foundation for a deep, lasting, loving marriage.' She paused and added in an apologetic tone, 'And sometimes it's the best foundation for a deep, lasting, loving friendship.'

'You think we're more like friends?'

'I did, but I'm not sure you're even that at the moment. Not all friendships are designed to last. I've got Angie and you've got Katie and those two are solid, dependable, always-there wonderful friends. But how many other friends have come and gone over the years? Sometimes that's because the main thing you have in common changes – school, work, the place you live – and sometimes it's because you change as individuals. You think differently, you want different things, you're at different stages in your life.'

'And you reckon that's the case for Craig and me?'

'I'm sorry to say it, but yes. You're *very* different people and I suspect that's what worked for you initially, but I think it's now pushing you apart. You're both ambitious and career-driven but that doesn't manifest itself in the same way. For Craig, it's about a big salary, massive house and flashy lifestyle. For you, it's knowing you're running a successful business with happy customers. I never realised that about him until he sulked about you choosing the café over the cash.'

'He's still annoyed about that.'

'See! Different things. Sometimes those differences make a relationship work and sometimes they drive a wedge.'

'Katie said pretty much the same thing the other day.' I filled Mum in on the conversation I'd had with Katie and what triggered it.

'I'm disappointed in Craig,' she said. 'I'd have credited him with more empathy than that. So how do you feel about what Katie and I have said?'

I bit my lip. 'Like you could be right.'

Mum sighed. 'I'm sorry, Angel. What are you going to do?'

I held up my left hand. 'I think it's time to return this.' A giggle unexpectedly erupted from me. 'Maybe he can return it to the Christmas cracker it came from.'

Mum clapped her hand over her mouth as she giggled with me. 'I didn't like to say anything. But it is a bit, erm...' She winced.

'I think the word you're looking for is hideous. Bless him, he thought I loved gold because of Granny's ring and the necklace so, even though it's absolutely not me, it did come from kind intentions and I love that.'

'But you don't love Craig anymore?'

'I don't know if I do or not, but you're right about me not liking him much at the moment and I think that's for the reasons you and Katie cite. We're too different and it's now pulling us apart. The help he's given these past few weeks has been amazing, but the support hasn't been there. I can't be married to a man who isn't properly there for me when I need him.'

'I'm so sorry. I know the heartbreak of a relationship ending is not what you need on top of losing your dad and brother, but if we take anything from the accident, it's that life is too short and we really do have to live every day as though it's our last because we never know when it will be.'

The tears I'd managed to hold back for most of the wake burst through the dam.

'Aw, Angel.' Mum put her mug down and rushed over to cuddle me. 'It's for the best and you've still got me, Angie, Katie and Bex. We all love you and we're here with a ready supply of hugs.'

'Craig's not a hugger. Even in private.'

'Then he's not right for you, but one day you'll meet someone who is. Someone who makes you laugh every day, hugs you simply because it's Tuesday, holds you when you cry, and dances in the rain with you. And men like that exist. I found mine. Bex found hers and it seems like Katie has too. When you're ready, you'll find him.'

'What if I'm never ready?'

'Then he'll find you. True love will always find a way.'

She kissed my head and I gratefully snuggled in her arms. This was how it should have been with Craig. I didn't want to let him go but, if I didn't, our differences would eventually destroy us. I'd call at his house after work tomorrow and say another goodbye.

27

HOLLIE

Present day

On Saturday, the sky darkened and the heavens opened a little before half two. It would go one of two ways: either we'd be taken over by walkers keen to escape the rain or we'd barely see a soul.

Half an hour later, with no sign of the rain subsiding, it was definitely the latter. Our only customers were a lone dog walker tucking into a toasted teacake and an elderly couple who came in for afternoon tea every Saturday whatever the weather.

Jake had said he'd come in with Mr Pickles, but would the bad weather keep them away? I leaned on the counter, staring out at the rain hammering against the glass. The sea was a blur through the torrent. Oh well, not long until closing time.

The door opened and, the moment I saw them, I felt the cloud hanging over me float away.

'We've been sitting in the car for ten minutes hoping the rain would stop,' Jake said, running a hand through his wet hair. 'We decided to make a dash for it.'

As I stepped through the counter gate, Jake released Mr Pickles from the shelter of his waterproof and placed him onto the floor. The dog immediately raced up to me.

'I'm so glad you still have him.' I scooped him into my arms and cuddled him. 'Is this permanent?'

'I don't know. I'd still like to talk it through with you if you're not too busy.'

I nodded my head towards our three customers. 'Absolutely rushed off my feet.'

'I can hold the fort so you two can talk,' Angie said, in a tone that I knew clearly meant 'introduce us'. She'd been gutted about not having a formal introduction earlier in the week.

'Jake, this is Angie, lifelong friend and assistant manager. Angie, this is Jake, the one who found this gorgeous bundle of fluff abandoned on the beach.' I waved one of Mr Pickles' paws at her.

'Hi, Jake and hello, Mr Pickles.' She reached over the counter to stroke the dog's ears. 'I've been dying to properly meet you both.'

'Good to meet you too, Angie.'

She beamed at me and the slightest flick of her head in Jake's direction indicated exactly what was running through her mind. If I didn't get him away from the counter quickly, she'd say something completely unsubtle about me being single or what a stunning couple we'd make.

'Let's grab one of the booths before they all go,' I joked, making a beeline for the corner one.

While Jake was distracted removing his waterproof, I turned back to face Angie. She crossed her arms and mouthed 'spoilsport' at me.

'Are you still after a scone or would you like to see the menu?' I asked Jake.

'I'm a sucker for a scone. My nanna used to make them all the time and I miss them now she's gone.' He grimaced. 'I should probably emphasise that I also miss my nanna and not just her scones.'

'Sorry to hear about your loss.'

'Thank you.'

'What sort would you like? We've got cheese, plain, fruit or blueberry.'

'Just plain, please.'

'Jam and cream?'

'It would be rude not to.'

'And to drink?'

'Black coffee.'

'I'll be back in a moment.' I placed Mr Pickles on the floor. 'Sit. Good boy. I'll fetch you something, too.'

'No wonder you were pining after him on Tuesday,' Angie said as soon as I returned to the counter.

'I was *not* pining after him.'

'He's got beautiful eyes.'

'Can't say I've noticed.'

'Hollie Gabrielle Brooks, you are such a hopeless fibber. Tell me what you want and I'll bring it over.'

'Oh, no you don't. You'll try to set us up on a date.'

'And that would be a bad thing because...?'

'Angie!'

She drew a cross over her heart with her hand. 'I promise not to say anything to him.'

I removed a few dog biscuits from the barrel. 'Okay, but you'd better mean it or you'll be job hunting next week.'

'Not a word. You go and have a cosy chat with the extremely handsome young man.' When I raised my eyebrows at her, she shrugged her shoulders. 'What? I only promised not to say anything to Jake.'

'Angie will bring everything over shortly,' I said, returning to Jake after I'd given her our order. 'But I've got your treats already, Mr Pickles. Would you like them?'

Mr Pickles followed various instructions to sit, give paw, turn round and roll over to get his biscuits.

'You're brilliant with dogs.' Jake sounded impressed. 'I never thought to try any of those tricks with him.'

'It's only because I'm used to being round dogs.' I shuffled into the booth as Mr Pickles stretched out on the floor beside us. 'So how can I help you?'

'It's all official. Mr Pickles is my dog now but I don't know how practical it is for me to give him a permanent home.' His shoulders drooped and I got the impression he hated saying those words. 'I've been back on shifts this week and, like I said in my message, my next-door neighbour Irene has been looking after him. She's always had a dog until recently so she's loved having him, but she's moving into Bay View Care Home at the start of December and they don't take pets.'

'That's a shame.'

'I know. Not that I could have expected her to do it long-term even if she was staying. That wouldn't be fair. I'm not sure what to do next.'

I could see the worry of the decision and suspected I already knew the answer to my question but thought I'd best ask it anyway. 'If shifts weren't an issue, would you want to keep Mr Pickles?'

Jake looked down at the little dog and a smile lit up his face. 'Look at him. Who wouldn't want to keep him?' He looked back at me and rolled his eyes. 'Apart from Carole Jessop.'

'How long are your shifts?'

'It varies. The shortest is eight hours but the longest is thirteen, which is obviously too long to leave him on his own. The challenge is finding someone to look after Mr Pickles when I have no set shift pattern and sometimes work nights. Does such a person even exist?'

We paused while Angie brought over our order and I steeled myself against any potential meddling, but she was on her best behaviour as promised. She placed our drinks on the table and I raised my eyebrows at her as she added a wooden tray containing four scones and accompaniments.

'No arguing,' she said, laying down a plate in front of me. 'You missed lunch.'

I rolled my eyes at Jake when Angie was out of earshot. 'She's obsessed with feeding me. She somehow notices every skipped lunch and is oblivious to me spending the rest of the day grazing and sampling.'

'She obviously cares a lot.'

I glanced across at her settling the bill for the dog walker and smiled. 'She does. I'm very lucky. So where were we?'

'We were discussing my shift pattern but it's not just my job that concerns me. I've got another commitment outside of work so I need to factor that in too.'

I wondered what he meant by that. A night out at the pub with the lads? Time with his girlfriend? It was none of my business, but I found myself wanting to know and I couldn't think of a way to ask that didn't sound too intrusive.

'So basically you want to keep Mr Pickles but you're worried about him spending too much time on his own?'

He nodded. 'If Margaret Hamilton – his proper owner – did the whole competition circuit thing with him, I'd imagine they were always together. I wanted to see how he fared left alone for a few hours and he seemed fine with that, or at least I presume he was. There was no damage to any of my furniture and no dirty protests anywhere.'

I laughed at that expression. 'That's lucky, then. Although have you checked *all* your shoes?'

He laughed with me. 'That's a good point. I'd better do that when I get home.'

As we ate, I told him about some of the dogs we'd had over the years, how there'd usually been someone around so they weren't left alone for too long, and how Willow had accompanied us to work. I chose my words carefully as the last thing I wanted to do was open up a conversation about my family. The more time I spent in Jake's company, the more I warmed to him. If he knew about my past and the accompanying pile of emotional baggage, I probably wouldn't see him for dust and I didn't like that prospect.

'You were right,' he said as he wiped his fingers after polishing off two cream scones. 'Genuinely the best coffee and scones I've ever tasted.'

'You'll be coming back really soon, then?' It was something I always said to new customers after they'd complimented the food in order to tout for future business. It wasn't usually accompanied by my heart racing, my cheeks colouring and a hint of desperation in my voice.

'Definitely.'

Jake held my gaze and my heart raced even faster. I hadn't held eye contact with a man for this long since Craig and it was exciting and unnerving at the same time. One of us was going to have to break contact. One of us was going to need to speak, but it couldn't be me. The only thought in my head was what it would be like to kiss him and I could hardly blurt that out.

A flash of light from my peripheral vision made me snap my head round to the window. I shuddered as the darkening sky was illuminated by several bright forks of lightning. Last thing I needed. I nibbled on my thumbnail as the accompanying thunder rumbled.

'You're not a fan of storms?' Jake asked.

'Not really. The thunder used to scare me when I was little and I never really got over it.' I'm not sure where that fib came from. As a child, I loved storms and would sit by the window with Isaac, wrapped in a duvet, counting the seconds between the lightning and the thunder to work out how close the storm was. Back then we'd been safe inside. We'd been protected. But now storms only made me think of one thing.

Jake peered through the window. 'I'd love to photograph a storm. I bet I could get some amazing pictures from your terrace.'

'Be my guest, any time you want. Mr Pickles and I will stay inside where it's safe and dry.'

'Very sensible.' He turned back to me with a smile. 'It's such a great view from here. Do you ever wish you could live here so you could see it all the time?'

'I love it here and the view is spectacular – or it is when it's not obliterated by rain – but I don't think I could live here *and* work here. It's good to escape occasionally. I've got a sea view at home too although it's not as stunning as this one.'

'Where do you live?'

'One of the streets off Sea Cliff so it's only side views and only from upstairs because of the trees but it's still sea views. Did you say you live in the Old Town?'

'Yes. My house is called Lighthouse View. Guess what I can see?'

'Hmm. That's a tricky one. I'm thinking maybe the lighthouse?'

'Nicely worked out, Sherlock!'

We were laughing as Angie cleared the table and she gave me that knowing look again.

'Can I get you anything else?' she asked Jake.

'No, thanks. I'd better settle the bill and let you both get home.'

'No charge,' I said. 'It's on me.'

Jake shook his head as Angie disappeared with the dishes. 'I can't accept that. How much do I owe you? And I mean for yours too because I want to thank you for helping track down the dog's owner.'

'Jake! There's no need.'

'There's every need. What do you say, Mr Pickles?' He stood up, picked up the dog and placed its mouth against his ear, frowning as though he was listening intently. Then he tucked Mr Pickles under his arm and turned to me with a shrug. 'If you insist on it being free, Mr Pickles says we'll never be able to come back for the best scones and coffee and the finest dog biscuits in the world because we'll feel too guilty.'

I laughed at his solemn expression. 'Oh, for goodness' sake. If Mr Pickles insists, then you can settle your bill but you're *not* paying for mine. As Angie pointed out, that was my lunch, and everyone who works here gets a free lunch.'

'You drive a hard bargain.'

We moved over to the till and I took payment then tutted when he slipped a tenner in the tips jar.

'Jake!'

'Mr Pickles insisted. He said it's bad manners not to tip and he's a Crufts winner so he mixes with the top dogs and knows what he's talking about.'

'Thank you for the exceedingly generous tip. It's very kind of you.'

'And thanks for the advice.'

'I'm not sure I helped find a solution.'

'Maybe not but you helped me decide one thing. I'm *definitely* keeping him and I'll somehow find a way to make that happen.'

My heart leapt. 'That's amazing news. But how did I help you decide that?'

'It was the way you spoke about your dogs. It was obvious how happy they made you. I've lived on my own for the past five years and I thought I was used to it, but this one...' He paused to ruffle the dog's ears, 'has been such good company and I don't like the thought of saying goodbye to him.' He cuddled Mr Pickles close to his heart. 'I just need to find the right carer for him. I'm sure there'll be a solution out there.'

I reached across the counter and stroked Mr Pickles' head but Jake moved his hand from the dog's ears at the same time and our fingers somehow entwined. An electrical pulse zipped through me and my heart started to race once more. I wanted to keep my hand there, feeling his warm skin against mine, and wondered if he felt the same. We laughed and untwined our fingers.

'Erm... so... yeah.' Jake cleared his throat. 'We'd better make a dash for it.'

'It was lovely to see you both and I'm so thrilled you're keeping him. I think you two were meant to find each other.'

'You could be right.' Jake adjusted Mr Pickles so that he was protected by the waterproof and made his way towards the door. He paused with his hand on the handle. 'Wish us luck.'

'Good luck.'

He pulled open the door and I felt a cool blast from the porch like a prod in my stomach. I didn't want him to walk out that door with no idea whether I'd see him again.

'Jake!' I called, rushing through the gate in the counter, no idea what I was going to say to stop him leaving.

'Yes?'

I glanced down at Mr Pickles and realised the obvious solution was right in front of me. There was a dog-shaped void in my life but getting another dog was a big commitment. What if I had a part-time dog? One who was exceptionally well trained and already comfortable in the café.

'I'll do it.' I stopped about a foot away from him.

He closed the door and turned to face me. 'You'll do what?'

'I'll look after Mr Pickles when you're on shift.'

He stared at me for a moment, mouth open. 'That's very generous, Hollie, but I can't ask you to do that.'

'I'd like to do it. Angie and I have been talking about me getting another dog and I wasn't sure about committing to one full-time but this would be the best of both worlds for everyone. I get to have a part-time dog, you get part-time care, and Mr Pickles has regular company. What do you say?'

Jake's eyes shone as he gave me the widest smile. 'I say yes, please. You've got yourself a part-time dog.'

I instinctively put out my hand to shake on the deal. Jake took my hand in his but leaned forward and lightly kissed my cheek. I held my breath as the feel of his hand in mine and the touch of his lips sent a tingle of longing throughout my body.

'Thank you so much,' he whispered, his breath warm against my ear, tickling the loose tendrils from my ponytail.

'It's my pleasure,' I whispered back. And it literally was. I'd never in my whole life felt such desire or longing. The scent of limes on his skin blended with the smell of woodsmoke on his waterproof was tantalising.

'I'm finished in the ki—' Angie called. 'Oops, sorry, kids. Ignore me. As you were.' I had my back to her but I knew she'd retreated into the kitchen. I could imagine her physically punching the air while metaphorically kicking herself for her lousy timing.

'I think that's my cue to go,' Jake said, stepping back. The smile was still there, although perhaps a little sheepish this time.

'Sorry about Angie. She's...' I shook my head. 'Let's not go there.'

'Thanks again. We're so grateful.'

'Have a think about what would work best for you and we should probably get together to talk it through.'

'I don't suppose you're free tonight or some time tomorrow to do that?' Jake asked.

Tonight? A Saturday night sounded too much like a date and, despite whatever it was that had just happened between us, the thought of dating again made me squirm. Which only left tomorrow but that was my beachcombing day.

Jake evidently picked up on my hesitation. 'Or I can come back between shifts next week if you prefer.'

I wanted to see him sooner than that, and ideally away from Angie's nudging and winking. 'I usually go down to the beach first thing on a Sunday. I could always make use of an extra pair of hands if you want to join me.'

'To do what?'

I grinned at him. 'You'll have to turn up if you want to know that. It's an early start.'

'Early's fine. Let me know which beach and what time and we'll be there.'

'I'll message you but, when I say early, I do mean early. Before sunrise. See you.'

Still grinning, I watched Jake sprinting across the car park, dodging the larger puddles. When he reversed out of his space, I turned towards the kitchen but my eyes were drawn out of the back window towards the sea. The storm had whipped up into a frenzy. The rain was battering the windows, the lightning was brighter, and the thunderclaps louder and closer. And yet I'd barely been aware of it moments ago. My fingers brushed down my cheek where he'd placed his kiss and butterflies swarmed in my stomach.

'Psst! Is it safe to come out now?' Angie peeked round the kitchen door.

'He's gone.'

'I'm so sorry. I didn't think. Did he ask you out?'

'No. It was nothing like that.'

'It didn't look like nothing.'

No. And it didn't feel like nothing either. Was it time to consider letting someone back in? The idea of that someone being Jake didn't make the prospect seem nearly as scary.

28

When my alarm sounded on my phone at crazy o'clock on Sunday morning, I lay back on my pillows, a knot in my stomach. What was I doing with Hollie? I only had two rules in life and I'd broken the first one: don't let anyone get close. Or had I?

I turned on my side and pondered. Yesterday had only been friendly advice over coffee and scones, although there'd been some sort of strangeness when I kissed her cheek. Nice strangeness. What was that? And why had I kissed her in the first place? After I'd touched her hand when we were both stroking Mr Pickles, I'd had this overwhelming urge to be close to her again and it had felt natural and right.

I wasn't sure what today was yet, but it wasn't a date. Although some might say watching the sunrise together was romantic. Were we even watching the sunrise? No idea.

So maybe I hadn't broken the first rule. I definitely wouldn't break my major self-preservation rule: don't talk about what happened. If I stuck to rule number one, it was easy to stick to rule number two. Avoiding getting close to anyone meant I could avoid discussing the past.

I never talked about my relationship status at the hospital. If they knew I was thirty-five and had only had a few short-term casual relationships they'd either think there was something 'wrong' with me or somebody well-meaning would make it their mission to find me my 'perfect match'. I'd heard several rumours ranging from me having a girlfriend overseas to going through a messy divorce to being gay. They could speculate however they wanted if it stopped anyone asking direct questions. Rumours didn't bother me. The truth did.

The great thing about casual relationships was that they were all about flirting and sex. They weren't about anything deep and meaningful; the one thing I was anxious to avoid. I'd chosen carefully, especially after the disaster with Cara. I'd only dated women I'd known from the outset were unsuitable or unavailable. Jenna was relocating to Switzerland with work so didn't want any commitments, Dawn was after a quick no-strings fling to make her ex-boyfriend jealous, and Tilly was on the rebound and just wanted a bit of fun. Fun? No strings? No commitment? I'd been happy to oblige, knowing each relationship had a natural expiry date, there was no danger of me hurting them, and they wouldn't be interested in knowing my life history or innermost feelings.

Conversations had remained superficial: music, films, food, holidays. There was never talk of meeting parents. If my parents were mentioned, I gave my stock answer: 'I don't see much of them,' before swiftly changing the subject. If I was asked about siblings, I claimed I had none, which was effectively the truth. If they asked where I'd got the scars on my cheek, I told them I'd fallen down the stairs when I was younger. They never questioned why there were three scars in perfect alignment and how falling down the stairs could have caused them because they weren't really interested. And the lack of interest was the appeal.

I pushed back the duvet. It'd be fine. Hollie and I were at the start of a mutually beneficial dog-sharing agreement and that was all it was. Today was simply about working out the logistics. And if there was a repeat of that strangeness from yesterday, I'd step away and that would be the end of it.

In the bathroom, I peered at my reflection and ran my fingers across the scars. Still noticeable but fading with each year. Hollie probably wouldn't ask. But if she did, I had the weirdest feeling that I might want to tell her.

* * *

There were no other vehicles in the car park in front of The Bay Pavilion so I had the pick of the spaces. Hollie must have walked down, which made sense if she lived just off Sea Cliff – a long road that ran along the esplanade on the cliff above and behind us.

'What do you think she does on the beach so early?' I asked Mr Pickles as I opened up the back door and released his seatbelt harness. She'd messaged to confirm the time and place but all she'd told me was to wear several layers and sturdy footwear.

Locking my car, I glanced back along the seafront. White lights above the beach curved round South Bay past the lifeboat station all the way to the harbour. Opposite them, facing the sea, were the lights of the arcades – more dimly lit than during the daytime but ever-present as a beacon to the boats.

I didn't feel confident enough to let Mr Pickles off the lead in the dark but he seemed content trotting alongside me as we made our way through the dimly lit stone covered walkway beyond the car park.

He yapped and tugged at the lead and I heard Hollie's voice before I spotted her. 'Is that my favourite little dog?'

She was silhouetted on the steps leading down to the beach. I released the dog's lead and he raced towards her. As I got closer, I could see she was dressed in a turquoise waterproof and a pink bobble hat with her long hair loose. Jenna, Dawn and Tilly hadn't liked the outdoor life. They'd have shuddered at the thought of an early start on the beach at any time of year, especially November. Seeing Hollie dressed like that, looking completely at home by the sea in the cold and dark, it struck me that the unavailability of those women hadn't been the only appeal. I'd been drawn to them because they weren't my type so I'd known I wouldn't fall for them. And now I was on the beach with someone who was. The thought made me both nervous and excited.

'I wasn't sure if you'd come,' she said as I sat down beside her.

'We couldn't stay away. Too intrigued as to what brings you down to the beach so early every Sunday.'

'This for a start.' She pointed past me up the coast where a band of orange blending into gold had appeared on the horizon beneath the deep blue sky. 'Sets me up for the day. Coffee?' She held up a flask.

'I'd love one. Thanks.'

She passed me two plastic cups and poured us both a drink. Mr Pickles clambered onto her knee as we sipped our coffees and watched the sun making its gradual ascent.

'Any change of heart about keeping him?' she asked after a while.

'Nope. Any change of heart about looking after him?'

'Definitely not. I'm really excited about it.'

'I have another dilemma I'd welcome your opinion on. Would it be too confusing for him if I changed his name?'

'You're not too keen on keeping... what was it again?'

'Mr Piccalilli Marmaduke Fluffington the Third. Oddly enough, no.'

Hollie laughed. 'That's so hilarious. Who thinks of these

things?' She tickled the dog's belly. 'What's he saying about your name?' she asked him in a sing-song voice.

She looked back at me. 'He's well trained so he'll probably respond to a new name fairly quickly. He's responded well to a new owner. Did you have anything in mind?'

'Not really. So that's another dilemma.'

'What about dropping the Mr and calling him Pickles or even just Pickle? That's sweet.'

I mulled it over for a moment and grinned at her. 'That's a sound idea. I'll try Pickle.'

By the time we finished our drinks, the beach was bathed in gentle golden light.

'Time to get to work,' Hollie announced, standing up. 'Sundays are all about indulging in one of my passions. Wood.'

I'm not sure what I expected her to say but 'wood' was not it.

She picked up her bag, I picked up Pickle's lead, and the three of us set off across the sand.

'It's a family thing going back several generations,' Hollie said, 'and my particular obsession is driftwood so, on a Sunday, I pick a local beach and go beachcombing. I was here last Sunday and I wouldn't normally come to the same beach quite so soon but we've had a couple of stormy days so the sea will have been all churned up. There's bound to be some good new pieces.'

'What do you do with the driftwood?'

'I make things. Picture frames, mirrors, coat racks, key hooks, Christmas tree decorations. Candle holders are one of my favourites.'

'Are these for you or do you sell what you make?'

Hollie stopped by a couple of pieces of wood and produced a large hessian bag from her backpack. 'Home is full to bursting with my creations so everything I make now is either sold in the café or on my website. I've built up a nice little sideline over the past few years.' She placed the wood in the bag and indicated we should walk again.

'Could you see yourself doing that full-time instead of running the café?'

'Gosh, no! I've got three passions in life – the café, dogs and wood – so I'd never let go of the café. Besides, I don't make any money from the wood. I split the profits across a few charities.'

I was about to ask which charities when she passed me another hessian bag. 'Let's see who can fill their bag first. The best places are usually around boulders and rockpools as the wood gets snagged. I use all sizes so don't worry about it being too small. If you spot any sea glass I'll have that as well, please. I sometimes look for shells and pretty pebbles but I've got quite a collection at the moment so it's just the wood and the glass today. Shove it all in together and I'll sort it out later.'

Did she want me to head off on my own? I felt a wave of disappointment, but I'd obviously misunderstood her as she pointed towards some boulders. 'Let's try over there.'

Pickle tugged on his lead. 'If I unhook you, will you stay close by?' I asked him. I'd have to hope he would because this was an enormous expanse of beach compared to Starfish Point and I didn't relish embarrassing myself in front of Hollie by chasing him up and down it.

* * *

Pickle did stay close by, running through the rock pools and dragging lumps of seaweed across the sand. Hollie occasionally strayed further from my side when something caught her eye but remained close enough to chat most of the time. She told me more about the love of wood passing down through the generations and how she could usually pick up a piece of wood and visualise what it could become but also how turning it over could completely change her vision. It reminded me of Philip Heslington talking about how different a photograph could look after changing position or camera settings.

'You see this piece?' she asked, huddling close to me and holding out a small piece of wood. 'If I hold it this way, it's a filler piece on a picture or a mirror frame but, if I turn it upside down and twist it round like this, there's a slight slope and these bumps at the end look like steps.'

I bent over to see where she was pointing, my pulse racing as I caught a trace of aqua perfume. 'Oh, yeah. I can see that.'

'This could become part of a harbour scene. It would go in a picture frame because it's quite small. There'd be a row of wooden painted houses and the steps would go down to the harbour where there'd be a sailing boat. And this piece...' She rummaged in her bag and pulled out a small tree branch. 'This, on the other hand, is sturdy and most likely to become a candle holder. I'd gather several branches together to make a unique piece.'

'I've always been fascinated by wood for my photography but I've never imagined it taking on a new purpose. It's really interesting.'

'How do you use wood in photography?'

'I'm a landscape photographer but that doesn't always mean taking photos of big sweeping instantly recognisable landscapes. Quite often it's about finding something within the landscape that talks to me and focusing on that. Therefore it doesn't actually matter where I am; it's what I find there that's important. Wood in any form – whether a tree, an old sailing boat with peeling paint on it, a groyne or a piece of driftwood – is great to work with because of the shapes, the texture, and the way the light falls on it.'

'You'll have to show me some of your photos.'

'Maybe. I'm still learning.' I'd welcome an excuse to spend more time with her, but I wasn't sure about showing her my photos. I'd never shown them to anyone since Cara questioned why I'd take a photo of 'some old washed-up crap' but from how Hollie spoke about wood, she'd never see it like that.

'Everyone has to start somewhere. You should have seen my first wood turning efforts. Disaster. But I reckon your photos will be amazing. One day when you're ready.'

I gave her a grateful smile. She'd managed to pick up on my insecurities, reassure me, and not push me. So refreshing.

We continued to forage and chat and I could have happily stayed down there all day. Hollie was so easy to talk to. She asked plenty of questions but nothing was invasive. Everything felt safe.

'You've done well,' she said, peering into my bag. 'Some good pieces there.'

I stretched out my back. 'I've enjoyed it but it's hard work.'

'Now you'll see why I roped you in. Same amount collected in half the time. I've got a favour to ask, too. Did you drive down?'

'Yes.'

'Last time I was here I spotted a slightly larger piece that I'd love to liberate, but there was no chance I could carry it up the cliff on my own. If I throw breakfast into the deal, would you mind helping me and driving me home?'

'What sort of breakfast?'

'Full English.'

I grinned at her. 'Lead the way.'

* * *

'Slightly larger?' I raised my eyebrows at Hollie as we stood on the beach looking down at a tree trunk with several branches sticking out either side.

Hollie giggled. 'I might have downplayed the size a bit. Do you think it'll fit in your car?'

'With the seats down, just about. If not, I've got some bungee cords in the boot so we'll be able to secure it.'

One end of the tree trunk was buried in the sand and disappeared under a rock. I pushed at it with my foot but there was no give.

'I think we might have to do some digging first.' Hollie held up a child's plastic spade.

'Loving the professional toolkit,' I said, laughing. 'How about we dump the bags in the car and put the seats down then come back for this?'

* * *

I might have laughed at it but Hollie's little red spade was just the ticket. She worked on one side and I started on the other with my hands but was soon shoved aside by Pickle, who was much faster at digging with his front paws, showering me with sand whichever way I moved.

Hollie and I moved to the top of the trunk and each wrapped an arm round it to try to pull it free but we'd obviously underestimated how far under the rock the other end went. That tree was going nowhere.

I took the spade and dug a little deeper and, confident there was more give, returned to Hollie. 'After three. One... two... three... heave!'

My feet scrabbled for a grip in the wet sand and still the damn thing wouldn't budge. I wedged my shoulder against a thick broken-off branch and Hollie pushed against a longer, narrower one.

'It's moving!' she cried.

But so were my feet. I could feel them slipping from under me and, as I fell forwards onto the sand, I heard a crack and a squeal from Hollie. She collapsed beside me, giggling.

'I think it might have defeated us,' she said, turning to face me, her eyes sparkling. She stopped laughing and reached out her hand towards my left cheek. 'You're bleeding. Did I do that?'

I'd felt a sharp scratch as we fell but there was no pain. All I could feel was my heart pounding. Her face was so close to mine, it would only take the slightest move forward to kiss her. Her lips looked so soft and her eyes, full of concern, had me mesmerised. I'd thought they were light brown but they were actually a blend of brown, grey and flecks of green. She had long thick eyelashes and a dark freckle just below her left eye, like a small beauty spot. Her cheeks were pink and, up close, I could see she was make-up free and naturally beautiful.

'I'm so sorry,' she said, breaking my trance. 'I must have caught you with this.' She tossed aside the branch in her hand.

I held my breath as she lightly touched my cheek then suddenly pulled back. 'I'd better not touch you. My hands are dirty. I don't think it's deep but we'd best get you back to mine and cleaned up.'

She didn't move and I knew what was coming next. 'How did you get those scars?'

Her hand twitched as though she was going to touch my cheek again. I definitely wanted to tell her. I actually wanted to share my story but this wasn't the moment.

'Long story.'

That seemed to placate her. She scrambled to her feet and I somehow managed to do the same. That strangeness had been back for a moment, like in the café when I'd kissed her on the cheek. What was going on? Why did she have such an effect on me?

Hollie planted her hands on her hips and shook her head. 'I think we're going to have to accept defeat.'

No way. Defeat wasn't part of who I was. I'd spent my whole life battling and I'd faced far worse adversaries than a chunk of dead wood.

'One more try,' I suggested, reaching for the spade. 'I'll dig a bit deeper.'

'Okay. But I'm putting a time on it. If we can't move it in ten minutes, we give up. Deal?' She offered her hand just like she'd done in the café yesterday.

'Deal.' Her hand was small and soft in mine and my heart raced again. The slightest tug and I could pull her into my arms. *Hollie Brooks, what are you doing to me?*

I knelt on the damp sand with the coldness seeping into my jeans but a warmth in my heart. I was in trouble. Was I ready to open up about my past to someone I'd only met just over a week ago?

Saturday 25th June, five and a half years ago

Returning from Nanna's will-reading and seeing Lighthouse View – my house – through fresh eyes, I realised how badly I'd neglected the outside this year. There was a small low maintenance garden out the front with a water feature and tubs of assorted sizes that usually burst with flowers but were now bedraggled with weeds.

Out the back was a small traditional lawn with shrubs and floral borders but I'd let that go, too. The gardens had been Nanna's domain. I'd carried bags of compost and relocated the heavier planters but otherwise left her to it. Irene's garden at Seafarer Lodge next door was always beautiful too and they used to chat over the fence while they worked.

Nanna said that creating colourful hanging baskets and tubs soothed her soul. Perhaps a spot of gardening would soothe my soul right now. It was a sunny late June Saturday and I had no plans as I'd assumed I'd be moving my stuff out and searching for somewhere new to live. I didn't have the energy to start unpacking. A couple of hours spent tidying up the front garden would be a good alternative. Several neighbours were out working on theirs and mine was letting the street down.

Half an hour later, I was on my knees weeding a tub when I heard the screech of tyres followed by a car door slamming.

'You odious piece of shit!' Larissa cried, bursting through the gate and storming up the garden path.

I stuck the metal fork in the soil and scrambled to my feet, my hands raised in surrender. 'I knew nothing about it. I swear.'

'Like I believe that. You know what the pair of you are? Sick! Probably thought it was hilarious, making me drive two hours to this grubby little shithole just so you could have some poncey solicitor tell me I was getting sod all.'

I winced at her high-pitched tone and glanced down the street. The neighbours were clearly trying to be discreet about watching us but some passers-by had actually stopped by the garden wall to gawp.

'Do you want to come in and talk about it?' I suggested, eager not to disrespect Nanna's memory by playing this out in front of our neighbours and a bunch of strangers.

'What the bloody hell would I want to do that for? No. Let's do it here.' She turned in a circle, shouting: 'Come on, everyone. Roll up, roll up, watch the drama unfold. You see this pathetic excuse for a human being here? This is my brother and I wouldn't piss on him if he was on fire. Do you know what he did?'

'Larissa,' I hissed. 'Not here.'

She turned back to me. 'Aw, am I upsetting you? Poor little Jake. Except you're not poor, are you? You're rich. You should be doing time, not living the life of Riley.'

'It wasn't my fault.'

'Stop saying that!' She stamped her foot. 'It *was* your fault.'

'It wasn't. Dad was an accident and Mum was told not to...' I tailed off as she took a couple of steps closer to me, her face purple with rage.

'Go on, you little runt! Finish that sentence. Mum was told not to what?'

I backed away a couple of steps, genuinely fearful that she was going to lash out and it wouldn't just be a light slap. She'd likely give me a beating.

'I'm waiting,' she snarled.

I've often wondered what would have happened if I'd left it there and retreated inside but I thought about the two decades of vicious, vindictive hate mail Larissa had sent and the toll that must have taken on Nanna emotionally and mentally and I couldn't help myself. Since I got back on track a few years after Dad died, I'd never lashed out or said cruel things. A childhood overshadowed by a bully had made me vow never to behave that way, but Larissa needed to hear some home truths. Maybe that would help her let go of her hate and find a way forward.

'Mum was told not to try for another baby after the problems having you.'

'Don't you dare say that. Don't you dare put it on me. It was you. All you!' She sounded hysterical.

It happened in a split second. Her eyes flicked towards the gardening fork I'd abandoned and, next moment it was in her hand and she was wielding it like a weapon. 'Take that back.'

I held my hands up and took another step back. 'Put the fork down, Larissa. You don't want to do this.'

'Take it back!' she screeched, raising her hand in the air.

I heard shouts and a scream and added my own cry as the fork struck my left cheek. Stars swam before my eyes as I staggered back, tumbled over one of Nanna's low pots and landed in a heap on the ground, the wind knocked out of me.

Larissa lunged for me again and I somehow managed to hold my arms out to protect my head in case she struck me once more, but she seemed to be floating backwards. There were more shouts and a barrage of expletives from Larissa and I realised she was being dragged away.

A couple of blurry faces appeared in front of me.

'Jake? It's Irene. Can you hear me?'

I blinked a few times as her face came into focus and I winced as she pressed something to my cheek.

'Yeah. I can. And that hurts.'

'Jesus! I'll bet it does. Who's the lunatic?'

Mild Irish accent. Blonde hair. Sarah's sister-in-law from Seashell Cottage. 'Clare?'

'Probably best not to talk,' she said. 'You're bleeding everywhere.'

'The police are coming for your sister,' Irene said, over the sound of distant sirens. 'So you're safe. We all saw what happened. She won't get away with it.'

Another reason for my sister to hate me, although she couldn't blame me this time. This was definitely her fault.

Present day

Victory! With a groan, Jake and I dumped the tree trunk in the covered wooden storage area running alongside the garage. I stored my large pieces of driftwood there next to the log pile for the fires.

'You score ten out of ten for perseverance and I'm so grateful,' I said, admiring the trunk. 'This is going to make something really special.'

'Is it talking to you yet?'

I ran my fingers along one of the branches. 'It's whispering at the moment. A few ideas. Nothing certain yet. I don't want to rush it so I'll probably keep moving it round and talking to it until it tells me its new purpose.' I clapped a hand against my cheek and shook my head. 'I'm saying the words and I'm thinking cuckoo! You probably think I'm totally mad.'

'Far from it. I might have spoken to a few trees in my time but don't tell anyone.'

I'd talked about my love for wood before but never in the way I'd spoken about it to Jake. I loved how he understood, the photographer in him appreciating wood just like I did.

'I can't believe how deep you had to dig. I was beginning to think you were making an escape tunnel.' He'd been a man on a mission, digging frantically in the sand at one side and then the other but it had been worth it in the end.

Jake smiled. 'I'll admit I wasn't expecting it to be so deeply wedged but that made me all the more determined to get it.'

'I'm very grateful.' I removed the two halves of plastic spade out of my pocket and held one up in each hand, tutting. 'Although you did break my extremely expensive professional toolkit.'

'Sometimes art comes with sacrifices,' he said solemnly. 'I owe you a replacement.'

'Best start saving, then.' We laughed as I deposited the pieces in the wheelie bin. 'Let's get Pickle and the rest of the stuff from your car and then get that cut on your cheek cleaned up.'

Willow's soft bed was still in the corner of the kitchen next to the fireplace and Pickle made a beeline for it as soon as I opened the side door. He padded round it, sniffing, then curled up in it and a lump caught in my throat. How lovely to see a dog in that bed again. I'd cleared out a lot of things over the years but had never been able to bring myself to remove the dog bed or the leads hanging by the door.

Jake looked up from untying his boot laces. 'Someone's made himself at home.'

I didn't trust myself to speak without blubbing, so I retrieved Willow's water bowl from under the sink, filled it and placed it near

Pickle. He lapped up some water then settled back into the bed for a sleep.

'Are you happy for me to clean you up or would you rather I point you in the direction of the bathroom?' I asked Jake, feeling in control of my emotions once more. 'I'm a first-aider but I think you significantly trump me on qualifications.'

'I trust you.'

He held my gaze for a moment and my heart began racing. Why did it keep doing that round him?

I suggested he sit at the breakfast bar at one end of the island.

'It's not deep but there's some sand in it.' Jake winced as I applied a little more pressure to clean it. 'I could do with swilling it out.'

He joined me at the sink set into the other end of the island and I poured saline solution from my first aid kit to flush out the cut. When he sat down again, I pulled up a stool opposite him and patted his face dry with a towel before misting some antiseptic spray over the wound.

I was still intrigued by the scars, but he'd said 'long story' on the beach, which could well be a way of evading the question. I wasn't going to pry as I knew first-hand how uncomfortable it felt when people tried to delve into the past.

Butterflies swooped and soared as he held my gaze. I sensed in him the same weight I carried. There was something in his eyes that I recognised so well: pain, loss, heartache. I could feel his leg warm against mine and I had an overwhelming desire to gather him into a hug and to tell him that, whatever it was he was hiding from, everything would be all right and I longed for him to do the same to me. But I was so scared. It wasn't fear of rejection. It was fear of acceptance and what that would mean: letting someone into my heart again and all the risks that came with that. Was I strong enough? Would I ever be?

'Breakfast,' I announced jumping up, fear spurring me into action. 'I believe I offered you a full English. Are you hungry? Do you eat meat? Do you like eggs and, if so, how do you like them cooked? And baked beans? Some people think they have no place on a breakfast plate but I'm team beans.' *Breathe, Hollie! Breathe!*

Hollie refused to let me help her cook but was happy to let me set the table, not that doing that took long. I watched her move round the kitchen with ease. She put some music on and, as she chopped mushrooms and laid the bacon out on the grill, she sang along, although she seemed to be making up half the lyrics, which made me smile.

The kitchen was enormous. I'd always thought the kitchen at Lighthouse View was a good size but it would probably have fit in Hollie's four times over. There was a real fire at the end where Pickle was sleeping, flanked by a couple of two-seater sofas. It was a relief that he clearly felt at home so quickly as he'd be spending a fair bit of time here. We hadn't discussed it yet, but I presumed Hollie's offer included having him at home when I was on night shift and not just at work when I was on days.

The cooking noises, the extractor fan, the music, and Hollie's singing meant there was no opportunity for conversation, which was probably just as well. I knew she'd been looking at my scars when she cleaned my cheek and, if she'd asked again, I'm sure I'd have told her about Larissa. What would I have done if she'd asked me why Larissa hated me? Would I have broken rule number two and let my tragic past tumble out? Probably. Because the longer I spent in Hollie's presence, the harder it was not to break both of my rules. I felt drawn to her. I felt like I could tell her anything and she'd understand. No idea why.

'I'd have helped you with that tree without the offer of the full English, you know,' I said as she placed a packed plate down in front of me a little later.

'I'd have offered to make you breakfast even if you hadn't helped me,' she responded, then bit her lip and widened her eyes as though she hadn't meant to say that. She averted her gaze but I could see her blushing. Maybe she was feeling the same things as me.

She nodded towards Pickle. 'He must be pooped if the smell of bacon hasn't woken him up. Tuck in before it gets cold.'

I hadn't realised how ravenous I was until I started eating. 'This is the best full English ever,' I told her between mouthfuls. 'And that's saying something because my nanna was a brilliant cook.'

'Thank you. It's all locally sourced from the farm shop we use for the café.'

'It's delicious. Have you always been a good cook?'

'I've always been a cook. Good couldn't be applied to my earlier efforts, but my mum was a brilliant chef so I learned from the best.'

I noticed the use of the past tense, the melancholy in her tone, and how the sparkle disappeared from her eyes. It would be normal to pick up on her comment and say sorry or ask her what happened but I couldn't seem to get the words out and I knew why. If I asked her about her mum, I'd be opening the way for questions about my own parents and rule number two was going to be smashed. Self-preservation aside, I couldn't intrude like that. I'd spent my life running from questions. I knew how hard it was to talk about loss. I wanted to make Hollie's eyes sparkle with happiness; not with pain. I fumbled around for a change of subject.

'So what are your thoughts on the logistics around our Pickle-share?' Hollie asked, her voice bright again.

Over breakfast, we discussed how best to cover my shifts at work in a way that would provide minimal disruption to Pickle. I loved how excited she was about having a dog in her life again and it reassured me that this was definitely something that she wanted, rather than feeling obligated because I'd found Pickle near her café.

I didn't mention my other commitment with the RNLI and she'd either forgotten about it or didn't like to ask. Nobody knew about that except Irene and, of course, the crew. When it did become official I'd have to open up at work and I was already dreading the inevitable question: *What made you do that?* I didn't want to answer that question. Whitsborough Bay wasn't that big. Somebody would know somebody who'd know about Binky and it would all come out. I couldn't go through that again.

Pickle woke up when we'd finished eating and tucked into the dish of poached egg Hollie had prepared for him.

'You said your house was packed with things you'd made,' I said. 'What's yours in here?'

She twisted round in her chair. 'I made the fruit bowl on the island. The dog lead hooks by the door were my first project. The picture frame by the window. I think that's it in here.'

'All from reclaimed wood?'

She nodded. 'The hooks were from where we were today, the wood for the picture frame came from Fellingthorpe beach and the bowl was a chunk of wood I found at Shellby Bay.' She twiddled with a strand of hair and lowered her gaze. 'I could show you my workshop if you want. You don't have to say yes. I probably bored you rigid on the beach.'

'I'd love to see it, and you didn't bore me at all. It was fascinating.'

She looked up, eyes wide. 'Really?'

'You sound surprised.'

'It's just that... well... most people aren't interested.' There was something about the way she said it that suggested to me it wasn't 'most people' at all and it was one particular person. I hoped he was a thing of the past.

'I'm not most people.'

'No. You're not, are you?' It seemed to be a rhetorical question and her words were barely audible. She held eye contact and, once more, that strangeness was there. A connection. A chemistry. So new.

Hollie pushed her chair out, breaking the moment. 'Boots back on and let's go to my workshop.'

* * *

Hollie's workshop was the large double garage set back from the house on one side of the garden against which we'd placed the tree trunk earlier. She unlocked a sturdy stable door on the side and I smiled at the wooden sign across it: Hollie's Wood.

'Is that your company's name?'

'Yes. I couldn't resist the play on words although when I first had the idea, someone told me it was crap and cheesy and would only have had the slightest chance of working if I'd been a Hollie with a Y.' She grinned at me. 'So when I started trading, I went with it just to piss him off.'

'Good for you.' I wondered if this was the same person who hadn't been interested in her woodwork. Sounded like an ex-boyfriend. Sounded like a knob.

She pushed the door open, flicked the lights on and I gasped as we stepped inside. It was a proper workshop with a couple of work-benches and lathes, tools hung neatly on racks, and a stack of shelving.

'This place is awesome.'

'Thank you. I love my workshop. I spend more time in here than I do in the house.'

While Pickle went to explore, Hollie pointed to the wall oppo-site us. 'That's my creative space. My tools, fittings, and my small lathe are over there and I use that workbench when I'm finishing off little items.' She turned and pointed towards the wall where we'd entered. 'These shelves are for completed projects, works in progress, and small pieces of driftwood.'

I took a step closer to look at some of her completed work. There were various styles of candle holder from a single piece of wood with a circle cut into it, presumably for a tealight, to large intricate designs consisting of several pieces of wood pulled together to create a candelabra with metal holders resting on the branches for church candles. Those were obviously the favourites she'd mentioned on the beach. I spotted bowls, picture frames, key hooks, boxes, keyrings and that seemed to barely scratch the surface.

'You made *all* of these?'

She smiled as she nodded.

'You're so talented.' I picked up a chunk of driftwood on which stood several pastel-painted cottages of varying sizes. 'This looks just like a street in the Old Town.'

'I'm so glad you said that. That's where I got my inspiration for that piece.'

'I bet these are popular.'

'Hopefully they will be. I haven't put any on my website yet. I wanted to make a range of styles and sizes first. The one you have is really neat but you see that one there? It's got more of a distressed appearance. And then I have smaller versions in picture frames like this.' She removed a white square photo frame from another shelf and held it up. 'That small piece with steps we found earlier would become one of these. So there's something for everyone. Or at least that's the hope.'

I looked back at the scene in my hands. The paintwork was immaculate and there were extra flourishes like climbing roses, animals in windows, and even a street name.

'So you're an artist too?' I asked, turning to face her again.

She blushed. 'That's stretching it. I have a good set of brushes and a steady hand but I don't think I'd be able to sit in front of a canvas and produce anything even half decent and it's not my thing even if I could. Unless I could glue chunks of wood all over it.'

'I'm kind of getting this vibe that you might like wood.'

'Do you think?'

She showed me a few more pictures she'd made, some with small wooden scenes and others with pebbles, shells and sea glass. Pickle had settled in a dog bed in one corner and we laughed as his snores interrupted us.

'I'm getting carried away,' Hollie said. 'Sorry.'

'Don't apologise. I'm fascinated to see what the stuff we collected on the beach earlier becomes.' I could listen to her talking for hours about her craft. She radiated enthusiasm and I genuinely was in awe of her talent.

'If you're sure I'm not boring you, I'll finish the grand tour.'

She pointed to a huge cabinet, which had to be at least seven feet square full of glass-fronted drawers, each with a handwritten label in a metal slot. 'That's my most treasured possession. Isn't it a thing of beauty? It's an old apothecary cabinet and it was in a shocking state when I bought it at auction but I had to have it. I stripped it back, gave it some serious TLC and returned it to life. I dread to think how many hours I spent on it but it was worth every last second. The drawers store pebbles, shells, sea glass, and small bits of driftwood. They're all cleaned and organised into size and colour so I can easily find what I need.' She laughed lightly, eyes sparkling.

'This is so impressive.' And the most impressive part of it was Hollie herself, doing all this alongside running a successful café.

'In the middle we have my main workbench and my large lathe and, at the back, the cupboards contain my big power tools.'

I nodded towards the front end of the garage where surfboards, bodyboards and a paddleboard rested against the metal garage door and several wetsuits hung from a rail. 'You're into watersports?'

There was an unmistakable sigh and, when I caught her eye, the sadness was back. 'No. That's my dad's and brother's stuff. I keep meaning to clear it out. Sometimes I forget it's there but sometimes...' She tailed off and frowned as she gazed at the pile of equipment, shaking her head. She reached for a chain round her neck and fiddled with what looked like a couple of rings dangling from it.

My mind was working overtime. I was certain her mum had died from the use of the past tense earlier, but had her brother and dad died too? Could her family have been killed in a car crash or something? It would explain the enormous house in which she seemed to live alone. It felt okay for me to bypass the comment about her mum earlier but there was no way I could ignore this second flag without coming across as cold.

'Your dad and brother aren't around anymore?' I asked tentatively, almost fearful of the answer.

She let go of the necklace, lowered herself onto a wooden stool, and ran her hands down her face. 'I don't know why I said that. I don't usually...' She exhaled deeply as she turned to meet my eyes. 'I'll say it quickly and then can we just forget about it?'

'Okay.' I sat down on another stool and waited, my stomach in knots. Had I found someone who'd experienced the same sort of tragedy as me?

'You have to promise you won't go weird on me when I tell you and suddenly decide that you don't want me to look after Pickle.'

'I promise.' Not a difficult promise to make if this was going where I suspected.

'And you won't ask me any questions?'

Another thing in common. I gave her a reassuring smile. 'No questions.'

'My dad and my older brother were killed in an accident nearly seven years ago and cancer took my mum a year later.' Her voice cracked and her eyes sparkled with tears. 'This was our family home and the café was Mum's and now they're both mine and I wish I could trade them both to have my family back.' Tears spilled down her cheeks and she wiped them with the sleeve of her hoodie. 'Sorry. I didn't mean to cry. This is one of the reasons why I don't tell anyone and why I can't cope with questions.'

'I can probably guess some of the other reasons. That sympathetic look? The panic in their eyes when they don't know what to say? The excuses to get away? Them avoiding you? Promises to meet always being vague and never coming to fruition?'

She looked at me, wide-eyed. 'All the above. You too?'

I nodded. 'I never knew my mum. She died within an hour of having me. My dad died on my ninth birthday. It was an accident but it was because he was doing something I wanted us to do. My sister Larissa blamed me for both of them which is why...' I pointed to my scars. 'She went for me with a gardening fork.'

Hollie stared at me for a moment, her cheeks damp, her eyes red. 'You're serious?'

'Sadly, yes. And not when we were kids, either. It happened at the start of summer five years ago after my nanna died. She left everything to me and disinherited Larissa. This was her reaction to that news.'

'Oh, my God, Jake! That's awful.'

She lightly ran her fingers across my cheek and I gulped as her touch fizzed through me.

'She didn't mean to...?' she asked.

That question had haunted me for a long time afterwards. 'I don't think so, but you never know with Larissa. She claimed that I provoked her but all I did was tell her something I thought she already knew. Whether she did or didn't, me saying it inflamed things. Anyway, like you, I don't talk about what happened with my parents or Larissa. Easier that way.'

'Can I ask you a question?'

She must have spotted panic in my expression because she added, 'It's not digging for details.'

'In that case, fire away.'

'Does it get any easier? It's been seven years and sometimes it feels like only seven hours.'

Another tear trickled down her cheek and I couldn't help myself. I slipped off my stool, gently cupped her face with my hand, and brushed the tear away with my thumb. 'Parts of it do.'

She didn't flinch at my touch, instead closing her eyes and nuzzling into my palm for a moment. She opened her eyes and gazed up at me. There was no ignoring the sparks between us, like the fireworks on the night we met.

Another tear trickled down her cheek, slipping between my fingers. 'I wish I could take your pain away,' I whispered.

'So do I,' she whispered back, her eyes searching mine. 'But this is helping.'

She parted her lips and I slowly lowered my mouth to hers in the gentlest of kisses. I could taste the saltiness of her tears. I ran my hands through her long hair as she slid off her stool and snaked her arms round my neck, pulling me close, her kiss deepening.

It felt like fireworks were exploding everywhere: in my stomach, my mind and my heart. I'd never experienced anything like it. I couldn't get enough of her and from the way she was responding, she felt the same. Was this how it felt when there was a real and proper connection with a person instead of a bit of no-strings fun?

On the beach earlier, I'd thought I could be in danger. Too late for that. I'd taken the leap and the only danger was if, for Hollie, this was a one-off because she was upset. If it was, I was about to experience my first broken heart.

I could scarcely catch my breath as Jake kissed my neck. It had never felt like this with Craig. My heart had sometimes beat a little faster but it had never pounded like it was doing now in Jake's arms. My legs had never turned to jelly like this. It had been very nice and polite and I'd put that down to us having been friends first. But if we'd really loved each other, shouldn't there have been the fire I felt burning inside me now?

I ran my fingers through Jake's hair, loving how soft and natural it felt. Craig's hair was always solid with styling products, which had left my hands feeling sticky. Not that he liked me 'messing up' his hair anyway.

Jake effortlessly scooped me up and sat me on the edge of the workbench then pulled away, hands still in my hair, his eyes searching my face, worry lines furrowing his brow. 'Is this okay?'

My heart melted. He'd asked my permission to continue. 'It's more than okay.' And to prove I meant that, I wrapped my legs round his waist and pulled him even closer as my lips found his once more.

The thoughts racing through my mind about where this could

lead both shocked and excited me. He hadn't attempted to remove any of my clothes or even to touch me anywhere intimate but there was no mistaking the passion in his kiss. He wanted me as much as I wanted him. I imagined us entwined together on the workbench and swiftly dismissed the idea. It might appear spontaneous and romantic in a film but the garage was cold and the workbench uncomfortable. We deserved better.

Was I brave enough to take him by the hand and lead him up to my bedroom? I'd never done anything like that before, but it was what I wanted. From the moment I saw Jake standing outside the café with Pickle in his arms, I felt a connection to him. It had deepened each time I saw him and, when he shared that he'd lost his parents too, I realised why. We instinctively understood each other. It was as though our broken hearts had found their match.

'Jake,' I whispered. 'Do you want to—'

Ding dong!

We looked towards the front of the garage where the sound had come from. With spending so much time in my workshop, I'd had the chimes for front doorbell wired up in here as well as the house.

'Expecting someone?' Jake asked, loosening his hold.

'No. Ignore it. They'll go away. Where were we?'

Jake's lips had barely grazed mine when the chimes sounded again. I grimaced. 'Really sorry. It's probably the kids from next door. They're always kicking their football into the garden. They'll have seen my car and they'll keep ringing. Back in a bit.'

Sighing, I slid down off the workbench and reluctantly left Jake. If it was next door's kids, I'd struggle to be polite this time. Talk about appalling timing.

The biting wind whipped my hair across my face as I stepped onto the drive and it was like a slap, bringing me to my senses. What had I just done? I gulped and ran my hand through my dishevelled hair, my heart still racing. It wasn't just that I'd kissed him. It was letting him know about my family. I *never* opened up like that.

'Can we get our ball?' I hadn't even registered that the two boys from next door were standing in front of me, staring.

'Er, yeah. Help yourself.' I vaguely waved my arm in the direction of the garden but couldn't seem to will my legs to follow them. I pressed my fingers to my lips and my heart leapt as I imagined Jake's lips pressed against mine. That kiss just now was without a doubt the best kiss I'd ever had but I had to stop there. There was no mistaking the chemistry or the intensity between us. If we did this, we'd be throwing ourselves fully into something, but I couldn't do it. Christmas was coming up and there couldn't be a worse time of year for me to get involved with someone. I needed to step back and make it clear that friendship and a dog-share arrangement was all that was on offer because I didn't have it in me at this time of year to offer anything else.

'Thanks, Hollie,' said the boys, walking either side of me, one of them with the ball tucked under his arm.

'You're welcome,' I muttered. *Oh God! What am I going to say to Jake?*

* * *

'We thought we were going to have to send out a search party,' Jake joked when I finally returned to the garage after pacing up and down on the drive for several minutes, my stomach and head in turmoil.

'I... erm... it...' Where had all the words gone?

Jake gave me a gentle smile as he rose from the stool. 'It's okay. Too much too quickly?'

'It's not you, it's me. And I can't believe I just said that! I'd like to explain.'

He held his hands up and shook his head. 'You don't have to. I understand. I really do. I'll grab his lead and my coat and we'll get out your hair. Pickle! Here, buddy!'

Pickle stretched and obediently trotted over.

'I'm sorry. It's really not you and I promise that's not a line. It's a timing thing. Across the space of five days in December, it's my birthday, Christmas Day, and three back-to-back days of anniversaries of losing my family. I can't...' My voice cracked and, next moment, he'd pulled me into his arms.

'For me, it was last Saturday,' he said, his voice soft and gentle. 'Birthday and two anniversaries on the same day. When I say I understand, I really, truly do.'

Pickle slumped across our feet as we stood in the cold garage, clinging onto each other and I thought about my conversation with Mum after the funeral:

'When you're ready, you'll find him.'

'What if I'm never ready?'

'Then he'll find you. True love will always find a way.'

The problem wasn't Jake. He was gorgeous, and lovely, and gave me all the feels. It absolutely was me. I wanted to be ready, but I wasn't quite there. I'd taken my first tentative steps onto that dance floor and now I needed to pause to catch my breath. The music was still playing and maybe, just maybe, I'd found the man who'd dance in the rain with me. If it was meant to be, it *would* find a way.

Six years ago

In early June, the year after we lost Dad and Isaac, Mum had a check-up with her oncologist and received the devastating news that the cancer was back, it had spread and, this time, it was incurable. It took her a fortnight to find the right moment to tell me the prognosis – not that there can ever be a 'right' time for news like that – and I wanted to stop the world and get off. I'd already lost Dad, Isaac and Craig and now I was going to lose Mum, very likely all in the space of a year.

I honestly don't know how I made it through the months that followed while I tried to remain strong for Mum and make her laugh like Dad would have done.

Her greatest wish was for me to continue to grow the business so she could say goodbye knowing I had job security. Each month she cut back on her hours at The Starfish Café and she worked her final shift in August.

The regulars wanted to say goodbye and threw her a party. It was touching and uplifting to see how much they cared, but so incredibly heartbreaking. It was hard for them, too. So many were much older than Mum and I heard all the clichés about only the good dying young and how it wasn't right or fair. No, it wasn't. None of it.

I spent my days off with Mum and Angie did the same. Mum insisted she didn't need company. She came from the Dad and Isaac school of thought that life had to go on, hard as that may be. She claimed she enjoyed the quiet time with Willow, but Angie and I both knew she was using it to get everything in order for me, sorting through clothes and paperwork and preparing her funeral wishes.

But then fatigue took hold, the pain intensified, her sense of taste faded, and her appetite diminished as she struggled to keep food down. She didn't argue with the suggestion that one of us should stay home with her each day – *we know you're fine, but Willow needs a walk* – when we knew the end was drawing ever closer.

One evening in mid-November, after she'd eaten a small bowl of chicken broth propped up in bed, she took my hand. 'I want to go into a hospice when the time comes.'

'You do?' I'd assumed she'd want to die in the home she loved and had already had conversations with her Macmillan Nurse about end of life.

'It's not fair on either of us,' she said. 'It's hard enough knowing you'll remember me like this but I can't leave you with a memory of me dying in our beautiful home. Your home. As for me, I'm all about the pain relief and the peaceful ending. Will you promise me not to fight that?'

'I promise.' I'd been through the denial phase early on – *you've fought it twice, you can fight it again* – but we both knew there was no battle left in her and, even if there had been, we knew from the consultant that it was a battle she couldn't win.

'I'll leave you to sleep.' I kissed her on the forehead and went to stand up, but her hand grasped mine with more strength than I'd felt in months.

'I need you to promise something else.'

'Anything.'

'Promise me you'll keep dancing in the rain.'

'Mum...'

'I know it might not feel like there's someone out there having a tougher time than you are right now but, believe me, there will be. There's still so much to be grateful for. The happiness we've had as a family and all the great memories of our time together is one of those things.'

I blinked back my tears. I knew I'd been really lucky with my family. My parents had clearly loved each other deeply and that warmth and affection had transcended into the positive relationship I'd enjoyed with Isaac.

She closed her eyes and I thought she might have drifted off. I gave her hand another gentle squeeze and released it with a sigh.

I lightly kissed her cheek. 'Goodnight, Mum,' I whispered.

As I stood up, her eyes opened. 'Craig wasn't the right dance partner, and you already knew that before you discovered what he'd done to you. The right one is out there somewhere. I'm sure of it.' She closed her eyes once more and drifted off to sleep.

I went downstairs and curled up on the sofa with Willow, the only light coming from the open fire and the red fairy lights on the Christmas tree in the bay window which Mum had still insisted we put up at the weekend as per tradition, even though Christmas wasn't something I wanted to celebrate.

She was right about Craig. When the rain poured, he'd retreated inside. He'd appeared as though he was there for me but it had been in the ways that worked for him – paperwork, sums, arrangements – and not in the ways I'd really needed. Yes, it had been helpful having him do all that, but we could have managed. Martin was good with things like that too. He could have helped. I'd needed a dance partner and Craig hadn't been there for me. Had he ever been? Probably not. Too busy 'dancing' with someone else.

I'd gone round to his house after work on the Friday, the day after the funeral. His car was parked in the street, so I knew he was home. One of his housemates arrived back from work at the same time so he let me in and, with no sign of Craig downstairs, I headed up to his bedroom.

I took a deep breath, telling myself it was for the best, and tentatively eased open his door then froze, my breath caught in my throat.

'Ah! Shit!' Craig cried, eyes wide as he spotted me.

The dark-haired woman on her knees must have taken that as a declaration of his pleasure as she moaned and continued what she was doing with greater fervour. Her hair obliterated her face but I'd recognise my best friend anywhere. How could they? How could she? Katie's betrayal stung more than Craig's.

My natural instinct was to flee but I wanted her to see my face and how much I despised them both right now.

'Oi, Katie!'

She tossed her hair back from her face and looked up. 'Hollie!' She sank back onto the carpet and narrowed her eyes at me, a smug smile on her red lips.

'Serena?'

'Oh, that's too precious. Wait till I tell my baby sister that her bosom buddy thought she was capable of screwing her fiancé behind her back.'

'Serena!' snapped Craig. 'Hollie! This isn't what—'

'Don't you dare!' I glanced down at Craig's crotch; my lip curled in disgust. 'Show some dignity and put it away.' I shot them both one more disgusted look then raced down the stairs. 'I hope you two will be very happy together.'

'Hollie!' Craig called but I wasn't going to stick around. I had no interest in hearing his lies and excuses, but he caught up with me before I'd even made it across the front garden.

'Please listen!' he cried, grabbing my hand.

I snatched it away from him, but spun round to face him, arms crossed. 'Why?'

'Because I love you.'

'And that's how you show it, is it?'

'She took me by surprise.'

'Oh, purlease. Don't insult me with that crap! How long?'

'Six months,' Serena called from the upstairs window. 'And he can't get enough of me.'

And suddenly it all made sense. More late meetings than usual. A lack of interest in the bedroom. I gasped as another puzzle piece fell into place.

'The argument on Bonfire Night. Katie knew?'

Craig looked as though he was going to feed me another lie, but Serena was clearly enjoying this. 'Avery saw us together and she thought I was Katie too.'

'Is this true?' I demanded, staring at Craig. 'You might as well be honest.'

His shoulders drooped and I knew I was going to finally get the truth. 'On Bonfire Night, when they left work, Avery told her she'd heard a rumour I was seeing someone else, although she didn't know who, so Katie confronted me about it outside the café.'

'So that's what you were really arguing about! Nothing to do with you and Avery arguing.'

He nodded. 'I could tell Katie had nothing solid—'

'So you played the innocent and tried to make out she was in the wrong?' I felt incensed for Katie and the difficult position he'd placed her in. If the roles were reversed and I'd heard a rumour about Trey, would I have gone straight to Katie? No. I'd have done exactly what she'd done and confronted him first.

'Then Avery actually saw me with Serena just before Christmas,' Craig continued. 'She mistook her for Katie and had a go at her at work. It was then that Katie realised it had to be Serena I'd been seeing. She told me she'd kill me if I ruined your birthday and Christmas, but I had until the end of the year to come clean or she'd tell you herself. And then stuff happened. I'm sorry.'

He genuinely did look sorry but it didn't move me. 'Do you love her?'

He nodded.

'Then why didn't you have the decency to end it with me?'

'I thought it would be one last quick fling, then I'd settle down with you because I love you, too.'

My jaw tightened and I looked from him to her, hanging out the window, victory written all over her face. 'In what screwed up little fantasy world did you think that "one last quick fling" could ever be acceptable?'

He lowered his eyes and shuffled on the spot.

'He needed a woman,' Serena called. 'Someone who knew what they were doing in the bedroom. Or wherever else the moment takes us.'

That stung but I refused to show it and I wasn't going to stoop to her level and retaliate.

'If you want to hang onto a man in future, you might want to watch a few videos or study some books.'

I clenched my fists. I still wasn't going to retaliate.

'That's what you said, isn't it, Craig?'

The final punch in the gut. He didn't even attempt to deny it.

'Thanks a lot, Craig.' I slipped the ring off my finger and held it up. 'You'd like this back?'

'Thanks for understanding.'

'And thanks for choosing a flashy ring. I can think of several charities who'll be very grateful for the donation.'

'You're not serious.'

'Do I not look serious?'

'You don't donate something like that to charity.'

'No, you're right. It's a faff for them.' I stuffed the ring into my jeans pocket. 'I'll sell it and give them the money instead. Goodbye, Craig.' I looked up at Serena and smiled as it struck me what a lucky escape I'd just had. I lowered my voice. 'And I'd better wish you luck because if you're shackling yourself to her, you're so going to need it.'

As I walked towards my car, head held high, I felt a moment's peace. I'd barely slept, feeling guilty for planning to end my engagement because Craig didn't live up to the dream I wanted, when the reality was he'd already chosen to enter his own nightmare. I knew Serena. I knew how she operated and I wouldn't wish her on my worst enemy. Craig needed all the luck in the world.

* * *

Mum went into the hospice two days before Christmas. I closed The Starfish Café and Angie and I each booked a relative's room so we could take shifts with Mum. Katie stopped by for hours at a time with a ready supply of drinks and hugs.

On Christmas Eve, Mum managed to mumble 'happy birthday' but was barely responsive after that. In the early hours of the morning on Boxing Day, with Angie and I sitting either side of her bed, each holding a hand, she peacefully drifted off to meet Dad and Isaac and rediscover the laughter.

We returned to an empty house, both too numb to speak.

I made us a strong coffee – something to do to take the focus away from the deafening silence – and we sat at the kitchen table, hands clasped round our mugs, cheeks wet with tears.

'I can stay tonight, if you'd like,' Angie suggested.

'Thanks, but that will only delay the inevitable. I need to get used to being alone.'

'You'll never be alone,' she whispered. 'Anything you want, you just have to say. Katie and I are here for you.'

I nodded. 'Thank you for everything. You've both been brilliant and I'm glad you were with me when she went.'

'I wouldn't have been anywhere else.' She stood up. 'I'll let you get settled, but call me if you need me.'

We hugged and, when she stepped away, she removed a card from her handbag. 'Your mum wanted me to give you this after...'

I took the cream envelope from her.

'What is it?'

'She wouldn't say. She just said I was to give it to you after the final goodbye.'

After Angie left, I sat at the dining table with the card in my hands for a good half an hour. At the hospice, there hadn't been any last poignant speeches but inside that envelope were her final words to me.

I swallowed back my pain and retrieved a knife from the kitchen drawer to delicately slit open the envelope. The card inside was a stunning watercolour image of a little girl wearing a pink tutu and red wellington boots, splashing in a puddle as the rain fell around her. A golden retriever, just like Willow, bounced beside her and an open red umbrella lay abandoned nearby.

'Dancing in the rain,' I whispered as I ran my fingers down the image.

With another deep breath, I opened up the card and a photograph slipped onto the table. I picked it up and smiled. It was from their wedding day and showed them in fits of giggles as Dad twirled Mum on the dance floor. Dad's cousin Josephine had taken it and they'd loved it even more than any of the official photos because it represented exactly who they were. An enlarged version hung in their bedroom. I'd frame this smaller one and put it by my bed.

I put the photo down and looked inside the card, both sides of which were filled with Mum's neat, sloping handwriting:

To my exceptional, beautiful angel, Hollie Gabrielle,

If you're reading this, we've said our final goodbye. The house may be empty and the family depleted but please know that you will never be alone. Your dad, Isaac and I will always be with you, in your heart and in your memories.

I have some final wishes:

Look after my wonderful Angie for me. She'll need a new best friend now and I can't think of a better candidate for the job than you. Look after my surrogate daughter Katie, too. I know they'll both be a tower of strength for you but they'll need your strength in return.

Take care of my precious café... but only for as long as it feels right. Get a manager in, knock it down and start over, sell it and travel. It's yours now but do what makes you happy, not what you think would make me happy, because what would make me happy is whatever makes you happy!

Live in the house, rent the house out, sell the house. Again, whatever feels right for you and makes you happy.

Don't dwell on the days we don't have together in the future. Remember instead the wonderful moments we all shared in the past.

Find someone who makes you laugh every day. If you do that, you can face anything that life throws at you.

Keep dancing in the rain. There is always, ALWAYS someone having a tougher time than you. And when you're ready, you'll find your dance partner and you'll never need to compare your relationship with someone else's because you'll know that what you have is special and true.

Smile. Sparkle. You've got this!

You and your brother made your dad and I so very happy and proud. We couldn't have asked for two finer children. I know you'll go on and do great things with your life and we'll be right by your side every step of the way.

Love forever,

Mum xxx

Through blurry eyes, I closed the card and gazed at the little girl in her wellington boots. 'I promise, Mum. I promise it all.'

Present day

I needed some air, so I took Pickle for a walk along the esplanade by Hollie's house before driving home. Bad timing. Yeah. Completely understood that. It would never have been a long-term thing with Cara, but it might have gone beyond that first date if I hadn't met her near my birthday.

I had so many questions I wanted to ask Hollie and so much I wanted to share in return. She wasn't ready yet. I understood that, too. After Dad died, I'd dreaded returning to school. It had been in all the local newspapers and on the news. They'd known my dad had drowned on my birthday and it was my fault. Nanna said they'd be nice to me but I knew different. I was already an outsider, occasionally hanging out with the other kids nobody liked, but even they abandoned me.

Throughout school and college, I remained an outsider and

struggled through a day at a time. It was only when I started at university that I felt a sense of ease round strangers. They didn't care about my background. They cared about my opinions on things, and I finally found a small circle of trusted friends in whom I eventually confided when we shared a student house together in our second year. They dragged me down the pub and we drank to my parents and nobody went weird on me and tried to avoid me. It was a first.

Last summer when I visited the lifeboat station, I wanted to be honest from the start. No more shying away from the past because that tragedy had shaped the person I was today; the person who Nanna was proud of.

'Why are you interested in joining the crew?' Chief asked.

'On my ninth birthday, I begged my dad to take me to the beach after school. The seas were rough and we should have gone home. I went down the old slipway on North Bay, got pulled into the water and my dad drowned saving me. I had a fear of the water for many years after that, but I visited the slipway on the twentieth anniversary of Dad's death and decided it was time not only to conquer my fear but to play my part in educating others and helping save anyone who found themselves in difficulties. I save people in my day job as a nurse and I want to do that at sea too. I've been the terrified person in the water and I know first-hand what the aftermath can be when it goes wrong.'

Chief ran his hand across his ginger beard and nodded slowly. 'You're how old now?'

'Thirty-three. I'll be thirty-four in November.'

'The old slipway on North Bay, you say? That would make you Bobby Reynolds' son.'

'That's right.'

He nodded again. 'I remember it well. I was crew that night. I'm sorry we couldn't save him.'

'Thank you. But you were there, and I know you tried. I want to try, too.'

'Everyone has different reasons for wanting to join us and yours is probably the most touching and personal I've heard. Your training starts on Monday at seven.' He thrust his hand out and shook mine tightly and vigorously. 'Welcome on board, son.'

Joining the RNLI had been the best thing that ever happened to me. They all knew, and they understood. We didn't talk about it, but I knew I could if I wanted to. I was a valued part of a team instead of an outsider and it had changed how I felt about myself.

Irene next door was the only person outside the RNLI who officially knew I'd joined, although I'm sure word would have spread round the Old Town after I'd been spotted in The Lobster Pot with the crew. She said I seemed calmer and less intense. I felt it. So I was going to stay calm about the situation with Hollie. It wasn't like she'd regretted the kiss; it was bad timing and I had no reason not to believe her. Nanna used to say the best things in life were worth waiting for and something in my gut told me that Hollie would be worth the wait.

Out of season, The Starfish Café closed on a Monday, giving me a two-day break. Sundays were typically spent beachcombing and creating in my workshop and Mondays started with a visit to the beach at Starfish Point to pick up litter and say hello to the seals.

The absence of vehicles in the car park hopefully meant I'd have the beach to myself as I didn't feel like chatting today, although it was still early which helped.

There was a biting cold wind freezing my cheeks and making my eyes stream as I made my way down the wooden steps beside the café. At the bottom, as it always did, the rugged beauty took my breath away and I paused to take it all in. A trio of grey seals lay between two clusters of rocks just ahead of me. Bigger and with longer bodies than the common seals, they also had longer, straight muzzles and their nostrils were almost parallel. Resting on one of the rocks above them was a white and grey common seal. I adored both varieties but the smaller common seals just nudged it for me. Their flatter faces and V-shaped nostrils gave them such adorable puppy-like faces and, as a dog lover, that had me smitten.

I rested my backpack against a rock, removed the litter-picker attached to the side, billowed out a bin bag, and swapped my warm gloves for some heavy-duty ones. There were no bins on the beach as the sea came right up to the rocks at high tide but there were a couple of bins further up the steps and visitors were pretty good at using them. Most of the litter I collected appeared to have been swept in with the tide.

As I worked my way round the cliff edge where most of the rubbish gathered, my mind was still on that kiss with Jake. That amazing kiss. And how understanding had he been about the whole timing thing? When he walked down the drive with Pickle, it took every ounce of willpower I had not to call him back and tell him I'd made a mistake. It was a battle of wills against head and heart. My heart was calling out to him, but my head was urging caution.

I'd honestly thought that the one thing that would make me more wary about a new man would be my past experience with Craig but, if anything, that was spurring me on. In the short time I'd already spent with Jake, I knew he was completely different. He was kind, sensitive, creative, cared for people, cared for animals and, boy, could he kiss! And that connection between us was so strong, but why had I had to meet him now? Why not in the spring when I was in a better place?

They all thought I was strong. They all thought I was coping. And most of the year that was how it was. Until Bonfire Night when the melancholy took hold as the countdown to Christmas commenced.

Time's a great healer. Life goes on. Platitudes I'd heard so many times, but they were right. The pain lessened a little each year as I found my way of living without my family by my side, but I still had my moments and, outside of work, the best way for me to get through the last two months of the year was to throw myself into my woodworking. The focus, the skill, and the sense of achievement from repurposing 'rubbish' into something beautiful helped me make sense of the loss. I needed to channel all my energy and enthusiasm into that and not into a relationship.

An hour later, I'd gathered four bin bags full of litter – predominantly plastic bottles – and placed them beside the steps. I rolled my shoulders then poured myself a coffee from the flask in my backpack and sat on a flat rock.

The wind had dropped a little, although it was still bitterly cold. The trio of grey seals had gone and in their place was a mother nursing its pup. I'd never grow tired of seeing that.

Mum had told me that Granddad loved the seals. She showed me photos of him stroking them and feeding them fish. The colony had only been about thirty-strong back then and he and Granny had named them all. The thinking behind the best way to treat wild animals had moved on since his time. I never tried to touch them or feed them, and asked visitors to maintain a safe distance.

Certain seals seemed to favour the beach more than Starfish Arc or Starfish Isle where the lighthouse was, and the locals had named a few of the more notorious characters. One of the common seals had been named Chaplin because he had small spots in a circle round one eye, looking like a monocle, and the largest grey seal was nicknamed Tank.

I watched the seals for a while as I sipped my coffee. The rolling of the waves against the shore and the occasional crunch of sand and shingle as seals moved along the beach soothed me but didn't give me any clarity. I needed someone to talk to about Jake. I needed Katie.

When I returned to Sandy Croft after finding Craig and Serena together, Katie was already parked outside waiting for me. Serena had wasted no time phoning her to tell her what a horrendous friend I was for thinking she'd do the dirty on me with my fiancé. Serena had thought it would come between us, but she underestimated the power of our friendship. Over a bottle of wine in the garden, we talked it over. Katie understood how I'd easily mistake Serena for her – especially when I didn't think Craig even knew Serena – and I understood why Katie had kept her suspicions from me, telling Craig he had to come clean.

Between them, Angie and Katie got me through those dark months after I lost Mum and they'd both been there for me ever since. Katie's boyfriend Trey was the best of the best as he'd never once complained about the amount of time she spent with me and, in the first couple of years, it was a lot! We'd then settled into a routine of every Thursday night together. It didn't matter whether it was a meal, a trip to the theatre, a walk, or a coffee round one of our houses, it was a good opportunity to catch up. I'd missed it so much this year. Katie and Trey had been granted a year's sabbatical from work and had flown out to New Zealand just after the New Year.

Even from the other side of the world, she'd stayed in regular contact, phoning, messaging me regularly and Skyping me every Thursday if her travel plans permitted. She was off the grid at the moment on the Inca Trail to Machu Picchu in Peru, although I knew she'd call me as soon as the trail was complete and she was settled in a hotel with a WiFi connection. Then it wouldn't be long until her return to Whitsborough Bay in mid-December. I couldn't wait to see her again.

The sky had darkened and, suspecting rain would be imminent, I packed my stuff away, grabbed the bin bags and began the trek back up to the car park. The climb could be a challenge for those not used to it but there were a couple of landing areas where wooden benches provided an opportunity for recovery. I was used to it and didn't need them, but I liked to pause by each simply to take in the stunning view. I'd paused by the second one when a voice startled me.

'Hollie?'

I twisted round. 'Jake! What are you doing here?' My heart thumped as I gazed at him. He hadn't shaved and the dark bristles were so alluring on him.

He looked as surprised to see me as I was to see him. 'Erm... we thought we'd photograph the seals.'

At the mention of 'we', I realised Pickle was with him and bent down to fuss the dog.

'Sorry. With the café being closed, I didn't think you'd be here,' Jake continued. 'I promise we're not stalking you.'

I smiled up at him. 'I come litter-picking on a Monday.' I straightened up. 'I'm sorry again about yesterday. I hadn't expected... I didn't mean to...'

He gave me a reassuring smile. 'It's fine. It's...' He frowned and wiped his cheek. 'Was that rain?'

'It might have been. Clouds are looking ominous.'

'I normally check the weather app and I didn't this morning. So you're okay?'

'I'm good. I realised after you left that we didn't make any arrangements for me to have Pickle this week. Unless you'd prefer me not to after...'

'No! Not at all!' Jake insisted. 'But don't feel you have to if you're uncomfortable.'

'You don't make me uncomfortable, Jake. Far from it. This time of year does and that's my issue that I keep trying to work through and—' I squealed as the heavens opened. 'Run!'

Jake grabbed two bin bags and I grabbed the others and we raced up the cliff as the sky darkened and icy rain pelted us. Muddy puddles quickly formed on the steps and I did my best to dodge them but I was already wet through.

'To the café!' I called to him as we reached the top. I tossed the bags in the direction of the wheelie bins to sort out later and fumbled in the front pocket of my backpack for the café keys.

We kept the heating on a timer and I was so grateful for the blast of warm air as we burst through the doors.

'That's the last time I forget to check my app,' Jake said, peeling off his sodden jacket.

'I'll grab us some towels.' I raced to the kitchen and returned with a pile of hand towels.

I tossed a couple to Jake and crouched down to rub Pickle dry.

'That was some impressive running,' Jake said when I'd finished with Pickle. 'I could hardly keep up with you.'

'I've done that in the rain more times than I care to remember. And hail. Snow. Storms.' I simultaneously slipped off my jacket and rubbed a towel over my hair as I spoke and momentarily unbalanced.

'And you don't like storms,' Jake said, his voice husky as he placed his hand under my elbow to steady me.

'No. I don't.' Except our own personal lightning storm, which was back, sparking between us, fizzing with anticipation.

'Your face is wet,' he said, gazing down at me with an intensity that made me breathless.

'So's yours.'

We edged closer to each other, eyes locked. I was desperate to kiss him and, from the look in his eyes, he felt the same, but I couldn't hurt him by repeating yesterday. It wasn't fair to either of us.

'You have no idea how much I want to kiss you right now,' I whispered, lightly dabbing my towel against his damp cheeks.

'And you have no idea how much I want you to, but I know you need time.'

I held my breath as he stroked the back of his hand across one cheek followed by the other. 'And I'll be right here waiting for you.' He smiled and his eyes twinkled. 'Was that a song lyric?'

I smiled back. 'It sounds familiar.'

'Well, I mean it.'

'Thanks for understanding.' We were standing so close and his lips looked so inviting that I couldn't resist stepping up on my tiptoes and giving him the briefest of soft kisses.

'I'd better make some drinks.' My cheeks felt on fire as I stepped away from him, realising I needed some distance as I was in danger of grabbing him, all thoughts of bad timing flown out the window.

* * *

Two hours and three drinks later, the rain had eased to a steady drizzle. I waved Jake and Pickle goodbye and ran my hands through my dry but tangled hair.

He'd asked about the seals and whether they were popular with photographers and we talked about the sorts of photos he was interested in taking. I told him about the differences between the grey and common seals, showing him photos I'd taken on my phone including ones of Chaplin and Tank.

I don't think either of us would have noticed how long we'd been talking if he hadn't received a text, interrupting our flow and drawing our attention to the time. I could have happily spent all day chatting to him but we both had things to get on with so we made arrangements for him to call round with Pickle on Wednesday night as he'd be working two long day shifts on Thursday and Friday. I couldn't wait for Pickle to have his first sleepover. But I also knew I couldn't wait to see Jake again. And the thought of him having a sleepover inflamed my cheeks once more.

Back at Lighthouse View, I dug out my phone and my stomach lurched as I re-read the text that had arrived while I was at The Starfish Café:

⊠ From Chief
Final assessment confirmed for a week on
Saturday — 27th Nov — starting 9.30am You've got
this, Mouse. See you tonight

Two more training sessions to go. I'd been ready for months. Chief had said so and I felt it myself. But that didn't stop me bricking it. I wasn't sure if that was because of the formality of being assessed or because it meant that I'd need to share that part of my life with others outside the RNLI. Probably the latter.

Irene had wanted me to let her know as soon as I had a date, so I went next door to give her the news.

'That's exciting,' she said, handing me a cup of tea. 'This is still a secret, yes?'

'Yes, please.' Despite her curtain-twitching and love of gossip, Irene could be trusted to keep confidences.

'Such a shame your nanna isn't around to see you passing out as crew but I bet she'll be watching you a week on Saturday and cheering you on. Are you worried?'

'About Nanna watching me or the assessment?' I grinned at her. 'No. The training we get is exceptional and I'm confident I know my stuff. I'm just nervous about what comes next.'

'Telling people?'

I nodded. 'It's a big thing.'

'I know it is, but I really think it's time you started letting people in. It's not right, you know. Handsome young man like you, living all alone because the past keeps haunting you.'

'I might not be alone for much longer.'

She put her cup and saucer down on a side table with a clatter and leaned forward, eyes wide. 'You've got a girlfriend?'

'Not quite. I've met someone and I think she...' I paused, hardly able to believe I was going to say the words out loud. 'I think she could be the one.'

'Oh, my! Oh, Jake!' Irene clasped her hand over her heart. 'You've never said that before. Not even close.'

'We're not together. We're friends at the moment. She's got a tragic past like mine and it's a bad time of year for her, so she doesn't want to leap into anything, but she's going to look after Pickle while I'm at work. When she's ready, hopefully...'

Irene gazed fondly at me. 'She'd be a fool not to have you, Jake MacLeod.'

'We'll see. When the timing's right, things will hopefully work out.'

'Take care of that heart of yours. I've seen it broken over your dad. I don't want that to happen again.'

'Me neither. I'll be fine. She's made me no promises, so I've got to relax and take it slowly.'

'Slow and steady wins the race,' Irene declared brightly.

'Let's hope so.'

From the moment I said goodbye to Jake on Monday, I couldn't stop thinking about him. I ricocheted from regretting not kissing him properly to congratulating myself on an impressive and sensible display of willpower.

When I arrived for work on Wednesday morning – my first day working with Angie, who'd taken annual leave on the Tuesday – I was determined to act casual and not mention the one man and his dog who occupied my every waking (and sleeping) thought. But Angie wasn't going to let it go that quickly.

'How was beachcombing with Jake?' she asked as soon as she'd hung her coat up.

'Good.' I glanced up from the fruit scones and couldn't prevent the stupid grin spreading across my face. There was no way Angie was going to miss it.

'I haven't seen that smile for a long time,' she said, eyeing me with suspicion. 'Are you two together?'

'No.'

'But you'd like to be?'

'No. Yes. I don't know. It's complicated.' The grin was still there.

'It doesn't have to be.'

I raised my eyebrows at her. 'Says the woman who misses her husband and hasn't made any steps towards a reconciliation.'

She sighed as she tied her apron. 'Okay, so sometimes things *are* complicated. Tell me why you and Jake are complicated.'

'You know why.'

'Surely not Craig.' She narrowed her eyes at me. 'Your parents and Isaac? Hollie!'

'This time of year's hard,' I muttered, realising too late that I'd given away more than I intended.

'How hard?'

I lowered my head and resumed pressing the cutter into the fruit scone mix.

'Hollie? How hard?' She eased my grip off the cutter and twisted me round to face her. 'Oh, honey! Why didn't you say anything?'

'You all kept saying how strong I was being and how brilliantly I was coping and I didn't want to admit that I wasn't because I *do* cope most of the time but, when Bonfire Night arrives, I find it becomes a bit too overwhelming. I manage to keep it together at work but, when I get home, I sometimes lose it.'

She took my hand in hers and squeezed it. 'Should I let you into a little secret? So do I.'

'You're not just saying that to make me feel better?'

'You can ask Felix and Pixie if you don't believe me. I'm a mess. There's snot everywhere. In the run-up to Christmas, I go through twenty boxes of tissues and four family tubs of chocolates.'

'You do not!'

'Okay, maybe it's just the nineteen boxes. But do you know what? It's okay to do that. When you have the good fortune to have known three of the best human beings in the whole wide world, there's going to be a great big gaping hole without them and it's okay to get upset about it. There's no rule book that says that at year three or four or five you've got to stop crying and move on.'

She drew me into a hug, and I wished I'd said something to her before now. I didn't need to ask her why she hadn't shared her pain because I knew; she'd been trying to protect me.

'Four family tubs of chocolates?' I asked, giving her a last squeeze.

'Yes, but not full tubs. I leave the coconut ones.'

'That's all right, then.'

We smiled at each other, and it struck me that we were both strong. Getting upset wasn't about being weak. It was about caring.

'Do you know what's not okay?' Angie said, her voice serious. 'Letting the tragedy from the past – or fear of it repeating itself – stop you from having the happy future you deserve.'

'That's good advice. You should probably listen to it.'

She frowned at me then I saw realisation dawn. 'I probably should.'

'So will you?'

'I will if you will.'

I'd walked into that one. 'I want to,' I admitted in a quiet voice.

'And so do I. First steps are always the hardest.'

'I've already taken the first steps. He knows. He doesn't know how Dad and Isaac died, but he knows. He lost his parents too when he was little.'

'Then it sounds like you might be kindred spirits.'

I turned back to the scone mix and picked up my cutter. Kindred spirits? We probably were. What a comforting thought.

* * *

By mid-morning, the sun was out; a welcome sight after two wet days. With it came a steady stream of customers taking advantage of a break in the weather to get some fresh air.

Betty and Tommy arrived for their usual tea and scones and bought a few of my tree ornaments, telling me two of their great-grandchildren were visiting on Saturday so the Christmas tree would be going up.

'It's a little earlier than usual,' Betty said, 'but they have so much fun doing it.'

'And then you rearrange all the ornaments when they've gone,' Tommy said, patting his wife's hand affectionately.

'I can't help it, Hollie. They haven't quite mastered the art of spreading things out so we tend to have a small section with about fifty decorations on it and the rest of it's bare.'

'How old are they now?' I asked. I prided myself on remembering most details about their family but, with three children, seven grandchildren and nine great-grandchildren, I couldn't keep track of names and ages. Betty and Tommy often joked that they couldn't either.

'Ferne is six and Lola is four. They're so adorable.'

'Tell Hollie what you found in town,' Tommy prompted.

'Oh, yes. I was inspired by your wonderful mum's mission to find an angel who looked like you and I found a Ferne and Lola angel. I can't wait to see their faces.'

'Mum would have loved that,' I said, feeling touched that she could still have an impact on our customers six years on.

'Will you carry on the tradition when you have children?' Betty asked.

'Children? I need to find a man first.'

'We thought you already had, my dear,' Tommy said.

'What would make you think that?'

'Because you have your sparkle back,' Betty said. 'And it's far brighter than it was when that Craig was around. It's such a thrill to see you in love again.'

'I'm not in love. We're not even together. We've just met. We're friends.'

'The lady doth protest too much, methinks,' Tommy said, winking at me.

'Tommy!' I cried, wagging my finger at him. 'Stop stirring! Now, what can I get you today?'

While I prepared Betty and Tommy's order, the conversation about children replayed in my mind and suddenly it wasn't just Pickle and Jake I pictured at Sandy Croft but two children running round, playing pirates and smugglers like Isaac and I had done. It was a family home. It should be filled with children's laughter instead of my sobs. But as for me being in love with Jake, they were being ridiculous. Weren't they?

'I'm nervous, Pickle,' I said, glancing at the dog in the rear-view mirror as I drove across town on Wednesday evening. 'Why am I so nervous?'

Pickle's ears twitched and he yawned.

'Oh, I'm sorry! Am I boring you with my problems?'

The biggest problem was probably that I was talking to my dog and half-expecting an answer.

'Slow and steady wins the race,' I muttered, repeating what Irene had said to me. 'Let's hope so, eh?'

Pulling to a stop on Hollie's drive, my stomach did a loop the loop. I'd never experienced feelings like this before. Not even close. It hadn't gone unnoticed. In the pub after training on Monday, I'd had several comments: *Why the big grin? Did you win the lottery at the weekend? What's perked you up?* I hadn't been aware I was grinning. It's not like Hollie and I were even together, and it concerned me that I must come across as a right misery most of the time. I needed to get a handle on that.

When I opened the car door to release Pickle, the kitchen door on the side of the house opened and Hollie stepped out. My breath caught. She looked gorgeous in ripped jeans and a baggy white sweater with rainbow stripes across it. Her hair was piled messily on top of her head and I imagined unclipping it and running my hands through it... and I had to stop thinking!

She scooped Pickle up and showered him with kisses. Was it wrong to feel jealous of my dog?

'How have you been?' she asked me as I joined them.

'Good. You?'

She held my gaze. 'Good. Do you need to rush off?'

'No.'

'Come in, then. Kettle's on.'

She put Pickle down and he went to explore while she made the drinks. We made small talk about how our day had been but she seemed a little tense, as though there was something she wanted to say. When she handed me a mug and we sat down in front of the fire, there was a moment's silence as she stared into the flames. She was definitely building up to something.

'I was engaged once,' she said eventually, turning to face me.

My stomach lurched and I reminded myself she'd used the past tense.

'His name was Craig. He was the grandson of one of my regulars at the café and we were friends for a few years first. Looking back, we probably should have stayed friends, but it became more and it was good for a while. And then it wasn't.' She gazed down into her mug and sighed. 'We were too different. We wanted different things from the relationship and from life and it turned out he was already getting some of those different things elsewhere.'

'He was cheating on you?' The man was clearly an imbecile.

'With my best friend Katie's sister. I had no idea there was someone else but that wasn't the worst part. The worst part was that it had been going on for six months and it never stopped after we lost my dad and brother. He spent his days here helping with the paperwork and funeral plans and his nights with her. I found them together the day after the funeral.'

'That's bang out of order,' I said, disgusted for her.

'When I had some time and space to reflect on it, do you know what hurt the most? It wasn't that he was seeing Serena or even that he was seeing her at the worst time in my life. It was the lies. While they were seeing each other, Craig and I had confirmed the wedding date, booked the photographer and the car, chosen where to go on honeymoon so we were busy making plans for the future together and he was secretly destroying it.'

Incensed for her, I wanted to call him a string of names, but I sensed there was more to come.

She gazed into the flames. 'Then I realised I was just as bad. I wasn't seeing someone else. I could *never* do that. But I was merrily making plans for the future when it was a future I wasn't convinced about.' She looked back at me with a weak smile. 'I'd swept under the carpet all the things about our relationship that didn't make me happy, trying to convince myself that the things that *did* make me happy were enough. I was lying to myself and I was lying to him. For a while, I thought I was no better than him, but the difference between Craig and me was that I made the decision to end it when I realised. Funnily enough, that's how I caught them together. Unplanned visit. After that, I promised I'd always be honest with myself and others, but old habits die hard. I had a conversation with Angie today and I admitted that I've not been honest with how I cope – or occasionally don't cope – with this time of year and I haven't been honest with myself about a few things, starting with how I feel about you.'

The temptation to kick in the defence mechanism and say something flippant was strong – *you can't stand the sight of me and you're going to dognap Pickle* – but I somehow managed to say something sensible instead. 'And how is that?'

Hollie put her mug down beside her and leaned forward. 'I really like you, Jake. *Really* like you. The moment I met you, there was something there and it's got stronger every time since.'

Her eyes were wide and her vulnerability was clear to me. This was huge for her. 'I felt it too,' I assured her.

'I thought I loved Craig, but...' She shook her head. 'This is new and it's exciting but it's also a little scary.'

'Completely uncharted territory for me.'

'You like me, then?'

Slow and steady wins the race. But this was a conversation about honesty, right? 'Like you? Hollie, it's so much more than that.'

A pink tinge shaded her cheeks and her eyes sparkled.

'We can take things as slowly as you want,' I said. 'We can just be two new friends who share a dog and enjoy each other's company for now and see where it takes us if you like. If and when you're ready for more or if your feelings change and you don't want more, just keep being honest with me. What do you think?'

'I think I might *like* you even more than I did before.'

As she gazed into my eyes, my heart thudded.

'If we're being honest right now,' I said, my voice coming out all husky, 'all I can think about is kissing you again.'

'Me too, but that's not taking things slowly.'

'Which is why I'm staying firmly on this sofa.' A line from one of Nanna and Irene's favourite films sprung to mind although I couldn't remember the exact wording. 'This is my dance space and that's yours. I don't step into yours and you don't step into mine.'

'*Dirty Dancing*,' Hollie whispered, tears glistening in her eyes.

'Did I say the wrong thing?'

She smiled and sniffed as she brushed away a couple of tears. 'No. It was perfect. I know the tears wouldn't suggest that, but it really was. I'll explain why another time.'

'Whenever you're ready.'

She twiddled with her necklace. 'Which brings me onto the next thing I want to talk to you about. I want to ask you about what happened to your parents and I want to tell you about my family, but would you mind if we don't share our stories just yet?'

'Fine by me. I know how hard it is.'

'I want to enjoy getting to know you. I want to feel normal again and I know it might seem strange saying let's not share our pasts when our losses are something we have in common and are possibly the thing that's drawing us together. Does that make sense?'

'Every word of it. Look, I know this is a difficult time of year for you, but can I give you some advice?' When she nodded, I continued. 'Someone once asked me this question: *Do you want to live in the past or live for the future?* Every time I feel the dark aspects of the past clawing at me, I ask myself that. I'm not saying I've cracked it because that would be a lie, but I'm getting there and I'd like to help you get there, as a friend or as something more.'

She chewed on her lip. 'I *do* want to live for the future. And I'd like you to be in it.'

I smiled at her, my heart racing once more. 'In that case, do I have permission to invade your dance space to give you a hug?'

'Definitely.'

HOLLIE

As Jake held me, my recent words to Angie came back to me: *We both know that a man – even a gorgeous, amazing, sweep-me-off-my-feet future-husband-material one – is not going to magically make the sadness go away.* Yet here he was with his arms round me. Definitely gorgeous and amazing. Potential future-husband-material given the intensity of my feelings towards him already. And, although he hadn't magically made the sadness go away, he had helped me find moments of pure happiness. I'd smiled and laughed – genuinely rather than polite customer interactions or convincing Angie and the team I was fine – more in the twelve days since I'd met Jake than I had in the previous six years.

And, to top it all, he understood why I might want to be cautious and hang onto that happiness for a little longer. We would share our stories. It might even be in the next few days or weeks but, for now, it felt right to just live in the moment and see where it took us.

* * *

The house felt empty when Jake left, which was crazy when he'd only been in it twice and had ventured no further than the kitchen.

'How about a tour of your new half-home?' I asked Pickle. 'Come on.' He raced me upstairs and sat on the landing, tail wagging.

'This was Mum and Dad's bedroom,' I told him, pushing the door wide open. He padded into the room and sniffed the furniture and rug. 'They're not with us anymore. They'd have loved you.'

After Mum died, I kept the door to my parents' bedroom closed and the room completely untouched, but Angie pointed out that the last thing they'd have wanted was for me to keep it as a mausoleum. Mum and I had sorted through and cleared out Dad's belongings a couple of months after he died and she'd have wanted us to do the same for hers, although she'd already done a lot of the sorting herself.

The Mother's Day after Mum died made sense to Angie and me. I was going to be upset that day anyway and it wasn't something Angie celebrated. She didn't have children and was barely in touch with her own mum, who'd run off with another man when Angie was thirteen. It was fitting that Katie joined us too, with my mum being more of a mother to her than her own.

There'd been tears but plenty of laughter, too. Certain clothes triggered memories of nights out or holidays and pieces of jewellery reminded me of birthdays, anniversaries and Christmases. It was hard, but it needed to be done.

Angie and Katie insisted I redecorate. Martin and Trey helped us paint and move the furniture around. We completed the fresh look with new bedding, curtains, a rug, lamps and pictures, although I retained a few special items like the framed photograph of my parents laughing on their wedding day and Mum's jewellery box.

I'd been unsure about changing quite so much, but Angie and

Katie were right to push. I was never going to make it my bedroom, but it was no longer a shrine, which helped me feel more comfortable in our family home without my family, even though I still only ventured inside occasionally to clean or air the room.

We also redecorated Isaac's bedroom on the top floor and relocated my bedroom to the larger front room on the middle floor. It didn't make sense to confine myself to what Isaac had jokingly called 'the attic' when I was living alone.

Pickle and I went up to the top floor and into Isaac's old bedroom at the front of the house. The wall opposite the window was still covered in the cork tiles from 'The Smuggler's Key'. Darker shapes on the cork showed where my brother had pinned things for the longest, the limited space round them having faded in the light. I ran my fingers down the tiles, feeling the indentations where pushpins had punctured the cork.

I scooped up Pickle, sat on the bed and rested him on my knee, stroking his ears and back. He really was the most gorgeous dog. 'Isaac would have loved you too. And he'd have loved Jake. Like I do.'

My phone pinged and I smiled at the GIF Jake had sent of the dance space scene from *Dirty Dancing*. He'd captioned it: *My dance space is ready whenever you are.* Of all the things he could have said to me, he'd picked something about dancing. Was that a sign?

'Oh, my goodness, let me have cuddles with you!' Angie said, picking up Pickle moments after she arrived at work the following day. 'You are absolutely gorgeous.' She turned to me. 'I didn't get a good look at him on Saturday, but you're right about him looking like a teddy bear. He's adorable. How was his first night at yours?'

'Amazing. He slept in Willow's old bed and was as good as gold.'

'And how was Jake?'

'Also amazing.'

'And...?'

'And have you phoned Martin?'

She laughed. 'Point taken.'

The morning flew by. It was another bright day, so several walkers dropped by along with our regulars. When the lunchtime rush died down, Mrs Sultana appeared. She unwound her striped scarf as she made her way towards a window booth.

I gave her a couple of minutes to settle then headed over to take her order. 'Hello! Good to see you back. Is it the usual?'

She tore her gaze away from the sea. 'Yes. Large pot of tea, fruit scone, flapjack, please.' Her grey eyes were clouded with tears and her soft voice merely a whisper.

'Are you all right?' I asked, my gut telling me she wasn't.

She turned away and looked out of the window once more. I hesitated, wondering whether she was going to share something or whether I should push. I didn't want to make her feel uncomfortable, so I returned to the counter to prepare her order.

'I'm worried about her,' I said to Angie in hushed tones, making sure no other customers were in earshot. 'I think she's upset. I asked if she was all right, but she didn't answer.'

'At least you asked. That could mean something to her.'

'I hope so. There's always been an air of sadness about her, but I've never seen her like this before. Do you think she's lonely?'

'Possibly. I've never seen her with anyone.'

I placed her scone on a plate. 'I hope she isn't lonely. It breaks my heart thinking we might be the only people she sees all week and we still don't even know her name.'

'We've all tried, though. We can't force someone to interact with us.'

As I carried Mrs Sultana's order across the café, I resolved to try again, and was surprised when she beat me to it after I'd placed her items on the table.

'I expect you wonder why I order a fruit scone and pick the fruit out of it,' she said, still facing the window.

'The thought had crossed my mind.'

She turned to face me. 'It's a silly thing. My husband and I always went to a café on the seafront. The Harbour Tea Parlour. Did you know it? It closed about six years ago.'

'Is that the one that's a vegan restaurant now?'

'Yes. Albert and I would go there every week for tea, a scone and a flapjack. They only ever did fruit scones and Albert hated fruit but he loved scones so he'd pick the sultanas out. We'd sit in a window seat overlooking the sea and have a nice chat. Then, one morning, he didn't wake up.'

Tears rushed to her eyes, and I instinctively offered her a napkin. 'I'm so sorry for your loss.'

She dabbed at her eyes. 'Thank you. He'd have been ninety today. We were together for sixty-one years, married for fifty-nine. We never had children. We couldn't, but that was okay because we had each other, but...' She dabbed her eyes again. 'When he died, I still went to the Harbour Tea Parlour every week and ordered the same thing and I found myself removing the sultanas, just like he'd done. Looking down at a tea plate with a few crumbs and a pile of fruit made me think of him. As I say, it's a silly thing.'

I swallowed the lump in my throat. 'I think it's lovely. I bet he would have done that too.'

She smiled – something I'd never seen her do before. 'I'd like to think so. Anyway, the café closed and I wasn't ready to let go. I tried others but they weren't right and one day I drove out here, saw the sea view, and it was perfect. So I come here and, even though Albert never visited, I look out at the sea and pick out the fruit and hold the scarf I knitted him and I can imagine he's here with me.'

I was in danger of needing one of the napkins too. I blinked back my tears. 'I'm sure he is. He's probably laughing and joking with my mum.'

'Oh! I'm sorry. I thought that other lady was your mum. You seem so close.'

'She was my mum's best friend and she's like a mum to me. Mum died before you started coming here. Nearly six years ago.'

'The same year as my husband.'

Silence fell. 'I'll leave you to eat.'

'It's Sylvia,' she said. 'I know you've all asked before. I don't know why I didn't say.'

'That's okay. I'm Hollie.'

'Thank you for asking, Hollie.'

'About your name?'

'No. Earlier. For asking if I was all right. I can't remember the last time anyone asked me that. And I don't think I've spoken for this long since Albert died.'

She reached for the teapot and poured it into her cup while I fought back the tears once more. That had to be the most heartbreaking thing I'd heard in a long time.

* * *

There were only a few customers left when Sylvia had finished her final cup of tea. I added a cupcake with a candle sticking out of it and a fresh pot of tea to a tray and carried it over to her.

I placed the cake in front of her and lit the candle. 'I thought you might like to wish Albert a happy birthday. On the house.'

She looked up at me, eyes wide, her hand pressed against her throat. 'That is so kind.' She closed her eyes for a moment, presumably making a wish, then blew out the candle.

'I brought you a fresh pot of tea too,' I said. 'And a listening ear if you'd like to talk about him.'

'Don't you have things to do?' she asked, sounding surprised.

'Loads of things, but my number one priority is my customers and, right now, I'd love to hear about Albert.' I made sure I didn't sound pushy and the choice was completely hers.

'I think you'd better get an extra cup.'

I whipped a mug out of the pocket in my apron. 'Already came prepared.' I sat down and smiled at her. 'So what was he like?'

* * *

'That was a beautiful thing you did this afternoon,' Angie said as we walked across the car park early that evening.

'What sort of world do we live in where six years pass without someone asking an elderly lady if she's all right?'

'I know you'll be feeling guilty for not chatting to her all the times she's been in here but remember you've tried for conversation before, loads of times. The difference is that today she was ready to answer the question and admit she wasn't all right and was actually really lonely.'

'I feel bad about calling her Mrs Sultana now.'

'Don't. It was never a name used vindictively. You asked her real name and she didn't share until today. You did nothing wrong.' Angie shivered. 'It's freezing out here so I'll say good night and you know what else I'm going to say?'

'Mum would be proud of me?'

Angie hugged me. 'Every single day, but with cream and sprinkles on the top today.'

* * *

Pickle and I hadn't been home for long when my phone rang. I squealed as Katie's face appeared on the screen with a FaceTime request.

'Oh, my God! I wasn't expecting to hear from you tonight. Or is it day for you? And where are you?'

'It's late morning and we've flown to Lima to rest for a few days by the sea after all that walking. I'm in my hotel room and Trey's in the shower.'

'How was the Inca Trail and Machu Picchu?'

'Amazing...'

Katie gave me an overview of the trip, said she'd added some photos to Instagram, and we chatted more about the rest of her travel plans.

'Enough of me wittering on,' she said. 'How are you doing?'

'Work's busy. We've hit that excited Christmas vibe.'

Katie tutted. 'Did I ask you about work? I could have sworn I said *how are you doing?* Emphasis on *you*.'

'Okay. I'm good. Actually, I've met someone and...'

She squealed so loudly that Trey came running out the hotel bathroom to check she was okay, which had us both in peals of laughter, as he wasn't even wearing a towel.

'Well, that was more than I'd bargained for,' I said when she'd shooed him away, reassuring him she wasn't hurt.

'I can't believe you let me witter on about ancient monuments when you're seeing someone!'

'Not seeing. Just met...' I filled her in on Jake and Pickle, smiling at her facial reactions. I had such a warm and fuzzy feeling as I spoke, picturing them both so clearly. Especially Jake.

'Two things. Firstly, I need to see photos. Secondly, and much more importantly, what's wrong with you? Why haven't you jumped his bones?'

'Katie!'

'Hollie! I'm serious! You're in love with the guy!'

'I never said that.'

'You didn't have to. It's obvious. Even Trey can tell that.'

Trey, now wearing clothes, appeared on screen and waved at me. 'I heard it.'

'See!' Katie cried. 'What's with the *let's take it slowly and see what happens* attitude? I say dive right in and *enjoy* what happens.'

I heard a knock on their door. 'That's the cleaner so we need to head out but, when he picks up the pooch tomorrow, I say drag him upstairs and have your wicked way with him. Exorcise the ghost of Craig the tosser and start living again. Promise?'

'I promise I'll think about it. Have a good day.'

The call disconnected and, moments later, a text arrived:

⊠ From Katie
I'll call you again soon and I expect juicy details!!!!! Stop over-thinking & rip off that sticking plaster! Love you xxx

'Jump his bones,' I said to Pickle. 'What kind of expression is that?' Where would I even begin? My sex life with Craig hadn't exactly been a thrill a minute or very regular. He claimed he didn't like the idea of sex while my parents were in the house, which was fair enough. But if we went to his, it was his housemates. If I tried to make advances, he'd often shrug me off, saying he was tired or he had an early meeting.

He'd been my first and it had all been very nice and gentle but I'd often wondered if my lack of experience was why he'd turned to Serena, who was the other extreme according to Katie. And I hadn't appreciated him discussing our disappointing sex life with Serena; one of the many unforgiveable things he'd done.

I couldn't help wondering if the problem was actually me; that I'd somehow turned him off rather than on. But Jake hadn't acted like that. From the way he held me and kissed me in the workshop, I'd already felt more passion from him in the space of an hour than I'd felt in two and a half years with Craig. Maybe Katie was right. Maybe I really did need to rip off that sticking plaster and exorcise all my demons.

✉ From Hollie
We're in the workshop so come straight in when
you get here. Pickle's missed you. And so have
I x

The text arrived as soon as I got home from my shift on Friday evening, and I couldn't get showered and changed quickly enough.

I could hear machinery as I approached the side of her workshop and eased open the door. Hollie had her back to me and was cutting or drilling a long chunk of driftwood, sending sawdust flying everywhere. I didn't want to make her jump while she was wielding a power tool so I waited until she put it down before I fully pushed open the door.

'Hello?' I called.

'Jake!' She whipped round to face me and pushed her hair back with her safety goggles. 'You're earlier than I expected.'

'I missed you both, too.'

She grinned. 'You got my text.'

'I thought I'd get here quicker if I didn't reply.'

She hugged me and kissed me lightly on the cheek, sending a ripple of warmth through me. I knew it was only a hug of friendship, but I couldn't help wishing it was more.

'Where's Pickle?' I asked, stepping back and glancing round the workshop.

'He was with me at first, but I took him over to the kitchen when I started with my tools. I wasn't sure if he'd like the noise and I'd rather check that out while you're here as I can't make the noise and keep an eye on him at the same time.'

'Good thinking. What are you making?'

'Tealight holders. Easy to make but really effective,' she said. 'And, of course, each one is unique because of the wood. I've got a crate of chunky driftwood in assorted lengths over there, already cleaned and treated to annihilate any lurking creepy crawlies. I add my hole saw bit to my drill and away we go. Do you want a go?'

'Okay. I've never used that drill bit before.'

'Then you're in for a treat. It's so satisfying.'

We each selected a piece of wood from the crate.

'Mine's a good length for five tealights in it and yours will suit three,' Hollie said. 'I used to carefully measure them out but now I instinctively know how to space them.'

She pulled down her safety goggles and handed a pair to me. 'Pop these on. It's not the sexiest of looks but, as you saw, the sawdust goes everywhere so safety first.'

I watched in awe as she pressed the drill into the wood, the drill bit spinning to carve out a tealight-sized circle. Sawdust covered her hands and workbench and segments lodged on her hoodie and in her hair as she expertly spaced five holes across the wood. As she worked, she chewed on her lip as though it helped her to concentrate.

When she'd finished, she placed the drill down, removed her goggles and shook out her hair. 'What do you think?'

'Of the candle holder or how impressive you are with a power tool?'

She giggled. 'Both.'

'Full marks for each. As for what you were saying earlier about safety goggles not being the sexiest look, I might have to disagree.'

'Really?' She looked doubtful.

'I think it's the whole goggles, sawdust-in-the-hair, creative genius at work, power tool combo that does it for me.'

'If this turns you on, you should see me operating the lathe.'

'Now you're being a tease.'

She gave me a sultry look then sashayed over to a shelving unit next to her apothecary drawers and removed a rectangular chunk of pine from it. 'It's going to have to be my *big* lathe.' She placed massive emphasis on the word 'big' and her eyes sparkled with mischief as she ran her fingers down the wood then placed it on the workbench.

'What are you going to do with the wood?' I was going for seductive, but Hollie was fighting to keep a straight face so suspected I sounded more like a cheesy porn star.

'We're going to turn this bad boy,' she said, mastering the seductive tone. 'We're going to start by smoothing off his rough edges.'

Hollie tried to talk me through what she was doing but she struggled more and more to supress her giggles. I had no idea words like 'pulley', 'motor', 'tool rest' and 'lever' could sound quite so dirty. And don't get me started on 'head stalk' and 'tail stalk'. But when she produced a long tool with a wood handle and curved metal end and introduced it as a 'spindle roughing gouge', we both lost it.

She removed her goggles and sank onto one of the stools while tears streamed down her face. I held onto the workbench, barely able to catch my breath. Every time we came close to composing ourselves, all it took was for one of us to glance at or touch the spindle roughing gouge and we were off again.

'Oh, my God, Jake!' she cried, wiping her damp cheeks when we'd finally calmed down. 'I haven't laughed like this in years. Thank you. I needed that.'

'Me too. I honestly don't remember laughing this much in my whole life, so thank you.'

Her eyes widened. 'Ever?'

I sank onto the stool as I realised how true it was. 'Ever.' It wasn't like I'd never laughed. Nanna had a great sense of humour and was always laughing and joking. Sometimes patients or colleagues at the hospital made me laugh, although not always intentionally, and there was always banter with the crew. But I'd never experienced proper deep, belly-aching-can-barely-breathe laughter like just now. With Nanna, guilt had held me back. With everyone else, I was always on high alert, not wanting to fully let go. With Hollie, I was able to be completely me. I felt relaxed. I didn't need to worry that she'd suddenly throw in a difficult question that would kill the mood and remind me what had happened.

Hollie pressed her fingers to her lips. 'Oh, Jake, that's heart-breaking.'

I shrugged. 'I *have* laughed before. Just never like that and I can't tell you how good it felt. When I get home, I'll finally be able to...' I tailed off, stunned it was going to happen. I hadn't thought about it in so long, but it had to mean something that I'd rediscovered it at the same time Pickle and Hollie came into my life.

Hollie looked at me expectantly.

'Did you ever have a Rubik's Cube?' I asked.

'No, but Isaac did. He could solve it, but I was useless. I used to have to take it apart. Why?'

'For my seventh birthday, I begged Nanna to buy me a Rubik's Cube. She thought I was too young for one but I had my heart set on it. She was right, as always. It was far too complicated but Larissa said she'd show me how to do it. I should have known she was up to something because she was never nice to me but I naïvely handed it over. She took it apart and dropped the pieces on my bed, saying "and now all you have to do is work out how to put it back together" then left my room, laughing.'

'That's awful.'

'That was mild for her. Obviously I had no idea how to put it back together, it wasn't worth telling on Larissa as she'd get her revenge, and I didn't want to tell Nanna I'd broken it so soon so I shoved the pieces in the back of a drawer and forgot about them. Nanna found them when she helped me clear my bedroom after Dad died. I didn't need to say anything. She knew Larissa was behind it. She put the bits in a plastic bag and said she'd fix it later but we both forgot. The next few years were a struggle although I'll explain more about why another time. When I started senior school, they found me a counsellor but I wasn't interested. I thought that talking to some random stranger wasn't going to bring my parents back so what was the point?'

'I know that feeling,' Hollie said when I paused.

'I reluctantly agreed to give it a try for Nanna's sake. I got home from school the day my first counselling session was scheduled and found Nanna with the bag of Rubik's Cube pieces. She said that the cube was like my heart. It was broken but the pieces were all still there. The point of the counsellor was to help me put the pieces back together and that Nanna would keep helping too. She suggested that sometimes progress would be good and two or even three pieces might be fixed and sometimes there'd be hitches and a piece might fall out but, over time, we'd end up with a whole Rubik's Cube.'

'That's such a beautiful analogy.'

'Isn't it? She poured the pieces into a glass bowl and placed it in the middle of the kitchen table. When I got back from my first session, she asked how my pieces were doing. I swirled my hand round the bowl and shrugged. She said to give it time. The same thing happened after the second time but, after the third session, I picked up a piece and added it to the centre stalk. Nanna cried.' Tears rushed to my eyes as I pictured the look of relief on her face. That woman had been nothing short of amazing.

'Do you still have the cube?' Hollie asked.

'Still in the bowl but it's on a shelf now.'

'And is it fixed?'

'There are still six pieces left but it's just struck me that three of those can be added to the stalk. One for finding Pickle, another for finding you and whatever it is we have, and the third for finding laughter. So you've just helped to fix me.'

'That's just made me feel all warm and fuzzy. If I had a broken Rubik's Cube, there'd have only been about six or seven pieces on the stalk but, after meeting you, there'd be a lot more. You're helping to fix me, too.'

We gazed at each other and then she was off her stool and in my arms, kissing me with fervour. I ran my fingers through her hair as I pulled her close, never wanting to let her go.

'I don't think we're going to get those tealight holders made tonight,' Hollie said, stepping back and smiling at me. 'And it's a bit chilly in here. Let's go in the house. Pickle will want to see you.'

I wondered if that was it – another sudden moment of passion before her head told her to stop – but she gently kissed me again. 'And then we can continue where we left off. If you'd like to, that is.'

'Is that a trick question?'

She switched off her drill, locked up the workshop, and led me by the hand into the house. Pickle raced up to me and I picked him up, feeling unexpectedly emotional at how much I'd missed my little buddy. I planted a kiss on his head and was rewarded with a lick. I could have done without that, but I was chuffed that he seemed pleased to see me.

'Let's go through to the lounge,' Hollie said.

An enormous high-ceilinged room, it was packed full of Victorian features including a curved bay window containing a sparsely decorated Christmas tree, intricate cornicing, and a real fire, although it wasn't lit. A warm cream was painted above the picture rail and a deep forest green below it. The room could have looked dark, but cream bookshelves and cupboards built into the recesses and light curtains made it feel warm and bright.

She indicated that I should sit on a dark grey two-seater sofa while Pickle flopped down on a rug in front of the fireplace.

'Where were we?' She knelt on the sofa beside me and ran her fingers through my hair and down my cheek, across my scars. 'My best friend Katie said I should stop over-thinking things, rip off the sticking plaster and go for it with you.'

'Your best friend Katie sounds wise.'

She searched my eyes. 'I'm scared.'

'What's more scary? Giving something a go and it not working out, or never trying and always wondering?'

There was a moment's pause. 'The second one.'

She closed her eyes and kissed me once more. It was a slower, more tender kiss than before, but just as fantastic. When I met her best friend Katie, I owed her a drink.

'Are you okay?' Jake asked as I pulled away a few minutes later. 'Did I hurt you?'

My heart glowed at his genuine concern. 'No but this sofa's too small to get comfortable on.' I extricated my limbs from Jake's, clambered in a somewhat undignified manner off the two-seater and slipped my hand into his. 'Come with me. Pickle, stay! Good boy.'

As he silently followed me upstairs, his hand clasped in mine, I wondered whether I should clarify that moving into the bedroom was about being comfortable and no guarantee of sex, but I thought about him asking if he'd hurt me just now, and checking it was okay to kiss me in the garage on Sunday. I didn't need to verbalise it. He wasn't going to make any assumptions.

Although who was I kidding about no sex? It wasn't a sure thing but, right now, it *was* what I wanted. I'd never wanted anyone like I wanted Jake. Not even close. Did it matter that I hadn't known him for long? Was there a rule?

I led him into my bedroom, silently congratulating myself for changing the bedding last night and making the bed before I left for work this morning. I'd never been a messy person so at least I didn't need to worry about discarded coffee mugs growing mould or dirty knickers on the floor. Butterflies chased each other round my stomach as I switched on the bedside lamp.

'You look nervous,' Jake said when I straightened up.

'I am. Sorry.' I ran both my hands down my jeans. 'My palms are sweating. I knew I'd mess this up.'

'What are you messing up?'

'This.' I sighed. 'Put me in a kitchen with a bowl, a spoon and some basic ingredients and I can whip up something delicious off the top of my head.' I lowered my eyes to the floor. 'But put me in a bedroom with a gorgeous man and I might need the recipe book.'

Jake tilted my chin so he could look me in the eyes. 'I haven't made any assumptions about what's going to happen. We can take things as fast or as slow as you want, Hollie. But if we did get to that point however soon or far down the line, are you saying it would be your first time?'

There was no judgement or laughter in his voice. 'No, but Craig was the only one. We slept together regularly, by which I mean slept. We were together for two and a half years and I can probably count the number of times it was anything more on two hands. My fault. Apparently I was rubbish in bed.' I felt so at ease with him and I knew it was my personal hang-ups because of my ex that was causing the nerves now; not Jake himself.

He brushed my hair back from my face with both hands and lightly kissed me on the forehead, then the tip of my nose. I felt dizzy as a surge of longing flowed through me. He eased me down beside him on the bed and took my hands in his.

'Listen to me carefully. Whatever he said to you or however he made you feel, he was very wrong. It takes two people to create the magic but, if he really wanted to apportion blame, it sounds like he needed to look closer to home.'

'I'm sorry.' I squeezed his hands. 'I know I shouldn't let the ghost of boyfriends past haunt me.'

'It's hard to not let the past haunt us and I don't just mean exes. We've both had much deeper losses than that. Remember that question I mentioned about the past or the future?'

'I *do* want to live for the future.'

He kissed my hand, which sent the butterflies scattering, then he looked round the room. 'Is it the bedroom? Does it feel too much? We can go back downstairs if you want. Or we can return to your workshop. There was a chill in the air but I don't think it was caused by the ghost of your ex.'

I laughed at that. 'Thanks, but it's not the bedroom. My bedroom used to be on the top floor and this was the guest room so Craig was never in here. Ignore me. I don't know what's come over me. I was fine in my workshop and downstairs. Why should this be any different?'

'Believe me, you were more than fine in your workshop both times. Way more. Close your eyes and imagine we're back there... Now take three really deep breaths, in through your nose and out through your mouth, relaxing your shoulders a little further each time you exhale.'

I could feel the tension flowing from me with each breath out.

'Keep your eyes closed. Keep breathing slowly and deeply and tell me what you can hear.'

I listened for a moment. 'The water gurgling in the pipes. Someone laughing outside. The clock ticking in the lounge.'

He lifted my hand and placed it over my heart. 'What can you feel?'

'My heart thumping.'

'Fast?'

'Yes.' I could feel his warm breath on my face, almost taste his kisses, and my heart rate quickened.

He placed my hand on his chest. 'What can you feel now?'

'Your heart. It's racing faster than mine.'

He lightly kissed my lips. 'That's the effect you have on me. You have no reason to be scared. You have no reason to doubt yourself. Fast or slow, I'm with you every step of the way.'

I opened my eyes and smiled at him gratefully. 'You might just be the kindest, most thoughtful and caring man I've ever met.' A frown creased his brow. 'Did I say the wrong thing?'

He smiled and shook his head. 'No. You just surprised me. Nanna wrote a letter to be read out with her will and she said those exact same words.'

'Then you'll know they're true.'

I leaned forward and kissed him this time. I wasn't ready to go all the way just yet – far too ambitious – but I was certainly ready to take a few baby steps. Hopefully the others would follow.

Jake stayed on Friday night and returned to Sandy Croft for when I finished work on Saturday evening. We didn't take that final step and it wasn't that I was afraid or worried. It was because I wanted to savour and enjoy each and every step as I fell deeper and deeper for him.

Sleeping together without the sex couldn't have been more different than sleeping with Craig. Jake held me and kissed me and made me feel like I was his complete world. We still didn't talk about what had happened to our parents, but memories seeped naturally into conversation and I was soon full of adoration and admiration for his nanna and his neighbour Irene who had clearly been such a strong and positive influence on his life.

'Did you ever hear from your sister again after she attacked you?' I asked as we lay in bed facing each other on Saturday night.

'No. I asked the police to drop the charges. I wanted it to end. I've never heard from her since. I wish her well and I hope she finds her peace somehow, but there's no chance of us ever having a relationship. It wouldn't benefit either of us.'

'Does she have a family?'

'She's married, but they don't have kids, which is a good thing. She's so angry and bitter, I can't imagine her being a good mum. What about your brother? Did he have a family?'

'He had a girlfriend. Bex. They lived together and he was planning to propose to her on New Year's Eve. She hadn't known.'

Guilt nudged at me. Every time I thought about Bex, I visualised her sinking to the floor, her body shaking with anguished sobs, after Mum handed over the stunning engagement ring Isaac had picked out for her. Their happy future was one of the many things that had been snatched away that tragic night.

I'd adored Bex but it had been too hard trying to support her through her loss while being there for Mum and dealing with my own grief. We stayed in touch and met up occasionally. She came to Mum's funeral, but she didn't stay for the wake. Had she made contact after that? Had I? It was all a blur. I shouldn't have let her disappear out of my life.

'I've made you sad,' Jake said, stroking my arm.

'I do feel sad, but it's not because of you. I'm a bit angry with myself. I haven't thought about Bex for such a long time. We lost touch less than a year after Isaac died and I shouldn't have let that happen.'

'Had they been together long?'

'Five years. I wonder what she's doing now. It's hard to believe it's been seven years since Dad and Isaac died. That sounds like so long ago yet sometimes it feels like only yesterday that it all happened.'

'The passing of time can seem fluid after losing someone you love.' He adjusted position so he could put his arms round me while I pressed my head to his chest, listening to his heart beating and thanking my lucky stars that Carole Jessop had abandoned Pickle that evening and brought them both into my life.

'I wonder if she's met someone else,' I said after a while.

'Would it bother you if she's moved on?'

'It would probably feel a bit strange at first, but I know it's what Isaac would have wanted. He was pragmatic about things like that. He'd have wanted her to find happiness.'

'Sounds like you miss her.'

'I do. I miss them all.'

'I can't do anything about your family, but you can do something about Bex. Do you still have her number?'

'Yes.'

'It's never too late to reach out.'

I gently kissed his chest, loving the way he asked questions, but didn't push for more, recognising that I needed to reveal details gradually.

He kissed the top of my head. 'If I could wave a wand and magic the pain away, I would,' he whispered.

'You have no idea how much you being here is helping.'

On Sunday morning, we were up early to catch the sunrise over Fellingthorpe Brigg down the coast – a narrow rocky peninsula stretching out into the sea. It could have been a scene from one of Nanna's romance films – arms round each other as we sat on a wooden bench on the cliffs above the Brigg, with Pickle draped across our legs, watching the sky turn gold. As the sun rose higher, it brought with it streaks of amber and red.

'It looks like the sky's on fire,' Hollie said.

'Like my heart.'

She looked up at me, wide-eyed, and I cringed before we both burst out laughing.

'I'd like to put it on record that I have *never* said anything like that before and have no idea where it came from.'

She kissed me. 'It was cheesy, but I love the sentiment.'

I nearly added, 'And I love you,' but something held me back. I felt it and I was certain she felt the same, but I'd promised not to rush things. There'd be a right moment and probably very soon.

After the sunrise, we went down to the beach and gathered some driftwood while Pickle raced up and down with a stick of seaweed in his mouth. It all felt so relaxed and comfortable, as though Hollie had always been in my life.

What a weekend it had been so far. For me, it was packed with firsts because I'd never had a regular relationship. I had no idea that little things like staying up into the early hours talking, holding hands while out walking Pickle, cooking together, and relaxing in front of a film could feel so special.

'It's a shame you didn't have your camera,' Hollie said as I drove back to Whitsborough Bay. 'That was a stunning sunrise.'

'It was. I'll come down another time with my camera, but seeing it with you beat seeing it through a lens any day.'

She rested her hand on my knee. 'Have you always been so romantic?'

'Was that romantic?'

'Yes, and so was the heart on fire comment, even though we laughed at it.'

'I had no idea I was romantic. I've never said things like this before. I've never felt like this before.' I glanced across at her and smiled. 'It's because of you.'

'I like it. Makes me feel special.'

'You are special.'

* * *

Hollie had originally planned to take photos of her painted houses and get them onto her website across the weekend and I didn't want her business to suffer because I wasn't ready to say goodbye so I suggested we go via Lighthouse View to pick up my camera and I could take the photos for her.

'Do you want me to nip in and grab my camera or do you want a tour?' I asked as I parked outside.

'A tour would be great. And can I see some of your photos, particularly the ones of wood?'

I hesitated. It was one thing offering to take photos of her houses – a straightforward piece of photography – but, aside from Nanna, I hadn't shown anyone my photos since Cara's critique. But this was Hollie. I doubted it was in her nature to say anything as cutting as Cara. If she didn't like something, I bet she'd convey that in a constructive way that still left the person feeling positive.

'Jake?' Hollie prompted.

'Yeah, I can do that.'

Pickle followed us as I showed Hollie round the downstairs and a quick look into my room and Nanna's, but my pulse quickened as we made our way up to the top floor.

'Wow! I love this room!' Hollie exclaimed. 'I love how the stairs come straight into it.' She rushed to the window. 'Lighthouse!'

I laughed. 'Told you.'

'It's a stunning view.' She stepped away from the windows and I bit heavily on my lip as she studied various framed prints on the walls.

'These are all yours?' she asked, her back to me.

'Erm... Yes.' I hated that I'd hesitated.

'Oh, my God! Jake! These are exceptional.'

'You really think so?' *More uncertainty. Get a grip!*

'Absolutely. I'm not just saying that because they're yours. This one here of the groynes? I feel like I'm in the photo, as though I could reach out and touch them and feel the grooves on the wood and the damp. And this one...'

Nanna had said she loved my photos, but Nanna was biased and would have said that about anything of mine, but hearing Hollie waxing lyrical about what she liked about the different images and, more specifically, how they made her feel, was more than a simple *they're really good.* She saw and felt everything I'd endeavoured to create. She understood. She believed in me and, for the first time since that summer with Dad when he'd raved about the improvements I'd made, I started to believe in myself.

* * *

Late that afternoon, I stood on Hollie's drive in the cold and darkness and kissed her goodbye. I didn't want to leave her and the feeling was mutual, but she had work to do and I wanted to check in with Irene.

'I'd love to see you tomorrow night, but there's something I do on a Monday that I can't miss.'

'What is it?'

I came so close to saying it, but it would have led to questions which would have meant opening up about my past and I'd promised to wait. I stroked a lock of hair behind her ear. 'I want to tell you, but it's connected to what happened in the past.'

She nodded. 'In that case, enjoy your evening and you can tell me all about it when we're ready to share our stories.' She kissed me. 'Thanks for understanding why that's important to me right now.'

'You don't have to thank me. I know it's hard.'

Pickle and I got in my car and I waved as we left. I hoped she'd feel ready to share her story soon because I felt ready to share mine. I wanted her to know. With Nanna gone, I still had Irene to talk to, but it wasn't the same as talking to someone my own age about the impact it had and was still having on my life. Hollie couldn't be a more perfect person with whom to do that.

Sharing my story with Hollie didn't feel scary. Sharing it with everyone else was what hurt but it was nearly time. I had my final assessment coming up and then it would be official. Everyone would know and I'd be the subject of gossip at the hospital. I'd rather they speculated about my sexuality or relationship status than know the truth about my past, but it had been inevitable it would come out at some point. With Hollie by my side, that prospect felt easier to deal with.

I couldn't stop smiling as I drove back to Lighthouse View with, already on a countdown until Tuesday when I'd drop him back at Sandy Croft and stay for dinner before starting two night shifts.

We visited Irene for about an hour and she pumped me for information about Hollie, eager to know whether I still thought she was the one. More than ever!

Back in the kitchen at Lighthouse View, I reached the glass bowl down from the shelves and lifted out the partially fixed Rubik's Cube. I let Pickle into the garden then sat down and carefully inserted three of the pieces, just like I'd told Hollie I would. Turning the cube over in my hands, I reflected on the day Nanna gave it to me and the various reasons pieces had been added or removed over the years.

'It's only taken twenty-three years but I'm nearly fixed, Nanna,' I said. 'I wish you were here to see it.'

Placing the cube back in the bowl, I picked up the three final squares.

'For when I'm officially crew,' I said, placing one back in the bowl. 'For when I tell Hollie I love her.' I dropped the second one in the bowl. 'And for when she says she loves me.' I released the final one.

I already knew I loved Hollie but feeling it and saying it were different things. Saying it meant I had finally let go of the past – of the regret and the guilt – and had given myself permission to accept love and happiness. That journey wasn't quite complete, but it felt like I could reach out and touch my final destination. Most unexpected.

'And all thanks to you, buddy,' I said as Pickle reappeared in the kitchen. I picked him up and ruffled his ears. 'Do you remember when Hollie said she thought we were meant to find each other. I think we were meant to find Hollie too. Don't you?'

Hollie was right up there with Nanna on the amazing woman stakes. Running The Starfish Café was impressive enough without her Hollie's Wood business running alongside it. She was smart, funny and confident but there was a vulnerability that I found endearing. An element of that understandably came from the loss of her family but it also seemed to stem from the way her ex-fiancé had treated her. His loss, my gain.

A bark from Pickle on Thursday night made me jump. I raced to the window to see Jake pulling his car onto the drive, then rushed to the kitchen door.

He exited the car, picked Pickle up and showered him with kisses. Craig hadn't been a dog person. I should have known then that he wasn't right for me.

I'd tell Jake what happened to Dad and Isaac soon but, for now, I would enjoy the laughter. After all, Mum said laughter was what made her relationship with Dad so strong.

Jake put Pickle down on the kitchen floor, then planted a soft kiss on my lips, making those butterflies soar once more. 'I've missed you both so much.'

'I've missed you too.' I closed the door and pulled him close to me. The back of his hair was still damp from the shower and he smelled deliciously citrussy fresh as I kissed him with longing. With reluctance, I pulled away when the oven timer pinged.

I told Jake to relax with Pickle while I dished up dinner. It was lovely seeing him sitting on the floor in front of the fire teasing the dog with a tugger toy, although Pickle seemed more interested in clambering over Jake instead of playing.

When we'd finished eating, Jake impressed me by gathering up the plates, rinsing them and loading them into the dishwasher. Craig would never have done that. If he was at Sandy Croft, he viewed himself as a guest to be waited on. Why hadn't that bothered me at the time?

'Nearly at the weekend already,' I said when Jake returned to the table. 'I have no idea where this week has gone. You're not working, are you?'

He ran his hand through his hair and took a couple of glugs from his water.

'Are you okay?' I asked, concerned that he seemed nervous but flummoxed as to why asking him about his shifts would warrant that reaction.

He grimaced. 'You know how we agreed that we wouldn't talk about what I do on a Monday night because I said it relates to what happened in the past?'

'Yes.'

'Well, I'm doing something on Saturday morning that connects to the thing I do on a Monday night and, once I've done it, the thing I do on a Monday night won't just be a Monday night anymore.' He relaxed his shoulders. 'I just heard what I said. It sounds all cryptic and mysterious and I don't mean it to be, but I promised you I wouldn't talk about it until we're both ready to talk about our pasts.'

My stomach dipped into spin cycle. He obviously wanted to come clean about whatever it was, but I just needed that little bit more time. Last weekend had been amazing and, even though I'd only seen him for an hour and a half on Tuesday when he dropped Pickle off, that had been special too. I just wanted to hold onto that feeling of happiness for a little longer. But that wasn't fair on Jake.

Who did I think I was dictating what subjects were taboo just because of my own emotional baggage?

'We can talk about your story if you're ready. I'm listening.'

He gazed at me for a moment then smiled. 'No. When the time's right, we'll do it together. Actually, there's something I wanted to ask you. Do you have plans for Saturday night?'

'No.'

'Would you like to go out with me? I can pick you up and we could have a few drinks in town.'

A date? My heart raced. 'I'd love that.'

We topped up our drinks after dinner and moved into the lounge.

'I was talking to Angie earlier,' Hollie said as she lay against my chest. 'Remember I was telling you about her and Martin? His sister turned sixty this week and she's having a party on Saturday night. She sent Angie an invite and Angie turned it down, but she's changed her mind. She's decided it's time she and Martin came face to face again.'

'Is she going to ask him for a divorce?'

'She doesn't want one. She still loves him and I wouldn't be surprised if he still loves her. I'm hoping they'll see each other, realise they've been idiots, and try again. Actually, what I really want is for them to admit they still love each other and take it from there. It's only three words. It's not difficult.'

'You think people should be honest about their feelings?' I asked, unable to resist testing the water.

'Completely. Unless it's inappropriate and could cause problems. When Isaac met Bex, she was with someone else. He never told Bex how he felt about her until she'd split up with Sean. It wouldn't have been fair on her while she was in a relationship. But under normal circumstances I say go for it, as long as the person is saying it because they absolutely 100 per cent mean it.'

'You don't think there's any sort of time that needs to pass before it's said?'

'Dad knew he loved Mum by the end of their first date. He bottled telling her when he walked her home and ended up returning an hour later and throwing some gravel up at her window to get her attention because he couldn't bear her not knowing.' She smiled dreamily. 'Isn't that so romantic? My dream is for Angie and Martin to admit it to themselves and to each other and move back in together. I'm determined I'm going to make it happen.'

'You little meddler! I seem to remember a certain café owner apologising to me for Angie's matchmaking attempts between us two.'

Hollie laughed. 'That was different. I'd only just met you and, at the time, I was adamant that I didn't want to let anyone in.'

'And now?'

She twisted round to face me. 'It's too late. You're already in.'

She held my gaze and my heart began to race. This felt like the right moment. I brushed my thumb gently across her cheek. 'I love you. And I promise I mean that 100 per cent.'

A smile slowly spread across her face. 'I believe you. And I love you, too.'

As we kissed, I don't think I've ever felt so happy or relaxed.

'I can put another two pieces in my Rubik's Cube now,' I said, stroking her hair back from her face. 'You've nearly fixed me. Thank you.'

She looked at me with such tenderness then kissed me with passion. Moments later, she pulled away, her breathing rapid, grabbed my hand and tugged me towards the door. 'There's something else you can help fix right now.'

'Are you sure? There's no pressure.'

'I've never been more certain about anything.'

We raced up the stairs and along the landing to her bedroom. She lifted my T-shirt over my head and ran her hands down my chest to my stomach then raised her arms so I could remove her T-shirt. Her eyes never left mine and that connection between us felt more powerful and arousing than anything I'd ever felt before.

I had finally let love in and, assuming I passed my assessment on Saturday, I'd be able to insert the last piece in the Rubik's Cube and it would be fixed. I never thought that day would come.

My stomach was in knots as I made my way down to the seafront on Saturday morning. This was it. My big moment. I'd been training for over a year, but I'd really been building up to this for twenty-six years since that stormy night when I lost Dad and nearly lost my own life.

Chief was waiting for me outside the lifeboat station and he greeted me with a strong handshake. 'How are you doing, Mouse?'

'Bricking it.'

'You've got this, son. We'd never have put you forward if we didn't think you were more than ready.' He clapped me on the back. 'Come on then, let's get you sorted.'

As he led the way into the building, I took a backwards glance towards the Old Town. I could just make out the roof of Lighthouse View near the top. Nanna hadn't lived long enough to see me start my training but she'd been there every step of my journey before that, cheering me on while I progressed through an intensive course to overcome my fear of water and keeping me strong each time I took a backwards step. She'd joined me at early bird swimming sessions at the pool and undertook a steady breaststroke up and down the slow lane while I built my strength and speed in the fast lane. She gave me a surprise Christmas gift of a lifesaving skills course with one of the pool lifeguards and I took to it so quickly that when a position became available for the children's afterschool classes I jumped at it, eager to put myself in the best possible position to join the RNLI. At least Nanna died knowing I was on a mission, and it would happen.

* * *

'What made you want to join the crew?' Gavin, the assessor, asked after I'd kitted up and the introductions had been made.

I glanced at Chief, who gave me an encouraging nod. *Stand tall, shoulders back, eye contact, and just say it.* 'When I was nine, my dad drowned trying to save me...'

'That's a powerful incentive to join,' Gavin said. 'Sorry for your loss, but thank you for channelling that traumatic experience into something good.'

'Jaffa and Simba will be your crew today,' Chief said. He clapped me on my back again, then Gavin and I made our way over to the ILB. They'd both have my back and they'd follow my guidance to the letter, willing me to pass out.

Sharing my story with Gavin didn't seem nearly as hard as sharing it with Chief when I enquired about volunteering, or with the rest of the crew when I first started.

I wished Hollie knew and kicked myself for not sharing it with her the other night, but I'd seen the fear in her eyes. She wasn't ready and I wasn't going to insist she hear my sad story just because it fit in with my timetable. She'd shared more and more memories of her dad and brother, mainly from childhood, so I sensed it wouldn't be too long. Just as well because, from Monday, assuming I passed my final assessment, I could be paged at any point when

Hollie and I were together. I needed to explain that I was an RNLI volunteer before that happened, even if that meant I didn't explain why I'd joined up.

* * *

We were in the middle of a scenario when the pagers went off. Gavin turned to me and shrugged. 'Sometimes happens that way. We'll keep going with the assessment but it's now a real-life rescue.'

I radioed the station for details. The coastguard had received a 999 call from a member of the public reporting an empty kayak in the sea at North Bay. Reports of empty vessels usually indicated a casualty in the water. As I steered the ILB up the coast to North Bay, adrenaline pumping through me, I hoped we'd find the casualty fast and that they were wearing decent kit and a lifejacket. On a choppy sea in late November, the right kit could mean the difference between life and death for a casualty in the water.

It didn't take long to find the casualty, but the rescue was a challenging one. After being capsized by a rogue wave which then separated him from the kayak, he'd had an exhausting swim against the current to the giant boulders that acted as sea defences. He'd gashed his leg when clambering to safety and, suffering from hemophobia – a fear of blood – he'd had a panic attack. Thankfully he'd been wearing a thick wetsuit or there'd have been a severe case of hyperthermia to cope with, too. It was tricky getting close enough to the rocks without damaging the ILB but we'd practised this sort of manoeuvre plenty of times during training nights so I had the expertise and I had the support from Jaffa and Simba.

We finally retrieved him and his kayak (to avoid a false alarm), transferred both safely to shore, and moved the casualty to a waiting ambulance as he was going to need stitches.

I thought I'd be nervous throughout the rescue because of the assessment, but everything I'd been taught by Chief and the crew, coupled with my nursing background, helped me stay calm and completely in control of the situation.

I was buzzing with adrenaline when we returned to the station. A real-life rescue and I was now officially a helmsman. Nanna would have been 'tickled pink', to use one of her favourite sayings.

I had a debrief with Chief and he shook my hand. 'Pleasure to formally welcome you as crew. You did a great job today.'

'Thank you. I loved it. I'm so grateful to be part of the team and I promise to work hard and never let you down.'

'Just keep doing what you're doing, and you'll be fine. Off you go and celebrate and we'll do drinks with the crew on Monday.'

* * *

My entire body ached as I traipsed up Ashby Street, but I was chuffed to bits and couldn't stop grinning.

Irene must have been watching out for me because she rushed out of Seafarer Lodge with Pickle hot on her heels. 'How did it go?'

'I passed out. Officially crew!' I'd done it! I'd honoured Dad's memory.

'Oh, young Jake, I'm so proud of you.' She launched herself at me. Irene wasn't usually demonstrative like that, so I knew how much it meant to her. 'Have you got time for a brew?'

'Do you have biscuits?' I asked, bending down to stroke Pickle.

'Always.'

'Then let me get showered and changed and I'll be back round.'

'So proud,' she repeated, making her way back indoors with Pickle.

I chuckled to myself as I unlocked the door to Lighthouse View and rolled my stiff shoulders. What would Hollie's reaction be? I was itching to tell her how I'd spent the day and to let her into that part of my life. Would I have the chance to do that tonight?

Before I went upstairs to shower, I removed the Rubik's Cube from the glass bowl and, taking a deep breath, inserted the final piece. Tears rushed to my eyes and I could barely breathe as I flopped down into the chair. Another major achievement! After all these years of battling, I'd finally come through the other side. My broken mess was whole again and it would never have happened without the two strongest and most inspiring women I'd ever met: Nanna and Hollie. And a lost shih tzu.

'We heard you singing in the kitchen,' Betty said as I carried the order over to her and Tommy on Saturday morning. 'You have your sparkle back.'

I hadn't realised I'd been singing that loud. 'I'm just in a very good mood today.'

They both studied me. 'She's definitely in love!' Tommy declared.

'I am not! I... okay. This time, you're right. How can you tell?'

Betty chuckled. 'When you get to our age, you've seen it enough times to recognise it. Is it the young man with the shih tzu?'

'Yes. His name's Jake and he's...' Amazing, warm, gorgeous, funny, considerate, talented and... I flushed from head to toe as I thought about the last two nights. Oh. My. God! What an eye-opener!

'Definitely love,' Betty said, saving me from answering. 'I'm thrilled for you, my dear. You deserve this so much.'

'Thank you.'

* * *

Mrs Sultana – Sylvia – appeared later that afternoon. I hadn't seen her all week and I'd been worried she might have felt awkward about opening up to me and decided to stay away.

She came straight up to the counter and I did a double take. She'd had her long white hair styled into a sleek bob and she was wearing a navy chiffon scarf with silver stars on it instead of the woollen one.

'Sylvia! We missed you this week.'

She smiled and her whole face lit up. 'I've had a busy week. Talking to you, I came to a huge realisation. I have no idea how long I have left on this earth – none of us do – and I can't spend the time living in the past and pining for Albert. Everything I've done for the past six years has been influenced by him and it's time to stop. I'll never forget him or our time together, but I need to move on. I've cleared out his things, put our house in part-exchange for a flat in a retirement home, had my hair cut, and been shopping for new clothes.'

'You look amazing,' I said, smiling at her. She looked about ten years younger. 'But does this mean we won't see you again?'

She shook her head. 'The Starfish Café has become very special to me. I've always felt I was welcome, never felt rushed, and you were wonderful last week. I'll be back but I think I might try a different scone and a piece of sponge cake next time.'

'That's brilliant to hear. I'd have been sad if you hadn't returned. You're part of what makes this place special.'

She looked touched by that.

'I have something for you.' She lifted up a small gift bag.

'I can't take anything from you.'

'I really want you to have it. Albert gave me it and it's time it had a new home.'

I took it from her and smiled. 'Thank you. That's very kind.'

'You're the kind one. It's not for opening now. It's for a time when life tests you and you're not sure which way to turn. I hope you don't need it but, if you do, it's there for you like you were there for me. I'll see you next week.'

With a smile, she left, leaving me holding onto the bag and feeling a little emotional.

'What did she give you?' Angie asked, sidling up to me.

'I don't know.' From the weight and shape of it, I suspected it was a book. 'I have to keep it until I feel tested.'

'Intriguing.'

'I think our Mrs Sultana might just be a very intriguing lady.'

My curiosity was definitely piqued but I respected her too much to open the gift. I'd store it safely in my bedside drawer and hope I didn't need to call on it.

* * *

'Good luck at the party tonight,' I said to Angie as we walked across the car park at the end of the day. 'Nervous?'

'Terrified!'

'Does Martin know you're going to be there?'

'I don't know if Candice has told him or not. She's assured me he isn't bringing a guest. That was my biggest worry.'

We paused by the cars, our breath hanging in the air.

'I'm sure it'll go brilliantly but, if you need me, you must ring me.'

Angie shook her head. 'As if I'd do that when you're out on a date.'

'Jake would understand. I can't bear the thought of you being upset.'

She hugged me. 'Have an amazing time tonight and how about I drop round after work tomorrow and we can share stories?'

'I'll hold you to that.'

* * *

With Jake and I both living a short walk from town but in opposite directions, we decided it would be easiest if he drove to Sandy Croft, left Pickle there, we walked into town, and he slept over. When I opened the door to him and saw him freshly shaved, wearing a shirt and smelling divine, I nearly suggested we ditch the drinks and go straight to the sleeping over. With little emphasis on sleeping.

'You look stunning,' he said, stepping into the kitchen and catching me in a dreamy kiss. My wardrobe had a distinct lack of going-out clothes, but I'd found a black dress with white spots on it which I'd teamed up with a deep red cardigan and a pair of brown suede boots. I'd even put curls in my hair with my styling wand.

'You look pretty amazing yourself,' I said, and laughed as Pickle pawed at me. 'And you do too, sweetie,' I said, picking him up and giving him a scratch behind the ears.

We gave Pickle some attention, then left him in Willow's bed.

'Where do you fancy going?' Jake asked, taking my hand in his as we set off into town.

'I like Minty's or Ruby Fizz best.'

'I've never been to either, so I'm guided by you.'

Ruby Fizz was closer. Recently under new ownership, it had been extended and refurbished in a 1930s style with art deco lamps, dark wood, green leather seats, and a cosy atmosphere. Jake got the drinks in while I secured a table in the back room not too far from the real fire.

We had such a lovely evening together, chatting, laughing, exchanging tender kisses, that I made a decision. Tomorrow I'd tell Jake everything. I'd already let him into my heart and, much as I'd have loved to stay cocooned in that bubble of happiness, it was time to fully let him into my life.

'To the person who fixed my Rubik's Cube,' Jake said, toasting his pint against my glass of wine when he returned from the bar with a fourth round of drinks. I pushed the six empty glasses to one side, wondering if anyone was going to ever clear the tables.

'Is it fully fixed now?' I asked.

'The thing I did this morning put the final piece in place.'

He had that nervous look again and I placed my hand over his. 'I've made a decision that I'm going to tell you what happened to my dad and Isaac tomorrow so it's fine. You can tell me.'

He squeezed my hand. 'In that case, let's keep tonight as it is, and we can talk properly tomorrow.'

'You're absolutely sure you don't want to tell me now?'

'I'm sure. It'll keep till tomorrow.'

Hollie seemed to be taking forever in the toilets. The pub was busy so there was probably a queue. I sipped on my pint and took in the surroundings. I could see why Hollie liked it in here. It was from a different era, but it had the same warm feeling as her home.

'Mouse! Mate!' I hadn't noticed Jaffa approaching until he was standing right beside me. 'That's some major celebrating!' He indicated the six empty glasses. 'Are you drinking the bar dry?'

I smiled. 'They're not all mine. I'm with someone.'

'Girlfriend?'

'Yeah.' My stomach lurched. Hollie would surely be back from the toilets any second and, even though we had plans to get it all out in the open tomorrow, I didn't want her to hear it from Jaffa first.

Hollie slipped back into her seat. 'Sorry about that. Bumped into a customer. Hi, I'm...'

She looked up at Jaffa... *Don't mention crew. Don't mention crew...* and the smile slipped from her face.

'Kyle!'

'Hollie!'

'You two know each other?' she asked, her voice high-pitched, the colour draining from her cheeks as her eyes flicked from Jaffa to me.

Jaffa looked as shocked to see her as she clearly was to see him. He ran his hand across his stubble. 'Jeez, Hols, it's been ages. How are you doing?'

My heart thumped. They knew each other and from the anguished expression on Hollie's face, I suspected it wasn't because Jaffa was a customer she recognised. And I knew there were no exes other than Craig.

This wasn't looking good.

Kyle Bradbury. I stared at him, my heart thumping. I hadn't seen him since Dad's and Isaac's funeral. I hadn't seen any of them. It wasn't that I blamed them, but it was too difficult and not just for me either. I knew they felt the burden. I knew they were hurting too and we had no idea how to act around each other.

He hadn't answered my question. I was about to ask it again when Jake spoke.

'How do you know each other?' he asked.

I couldn't find any words to explain it. I'd always known this day would come. Whitsborough Bay wasn't big enough to avoid them all but I shopped online, stayed away from South Bay, and had a limited social life so the chances of bumping into one of them had been miniscule.

'I was gutted to hear about your mum,' Kyle said. 'I'm so sorry. She was a lovely woman.'

'Thank you,' I whispered.

'I wanted to come to the funeral but I wasn't sure... I didn't want to...'

I nodded. I understood. I deliberately hadn't placed the funeral details in the paper, hadn't let them know, even though Artie, the full-time coxswain at the lifeboat station, had asked.

I was aware that Jake had asked how Kyle and I knew each other and I hadn't answered, but I was more interested in how they were connected. I tried again with my question, the three glasses of wine I'd drunk swirling uncomfortably in my stomach. 'You two know each other?'

'Yeah! He's one of us. He's crew.' Kyle clapped Jake on the back. 'Just passed out today.'

Jake's shoulders slumped.

Oh, my God! 'You're lifeboat crew?' I asked Jake, the words coming out husky.

'It was my final assessment this morning.'

The room started to spin as beads of perspiration pricked my forehead. I was going to be sick. Clapping my hand over my mouth, I dashed back to the toilets and only just made it into the first cubicle.

I felt as though all the energy had seeped out of my body as I slumped on the floor tiles. I grabbed at some loo roll and wiped my streaming eyes and my mouth, flushed the toilet, kicked the door closed and rested my head in my hands. Why? When things were going so well and I finally felt happy and in control again, why had that had to happen?

'Hollie!' I called, pushing my chair back, but she was heading towards the toilets so I could hardly run after her.

I turned back to Jaffa, mouth open. 'What was all that about?'

'Oh, mate! I'm sorry.' Jaffa had his hands pressed against his temples. 'I assumed she knew.'

'She didn't. But why...?'

He frowned at me. 'She hasn't told you about her dad and brother?'

'I know they died in an accident. We were...' I stopped, my stomach sinking. 'Don't tell me...'

'Sparky and Silver,' he said, his voice flat, his eyes full of pain.

I gripped the back of my chair, my breathing coming rapidly. How had I not realised? The information had all been there – the watersports, her dad's job, Isaac's hobby, the timing – but I hadn't connected it. Maybe I hadn't wanted to. Hollie had told me her dad was an electrician – a sparky – and that Isaac worked with him. When she'd talked about her brother, she'd told me about his love for smugglers and pirates and that his favourite book was *Treasure Island*; a book featuring the fictional pirate Long John Silver.

The tragedy of Sparky and Silver was still raw for the lifeboat crew, especially those who'd been on the shout that fatal night. Their real names would never have registered with me, but I should have made the connection to the nicknames and now it was too late. The woman I loved, who I'd been careful to protect from my story until she was ready, had just been slapped with the truth.

Seven years ago

Dad joined the RNLI crew at Whitsborough Bay Lifeboat Station when he was nineteen, a year before he met Mum. He was third generation crew, and it was inevitable that, with his love for watersports, Isaac would follow in the family footsteps. He joined the Sea Cadets as a lad – which is where he met Kyle – and they both started training with the RNLI when they were seventeen, passing out at nineteen.

Dad taught me to swim when I was a toddler and for several years I attended lifesaving classes. I never caught the water bug like the male side of the family, but was a strong swimmer and confident on what to do if I found myself in difficulties. I knew how powerful the sea could be, even on what appeared to be a calm day, and always had tremendous respect for it. I knew never to venture down to the seafront on a high tide when there was overtopping, and I cringed at the risks people took wave-dodging. The danger in which they put themselves had escalated since social media took off. Was the 'perfect' photo or video really worth risking their lives for?

From a young age, I knew how to access and read the tide timetables and which beaches and coves along the coast got cut off at high tide. Safety was drilled into me: how to spot a riptide, never to play with inflatables in the sea, to calmly lie on my back in a starfish position if I was swept from shore.

If Dad's and Isaac's pagers sounded when they were at home, I always felt a tingle of nerves for whoever was in trouble, praying the coastguard hadn't been alerted too late, but I never felt worried for Dad or Isaac. They knew what they were doing. The whole crew were highly trained, extremely competent, and looked out for each other. Every rescue put them at risk, but I never imagined they'd lose their lives saving others. Others whose actions had been reckless.

* * *

We'd had such a lovely Christmas, perhaps the best ever. Isaac and Bex had come over for dinner and Craig, Angie, and Martin joined us on the afternoon. We played silly games, ate and drank too much – basically a typical Christmas – and the house had been alive with laughter.

Two days later, a storm was brewing and there were red weather warnings along the Yorkshire Coast. During the morning, the wind speed picked up considerably and the slow and steady rain became torrential. The local news and social media showed business owners along the seafront on North and South Bay weren't taking any chances and were closing early. They often did that for red warnings or extremely high tides; a good deterrent to the public to stay home and stay safe. Strong metal flood barriers were pulled down on the larger, more successful businesses and the smaller ones closed their shutters, piled up sandbags in their doorways and hoped nature wouldn't do its worst.

Early that afternoon, with the sky blackening by the minute, Dad and Isaac headed down to the lifeboat station saying they could make themselves useful and be on hand for any incidents. Mum and I said goodbye and waved as the van pulled off the drive.

That was the last time we saw them alive.

* * *

It was shortly after 8.00 p.m. when the front doorbell rang. Mum and I exchanged nervous glances. Anyone who knew us always knocked on the kitchen door.

I peeked round the Christmas tree and my stomach lurched as I spotted two police officers on the doorstep. I switched the television to mute and heard one of them asking if they could come in. That wasn't good.

Mum brought them into the lounge. 'This is my daughter, Hollie.'

There was a man and a woman. He introduced them but I wasn't paying attention.

Mum sat on the larger sofa beside me and they perched on the two-seater.

It was the woman officer who spoke. 'I'm very sorry to inform you...'

I pressed my hand to my chest as words jumped out at me. Rescue... capsized boat... accident... and then came the chilling word that I swear made my heart stop for a second. Dead. Isaac was dead and Dad had been rushed to hospital in a critical condition. Critical. Another chilling word.

Artie met us at the hospital, the toll of the evening showing in his grey pallor and red eyes as he gathered us into his embrace. Dad had crashed and been rushed into surgery. There was nothing we could do except huddle together in the waiting room, praying we wouldn't suffer a second loss, while the officers who'd taken us to hospital left to deliver the tragic news to Bex.

'What happened?' Mum asked Artie. 'Were you there?'

'Yeah. I was there.' That giant bear of a man seemed to have shrunk that evening, broken by what he'd seen, his voice shaking as he told us about the rescue gone wrong.

They'd responded to a mayday call from a sailing boat: *Siren's Bounty*. Four casualties. Claims of a body in the water. The all-weather lifeboat (ALB) was launched and, within twenty minutes, they found the *Siren's Bounty* listing dangerously with three men on the deck without life jackets. There was no sign of the fourth.

The plan was to position the ALB alongside *Siren's Bounty* and for Dad and Isaac to go aboard with life jackets, help the men transfer safety to the ALB, then either steer the boat back to the harbour or have a tow.

Trying to bring both boats together was a tricky manoeuvre, especially in rough seas, but the lifeboat crew were highly experienced and had done it many times before. But at this point, they had no idea who they were dealing with.

The men, all in their fifties, had been on an all-day drinking binge and, unable to stay in any of the seafront pubs which were closing ahead of the storm, they continued their party on board the boat that one of them owned. The boat had been a recent purchase, the owner wasn't an experienced sailor, and even an experienced sailor would not have gone out in that storm. It was a disaster waiting to happen.

As Isaac was transferring across, one of the men emerged from the cockpit erratically waving a lit flare. Moments later, he was on fire. The crew looked on in horror as he staggered across the deck before tumbling overboard. He must have dropped the flare in the cockpit as that burst into flames.

Knowing it was unlikely he'd have survived the double shock of burns and water, the priority had to be rescuing the two men still on board. Isaac made it safely across and they prepared for Dad's transfer.

Casualties sometimes panicked about drowning and made a grab for the crew, which was exactly what happened here, with both men launching themselves at Isaac. He had life jackets for them, but they seemed intent on having his and his helmet.

The ALB did another pass and Dad transferred onto *Siren's Bounty*. Isaac had been overpowered and knocked to the deck. The men had managed to remove his helmet but it had rolled into the sea. One of them was pulling on the stolen life jacket. Dad was helping Isaac to his feet when the other man lunged at him, presumably wanting his life jacket.

All the while the storm intensified, the fire burned despite the rain, and suddenly the boom broke free and knocked them all into the water. The boom hit Isaac on the head and, without the protection of his helmet, he stood no chance. It caught Dad across the body.

Despite our hopes and prayers, Dad never regained consciousness and died the following day. Significant internal bleeding. Hypothermia.

53

Present day

Muttering his apologies, Jaffa beat a hasty retreat. I pulled on my coat, gathered together Hollie's belongings and waited near the toilets.

The door to the ladies opened and Hollie stepped out, red-eyed, pale-cheeked, her hair dishevelled.

'Let's get you home,' I said, gently, holding out her coat so she could easily slip her arms into it.

I handed over her scarf. 'I'm so sorry. I should have told you sooner. I didn't realise.'

Hollie shook her head. 'My fault. It was a stupid idea not to share our stories. I thought I was protecting us both.'

She took her bag from me and I followed her out of the bar.

'Do you want to walk or get a taxi?' I asked.

'Taxi. I just want to get home.'

She looked up at me and I knew what was coming. I tried to keep my voice strong. 'You want to be alone.'

'I'm sorry. I can't do this tonight.'

We set off towards the taxi rank. 'What if I just keep you company? No talking. I'm worried about you.'

'I'll be fine. It was a shock. I need some time to process things.'

I ran my hand through my hair, my stomach in knots. Process things? That didn't sound good. What must be going through Hollie's mind right now? What were the odds of her falling in love with someone who'd just joined the RNLI after losing her dad and brother at sea?

I desperately wanted to say something helpful, meaningful, but my mind was blank. I was so out of my depth. My casual relationships had taught me nothing valuable about how to deal with an emotional situation like this.

As the taxi pulled away a few minutes later, Hollie gave me a weak smile through the window. I smiled back, but I couldn't shake the feeling I'd just lost her. All these years to find my happy future and my damn past had just screwed it all up again.

54

Seeing Kyle after all these years had been a hell of a shock and a sobering one at that. The crew typically frequented the pubs along or near the seafront, favouring The Lobster Pot, opposite the harbour. Isaac and Kyle had never been fans of the bars in town, saying they were noisy and soulless, so Kyle had been the last person I'd have expected to see in Ruby Fizz tonight. Then to hear that Jake had joined the RNLI. I hadn't seen that coming.

I made a mug of strong tea and took it upstairs. Feeling shivery, I pulled on a snuggly onesie, sat on top of my bed and cuddled Pickle. I hadn't thought about Pickle being at Sandy Croft when I'd caught the taxi. Jake would probably have appreciated his company tonight. There was nothing I could do about it now.

I took a couple of glugs of tea then rested my head against the headboard. As soon as I closed my eyes, I pictured Jake but it wasn't his horrified expression in the bar earlier. It was the way he'd looked at me so tenderly when he told me he loved me. I could imagine his gentle kisses and the touch of his hands.

I snapped opened my eyes. I had to stop thinking about him in that way and focus. I felt terrible for him. None of it was his fault.

He'd kept his promise not to talk about the past and neither of us could have known it would creep up like that. He'd told me his plan for today was connected to his regular Monday evening commitment and that both were linked to his past, so he hadn't lied to me; he simply hadn't told me the details because I'd asked him not to. He'd have had no idea about my connection to the RNLI because I'd kept that hidden for the same reason.

I grabbed my laptop and paused to do the maths. He'd been nine when his dad died and if joining crew was linked to his past, it had to be connected to his dad's death. I typed in some search words and the year and clapped my hand across my mouth as I scanned various headlines and took in the photos of a smiling dark-haired boy clutching a soft penguin, a police sergeant, and the old slipway at North Bay.

'Jake Reynolds,' I whispered as I read the first article. 'You even changed your name afterwards.' I could relate to that. I hadn't wanted people to know because I hadn't wanted their sympathy and, most of all, I hadn't wanted their opinions. I had enough opinions – and anger – of my own without dealing with anyone else's.

A tragic accident, they called it. Murder, more like. Who took a boat out in a storm, especially when drunk and inexperienced at sailing? And who attacked their rescuers like that?

It felt like adding insult to injury that the two men who'd attacked Dad and Isaac survived with only a broken arm and a couple of cracked ribs between them. The one who'd set on fire didn't make it and the original body overboard washed up ashore two months later. Four lives lost that day and a hell of a lot more lives destroyed. For what?

After it happened, I wanted to be anonymous. I wanted to hide. But, as per Dad's and Isaac's philosophy, life had to go on, so I smiled and thanked the well-meaning customers and refused to engage in conversations about the 'accident'. But as the years passed, I called it that too. What other choice did I have? Killings? Murders? 'Accident' didn't hit such a harsh blow.

Reading the various articles about Jake now, my heart broke for the little boy who must have been terrified when he was swept into the sea, who'd lost both his parents by the age of nine, each dying on his birthday. And my heart broke for the man he'd become, who'd had to build up that protective wall so high that he'd even changed his name.

I was seven weeks younger than Jake so had been approaching nine myself when it happened, and I remembered it well. Dad had taken it as another valuable opportunity to talk about the importance of respecting the sea and never venturing down to the seafront in a storm.

I recalled that Jake's dad had managed to pull him to the surface and a dog walker had thrown in a life-ring, pulling Jake to safety, but his dad was swept out to sea before the man could throw the ring again. There was nothing he could do without risking his own life. A passing jogger had alerted the coastguard and Dad had been on that shout. He'd been the one who'd found and pulled Jake's dad from the water. He was the one who'd tried CPR, but to no avail. They'd known that when they found him. Nobody could survive that long in the North Sea without succumbing to hypothermia.

I picked up my phone. I needed to speak to him. I wasn't strong enough to do it tonight, but it wasn't fair to prolong it.

✉ To Jake

I'm so sorry about abandoning you. Can you meet me at sunrise at South Bay tomorrow? Same place as last time xx

His reply came straight back:

✉ From Jake
I'll be there but my phone's on if you want to
talk sooner. Is Pickle OK and, more importantly,
are you? xx

✉ To Jake
Pickle's fine and sends his love. As for me,
that's a more complicated question but please
don't worry about me. We'll talk tomorrow xx

My head thumped and my eyes felt sticky with sleep when my alarm sounded on Sunday morning. I reached for the blister strip of paracetamol I'd left on my bedside drawers last night and swallowed two with a glug of tepid water.

I hadn't expected to get any sleep but exhaustion had claimed me and I'd dropped off on top of the duvet, still wearing my onesie and fluffy socks, with my laptop open beside me and Pickle sprawled out on the bed.

As I showered, I felt surprisingly calm. I couldn't help feeling like there was a certain inevitability that things had been going too well between Jake and me and that a major obstacle had to present itself. It had been careless of me to throw myself into a relationship so quickly and to fall so deeply. That approach might have worked before I lost my family, but it was reckless now.

I was 99 per cent sure about how this was going to play out but I would make my final decision once I spoke to Jake.

* * *

I was leaning against a column in the covered walkway beyond The Bay Pavilion looking out to the dark sea when Pickle barked excitably and ran off, indicating Jake's arrival. My heart raced and butterflies did somersaults in my stomach as Jake emerged from the darkness with Pickle bouncing round him.

'Hi,' he said, pausing and thrusting his hands in his pockets. I could imagine him struggling with how to greet me, but there was no reason to act like strangers. I held my arms out.

My heart continued to race as he held me tightly and rested his chin against my head. Words tumbled round my mind but I couldn't string any of them into a coherent sentence so I clung onto him, willing myself not to cry. I could have stayed like that forever, feeling warm and safe, listening to the soothing sounds of the sea.

I withdrew from the hug and we sat on the steps, which were still wet from high tide. Pickle scampered down to the beach and sniffed some nearby boulders.

I grappled for where to begin. 'Did you manage to get any sleep last night?' It felt inadequate.

'Not much. You?'

'Same. I'm sorry for running out on you. It was a shock.'

'I can't believe I didn't work it out sooner. Sparky and Silver.'

'Now there's a couple of names I haven't heard in a long time.' I turned to look at the sea. The tide was on its way out so the waves were gentler and flatter than they would have been earlier, and I could just make out the ebb and flow in the lightening sky.

'After it happened I hated the sea,' I said, 'but our house and the café overlook it so I couldn't escape. And then I realised I was directing my anger in the wrong place. The sea didn't kill them. It was a tragic accident. It was caused by reckless stupidity by a couple of drunk idiots, but I accepted it was an accident. So I made peace with the sea and it's my happy place now. They both loved it so much and I feel close to them every time I'm here.'

Pickle scampered back up the steps and plonked himself down, panting, between us. I stroked his back then looked up at Jake.

'Did you hate the sea for taking your dad?'

My eyes widened at Hollie's question. 'You know?'

'You're not the only one who joined the dots last night.'

'I did hate the sea for a long time, but not as much as I hated myself.'

'Tell me about it.'

So I did. As the sky gradually lightened, I told her all about my parents being desperate for another child and how the risk hadn't paid off. I talked about my birthday being too hard for Dad and how I'd begged Nanna to intervene; a move that had proved fatal. And I talked about Binky the penguin.

'Kids started following me round the playground waddling like a penguin. They called me "penguin-boy" and laughed at me for being too old for soft toys. Some kids said I'd jumped in to save my "precious teddy bear" and my dad drowned saving me. The nastier ones said I'd killed my dad.'

'Oh, Jake. That's horrific.'

'Larissa accused me of killing him too and those kids were so close to the truth about Binky. I hadn't jumped in, but I *had* been leaning forward to rescue him when a wave took me and Dad *had* jumped in to save me and died as a result.'

'I noticed you changed your name.'

I raised my eyebrows at her. 'You've done your detective work.'

'Hours spent with Isaac while he tried to solve the mystery of Tingler's Treasure must have rubbed off.'

'I got into several fights. Parents complained and, even though it wasn't me who'd started it, I was the common denominator and the one who threw the first punch so the school had no choice but to exclude me. Each kid I hit claimed they'd never be mean enough to poke fun at the orphaned kid, so it was my word against theirs.'

I paused to give Pickle a belly rub, feeling lighter for having shared that buried part of my past with Hollie.

'Nanna was worried that if she moved me to another school straight away the same thing could happen, so she home-schooled me for the rest of that school year and changed my surname. Reynolds was my family name but MacLeod was her maiden name and she'd reverted to it after my granddad left her. I did my last two years at Chemsby Hill School in town. It was closer to Lighthouse View and, being the biggest school in Whitsborough Bay, I could become invisible. I've been perfecting that skill ever since.'

We sat in silence for a while and that feeling of relief grew stronger, although my stomach wouldn't stop churning for fear of what might happen now between Hollie and me.

She stood up and brushed the sand off her jacket and jeans. 'I can feel the water seeping through my jeans. Fancy a walk?'

The sky was lighter now that the sun had appeared over the horizon, bringing streaks of baby blue and pale lemon. It felt romantic, hopeful. I automatically raised my arm to place round Hollie's shoulders but paused and turned it into a stretch before thrusting my hands back into my pockets. I didn't know where things stood between us. Best not make an idiot of myself when I suspected Hollie was building up to saying goodbye.

'What about your story?' I asked as she guided us across the beach in a southerly direction.

'You probably know most of it but here goes…' She filled me in on her dad being third generation and Isaac being fourth generation lifeboat crew and how her dad had hoped she'd become the first woman in the family to join but the sea hadn't called to her like it had to Isaac. I heard how her dad taught her about water safety and respecting the sea and had to stop my mind from wandering, wishing I'd known what she'd known back then. And she admitted the real reason she hated storms – because of the stormy day two days after Christmas when two police officers turned up at the door and their lives were turned upside down.

It was heartbreaking hearing her describe the agonising time in the waiting room at the hospital, knowing they'd already lost her brother and clinging onto the tiniest shred of hope that her dad would make it. I'd seen family members in pain like that so often and had delivered tragic news on so many occasions.

'When I was sixteen, I'd carved them a wooden starfish to hang in the van so they could always feel close to Mum and me when they were out and about with work. When Isaac started his lifeboat training, I made them one each. They kept it in their kit as a good luck charm. We were handed Isaac's personal effects and I got his starfish back. I've never thought of myself as religious, but I had nothing left that day. I held his starfish, closed my eyes and prayed to God, the universe, Poseidon … whoever or whatever could hear me … to save Dad.' She sighed. 'But none of them could.'

There wasn't much more beach left. Ahead of us were boulders either side of a slipway after which the land jutted out. We changed direction and set off again.

'You said you were scared of water after what happened to your dad...' Hollie began and my stomach lurched. This was the part that I'd been dreading. 'So what made you want to join the RNLI?'

I told her about the visit to the slipway on North Bay on the twenty-year anniversary of Dad's death, my epiphany moment, and the challenges I had in overcoming my fear of water.

'It sounds like it was a proper calling,' she said.

My stomach lurched once more, but I wasn't going to lie to her. 'Yes.'

We walked in silence for a while. It was light now, the pale blue sky streaked by dark grey clouds. The forecast for this afternoon was for rain but I could already sense the storm brewing between Hollie and me. I didn't want to push the conversation because I didn't want to face it. Pulling a ball out of my jacket pocket, I tossed it along the beach for Pickle. Several rounds of catch were the perfect distraction.

'When I realised who you were yesterday, I realised something else,' Hollie said. 'It was my dad who pulled your dad out of the water.'

'Seriously?'

'He tried to save him, but he was already gone. I remember the night it happened. I couldn't sleep so I'd gone downstairs to ask for a glass of milk and my dad was in the kitchen with Mum and he was crying. I'd never seen him cry before. He didn't try to hide it or shoo me away. He pulled me onto his knee and said he was sad because he hadn't been able to save somebody's daddy and that his little boy had nearly drowned too. I think it hit him extra hard because you were my age and your dad was about his age. It could have been our family.'

'Neither you nor your brother would ever have been daft enough to play with the sea.' I could hear the bitterness in my tone. I couldn't revert to blaming myself again. I'd come too far.

Hollie grabbed my hand. 'Don't think like that. We might have been if Dad hadn't joined the RNLI. It's only when you've seen what can happen that you appreciate how powerful and dangerous the sea really is.'

Her hand slipped away, and my heart sank at the realisation that we'd already transitioned into friends talking a walk with the dog instead of two people who'd said 'I love you' days earlier. Pickle dropped the ball by my feet, and I threw it for him again. In the distance, I could see a couple more dog walkers.

'So it seems that our lives were connected from childhood,' Hollie said. 'Which makes the next part even harder to say.'

I closed my eyes for a moment. *Here it comes.* 'Then don't say it.'

'I have to. I'm really sorry, Jake, but I can't do this. I love you but I've already lost two people I love on a shout, and I can't risk losing another. It's taken me seven long, difficult years to get to where I am today and I can't go back. And I know you understand that because you've had a similar tough journey yourself. If we stayed together, I'd be anxious every time there's bad weather. Every time your pager goes, I'd be a nervous wreck. It would destroy us both so it's better to walk away now, be grateful we met and had the most incredible week together, and accept that there can't be a future for us.'

'You can't mean that.'

'It's the only way.'

'It's not. There's another way. I could stand down.' I probably sounded desperate and needy, but I didn't want to lose her.

She shook her head vigorously. 'I can't let you do that. You said it yourself. It was a calling. I'm from a family with the lifeboats in their blood so I know it's not something you can just walk away from. The crew are your team, your family. There's no way you could let them down.'

'I *would* walk away for you.' But as I said it, my insides contracted. I pictured the crew, the banter, being part of a team where everyone accepted me without question, the elation at making a difference, and I knew it would hurt to step down. But not as much as the pain of losing Hollie.

She lightly touched my arm. 'I know you would, but I can't and won't let you because that would come between us too. You'd have the regret and I'd have the guilt.'

'So it's Catch-22? We can't be together if I'm in the RNLI but if I leave we'll break up anyway?' I fought hard to keep the frustration out of my voice but this was doing my head in.

'I'm sorry.'

My shoulders slumped. It was pointless me getting het up with Hollie. I respected her honesty, it was obvious this wasn't an easy decision for her and, even though I hated the situation, her logic wasn't flawed.

'Is there anything I can say or do to help you change your mind?'

'I wish there was, but I think both our pasts have caught up with us and, even though we're connected, we can't stay connected. I can't do it, Jake.'

Pickle charged towards us with a stick of seaweed in his mouth, did a lap round us then flopped down on the sand. I couldn't muster the energy to bend down and pick up the seaweed or the ball to throw for him. I felt numb, lost, weary. Then Hollie threw a lifeline.

'Not yet, anyway.'

Not yet, anyway. Where on earth did that spring from?

The hopeful expression on Jake's face was almost too much to bear. What was wrong with me? I'd already done the hardest bit. I'd explained it, I'd declared it, and it was out there. So why had I effectively retracted it?

'I shouldn't have said that, Jake. I'm sorry. Please forget it.'

The anguished look in his eyes broke me, but he didn't say anything. He held out his arms and we stood there on the beach holding onto each other as the sun rose and the sky brightened and Pickle raced up and down the sand.

It was Jake who eventually pulled away. Tears glistened in his eyes. 'I don't want to lose you, Hollie.'

I nearly threw out the 'we can still be friends' line but it sounded so trite. 'If there was any other way...'

'I know. I do understand.' He seemed to deflate before my eyes. 'I'd better go. Have you got the dog lead?'

I pulled it out of my pocket.

'Pickle!' Jake called. 'Let's get you clipped on.'

I swallowed hard on the golf ball in my throat as Pickle raced towards us. I'd been so focused on losing Jake, I hadn't even considered what that meant for Pickle.

'I'd still like to help out with Pickle.' The words were strained as I fought back more tears. 'But I understand if that would be too hard for you.'

Jake bit his lip and looked away for a moment before turning his gaze to me. 'Can I think about it?'

'Of course. There's no rush.'

'Say goodbye to Hollie, Pickle.'

I crouched down beside him and lifted him to my chest. That adorable teddy bear face looked at me with such unconditional love and trust and all I could think was how I'd let him down. I breathed in his doggy scent for what might be the last time, tears dripping onto his fur as I kissed his head and his ears.

'We'd better go. I'll collect my car from yours.'

I put Pickle down and hastily wiped my cheeks before straightening up.

'Take care of yourself, Hollie.'

'You too.'

He held my gaze for a moment, his eyes full of pain, just like my heart. Then he turned and strode down the beach, Pickle beside him.

I couldn't watch them. It hurt too much. I wrapped my arms around myself and turned to face the sea. Why did I lose everyone and everything I loved?

* * *

I stayed on the beach for twenty minutes or so then trudged back up the cliff path towards home. A part of me had hoped to find Jake's car still on the drive, him presenting a way it could work, but Jake, Pickle and the car were gone.

I made myself a cappuccino, and sat at the breakfast bar, staring into nothing, absent-mindedly stirring a half teaspoon of brown sugar into my drink.

I'd had nearly six years without other humans and five and a half without any furry companions, yet the house had never felt as empty as it did now. A sob escaped from me as I glanced towards Willow's dog bed and pictured Pickle curled up in it. I needed a distraction and glanced at the clock: 9.47 a.m. In my life before Jake and Pickle, I'd normally have spent the day in my workshop so that was exactly what I'd do.

Outside, I paused by the tree trunk that Jake and I had liberated. Had that really only been a fortnight ago? I ran my hand along the bark, a shiver of anticipation running down my spine as I started to envisage what it could become, but then my mind became clouded with visions of Jake and Pickle.

Stepping away, I unlocked my workshop. I couldn't rush the trunk and regret it later. I needed more time. Right now, with no boyfriend, probably no dog, and my best friend still overseas, I had plenty of that.

* * *

I broke for a late lunch and returned to the house to heat up some soup and have a drink. A text came through from Angie and I remembered with a jolt that we'd said we'd meet up tonight. I couldn't face that. Thankfully I didn't need to:

🖼 From Angie
Hope your date was amazing. I'm sure it will
have been! Candice's party was awkward at first.
He walked in with another woman & I thought they
were together. Turns out it was coincidence &

they didn't even know each other! Finally got
talking & there's lots still to say. He asked if
he can come round after I finish work. Are you
OK to take a rain check? x

I breathed a sigh of relief.

✉ To Angie
Definitely! Hope it goes well tonight. Hugs x

58

JAKE

Irene took Pickle overnight on Sunday while I worked a night shift. It was the worst shift I'd ever done. All the patients seemed to be aggressive. Three fights broke out, a drunk vomited on me and two of my patients died. The shift couldn't come to an end soon enough.

As I was leaving the hospital on Monday morning, I spotted a couple of ambulance technicians taking a break. I recognised them as the ones who'd responded to the incident where the cyclist ploughed into the elderly pedestrian, Geoffrey, so I asked after him. He hadn't made it. Ruptured spleen. Internal bleeding. Gone.

Everything was falling apart again, and I felt like that child once more, full of anger and confusion. I wanted to lash out. I wanted to scream.

I slammed the door behind me at Lighthouse View, stormed into the kitchen, grabbed the Rubik's Cube and hurled it against the back door. Colourful squares bounced across the tiles and I sank to the floor, head in hands, and properly cried for the first time since Nanna died.

A text came through from Jake round Monday lunchtime. My heart raced as I opened it, not sure whether I had the willpower to keep pushing him back if he begged me to reconsider.

✉ From Jake
I'm off now until Friday so I can have Pickle this week and Irene has asked to have him on Friday and Saturday. I think she wants her final dog-fix before she moves into Bay View next Monday. Probably good timing to have a week apart but Pickle really misses you and hopes you'll still be his half-owner next week. We understand if you'd rather not and we'll make other arrangements

He included the thoughtful emoji and a set of pawprints. Moments later, a second text arrived:

✉ From Jake

Pickle isn't the only one who misses you. Hope
you're OK xx

'I miss you, too,' I whispered.

✉ To Jake
Hope Pickle has a good week with you and Irene.
If it's OK with you, I do still want to be his
half-owner so let me know how you'd like that to
work. Take care xx

I had typed in 'I miss you both too' but I deleted it. I'd already
given him false hope on the beach and had to retract it. I wasn't the
sort to play games. I couldn't not include the kisses, though. I only
wished they were real ones and we could be together but there was
no way. It would destroy me.

Since I'd discovered photography, the best thing about working my type of shifts was all the time off in between. Not this week. This week, it felt like the worst thing in the world. Too much time to think, to dwell, to agonise.

Training on Monday night had given me something to do but Hollie was ever-present. I studied the photos of her dad and brother on the memorial wall in the training room and could see the obvious family resemblance.

Jaffa bombarded me with questions: *Is Hollie okay? Why didn't she know you were crew? Why didn't you know about her family?*

What was I supposed to say? I knew he'd been Silver's... Isaac's... best mate and had been on the shout that night but it was obvious from his brief exchange with Hollie in Ruby Fizz that he wasn't part of her life anymore and hadn't been since the incident.

'We're just friends,' was my pathetic response before walking away. Did a week of passion and an ongoing dog-share even constitute friendship?

I went to The Lobster Pot after training to celebrate passing out, but it didn't feel like much of a celebration when I'd lost Hollie because of it. On what should be the happiest of days, I had nothing to say and felt like a fake, smiling as Jaffa and Simba relayed what had happened during the rescue.

Yesterday, I went next door and offered to help Irene pack. She'd already done it all but she invited me in for a coffee. I stayed all morning while she talked excitedly about the activities she was looking forward to at Bay View and the friends she knew there. I nodded and smiled, but my mind was elsewhere.

I'd taken my camera down to the beach every morning and the conditions had been ideal for some great shots, but my inspiration evaded me and I hadn't even bothered taking it out of my backpack.

It was now Wednesday lunchtime and there'd been no shouts. I stood in the middle of the lawn out the back of Lighthouse View, my hands clasped round a mug of coffee. The wind had picked up, blowing leaves across the garden, which Pickle was chasing and pouncing on.

'Not sure what I'd have done without you this week, buddy,' I said, picking at a stiff brown leaf caught in his tail. It disintegrated in my hands. I pushed aside the dramatic *just like my relationship* that sprung to mind as I let the wind take the broken pieces.

I wanted to see her, but I didn't want to be *that* guy; the needy, pushy one who was all about his agenda and wouldn't give the woman the time and space she needed.

My pager sounded and my heart leapt. At last! Something to do!

I dropped Pickle next door and sprinted down the hill. I'd just made it to the bottom when my pager sounded again. Hoax call. I paused for a couple of minutes, catching my breath as I gazed along the seafront towards the lifeboat station. Simba lived at the bottom of the Old Town and had made it as far as the forecourt when the second page came through. He threw his arms in the air and I felt his exasperation. Hoax calls were such a waste of time and resources, not to mention dangerous. While we were out on a wild goose chase, a genuine call could come through and lives could be at risk. At least this hoax had been detected before either boat was launched.

Simba headed inside the station. Jaffa and Chief were permanently based there so he could chat to them and help out. I could have made myself useful, too. There was always something to do – cleaning, organising, fixing – but I couldn't face it. Too connected to Hollie.

I traipsed back up the hill.

By Thursday evening, I was going stir crazy. I'd been out for a morning and an afternoon run but nothing could ease the restlessness. I'd picked up my phone to call her a dozen times and started and scrapped maybe thirty texts.

'I've got to see her, buddy,' I told Pickle as he watched me pacing the kitchen floor. 'We could casually drop in, saying we happened to be in the area.' I slapped my palm against my forehead. *Pathetic excuse. And you can't use Pickle like that. Think!*

Pickle cocked his head to one side and I swear he was judging me. I was judging me too.

Early on Sunday, before the sun rose, I drove up the coast to Shellby Bay – one of my favourite beaches outside of Whitsborough Bay. I usually came back with an impressive haul of driftwood and sea glass and this morning was no exception. I was all set for a long day in the workshop, getting lost in the world of wood.

As I drove back along Sea Cliff towards my house, I noticed a red hatchback parked outside, which hadn't been there when I left. It didn't look familiar and, as I reversed onto the drive, I peered through the windscreen, but the car was empty.

I removed my hessian bag from the boot and plonked it down in the garden. I'd have some breakfast, then crack on. As I turned to close the boot, I squealed. There was a woman standing on the drive.

'Sorry! I didn't mean to scare you.'

I clutched my throat, stunned at who it was. 'Bex?'

She shrugged and gave an awkward wave then planted her hands in her coat pockets. 'It's been a long time.'

'Too long,' I said, tearing up as I took a few steps closer.

Next second, we were clinging onto each other, sobbing.

* * *

I handed Bex a mug of tea and sat down opposite her on the kitchen sofas.

'Kyle told me he saw you in Ruby Fizz last Saturday,' she said. 'I wanted to come round the next day, but I wasn't sure. I've been blowing hot and cold on it all week, wondering if too long had passed, but I woke up this morning and decided today had to be the day.'

'It's great to see you and so spooky because I was just thinking about you the other week and wondering about making contact.' My voice caught in my throat as I pictured Jake suggesting it was never too late to reconnect. 'So you kept in touch with Kyle?'

She grimaced. 'I married Kyle.'

If I'd had a mouthful of tea, I'd have spluttered it everywhere as those were words I'd never expected to hear from Bex.

'You look shocked.'

'Sorry. I don't mean to. And it's not because you're married. I'm delighted you've found someone. It's what Isaac would have wanted. But Kyle? I thought you couldn't stand each other.'

She visibly relaxed. 'I'm so glad you're not disappointed. It's one of the reasons I've stayed away.'

'Aw, Bex, I could never be disappointed in you finding love again. Not at all. I'm just surprised that it's Kyle.'

'Not as surprised as we both were. I had him pegged as a right lad who was all about jokes, pranks and a different woman every night. Isaac would say it was a front and he was shy and insecure, but I wasn't buying it. He dropped off some of Isaac's things a couple of weeks after the funeral and he looked so haunted that I invited him in for a drink. He broke down. He felt guilty that he'd been the one who'd survived. He'd been on the ALB and it was a split-second decision as to whether Isaac or Kyle would go over to

Siren's Bounty. He wished it had been him. We saw each other every so often after that and I discovered Isaac was right about him. All the bravado was a front and we became friends.'

She paused and took a sip of her tea. 'Are you okay hearing this?'

'I thought it might be a little weird but it's not at all. When did it become more?'

'It was the start of summer, eighteen months after Isaac died. We were walking round The Headland like we often did and, as we approached Stanley Moffatt, there were a couple of families – maybe six or seven children – clambering over him. One of the mums asked if Kyle would take a photo of them all and he had them in hysterics, pretending to be a professional photographer, instructing them to do all sorts of daft poses.'

Her eyes shone as she described it and I could hear the warmth in her voice.

'When we left them, he had a big grin on his face and was gushing about how adorable the kids all were and it struck me how amazing he always was round children. So why was he wasting his time with me when he could be out meeting someone and starting a family of his own? I wondered if it was because of the guilt he felt for Isaac being taken instead of him so I decided to insist he focus on finding himself a girlfriend instead of devoting all his time to me. But the more I thought about him not spending time with me and being with another woman instead, the more panicky I felt and I realised that somehow I'd fallen in love.'

'That's so sweet.'

'I honestly didn't think it would happen because I loved your brother so very deeply.'

'I know you did.'

'I had no idea how Kyle felt about me. He'd not tried anything or given even the slightest hint he'd be interested in more than friendship. I suspected he wouldn't make a move out of respect for Isaac and any first move would have to come from me, so I told him how I felt. Thankfully it was reciprocal. We got married the following June.'

She took her phone out and passed it over. I smiled at the gorgeous photo of the bride and groom. She took her phone back and searched for another image to show me. 'And this is Mia. She'll be three in March.'

I gazed down at the cutest little girl with pink cheeks and blonde bunches wearing a pink tutu and red wellington boots, just like the girl in the card Mum left for me after her death.

'She's gorgeous.'

'Scroll on one.'

I did and my gaze fell on a beautiful baby boy holding a wooden boat.

'That's Isaac. He's eighteen months now.'

Tears welled in my eyes. 'You named your baby Isaac?'

'We both loved your brother so much, it felt right. Aw, don't cry, Hollie. You'll set me off again.'

I waved my hand at her. 'They're happy tears. I promise you. Isaac would be delighted for you and he'd love that you used his name.'

'Thank you. That means a lot to me.'

We chatted some more about her new family and Bex asked me about the café, Katie and Angie. And then came the inevitable question.

'What about you and love? Kyle said you're seeing Mouse. I'm sorry, but I don't actually know his real name.'

'It's Jake, but it's over.'

'Oh. Sorry.'

'Can I ask you a question? Isaac was crew and he died on a

rescue and now you're married to Kyle who's also crew. Do you not worry?'

'About what? Losing him on a rescue? No. It was a very unique set of circumstances with Isaac and your dad and, ultimately, it wasn't the sea that took them, it was those men being idiots. I genuinely don't think I'll lose Kyle on a shout. Yes, I get butterflies when his pager goes but it's partly adrenaline. None of us know how long we have or how we're going to go and, if we worried about it, we'd never do anything or go anywhere. I love that Kyle cares enough to risk his life for others. That's such a gift to give and it takes a special person to give it. I'm happy to cheer him on.'

I made another drink while I mulled over what she'd said. That comment about it not being the sea that took them was exactly what I'd said to Jake when I told him how I fell back in love with the sea. But I didn't feel calm about it like Bex did.

She took the fresh mug from me. 'The other thing that helped was time,' she said. 'I'd had eighteen months of friendship with Kyle, all that time with him as serving crew, before I realised how I felt about him.'

'Yeah, I didn't get that with Jake. I only found out on Saturday. That was a shock.'

'Are you saying it's over with Mouse because he's crew?' She sounded more curious than critical, and she was perhaps the only person I knew who'd truly understand.

My shoulders slumped and I lowered my head. That was absolutely the only reason, but it was a huge one. 'Yes.'

'Do you love him?' she asked gently.

'Yes.'

'And does he love you?'

'Yes.'

'Then you should be together. Not everyone finds love, Hollie, and my experience of it is that, if you do find it, you grab onto it and live every day as though it's your last because, one day, it really could be.'

'You make it sound simple.'

'It is. But this,' she tapped her temple, 'has a habit of making it complicated. As soon as I realised how I felt about Kyle, I told him. I could have spent weeks or even months debating it and over-thinking it, but my heart told me the truth and I shared that with Kyle. What's your truth? And I don't expect you to answer that right now. It's something to ponder on.'

Her phone beeped and she stood up. 'I'm sorry. I need to get home to take Mia to a birthday party.'

We hugged goodbye and promised to stay in touch. I was anxious to meet Mia and baby Isaac.

I loaded the mugs into the dishwasher. 'What's my truth?' I muttered to myself. My truth was that I loved Jake more than I'd thought it was possible to love another person, but my truth was also that my head was in charge and, right now, I could not let go of my worry. No, not worry. It was stronger than that. It was fear. Until I got my fear under control, there was no chance for us.

I paused in the lounge doorway on Monday morning, a mug of tea in either hand, feeling quite emotional at the sight of Irene standing in my bay window watching two men and a woman empty the contents of Seafarer Lodge into a small removals van.

She'd been Nanna's next-door neighbour the whole of my life and now she was moving out and a young couple with a baby would be moving in. I was going to miss her. She wasn't going far but I hadn't appreciated until recently quite how many conversations we had in passing on the doorstep or by the gate or that I'd looked upon her like family. I'd have to make sure I visited her regularly. Wouldn't be difficult to find time.

She turned away from the window and smiled at me. 'Ooh, I'm ready for a brew. Thanks, love.'

'Does it feel strange moving out?'

'Not as strange as I thought. I was born next door. I've lived there all my life except for one year when I first married my Derek. Mum died a year later so I moved back. Folk back then didn't move about like they do these days. Houses often stayed in families. Now it's all changed. Kay moved out and her nephew and his Irish lass moved in, your nanna passed, other friends have passed or moved into their kids' houses, retirement or care homes, and now I'm doing the same.' She shrugged. 'I always thought the only way I'd leave Seafarer Lodge was in a wooden box.'

'I thought you were looking forward to moving into Bay View.'

'Aw, bless you, lad. I am. I'm just being nostalgic. I've more friends in there than I have round here now. The time's right to move on.' Her eyes clouded with tears. 'I'll miss you, though. You're the closest thing I've got to family.'

'Same here. I promise I'll visit. We could go on days out like I used to with Nanna.'

Her bottom lip wobbled, and I panicked that I'd made her cry, but she seemed to pull past it. 'That'd be smashing, love. Better than you spending your time between shifts moping after that young lass of yours.'

'I'm not moping.'

'Pull the other one. It's got bells on. You've had a face like a wet weekend all week.'

'That's because I'm sad to see you go,' I quipped.

'I should think so, too.' She glanced out the window again. 'I've got plenty of time till they're done next door. Talk to me...'

* * *

'Mouse!' Jaffa fell into step beside me after training that evening. 'Drinks in The Anchor after training tonight.'

'Not The Lobster Pot?'

'The others are going there as usual but you and me are off to The Anchor. We need to talk about Hollie.'

'I should get home to check on my dog.'

'He'll be fine for another hour. It's important. Although we could go to The Lobster Pot and discuss it in front of everyone if you prefer.'

'Okay. The Anchor it is.'

* * *

'Get that down you.' Jaffa plonked a pint of real ale on the table in front of me. 'Great work tonight. You made some good calls.'

'Thanks. It was an interesting scenario.' Except for the location. We'd been to Starfish Point again and, as we sped towards there on the ILB, all I could think of was Hollie. I kept looking up at the cliff, as if expecting to see her standing on the terrace outside The Starfish Café, waving at us.

He glugged down half his pint in one and wiped the froth from his upper lip. 'I needed that.'

I raised my glass towards him and took a sip. 'Cheers.'

'I love every part of being lifeboat crew,' he said. 'From the buzz of the search to the thrill of the find to the satisfaction of being part of a team that saves lives. I love that we're an eclectic mix of people – different ages, jobs, backgrounds, personalities – who might not otherwise have crossed paths but being crew has brought us together as a family.'

I nodded, curious as to where this speech was heading.

'Some of us are second, third or even fourth generation and others, like you and me, are first. Thing about being on crew is it's a lifestyle and sometimes life and crew don't lie comfortably in the same bed. I reckon everyone thinks about walking away at some point, but most don't. Most *can't* because, whether crew is a family tradition or not, it's in our blood and it's who we are.'

I nodded once more and took a sip on my drink.

'Me and Isaac – never could get used to calling him Silver – met at Sea Cadets when we were ten, joined the RNLI when we were seventeen, had our final assessment on the same day at nineteen, and were on most shouts together. Seven years on, I still expect to find him right beside me. Feels weird that he isn't.'

'Must have been tough losing your best mate like that.'

'Worst thing I've ever experienced. The loss was bad enough but there was all this guilt too. Why him and Sparky instead of me? It wasn't right. I wanted to look out for his girlfriend, Bex, and make sure she was doing okay. I must have done a pretty good job of it 'cause she's my wife now.'

I couldn't tell if he was joking or not. He took a few more gulps on his pint and shrugged. 'That was flippant of me. I *am* married to Bex, but I didn't jump into Isaac's grave. We were friends for a long time and even when I knew it was more for me, I never said or did anything. But I did think about leaving crew.'

'Why?'

'Because I figured Bex had already gone through enough losing Isaac and she might not want to get involved with me in case it happened again. And do you know what I realised?'

He bent his head closer and I found myself leaning in, my curiosity piqued.

'I realised I couldn't give it up. I wouldn't be me if I wasn't crew. It was Bex who made the move on me and we had a long talk but she was good with it. She knew who I was. It was one of the reasons she loved me.'

'Why are you telling me this? Do you know something?'

'Bex saw Hollie yesterday. They'd lost touch. We all had. Hollie found it too hard to keep the connection going and we had to respect that, but Bex wanted to make sure she was okay. They had a good catch-up. Don't know all the details but I do know that Hollie's in the avoid crew camp like I thought Bex would be and I'm thinking that, because you've been even quieter than usual recently – which I hadn't thought was humanly possible – maybe you're thinking of hanging up your life jacket. As I've had those same conversations with myself, I thought you might like a sounding board.'

Jaffa finished his drink. 'I'll get another one of these then the floor's yours, mate. I know I can yack, but I can listen too. Another pint?'

I shrugged. 'Go on. I might need one if you're going to make us have a heavy heart-to-heart.'

He laughed. 'I wouldn't go quite that far.'

* * *

When I got back from The Anchor, Pickle greeted me in the hall, wagging his tail. I loved that warm welcome. We were about to walk down to the seafront when Sarah's brother Ben and his wife Clare pulled up outside Seashell Cottage and called me over.

'We saw your photo in the paper,' Clare said. 'Congratulations! We didn't know you'd joined the RNLI.'

I shrugged. 'I kind of wanted to keep it quiet until it was official.'

'I'm sorry about your dad,' Ben said. 'I remember it happening but never realised it was you.'

'Thanks. I wanted to keep that quiet too, but I guess that was unrealistic.'

Everyone knew now. There'd been a double page spread in last Thursday's *Bay News* celebrating my passing but also dredging up Dad's death and the other two tragedies on the slipway afterwards.

I'd known it was coming. Chief had phoned to warn me and to assure me they hadn't heard the story from him, but I'd already guessed. A reporter anxious to speak to me had left a stack of voice-mails earlier in the week. I wasn't interested in raking over the past or being made out to be a hero so I ignored his pleas to return his calls. A reporter worth their salt would have been able to piece it all together and I'd decided to let him run with it.

Now that my story was out there once more in the public domain, I felt surprisingly relieved. I'd battled so long and hard to keep it secret that it felt like a weight off my shoulders. The reporter might not have been able to speak to me, but he'd done his homework, even tracking down my old primary school teacher Miss Lemmings and my swimming instructor from when I'd braved the water again. No stone was left unturned although, thankfully, there was no mention of any connection to Hollie. I'd have been devastated if she'd been dragged into it.

At work, I'd already told my manager in case I was paged but now my colleagues knew. I'd dreaded going into shift on Friday, the day after the story broke, but instead of sympathetic looks I had handshakes and congratulations for facing my fears.

'Why the big secret?' Clare asked.

'I hated the way people acted around me when they knew. You'd think I'd just announced I had a highly contagious disease the way some of them scuttled off.'

'Why do you give a bollocks what other people think? If they can't hack hearing about something that happened when you were a kid, are they people you want in your life?'

'Probably not.' Pickle tugged at his lead. 'Sorry. I'd better take him for his walk.' I was about to set off when it struck me that I was in default mode and I didn't need to be anymore. The truth was out there in a double page spread so there was nothing to hide from now. I needed to stop running away and start letting people in. 'You're welcome to join us if you want.'

The three of us walked down Ashby Street and along the seafront and it all tumbled out, including the situation with Hollie, which I hadn't expected to share.

For someone who didn't talk much or let people in, I'd managed to open up and have the same conversation three times in one day and each of the listeners gave me further food for thought. But they all challenged me on the same thing: whether I really, truly could hang up my life jacket without also letting go of a little part of my soul.

'It's like that old Meatloaf song they're always playing on Bay Radio,' Clare said. 'I'd do anything for love...'

'But I won't do that,' Ben finished.

We laughed but they made a good point. I had absolutely no doubt about how deeply I loved Hollie, but I loved being part of the RNLI too. Truth was, I didn't want to give either of them up but one of those decisions had already been made for me.

A couple of days later, I was on the last of my days off between shifts and I was going stir crazy. A shout yesterday had broken up the monotony and I longed for another one today to take my mind off seeing Hollie tonight. Pickle was staying with her until Friday evening – lucky dog – while I did two long day shifts.

'Fancy playing with your ball down on the beach?' I asked Pickle after lunch. Poor dog was probably shattered after all the walks we'd been on to try to pass the time, yet the mention of 'ball' still had him circling the kitchen in excitement.

We joined the beach by the lifeboat station and played ball, gradually making our way south along the sand. It was a grey day with a chilly breeze but there was no rain forecast, so there were several people walking along the beach, wrapped in thick coats and hats, some with dogs, some just out taking in the fresh air.

Several said 'hello' or smiled as they walked past. An older man and woman came towards me with a Dalmatian and both greeted me. I said 'hello' in return and frowned as I passed them. Had that been...?

'Jake?'

I stopped and turned to face the couple.

'Auntie Maggs?'

'Oh, my goodness,' she exclaimed, clapping her hand across her mouth. 'It *is* you! Oh, how you've grown. Can I...?'

She held her arms out tentatively and I had no hesitation in hugging her. 'It's so good to see you again,' she cried.

We pulled apart, smiling.

'If you're dishing them out...' Uncle Adrian said, raising his arms, and I hugged him too.

Twenty-four years had passed since I last saw them, but Auntie Maggs, now in her late sixties, looked exactly how I remembered: kind grey eyes, large glasses and shoulder-length wavy hair, although it was grey rather than brown now. Uncle Adrian would be early seventies. He still had a full head of hair but it was white instead of blond and the beard and glasses were new.

'We might have walked straight past you if it hadn't been for your photo in last week's paper,' Auntie Maggs said. 'Congratulations on joining the RNLI. We always knew you'd go on to do amazing things, didn't we, Adrian?'

He nodded. 'Chuffed to bits, we were, when we read about it. Your dad would have been too.'

'I did it for him.'

'We thought that might be the case.' Auntie Maggs seemed to be studying my face. 'Oh, Jake, you look just like your dad did when I first met him. It's really wonderful to see you again and you've saved us a walk up the hill.'

Uncle Adrian nodded. 'We were planning to call at Lighthouse View after our walk on the off-chance you were still there. We'd have come sooner but we've been away and only saw the paper when we got back yesterday.'

'You were really on your way to see me?' I asked, touched by the idea.

'We've wanted to for years, haven't we, Maggs?'

'Yes, but we weren't sure whether we should. We didn't want to make anything difficult for anyone, especially your nanna, bless her. We wondered about reaching out after she died. We're so sorry about that.'

'Thank you. She was the best.'

'I saw the article,' Uncle Adrian continued, 'and I showed it to Maggs and we both agreed it had to be now.'

'We just hoped you'd remember us.'

'I remember you both so clearly. And you're not the only one who thought about getting in touch, but after the way I behaved—'

'You had every right to behave how you did after what you'd been through,' Auntie Maggs said, her voice as gentle and reassuring as I remembered it. 'Please don't worry about it for a single moment.'

Hearing her say that felt like another weight had been lifted. 'There's a decent dog-friendly café over there,' I pointed to the promenade. 'Fancy a catch-up over coffee?'

'We'd love that,' Uncle Adrian said. 'We really would.'

* * *

An hour flew by and we barely scratched the surface of the last twenty-four years.

'I wish we could stay longer,' Auntie Maggs said, 'but we have to get to an appointment. Do you have plans for Sunday?'

'Not yet.'

'Then you must come to our house for Sunday lunch.'

'I'd love that.'

Uncle Adrian and I swapped numbers.

'We moved house a few years ago,' he said. 'I'll text you the new address.'

We exchanged goodbye hugs and I had yet another emotional moment. I hadn't realised how much I'd missed them being part of my life. I'd thought about them a lot over the years, but I hadn't known whether they'd want me in their lives, and I knew I wouldn't have dealt well with the rejection if not. Clearly they'd never forgotten about me either.

They'd asked if I was with anyone and I'd glossed over it, but seeing them again reminded me how easy it was to lose people you cared about from your life. Hollie had regretted doing it with Bex and I regretted it with Uncle Adrian and Auntie Maggs. I wasn't going to add Hollie to that list of regrets.

Pickle and I walked in front of the arcades and cafés in the direction of the Old Town. We paused by the corner shop at the bottom of Sandby Bank – the road from the seafront up to the town – waiting for the pedestrian crossing to change to green. I glanced to my left at the bags of pink and blue candyfloss pegged outside the shop, swaying in the breeze. Net-wrapped sets containing brightly coloured buckets, spades and plastic moulds hung from a plinth and I smiled to myself as I spotted what was hanging on some hooks beside them. Perfect.

* * *

I sat at the kitchen table back at Lighthouse View late that afternoon, sipping on a glass of water and staring at the squares of Rubik's Cube, which I'd retrieved earlier in the week and returned to the glass bowl.

I picked up the stem and twiddled it for a while, reflecting on the final six pieces I'd recently added to complete it. When I'd inserted the first three, I'd felt genuinely happy for the first time since losing Dad. For the final three, I'd been elated. But now I'd lost Hollie and I didn't know what to feel. I dropped the stem back into the bowl.

Since meeting her, I'd changed. I'd become a different person – one who'd stopped hiding who I was anymore. I was finally letting people in. I'd opened up more to Irene in the past few weeks than ever before, I'd had that long chat with Jaffa, I'd even told Ben and Clare everything and we'd made plans to go out for drinks. I was building my existing friendships and making new ones and I wanted Hollie to be part of the new life I was creating.

The fact that she wanted to continue to share ownership of Pickle was a good thing as it meant we needed to be friends. Friends was better than nothing and things might build from there again. Clare and Ben told me they'd started off as friends, as had Sarah and her husband Nick. Jaffa and Bex had too. Hollie and I had managed about a fortnight as friends first. Maybe she could get used to the pager going when we weren't involved and realise it wasn't that bad.

I could do friends. Probably.

I grabbed the stalk of the Rubik's Cube again and inserted a piece. All the experiences that had made me add a piece before I met Hollie couldn't be taken away from me. They'd shaped me. They'd changed me. I added another and another, working frantically until it was back to how it had been before. Six pieces remained in the bowl. My shoulders slumped. Would I ever be able to replace them?

I hated how nervous I felt about Jake coming round and wished I'd suggested earlier than 7 p.m. because then I might not have worked myself into such a state. I'd changed my outfit twice, put on some make-up and wiped it off again, straightened my hair then back-combed it to make it look more natural before dragging it into a casual ponytail. Anyone would think I was going on a first date.

There was an explosion of butterflies in my stomach when he knocked on the kitchen door. *Deep breath. Act casual.*

Pickle launched himself at me the moment I opened the kitchen door, so I barely had a chance to look at Jake. I picked Pickle up and stepped back to let Jake inside.

'I have something for you,' he said, producing a bouquet of flowers from behind his back.

Tears rushed to my eyes. Craig had never bought me flowers, despite copious hints at how romantic I thought they were. Guilt swept through me, too. Here was Jake being kind and lovely giving me flowers and I hadn't even done him the courtesy of messaging him last week when that article appeared in *Bay News*. I'd thought about it. I'd started and deleted a dozen messages and my thumb had hovered over the call button so many times, but I hadn't known what to say so I hadn't said anything at all. Coward.

'They're gorgeous, but why?'

'Two reasons. Firstly, to say sorry about everything that's happened. I never wanted to hurt you.'

'Aw, Jake. You did nothing to hurt me. You weren't to know.'

'Even so. I feel bad. And secondly, I owe you something and I need to settle my debt.'

He tipped the bouquet forward and I laughed out loud. Nestling among the white roses, thistles and eucalyptus foliage was a bright red plastic child's spade.

I put Pickle down and took the bouquet from Jake. 'The flowers are beautiful, but that centrepiece definitely makes it.'

'I'm friends with Sarah who owns the florist. She said she can't believe she's not integrated a spade into her bouquets before and thinks I might have started a trend.'

'Thank you so much. I'll pop them in some water.' I marvelled at how friendly and thoughtful he could be towards me when all I'd managed was a few brief texts about looking after Pickle. I was a bad person. I needed to make it up to him. He hadn't hurt me – the situation had – but I'd definitely hurt him and he hadn't deserved it.

'Do you have time for a coffee?'

'I don't need to rush off, but I don't want to make things awkward for you if you'd rather I didn't—'

'I want you to stay,' I said softly, cutting him off. I wanted so much more than to share some idle chit-chat over coffee but I had no right to feel like that when I was the one who'd said we couldn't be together. I had to stand by that. I'd had lectures from Angie and Katie and I agreed with everything they said. I loved him, I wanted to be with him, but it had to be the RNLI or me as I couldn't live each day in fear. Not when I was only just starting to live again.

We were halfway down our drinks when Jake's pager beeped.

My hands shook and I put my mug down, hoping Jake wouldn't have noticed.

'Hollie, I...'

That look of sympathy was almost too much to bear. My stomach was swirling and I felt lightheaded as I shooed him towards the back door with my hands.

'Go!' Even that one word was a struggle to force out.

'I'll see you on Saturday.'

The moment he closed the door, I dashed to the kitchen sink, knowing I wouldn't make it to the bathroom in time.

Weak and shaking, I sank to the floor tiles. Pickle clambered onto my knee and looked up at me with his big, brown eyes. I cuddled him to me. 'Thanks for being here.'

I rested my head against the sink unit and closed my eyes, cursing what had just happened. The conversation had been going well. It felt amazing to be in Jake's company again. But his pager going off proved to me that I couldn't do it. It didn't matter how much I loved him, there was no way I could let myself go back there. The memories of those two days were back in bright technicolour – the police at the door, the journey to the hospital, the waiting room – along with the same kaleidoscope of emotions from hope to despair to anger.

Feeling drained, I climbed the stairs to my bed and crawled under the duvet. Pickle snuggled up beside me and I relished his warmth and unconditional love.

I eventually drifted off to sleep but I was haunted by dreams of *that* night, only this time the police were there to tell me that Jake was dead. It was *his* pale face I gazed upon and his cold, limp hand I held while he lay on a metal table draped in a sheet. I woke up in the early hours, clinging onto a tear-soaked pillow. Those drunken idiots had already taken so much from me and, seven years on, they were still taking.

On Saturday morning, I turned the sign round to 'open', pushed open the door, and breathed in deeply. A fortnight today would be Christmas Day. In that brief window of time when Jake and I had been a couple, I'd felt hopeful about Christmas. I'd taken some giant leaps forward then and I was trying to cling onto that, but it was hard.

The car park was carpeted with thick frost and the branches of the pine trees sparkled with it. A squirrel scampered across to one of the picnic benches beside me, stared at me for a moment, then grabbed one of the monkey nuts I'd put out earlier. It stared at me again then leapt off the table and raced up a nearby tree.

It would be busy today. It was one of my favourite sorts of winter day – cold and crisp but with a clear blue sky. The walkers would be out and there'd be families desperate for respite from heaving shops.

I stepped back into the café and checked the display of wooden sailing boats by the till. I'd sold a lot in November, but I'd been asked if I could make the sails in different colours. A combination of more colour choice and the arrival of December had them flying out the door.

I'd added Jake's photos of my wooden houses and frames to my website and they'd proved popular, as he'd suspected. A selection I'd bought into the café had sold immediately so, at Angie's suggestion, I'd made some wooden plinths, bought some soft white material and created a snowy village scene, which I'd displayed on tables upstairs. I'd already made about six times as much money from Hollie's Wood as I usually did across the whole Christmas period. The three charities I distributed the money across – Whitsborough Bay RNLI, Macmillan Cancer Support, and Paws Rehomed, a local dog charity – would all benefit from the increased sales.

'What time's he coming?' Angie asked, carefully placing a red velvet cake into the display counter.

'Mid-morning.' I felt bad about texting Jake and asking if he could pick Pickle up from the café this morning instead of from the house last night, but I couldn't risk being alone with him for any stretch of time. What if his pager went off again? It was better for us both that we were surrounded by people. In typical Jake fashion, he hadn't objected, which made me feel even more guilty.

I kept picturing his apologetic expression when his pager had gone off on Wednesday evening. He shouldn't have to feel bad when he was doing something so admirable and worthwhile.

* * *

My heart leapt into my mouth when the door opened and Jake looked over towards the counter and smiled at me. The café was busy and I was in the middle of pulling an order together so I signalled to him to give me one minute.

'Pickle! Jake's here!' I called as I placed a couple of cups and saucers on a tray. The little dog was out of his basket before I'd finished speaking and ran over to Jake, who picked him up and hugged him. What I wouldn't give to be Pickle right now.

Jake walked towards the staircase, paused by the sign, then took the stairs with Pickle under his arm. My heart raced. I'd put them up there this morning. Would he notice?

'Was that your lovely young man going upstairs?' Betty asked as I placed their order on the table.

'Yes, but we're not together anymore.'

'Why ever not?'

I had too much respect for Betty and Tommy to fob them off with 'it's complicated', but there was no quick and easy way to explain things.

'Bad timing,' I offered.

'But you still love him,' Betty declared. 'I can tell. Your sparkle faded this past couple of weeks, but it was back the moment he walked through the door.'

'And he clearly feels the same way about you,' Tommy added before I could object that he might have gone off me.

I didn't have it in me to continue the conversation, so I gave them a polite smile. 'Enjoy your food.'

Betty grabbed my hand. 'Don't let love slip through your fingers. Whatever it is that's keeping you apart, I guarantee there's a way to resolve it.'

'Sometimes you need to look at the problem from a different angle,' Tommy said.

Great advice. But this wasn't something that could be worked out, no matter what angle I looked at it.

Jake and Pickle were taking ages upstairs.

'Go up,' Angie hissed at me.

'It's busy.'

'We've got it. Go!'

I crept up the stairs, my heart thumping. Pickle was sniffing in front of the window and Jake was crouched down in front of the display.

'The display was Angie's idea,' I said. 'We've sold a lot of them.'

He whipped round. 'I'm not surprised.' He pointed to one of the street scenes. 'You made Ashby Street.'

'The pieces spoke to me.'

'And you made the lifeboat station.' He straightened up.

I shrugged. 'Guess who's been on my mind lately?'

'And guess who's never out of mine?'

'I'm sorry, Jake. I wanted to... but then your pager went off.'

He sighed. 'I know. I saw the look on your face. Genuine fear.'

'I was sick again after you left.'

He held my gaze and I willed him to offer a solution – something that neither of us had considered so far – that would mean we could be together. But what?

'Can I have the Ashby Street one? I'm visiting Irene this afternoon. She'd love it. And can I have the lifeboat station for me?'

I removed them from the display while Jake picked up Pickle.

'People can overcome fears, you know,' Jake said after I'd taken payment downstairs. 'You know my story. I was terrified of water – and we're talking severe panic attack, stuff of nightmares, phobia-terrified here – and now I work on the lifeboats. I'm not saying it was easy, but fears really *can* be overcome. If it's what the person really wants.' He gave me a weak smile. 'I'll see you later.'

I was aware of Betty's and Tommy's eyes on me as I watched Jake leave. Their advice rang in my ears. Had Jake just presented me with an alternative way of looking at things?

'Young Jake!' Irene declared on Sunday morning when I stepped into the residents' lounge at Bay View Care Home. She hugged me. She did that every time I saw her now and I liked it.

'Callie! This is my surrogate grandson who I was telling you about.'

A short brunette smiled at me. 'Good to meet you, Jake. Irene has settled in brilliantly, haven't you?'

'Love it!'

'Are you going to show Jake your rooms today?' Callie asked.

'Yes!' Irene turned to me. 'I'm all straight so let's give you the grand tour and there'll be tea and biscuits by the time we're done.'

I thanked Callie and followed Irene along the corridor and into what she called her apartment – a good-sized lounge with a small dining table and kitchenette, a bathroom and a large bedroom.

'It's very smart,' I said.

'It's a lot smaller than I'm used to but it's ideal. Seafarer Lodge was too much to manage on my own. Besides, I'm hardly ever in here. I take most meals in the restaurant and there's always someone to chat to or something going on in the lounge.'

'I have a housewarming gift for you.' I handed her a paper bag containing the Ashby Street scene. 'Hollie made it.'

She removed it from the bag and gasped. 'It looks like our houses!'

'Look closer.'

Her glasses dangled from a chain round her neck and she put them on and peered more closely at the names above the doors. '*It is* our houses. This is wonderful. Your Hollie really made it?'

'She's not *my* Hollie, as you very well know and, yes, it's all her work.'

'What a clever girl.' She moved a couple of photo frames aside on a shelving unit and placed the scene between them. 'Have you reached a decision?'

'I keep going round in circles.'

'You'll make the right decision eventually,' she said.

'Yes, but right for who?' I asked, shrugging.

Sunday lunch with Uncle Adrian and Auntie Maggs was brilliant. The years slipped away and it was like being out with old friends. They wanted to know all about my life and my achievements and acted like proud parents. I'd thought of myself as a lone wolf for so long, so it was unexpected to go to bed that night realising that I wasn't just letting friendships develop but I was growing my family too. I now had surrogate parents back in my life and a surrogate nanna in the form of Irene.

But the idea of family had me thinking about Hollie once more. I wanted her to be my family. I'd never been open to the idea of marriage and kids because of my need to be closed off from the world, but that had changed since meeting her.

I'd set myself a deadline. I had until Christmas Eve to make the biggest decision of my life. Could I walk away from the RNLI without it destroying my soul? And if I could, could I walk away without it destroying Hollie's? I'd lived with guilt for so many years and I wouldn't be the cause of someone else's. If that meant I stayed in the RNLI nursing a broken heart, I'd rather do that than risk breaking hers.

I curled up in front of the kitchen fire with Pickle and a mug of hot chocolate on Wednesday evening. Jake had dropped him off last night but he'd had to let himself in with a key I left for him because it had been our staff Christmas night out. Probably just as well. I wasn't sure what I'd have said to him if I'd seen him in person. He'd be collecting Pickle from the café again on Friday morning but it would be busy so we wouldn't be able to talk. Was this what we were reduced to now?

A loud knock on the kitchen door made me jump and Pickle bark. I rubbed my tired eyes as I went to answer it.

A bottle of wine was thrust towards me. 'Angie? What's this for?'

'I have something for you.'

She stepped aside and Katie jumped into her space.

'Oh, my God!' I squealed, hurling myself at my best friend. 'I thought you weren't flying back until tomorrow.'

'I lied. I wanted to surprise you.'

'Best surprise ever. Come in.'

I closed the door behind them and grabbed three wine glasses as they removed their coats and scarves.

Angie poured the wine while Katie acquainted herself with Pickle, then we sat round the kitchen table.

'It's so good to see you,' I said, grinning at Katie. 'I can't believe you've been away for nearly a year.'

'You wouldn't believe how quickly it's gone,' she said. 'Such an experience.'

'Tell me everything.'

Katie shook her head. 'You'll be sick of me going on about it soon enough but tonight's not the night. We want to talk about—'

Another knock on the door interrupted her.

'I'll get another glass,' Angie said.

'It's not Jake, is it?' I asked, my stomach churning.

Katie shook her head. 'No. We wouldn't do that.'

I yanked the door open. 'Bex?'

'Sorry I'm a bit late. How are you doing?'

She grabbed me in a hug.

'What's going on?' I asked.

Bex ignored me and dished out hugs to everyone else.

'We're all worried about you,' Angie said when we were seated at the table.

'Oh, come on. You don't need to be. It's December. Somehow I make it through the other side each year relatively unscathed.'

'Yeah, but this year was going to be different,' Katie said, placing her hand on my arm. 'Because you had Jake and now you don't.'

'And you know why.'

'And we all understand,' Bex said, 'but do you understand what you're walking away from? We're here to listen and hopefully to help.'

So I told them all about it. I relayed every conversation I'd had with Jake and my jumble of thoughts and emotions. They asked questions but nobody lectured me.

'I guess this is the part where you tell me I've made a huge mistake,' I said.

'Do you think you've made a huge mistake?' Katie asked.

I shrugged. 'I don't know anything anymore. Advice? Suggestions? I'm all ears.'

'We don't think we're the best ones to give you the advice,' Bex said, looking at Angie.

'You know that card your mum asked me to give you after she died?' Angie said. 'There were two of them.'

The butterflies in my stomach took flight. 'Two?'

'She asked me to keep the second one a secret and only give you it if you lost your way and needed some help. I know you've had more than your fair share of difficult days, but I've never felt I needed to give you this until now.'

She reached into her bag and placed an envelope on the table. I recognised the same cream envelope so it was either a duplicate card or part of a set. My heart thumped as I stared at Mum's handwriting on the front: *Hollie. For when you're lost.*

I grabbed a knife, slowly slit open the envelope, and removed the contents. On the cover was a watercolour illustration of the same little girl in the pink tutu and red wellies splashing in a puddle. Behind her stood a first aid case and in front of her sat a teddy bear with its arm in a sling. She had a sticking plaster across her knee and was blowing kisses to the bear.

I opened it up.

To my exceptional, beautiful angel, Hollie Gabrielle,

I have always maintained that, no matter how tough things get, there is always someone having a tougher time than you. In many ways, I hope Angie never has to give you this card because, if she does, it means you've hit a particularly low point and it breaks my heart to imagine that for you.

I wish I was there to hug you and help you find your way through whatever challenges life has thrown at you.

I said that you should keep dancing in the rain and I hope you've managed to do that but there's an extension to that saying:

If you stumble, make it part of your dance.

Sometimes we get lost or we make decisions we later regret. Learning from those stumbles is what makes them part of your dance. Be brave, take risks, live life to the full and dance in the rain knowing that, if you stumble and fall, the pain will heal.

Always remember what Sir William Hillary said: 'With courage, nothing is impossible.'

Smile. Sparkle. You've got this!

All my love forever,

Mum xx

Tears coursed down my cheeks and dripped onto the table as I re-read the words until my eyes were too blurred to see them anymore. Sir William was the founder of the RNLI in 1824 and the quote had been what he'd used in his call to the nation a year earlier to set up a service dedicated to saving lives at the sea. As apt today as it had ever been.

'What does she say?' Katie asked.

I passed her the card and watched her face crumple. She passed it to Angie, who passed it to Bex, both of them sobbing at Mum's very last words.

'With courage, nothing is impossible,' Bex whispered. 'I really do believe that.'

'And we're all here to help you find that courage,' Angie added.

'We are,' Katie agreed. 'But I think it's already there. It always has been. You just need a bit more self-belief.'

They pushed back their chairs and surrounded me with hugs.

Mum's best friend, my best friend, and the woman who'd almost been my sister-in-law were there for me no matter what. They believed in me. Katie was right. I just needed to believe in myself more. Jake had said that fears could be overcome. He was right. He'd done it. It had taken a lot of courage and self-belief but he'd got there.

My friends sat down again and everyone took a much needed glug on their wine. As I looked round at them, it struck me that they weren't just friends. They were my family and they had my back. Just like the crew at the lifeboat station had Jake's back.

* * *

Some time later, after they'd all gone, I sat cross-legged on my bed with various items spread round me on the duvet: both of Mum's cards, the photo of my parents laughing on their wedding day, a framed photo of Dad and Isaac fully kitted out, posing in front of the all-weather lifeboat, the little crocheted angel bear that Betty had made me, and the gift bag that Sylvia had given me.

I picked up the bag. She'd said, 'It's for a time when life tests you and you're not sure which way to turn.' That time was now.

As I'd suspected, there was a book inside – a small dark brown leatherbound journal. I unfastened the leather strap and opened up the first page.

'Albert Braithwaite, devoted husband to Sylvia, lover of the sea, muser of musings, and loather of sultanas,' I read, smiling at the last comment.

I flicked onto the next page and did a sharp intake of breath as I read Sir William Hillary's quote written beside a skilfully drawn pencil sketch of a lifeboat being launched into the sea.

The next page had a drawing of the oversized statue of Stanley Moffatt on his bench in North Bay and a short poem under it about the legacy he'd left to the town. I settled back against the head-board, absorbed by more poems, quotes and illustrations. The over-riding themes across all the entries were courage, the sea, and love.

When my eyes started drooping with tiredness, I reluctantly closed Albert's journal and tidied away the cards, photos and the bear.

As I settled down to sleep a little later, instead of the swirl of confused thoughts that had clouded my mind for the past fortnight, I felt uplifted. Mum's card and that amazing journal couldn't have come into my life at a more perfect time and, encouraged by the belief my 'family' had in me, I knew exactly what I needed to do.

On Friday night, there was hardly anyone around at North Bay so I clambered onto the giant bench beside Stanley Moffatt and watched the rise and fall of the waves. One week today until my Christmas Eve deadline and I still hadn't made my decision.

I'd been to The Starfish Café to collect Pickle this morning but hadn't had a chance to speak to Hollie. Angie was full of apologies from Hollie, telling me a customer had taken ill and she'd accompanied them to the hospital. I was disappointed but it did make things easier. No awkwardness. No hopes being dashed. I collected Pickle and left.

I felt closer to Dad on Stanley's bench than I did at the cemetery. 'What do you think I should do, Dad?' I asked into the cold night air.

If only he could respond.

* * *

Christmas week arrived and, as well as my impending decision deadline, I was very aware of what the week or so ahead meant for

Hollie: her birthday on Friday on Christmas Eve, the six-year anniversary of her mum's death on Boxing Day and seven years since losing Isaac and her dad over the next two days. If we'd still been together, I could have been there for her. I still wanted to be there for her, but she hadn't mentioned anything about seeing each other this week and I didn't want to crowd her or make things awkward by suggesting it.

Having worked every Christmas since Nanna died and many of the ones before that, I'd booked the time off this year and regretted that now. When I'd started seeing Hollie, I'd got ahead of myself and dared to imagine a Christmas together. Instead, I'd be alone as usual.

On Wednesday night, I sat at the kitchen table staring at the wooden lifeboat station Hollie had made. I longed to talk to her about it. Had it been emotional making it? Had she made it in memory of her dad and brother or had she also been thinking about me?

I put it to one side and turned my attention to the Rubik's Cube, reassembled to how it had been before I met Hollie. Spreading out the six remaining pieces in front of me, I reflected on what each one symbolised; all key moments where I'd moved forward.

The first three had been for finding Pickle, Hollie, and laughter and I needed to add them back into the cube. Pickle was right here beside me and I still had Hollie in my life in some capacity. I might not have belly-laughed since things ended, but the memory of that day in her workshop couldn't be taken away.

I looked at the remaining three pieces. Hollie had told me she loved me and I'd told her I loved her so those pieces needed to go back in too. Which only left the one representing the RNLI. At the time, it had symbolised passing out but now it felt like it represented so much more.

I sighed as I sat back in my chair, twiddling that final cornerpiece cube between my fingers. One piece with yellow, orange and blue sides.

'RNLI colours,' I said to Pickle, who was curled up on a cushion on the table. 'How appropriate.'

Having tried not to think too much about my past in so long, I'd done nothing but think about it over the past fortnight. I'd thought about conversations I'd had with Dad and Nanna and things Auntie Maggs had told me about Mum when I was little. I'd reflected on more recent conversations with Irene, Jaffa, Clare and Ben, and over Sunday lunch with Auntie Maggs and Uncle Adrian, and the advice they'd all given.

I'd gone back and forth and round in circles but it was ultimately Nanna's final words in her will that helped me make my decision: *Life is all about choices. Some choices are easy and feel right, some are difficult but are ultimately for the best, and others cause too much pain to be right.*

With a sigh, I inserted the final piece into the cube.

I ran my thumb along a crack in one of the red pieces which must have happened when I'd tossed it against the back door.

'Hollie and I aren't broken,' I muttered. 'It's just a surface crack which can be fixed. And I can fix it.'

Or at least I hoped that was what would happen on the back of my decision.

Christmas Eve arrived with a glistening frost. I picked up my camera and took Pickle on an early walk along the river, taking photos of frozen spider webs and the intricate ice patterns stamped on leaves and trees. It was the first time I'd picked up my camera since taking the photos of Hollie's Wood. Looking through the lens once more gave me a buzz of excitement.

Photography was a part of who I was, and I shouldn't have neglected it.

I was due at the lifeboat station later for our Christmas Eve Extravaganza. I'd always thought 'extravaganza' was a bit of a stretch for the annual event, which ran from 11 a.m. till 2 p.m., but was usually well attended and good for fundraising.

Jaffa was dressing up in the RNLI's mascot costume Stormy Stan – a uniformed crew member with a big ginger beard who was the spitting image of Chief – and kids could have their photo taken with him in front of the ALB. There'd be tours of the station, a raffle, tombola, cake and craft stalls, and various activities.

I'd be back there again on Boxing Day as crew on the ILB, acting as the safety boat for the Boxing Day Dip and raft race. That just left Christmas Day to struggle through. Auntie Maggs said they'd have invited me to spend Christmas with them but they'd already arranged to join her sister on the Isle of Wight.

I had a Christmas dinner for one ready meal in the fridge and had chosen a couple of boxsets on streaming for a day of binge-watching. I'd get through it like I had done for the past five years since losing Nanna.

* * *

'I need to go down the lifeboat station for a few hours,' I told Pickle when we finished our walk by the river. 'I've got something important to do, so wish me luck.' I picked up the envelope I'd propped up on the kitchen table. 'I'll see you later, buddy.'

I took a slow, considered walk down the hill. The winter sun had melted the frost and the sky was blue and cloudless. The sea was calm and there were already plenty of folk about – the sensible ones avoiding the last-minute present or food-purchasing frenzy – so we should have plenty of visitors and raise valuable funds.

When I reached the corner I paused, checked the letter was still in my back pocket, and took a deep breath as I looked across at the lifeboat station. This was the last time I'd take in that view as crew. It was the right choice to make. The RNLI would always be part of me, so I wasn't going to step back completely. There were plenty of other things I could do as a volunteer – fundraising, working in the shop, cleaning, even dressing as Stormy Stan – and I'd willingly throw myself into them all, but I couldn't continue to save lives while sacrificing my own. I'd lived a half-life so far, shutting myself off from the world, believing I could never find love because I didn't deserve it, but I'd seen what a future with love could look like and I wanted that. Staying on as a volunteer would still help save lives at sea, just in a more indirect way. And, assuming she still felt the same way about me, *my* life would finally start with Hollie by my side.

The risk scared me. It could go the other way. But it was a risk I had to take. Getting back in the water had scared me but that had worked out. I had to believe this one would too, and that Hollie wouldn't resent me as she'd feared.

* * *

'You're early, Mouse,' Chief said when I found him in the training room.

'I wanted to catch you before everyone else got here. When I passed out, I said I'd never let you down, but now I'm going to have to. I'm sorry.'

He narrowed his eyes at the envelope I proffered.

'What's this?'

'Please read it.'

He sighed as he took it from me, ripped open the envelope and removed the contents. His eyebrows raised as he glanced at the cheque, then scanned down the letter. I knew how costly it was to put someone through training – particularly the time I'd spent at our training centre in Poole – and there was no way I wasn't going to repay that from my inheritance.

Without a word, Chief re-folded the letter, stuffed it back in the envelope with the cheque, and handed it back to me. 'You hang onto this for the moment. Let's see how you feel later.'

I shook my head. 'I've been thinking about this for weeks now. I'm not going to change my mind.'

He quirked his eyebrows at me. 'We'll see.'

When I refused to take the letter back, he placed it on the table. 'Seeing as you're here early, you can make yourself useful. The trestle tables need putting out in the forecourt, three each side.'

'But Chief...'

His phone rang and he left the room. I released a frustrated sigh, picked up the envelope and stuffed it back in my jeans pocket. I'd played out various potential reactions in my mind and most of them had revolved round him being annoyed, disappointed or both. I hadn't considered a refusal to accept my resignation and I was clueless as to what to do about that.

* * *

By noon, the lifeboat station was a hive of activity. There was a line of kids waiting to have their photo taken with Stormy Stan. I'd wondered if Chief might make me dress as Stan as punishment for letting him down, but I was manning the tombola as originally planned. Jaffa made a much better Stan than I would have, doing a dance routine with several of the children which even some of the adults were joining in.

'It's the latest TikTok dance craze.' Jaffa sidled up to me.

I stared at him, frowning, then glanced at Stormy Stan. 'I thought that was you in there.'

'It was meant to be, but why would I do that when we have a willing trainee?'

'I thought Spaniel was going away for Christmas.' Our latest recruit was joining us in the New Year but had been invited to The Lobster Pot for Christmas drinks after Monday's training so he could meet everyone before he started. He was so excitable and jumpy that he'd already been awarded his nickname.

'He is. That's not Spaniel.'

'Then who is it?'

He tapped his nose mysteriously. 'That's for me to know and you to find out.'

An influx of customers prevented us from discussing it any further. Every so often, I glanced across at the mascot. Whoever was in there, he had bundles of energy and some impressive moves. I might have to scribble out that part on my letter because no way could I do that. Stan must have sensed me looking as he waved in my direction and I waved back, cringing. Had I really just waved at a seven-foot mascot?

The crowds thinned out and we started clearing away. I watched Stan head inside the station, grabbed a couple of tables and followed him. He was talking to Chief.

'Mouse!' Chief waved me over. 'Perfect timing. I know you and I have some unfinished business, but I wanted to introduce you to our newest trainee first.'

Stormy Stan waved at me again.

'Hi,' I said, propping the tables against the wall. 'Nice moves outside. You must be melting.'

Stan fanned his face with an oversized hand.

'That's a point,' Chief said. 'Let's make you more comfortable.'

He stood in front of the mascot to remove the head, blocking my view.

'Ooh, that's better. I can breathe now. Thanks.'

My heart raced. No way! That's...

'I think you already know Hollie,' Chief said, stepping aside with the giant head in his hands.

She smiled at me. 'Surprise!'

'I don't understand. How are you the newest trainee?'

'If you can't beat 'em, join 'em,' she responded.

'Hollie will join us for Monday night training from the New Year. She might not go on to become crew, but she asked if she could experience it so that she can face her fears. I think you know something about that, don't you, Mouse?'

I stared at Hollie in astonishment. 'You don't have to do this for me.'

'I know I don't, but I want to, and I also think I need to do it for me. I have a few demons to lay to rest and I think you, Artie and Kyle can help me with that.' She held out her arms, tears sparkling in her eyes. 'Permission to come aboard?'

'Permission granted.' I rushed to her and tried to hug her but the giant padded suit didn't let us get very close.

'I'll leave you two for a moment,' Chief said, grinning at us both. 'About that unfinished business, Mouse... do you still want to give me that letter?'

'I might hang on to it a bit longer.'

'You do that, son. You do that.'

'What letter?' Hollie asked when he'd gone.

I took it out of my pocket. She pulled off her giant hands and took it from me, scanning down the page.

'You really were going to walk away from this, even though you had no idea how I still felt or whether I'd take you back?'

'I had to take that risk. Looks like you've taken a big risk of your own.'

'I learned to dance again.'

'That TikTok thing?'

She shook her head, smiling. 'I'll explain later. For now, there's something I desperately want to do, but I need your help first.'

'Name it.'

'Can you unzip this stupid costume so I can kiss you?'

I helped her out of the mascot and into my arms. I hadn't been sure whether I'd ever have the chance to do this again but it felt so right.

'Happy birthday,' I said as we pulled apart at the sound of wolf whistles and cries of 'get a room!'

Hollie grinned at me. 'It is now. And do you and Mr Piccalilli Marmaduke Fluffington the Third have any plans for Christmas Day?'

I kissed her again. 'We do now.'

For the first time in seven years, I woke up on Christmas morning with my heart bursting with love instead of breaking.

'Happy Christmas!' Jake said, nuzzling my neck.

'Happy Christmas to you too.' I turned over and kissed him. Happy? Thanks to Jake and Pickle, it really was.

'How are you feeling?' he asked.

I thought for a moment. 'Hopeful. You?'

'Same. And very lucky. What you've arranged with Chief is awesome. The courage that must have taken.' He pushed a tendril of hair back from my face, sending a ripple of excitement through me.

'Says the man who overcame his own fears to become crew and was about to leave that world behind for me. Both those things took tremendous courage. I still can't believe you were going to give it all up for me.'

'I couldn't live without you. Simple as that.'

I kissed him again. 'You don't have to. I've had my stumble and I've made it part of my dance.'

I smiled at his puzzled expression. 'There's something I want to show you.' I opened my bedside drawer and carefully removed the two cards from Mum along with Albert's journal. 'My mum asked Angie to give me this card after she died. I'd like you to read it...'

Jake went downstairs to let Pickle out and make coffee while I cleared the cards and journal away. The sound of claws tapping against the wooden floorboards as the little shih tzu scampered across the landing filled my heart with joy.

Sandy Croft was a family home and it needed to be filled with animals, people, love and laughter. My family had gone from one to three and it would grow again, in time.

'I wish I had some Christmas presents for you,' Jake said, returning with a couple of mugs of coffee and placing them by the bed.

'You've already given me the best gift I could ever ask for. Two gifts, in fact.' I rubbed Pickle's belly. 'This fluffy little thing right here. And you. Especially when I thought I might have lost you.'

Jake sat beside me and smiled tenderly. 'You didn't lose me, Hollie. You found me.'

He rubbed Pickle's belly too and our hands intertwined like they'd done that time in the café but, this time, they stayed that way.

'You once said you thought Pickle and I were meant to find each other,' Jake said. 'I think he was meant to find us both so we could find each other.'

I smiled down at the little dog. 'Happy Christmas, Pickle, and thanks for making this a happy Christmas for us both.'

Two months later

I stood on the second step in The Starfish Café on the last Friday in February, smiling at the sixty or so guests.

'Good evening, everyone. We'll be cutting the cake shortly but, before we do, Betty and Tommy have something special planned for you on this, their sixty-fifth wedding anniversary. I've seen the photos and I can't tell you how excited I am to be seeing this for real. So, if I could ask you to all spread around the café and make room for your not-so-newlyweds as they take to the floor as husband and wife, sixty-five years on.'

The guests cleared some space and Tommy led Betty to the centre of the café. He gave a slight bow and she curtseyed, then they moved into ballroom hold as Elvis Presley's 'Love Me Tender' started playing – a song they'd told me had been a hit shortly before their wedding.

Jake put his arm round my shoulders, and I rested my head

against his chest, blinking back tears as I watched my two favourite customers waltz round the café. They'd both turn eighty-four later this year but they still had the magic that had made them ballroom champions in their teens and twenties. It was an honour to be part of their celebration.

'We know sixty-five years isn't usually a big celebration,' Tommy said when they'd asked if they could host a party at the café for their friends and family. 'But we don't know if we'll still be around for our seventieth.'

'Every year should be celebrated, and sixty-five years is definitely cause for celebration.' I dug my phone out and Googled it. 'Blue sapphire apparently, and it says it's a rare, beautiful and exotic gem which symbolises loyalty and brings inner peace. That's gorgeous.'

And so we'd decked out the café with blue, silver and white balloons and flowers. Tommy was wearing a navy suit with a bright blue tie and Betty wore the most beautiful three-quarter length chiffon gown with a velvet bodice and floating chiffon sleeves. The pair of them were timeless.

The mesmerising dance ended and everyone clapped. We released the balloons from the ceiling then the still happy couple cut their cake.

I stood by the counter a little later, sipping on a glass of champagne, taking in the scene. All the staff and several regular customers had been invited to join in the celebrations alongside Betty and Tommy's friends and family. Mrs Sultana – Sylvia – turned and raised her glass to me and blew me a kiss. I'd introduced her to Betty and Tommy as soon as I'd spotted them in the café at the same time and it warmed my heart that they'd taken her into their lives and introduced her to their friends. She'd also made new friends in her retirement home. Not so lonely anymore.

'You've done an amazing job tonight,' Jake said, slipping his arms round my waist from behind and gently nuzzling my neck. 'It's a brilliant venue for functions.'

'I was just thinking the same. I'll post something on Facebook next month and see if we get any bookings.'

'I thought you might say that. I've taken some photos of the café and the food, which might help.'

'Aw, you star. You think of everything.'

'It's snowing!' someone cried, and all the children rushed to the window, squealing with excitement.

I peered outside and smiled at the thick flakes rapidly tumbling onto the terrace. It had been dry for the past week so it was going to settle well.

* * *

By 9.30 p.m. the final guests were gone and, as most of the tidying up had been done along the way, Jake and I sent the staff home too. He swept the floor and took out the rubbish while I finished clearing up in the kitchen.

There were about three inches of snow as we stepped out of the café and it was still falling heavily. The footprints and tyre tracks left by the guests departing were already covered with a fresh layer and the woods looked like an alpine winter wonderland with laden branches.

'I love The Starfish Café in the snow,' I said, breathing in the fresh cold air and laughing as a snowflake landed on the tip of my nose.

Jake took my hand. 'I may not be a ballroom champ like Tommy and I know it's not rain but snow is frozen rain and you know what we need to do in the rain?'

'Dance in it.'

He twirled me in a pirouette then dipped me back and brushed his lips against mine before pulling me to him and slow-dancing in a circle for a moment. We giggled together as we half-waltzed, half-jigged to the car.

He unlocked the car, grabbed my bag and placed it on the back seat then twirled me again.

As the snowflakes fell over The Starfish Café, we slow-danced in the middle of the car park. Jake softly sang the lyrics to 'Love Me Tender' then drew me into a slow and tender kiss.

'I love you so much,' he whispered, brushing my damp hair back from my face.

'I love you too. Thanks for dancing in the rain and the snow with me.'

'Thank you for letting me be your dance partner.'

'Before we go inside, I have something special for you in the workshop,' I said to Jake when we exited the car back at Sandy Croft. I took his hand and led him through the garden.

'Close your eyes,' I instructed as we entered the workshop. 'There's a project I've been working on for several weeks and I finally finished it a few days ago.'

I'd placed it on my workbench earlier and covered it in a piece of tarpaulin. I whipped off the cover. 'Open your eyes.'

Jake stepped forward and reached out his hand to stroke the wood. 'Is this our tree?'

'It is! I told you that pieces speak to me and that one spoke loud and clear. We found it the day we fell in love so the trunk represents our lives and the six candle branches are the most important people we've lost – three on this side for my parents and Isaac and three on that side for your parents and Nanna.'

He ran his fingers down the two intertwined channels I'd cut into the trunk. Each was filled with a resin, one containing sparkling grains of sand and the other containing glitter so it twinkled like the sea on a sunny day.

'The sand and the sea,' he said, 'and our lives being intertwined from the start.'

I smiled at him, touched that he understood.

'Come round the other side. This took a lot of practice, but I got there eventually.' I'd kept the intertwined theme going and had carved a vine but, instead of leaves growing from it, there were meaningful images: an anchor to represent the RNLI, a starfish, a penguin, paw prints, a Rubik's Cube, and a raincloud with a pair of wellington boots. Round the bottom I'd carved the quote from Sir William Hillary: *With courage, nothing is impossible.*

Those words, which Mum had quoted in her second card and which I'd found in Albert's journal, had helped me find the courage to phone Artie and ask if he'd accept me as a volunteer. It hadn't been easy and I'd had several wobbles and a major meltdown during the past eight weeks of training, but every time Artie mentioned me becoming the first female crew member from my family, my protests were a little weaker.

Hillary's quote also couldn't have been more appropriate for the journey Jake and I had taken and were still taking together.

Jake ran his fingers down the carvings and across the letters. 'I don't have enough words. This is exceptional. It's beyond anything I could ever have imagined.'

'Thank you. There's just one problem with it.'

He shook his head. 'Looks pretty damn perfect to me.'

'It's more of a practical problem. You see, it's *our* tree and it's about *our* lives so it really needs to be co-owned. It's one thing dropping Pickle off at each other's houses, but I think we might get some strange looks from the neighbours if we started dropping off our tree too. So I was thinking, you're always saying how much you love it here, how would you feel if we kept our tree here and you had permanent visiting rights because you also lived here?'

Jake's eyes shone as he smiled that wide, friendly smile that I loved so much. 'Are you asking me to move in with you?'

'It was Pickle's idea.'

Jake drew me into a tender kiss. 'Pickle knows his stuff. Crufts' winner, no less. I'd love to move in.'

We kissed again and I was now sparkling and shining just like Mum wanted. I didn't care that we were both soggy from the snow. The important thing was that I'd found my dance partner, the one who made me laugh every day, who hugged me simply because it was Tuesday, who held me when I cried and who danced in the rain with me.

Life had dealt us both so many hard blows but we'd found the strength to come through it. Most of those steps had been taken before we even knew each other but we'd needed to draw on each other's strength and encouragement to take those final few difficult steps together. We'd both stumbled but we'd got up and made it part of our dance. *With courage, nothing is impossible.*

ACKNOWLEDGMENTS

Thank you for reading *Snowflakes Over The Starfish Café*. I hope you enjoyed it. This is a very special book for me because not only is it my thirteenth (unlucky for some), but also the start of a brand new twelve-book contract with my amazing publishers, Boldwood Books. I feel so lucky to have joined Boldwood, so it's with them that I start my thanks.

Three days after the release of *Snowflakes Over The Starfish Café*, it's the two-year anniversary of the first of my Boldwood Books releases. What an incredible two years it has been! Joining Boldwood has quite literally changed my life. I am so grateful to the team for believing in my original submission of *The Secret to Happiness*, taking me on as one of their first twenty authors, giving me a contract to write new books and to breathe fresh life into my back catalogue, and giving me the secret to happiness in return. I've gone from being a struggling author selling very few books and trying to fit writing around a demanding full-time job to being an international bestseller who writes full-time. Every day I count my lucky stars.

Thank you to my amazing editor, Nia Beynon, for such

insightful feedback and for helping smooth out the creases in this story and the twelve that preceded it. Thank you to Boldwood's CEO and founder, Amanda Ridout, for building such a successful, supportive, forward-thinking business. And thank you to Claire for all the digital marketing and Megan for the behind-the-scenes support.

As this story includes a strong relationship between Hollie and her brother, Isaac, it seemed appropriate to dedicate it to my two brothers. Mike and Chris – we may not see much of each other and we're all shocking at picking up the phone, but it doesn't mean I don't think the world of you both. Sending hugs xx

Snowflakes Over The Starfish Café was a difficult book to write for so many reasons. Firstly, it originally started life four years ago with the intention of it being a novella and my first ever Christmas release. I visited my local lifeboat station (Scarborough) and interviewed one of the crew but, when I started writing the story, I realised it was much bigger than a novella, so I parked it. I'd only written about ten thousand words but they included the seeds for many threads. When I returned to it, I'd forgotten what some of those threads were. I often can't remember what I did yesterday so there was no chance of me recalling where I was heading in a story started four years ago!

Secondly, with so much time between the original idea and writing the full story, I'd been developing plot points in my head but, as a pantser, this went against my natural style to have a basic premise and just write. This massively slowed things down for me.

Thirdly, I hit that stage that many authors reach where I thought it might just be the worst book that I – or anyone in the whole world – had ever written and it took a while to get past that.

And finally, it turned out that the story I wanted to tell wasn't only too big to be a novella, it was actually too big to be a novel! I'd tried to cover far too much and, as such, hadn't done justice to either of the two main storylines. I've been very fortunate that I've never had to do a re-write before, but this book ended up being that. The main storyline still exists – the love story between Hollie and Jake and the courage needed for them to stop letting their pasts control their future – but another storyline running alongside that needed to go. Taking it out left enormous gaps and I had to write new scenes and chapters and knit the existing ones together in a different way. It's by far the hardest edit I've ever done but, with Nia's help, I finally got a polished story which I love. Nia – I cannot thank you enough for the reassurances, phone conversations, and emails as we explored how to make this work.

The good news (or at least, it's good news if you loved this story), is that we're now planning a sequel and the second storyline I removed will be the basis of that. Watch this space!

A massive thank you has to go to Scarborough Lifeboat Station for their time and support. Thank you to Dave Barry for arranging my visit several years back and answering my (endless) questions. Enormous gratitude to Matt 'Mouse' Marks for letting me interview him. I've used his job and his nickname (but awarded for different reasons) as the inspiration for Jake's character. I've also watched stacks of episodes of the BBC's brilliant *Saving Lives at Sea*, which follows the men and women of the RNLI; ordinary people doing extraordinary things.

Living in a popular seaside resort, I'm very much aware of the invaluable work undertaken by the RNLI, whether that is from crew, fundraisers or volunteers in other capacities, as well as the families of crew who support their way of life. I've been touched by tragic stories over recent years of lives lost along the coast and a couple of these have influenced aspects of this book.

My chosen charity is Scarborough RNLI and I'm going to be making a donation to them to help in some way towards the incredible work they do. The RNLI, both centrally and at a local level, are always appreciative of donations. Search https://rnli.org for more details.

Thank you to the lovely members of my Facebook group, Redland's Readers, for your thoughts around changing a dog's name. The discussion was really helpful.

There are so many parties involved in polishing my manuscript and getting it into the format you've read or listened to. Thanks to Cecily Blench and Sue Lamprell for the brilliant copy editing and proofreading, particularly Sue who has worked on all of my books so far! Thanks to Debbie Clement for the gorgeous cover. Isn't it dreamy? Thanks to Rachel Gilbey for organising the blog tour and all the bloggers and reviewers who took part and helped create a bang with this book's launch. Thank you to Lucy Brownhill and Gareth Bennett-Ryan for bringing Hollie and Jake to life with their amazing narration on the audio version of *Snowflakes Over The Starfish Café* and ISIS Audio and Ulverscroft for the production and distribution.

As always, I'm eternally grateful to my husband and daughter, Mark and Ashleigh, for their support and encouragement and to my mum Joyce who's my biggest fan. Mark has provided valuable inspiration for one aspect of Jake. He's an extremely talented photographer who takes the most stunning landscape photographs. I quizzed him about all sorts of details, from what a photographer might learn and how, to what they'd call their equipment, to how they'd be inspired by wood. Thank you for all your guidance and suggestions, Mark, even though I know you will now claim you wrote half the book! xx

Over the past year, I've been quite overwhelmed with some of the lovely messages I've received from readers who've discovered my books and wanted to thank me for a particular storyline that resonated with them or for the escapism my books have been, especially during the global pandemic. I have been thanked for keeping my books a Covid-free zone and they will remain that way. Reading provides a respite from the world around us, and we need that more than ever these days. I know it's our reality, but I don't want to write about a socially distanced world full of facemasks and hand sanitiser or a world without hugs, and I'm sure most readers don't want to read about it either.

My final – but oh so important thank you – is to you, the reader, for choosing this story. If you've loved going on Hollie's and Jake's journey, you might like to explore my other books set in Whitsborough Bay and Hedgehog Hollow on the Yorkshire Wolds. Please do tell your friends, family and the whole world. The best way to thank an author for a book you've loved (and to keep us writing) is to leave a review. A sentence or even a few words is amazing. Or just a rating. Every little helps.

Big hugs,

Jessica xx

MORE FROM JESSICA REDLAND

We hope you enjoyed reading *Snowflakes Over the Starfish* Café. If you did, please leave a review.

If you'd like to gift a copy, this book is also available as an ebook, digital audio download and audiobook CD.

Sign up to Jessica Redland's mailing list for news, competitions and updates on future books.

http://bit.ly/JessicaRedlandNewsletter

ABOUT THE AUTHOR

Jessica Redland writes uplifting stories of love, friendship, family and community set in Yorkshire where she lives. Her Whitsborough Bay books transport readers to the stunning North Yorkshire Coast and her Hedgehog Hollow series takes them into beautiful countryside of the Yorkshire Wolds.

Visit Jessica's website: https://www.jessicaredland.com/

Follow Jessica on social media:

facebook.com/JessicaRedlandWriter
twitter.com/JessicaRedland
instagram.com/JessicaRedlandWriter
bookbub.com/authors/jessica-redland

ALSO BY JESSICA REDLAND

ABOUT BOLDWOOD BOOKS

Boldwood Books is a fiction publishing company seeking out the best stories from around the world.

Find out more at www.boldwoodbooks.com

Sign up to the Book and Tonic newsletter for news, offers and competitions from Boldwood Books!

http://www.bit.ly/bookandtonic

We'd love to hear from you, follow us on social media:

facebook.com/BookandTonic

twitter.com/BoldwoodBooks

instagram.com/BookandTonic

Made in United States
North Haven, CT
31 December 2021